...she walked... into the Late Morning studio. She still wasn't sure why she was there.

When she'd gotten home the previous night, she'd convinced herself that she would forget all about Jacques. Especially since she still felt raw because his interest in her—his kindness to her—had all been a ploy to get her to help him.

She'd told herself she should have known. Her ex, Kyle, had been nice to her once upon a time. It was how she'd fallen for him—and how she'd learned niceness was never simple.

But still, it stung.

His dismissal felt like confirmation that she wasn't likable. And even though he'd claimed otherwise, his actions had shown her the truth. It had amplified all of her insecurities, and she'd been determined to escape it. She'd been determined to show Jacques she was as right for his plan as anyone else was. So she'd kissed him.

It was impulsive. It was hot. It was everything she'd expected from a man with Jacques's undeniable sexiness and charm. But there was something more, too. She remembered the scar above his mouth again, the fight he'd said he'd had with Kyle, and realized it was *dangerous*, too.

It both thrilled and terrified her that she seemed to be attracted to the danger she sensed in Jacques. And though she wanted to, she couldn't deny that it was part of the reason she was walking into a television studio at six in the morning to pretend to be his girlfriend. She knew this plan was a form of redemption for him.

THE MILLIONAIRE'S REDEMPTION

BY
THERESE BEHARRIE

First Published in Great Britain 2017
By Mills & Boon, an imprint of HarperCollins*Publishers*
1 London Bridge Street, London, SE1 9GF

© 2017 Therese Beharrie

ISBN: 978-0-263-92321-6

23-0817

Our policy is to use papers that are natural, renewable and recyclable products and made from wood grown in sustainable forests. The logging and manufacturing processes conform to the legal environmental regulations of the country of origin.

Printed and bound in Spain
by CPI, Barcelona

Therese Beharrie has always been thrilled by romance. Her love of reading established this, and now she gets to write happily-ever-afters for a living and about all things romance in her blog at www.theresebeharrie.com. She married a man who constantly exceeds her romantic expectations and is an infinite source of inspiration for her romantic heroes. She lives in Cape Town, South Africa, and is still amazed that her dream of being a romance author is a reality.

For my husband, who was the official consultant for this book (and the unofficial consultant for every other). Thank you for making me see that I am more than enough.

For my mother, who taught me that the best way to deal with bullies is to believe in myself and work even harder.
Thank you for helping me through it.

And Lunelle, who's always willing to defend me (even when it isn't necessary).
Thank you for your love and support.

I love you all.

CHAPTER ONE

'AND THE SOLUTION you've come up with is *marriage*?'

Lily Newman's steps faltered at the words. Not because she was at an engagement party—her best friend Caitlyn's—where marriage was supposed to be celebrated, but because of the anger that stiffened every word she'd overheard.

There was something familiar about the voice, though not because she knew the person speaking. It was just something in the tone… But that was ridiculous, so she focused on the fact that since she didn't recognise the voice entirely she couldn't be overhearing either of the individuals she was celebrating that evening.

She looked around to check whether she might be caught eavesdropping. Not that she *wanted* to be doing that. She had come upstairs to have some time alone. Yes, maybe it *did* have something to do with seeing her ex-fiancé Kyle arrive with the woman he'd cheated on Lily with. Okay, maybe it had *everything* to do with that.

Because she hadn't wanted to face it, she'd escaped the lavish party Caitlyn's wealthy fiancé Nathan was hosting at his newly purchased home, thinking she might as well explore considering the time she would spend there once her friend was married. But her exploration had ended fairly quickly when she'd heard those angry words from the room she was now standing outside.

'Mr Brookes, we think—'

Brookes was Nathan's surname, she thought, and realised why the man's voice had sounded so familiar. He was one of Nathan's family. Perhaps the brother Caitlyn had told her Nathan had a tenuous relationship with. The one she'd never met and knew not to bring up in front of Nathan after Caitlyn had told her not to. She knew she should give him his privacy, and was about to leave when the man spoke again.

'It doesn't really sound like you were thinking at all, Jade.'

The voice hadn't risen in volume, but Lily felt a chill go through her.

Poor Jade.

'We…we actually *did* put a lot of thought into this, Mr Brookes.' A male voice took over from Jade, though his words were no more confident.

'Then take me through your thought process.'

Careful, Lily thought.

She looked around again, saw that she was still alone, and leaned against the wall.

'We did the research.' Jade was speaking again. 'The file we mailed you has all the results from various avenues—test groups, opinion polls, social media. Yes, you're a successful businessman *now*, but you've done that largely outside of the public eye. People still remember you as the man who lost the Shadows Rugby Club their chance to compete internationally. They remember you as the man who would do anything to win a game, but took it too far in the end.'

There was a pause, and then Jade continued hesitantly. 'And then all the attention was on your suspension, and the partying you did during the year after your last game for the Shadows…'

'You're not telling me anything new.' The words were flat. 'I hired you because I knew that it would be difficult to…restore my image. But I'm doubting my decision now, since you're telling me marriage is the only way I can do that.'

'It's not the *only* way,' the other man Lily had yet to identify said quickly. 'But it's the fastest way. And considering that the buy-out is time-sensitive…' He trailed off.

There was silence for a while, and Lily pushed away from the wall. Guilt spread through her when she realised she shouldn't be listening to a private conversation. Sure, she wanted to know more about Nathan's mysterious brother—if that was who he was—but it was purely out of curiosity. There really wasn't a *reason* for her to listen to Nathan's family's business.

She turned away, forcing herself to act like the confident woman she was trying to be and face Kyle, but she paused when she heard the voices in the room again.

'I shouldn't have asked you to come to my brother's engagement party.'

So he *was* Nathan's brother.

'We can discuss this tomorrow, after the TV interview.'

Her thoughts froze when she realised the man was now walking towards the door, and her legs moved just in time to avoid being caught. She hurried down the passage and turned the corner that led to the stairs…

And then stilled when she saw the man she was trying to avoid walking *up* them.

Kyle.

His date—the other descriptions in her mind weren't

quite as polite—was giggling as he whispered something into her ear. Lily had never bothered to learn the woman's name—why would she need to know the name of the woman she'd caught naked in her fiancé's arms?—but she *did* remember the red hair and petite frame.

It made her pull at the dress Caitlyn had begged her to wear a few days ago. It was too tight, Lily thought desperately. She wished with all her might that it wasn't in a shocking red colour that did nothing to hide the curves Lily had plenty of—too many, in fact.

Her pretend confidence was already dwindling, she realised. And although there was a part of her that told her it was to be expected when she was about to face the man who had broken her down throughout their relationship—who had cheated on her—she had expected more of herself.

It also did her no good to notice how much *smaller* than Lily Kyle's date was. She watched the man she had once thought she loved slide a hand around the woman's tiny waist, pulling her close enough that there was no space between them. They were sneaking away to fool around, she realised, nausea fierce in her belly. How many times had she thwarted Kyle's attempts to do just that with *her* when they were at parties? He hadn't only found a woman smaller than her, Lily thought. She was also the risk-taker Kyle had always wanted and Lily would never be.

In the split second before Kyle saw her Lily decided to take a risk. She wanted Kyle to think that she had been making out with someone upstairs. That the thing she had refused to do with him—the thing he had found someone else for—she was now doing with someone *other* than him.

She would probably think that it was a terrible decision later, but as she fluffed her coiled curls and rubbed her lips together to smudge her lipstick she only hoped one thing—that Nathan's brother had a sense of humour.

'Lily?'

Kyle's voice immediately sent her skin crawling and her heart galloping. She couldn't believe that she'd once found that voice attractive. Now she heard the slime curl around every word.

She lifted her eyebrows. 'Kyle? I didn't see you there. How are you?'

The *of-course-you-saw-me* glint in Kyle's eyes set her teeth on edge and had a small part of herself recoiling.

'I'm well. How are you? I heard you managed to get that bookstore up and running eventually.'

'It's doing really well, actually. My initial investment was quite substantial, as you know.'

Kyle's eyes hardened, and satisfaction pumped through her. But then it gave way to the usual feelings of disgust at the thought of how their relationship had ended. At how she'd compromised her integrity, her dignity.

She ignored the fact that her self-confidence was deteriorating with every moment she spent in his presence.

'You've never met Michelle before, have you? At least not officially.' Kyle pushed the woman forward. 'We're getting married in a few months.'

'Congratulations,' she answered, and though ice stiffened her spine at the woman's cold look she felt nothing else at the news that Kyle was getting married.

That didn't mean relief didn't wash over her when she heard steps behind her.

Not even considering that it might be someone else, she spoke again. 'I didn't think you needed that much time to recover, honey...'

She turned around, and the words tailed off when she

saw her supposed 'boyfriend' for the first time. His skin was the colour of coffee with cream, complemented by dark hair tousled in a style that made her fingers wish they'd been the ones to style it. His dark eyes were stormy, and she realised she had taken a massive gamble with the man—he was clearly still upset about the conversation he had just had.

But the storm cleared immediately after that thought, and was replaced by a look of calm that made her feel even more uneasy. His eyes flickered over her, and then looked at Kyle before resting on her again. The calm then transformed into interest—amusement, too, she thought—with the faintest hint of some secret knowledge that made her skin heat.

He looked nothing like his traditionally handsome brother. His face was made of rugged planes that suggested he had a thousand stories to tell, and just above his mouth was a scar that she could imagine feeling during a kiss.

When the sides of the lips she was admiring curved upwards, she flushed. He might not be traditionally handsome, but he sure as hell was sexy.

'"Honey"? You and Jacques…you're dating?'

Kyle interrupted her perusal, and Lily felt her tongue stick in her mouth when she realised that Kyle *knew* Nathan's brother—Jacques.

You should have thought of that, Lily admonished herself.

She knew that Kyle was here because Nathan worked in Kyle's family's law firm. Nathan loved his job, and hadn't wanted to upset the prestigious Van der Rosses by not inviting the man who would one day become his boss. Caitlyn had assured her it was the *only* reason Lily's ex-fiancé had been invited.

'Yes, we're dating.'

The smooth baritone of Jacques's voice sent shivers down Lily's spine, and she struggled to shake the feeling.

'For how long?' Kyle said, and she turned back to see the smugness disappear.

It bothered him, she thought, her heart accelerating in an instinctual response to Kyle's anger. But then she paused, and told herself she didn't have to be worried about him lashing out.

She didn't have to worry about him at all any more.

'Almost six months now,' she said as Jacques moved down a step to stand beside her. He was a full head taller than she was, and she tried to ignore the awareness that realisation brought.

'Six months?' Kyle repeated, and she saw his eyes flash.

They'd broken up a year ago, and clearly he thought six months was too short a time for her to mourn for him.

'It doesn't feel like six months, though,' Jacques said, and she shifted her gaze to him. 'I barely feel like I've scratched the surface with you.'

So he *did* have a sense of humour, she thought, and smiled. When he responded with a smile of his own her breath caught and she thought something crackled between them. Her heart thudded when Jacques wrapped an arm around her waist, and for a moment she forgot that it was all a game and lifted her hand to brush at a piece of his hair.

'How did you two meet?'

Kyle's voice punctured the tension in the air and she looked at him with a foggy mind. It took her a minute, but when she came out of her Jacques-induced haze she noted the grim set of Kyle's lips. He *really* didn't like this, she thought, and waited for the panic. For that quick rush of trepidation that anticipated that she was about to be put in her place.

But nothing came. And somehow she knew it was because of the easy strength exuded by the man at her side.

'I'd love to tell you all about it, Kyle, but we were up there for far too long.'

Lily shot a flirtatious glance at Jacques, and briefly wondered how deep a hole she was digging when she saw a flash of heat in Jacques's eyes.

'We should probably spend some time with the happy couple. Enjoy the rest of your evening.'

Taking Jacques's hand, she hurried down the stairs, weaving her way through the guests. She only stopped once they were outside on the balcony, and then she immediately let go.

'I'm so sorry about that,' she said hurriedly, her chest suddenly tight.

Just breathe, Lily, it's over now.

'Care to explain?'

There was a slight breeze in the air and Lily walked to the edge of the balcony, turning her face towards the wind. It helped steady her, and when she opened her eyes—when she saw the view in front of her—that did, too.

Nathan's new house stood at the top of the Tygerberg hills in Cape Town, and she could see Table Mountain and most of the city from where she was. It reminded her of how small her problems were.

Even the after-effects of a bad relationship.

'How about we start with an introduction?'

Her words were said a little breathlessly, and she cleared her throat. Nerves had replaced panic, and she glanced around. No one was paying attention to them. That helped.

'Lily Newman—best friend to the bride-to-be.' She offered a hand.

'Jacques Brookes—brother of the groom-to-be.'

He took her hand and it was like touching the coals of a fire. It made her want to break the contact immediately, but he held on, shaking her hand slowly. The heat went up her arm, through her chest...

Before it could move any further she pulled her hand away. 'Nice to meet you,' she said, and folded her arms, constraining the hands that suddenly wanted more of the fire. 'It probably would have been better if that had happened before the whole debacle inside.'

'I don't know,' he answered with a sly smile. 'It was much more interesting than the way I usually meet girls.'

'I'm sure you must mean *women*, because clearly...' She gestured to herself, and then flushed when she saw appreciation in his eyes.

But he only said, 'Touché,' and made her wonder why she'd said those words.

They'd made her sound sassier than she was. As if she was in his league. As if she was used to playing the cat-and-mouse game of flirtation. She almost laughed aloud at the prospect of being in *any* league.

No, she thought as she took in how effortlessly Jacques's muscular body wore his suit. He was *way* too attractive to be interested in her. Someone who looked like him spent time with models and actresses—definitely not with women who had more than twenty-five per cent body fat.

She distracted herself by offering the explanation he'd asked for earlier. 'Kyle's my ex-fiancé—'

She broke off when he lifted a hand, and she saw that his ring finger was a little crooked.

'The one who dumped him a month before the wedding?'

'Yes.'

'I always thought the woman who did that had some balls.'

She smiled. 'Thanks.'

'It doesn't explain why you dated him in the first place.'

It was the same thing she'd asked herself when she'd realised how poorly he'd treated her. But that realisation had only come at the end—when she'd been *forced* to see the truth. She'd been blinded by how charming, how handsome he was at first. And at all the times when he'd switched it on again sporadically throughout their relationship.

But the simple truth was that the blinkers had been kept in place because he'd been *interested* in her. It had been intoxicating—until it hadn't been. And then she'd found him with a naked woman and regained the gift of sight. It had grown clearer with each hour that had passed after she'd ended it. With each phone call Kyle had made. With each threat...

She was ashamed that she'd dated a bully—that she would have *married* him—just because she didn't think enough of herself. She'd dealt with bullies her entire life—she should have known better. And then there was the guilt, the *indignity* of her actions after the break-up...

'Some things you only realise with time,' she finally answered Jacques.

'Touché,' he said again.

She watched him shift his weight from one leg to the other and frowned. The movement was so out of place for a man who clearly had an abundance of confidence. She thought of the conversation she'd overheard, wondered if what she saw was vulnerability, and felt it hit straight at her heart.

No! she commanded herself. She had her hands full with her own problems. Like the store she'd wanted all her life—had sold a piece of herself to start—which was failing. She needed to focus on fixing *that*—on fixing *herself*—before she could even *think* of getting involved with someone else's problems.

And yet when she looked at the sexy man in front of her the resolutions that she'd thought were firmly in place seemed hazy.

'Kyle didn't seem to like you,' Lily said to distract herself. 'Why is that?'

Jacques moved closer, and the breeze brought his fresh-from-the-shower scent to her nose. Her insides wobbled as attraction flowed through her, but she chose to ignore it.

Or tried to.

'We have history.'

Lily waited for him to continue. When he didn't, she said, 'That's all you're going to tell me?'

He chuckled. 'Apparently not.'

He leaned against the balcony's railing.

'Our families run in the same circles, so I'd met him a few times before Nathan started to work for him. Because I knew he was a—' He looked at her, as though checking what her reaction would be, and then continued with a grin. 'Because I knew he wasn't a very nice person, I used to make a game out of stealing his dates.'

Her heart raced. 'But you stopped?'

Something sparked in his eyes. 'A while before you, yes. Unfortunately.'

Her face heated and she leaned against the railing as well, looking away from the view he was facing towards.

She didn't want him to see how uncomfortable he made her. And heaven only knew why she was staying there with him so that he *could* make her uncomfortable.

'Why?'

'Why did I stop?'

She nodded, and he sighed.

'Because Nathan started working for Kyle's firm. Because I stopped going to events he would be at.'

Jacques fell silent, and Lily wondered if he was remembering why he'd stopped going to those events. Had it been because he'd started playing rugby? Because he'd stopped? Had it been during the year *after* he'd stopped?

She folded her arms again when guilt nudged her at the way she'd got the information to wonder those things at all.

'And,' Jacques said after a while, 'because I didn't have time to deal with the punches he tried to throw at me.'

Surprise almost had her gasping. 'Kyle tried to *hit* you?'

His lips curved and her pulse spiked.

'*Tried* being the operative word. It was entertaining for me...painful for him, I imagine.'

'You hit him back?'

'Don't sound so surprised. I was defending myself.'

It took her a moment to process that, and then she laughed. 'I would have *paid* to see that.'

He smiled. 'You could still see it.'

She gave him a look. 'I'm not *actually* going to pay you to hit my ex.'

Jacques laughed. 'It wouldn't cost you much if you wanted me to, but I wasn't talking about that. I saw the way he looked at us when he heard we were together. He *hated* it. So I bet if you and I go into that party right now and pretend to be a couple for a while longer his reaction would pretty much be the same as a punch in the gut.'

She'd barely had enough time to consider his proposal before he'd pushed up from where he was leaning and moved closer to her, sliding an arm around her waist. Her eyes widened and her mouth opened as she drew a quick breath. She watched his eyes lower to it. He only needed to dip his head—it was barely five centimetres away—and she would know if she could *really* feel that scar during a kiss...

He moved his mouth until it was next to her ear and whispered, 'Kyle's watching, so you might want to make that decision quickly.'

CHAPTER TWO

JACQUES COULDN'T DENY enjoying the way the woman he'd only just met shivered in his arms. Or the look her ex—a man he had a *very* low opinion of—was aiming at him. But those things were irrelevant to him at that moment. What *was* relevant was an opportunity to do just as his PR firm had advised. An opportunity that had just fallen into his lap, and would get him exactly what he wanted if he used it properly.

Lily shifted, reminding him that the opportunity wasn't an *it* but a *who*.

'If I say yes, will you let go of me?'

She asked it in a shaky tone, and he looked down into uncertain eyes. They became guarded a moment later, and he frowned, wondering where the spirit he'd admired earlier had gone.

'I'll let go of you regardless, Lily.'

He spoke softly, but forced his heart to harden. He couldn't feel anything for her—including empathy. It would make using her a lot more difficult.

It sounded harsh, even to him, but he knew he would do it if it meant he could redeem himself from the mistakes he'd made in the past. He'd been trying to do that since he'd realised he was only proving people right—

specifically his father—by acting the way he had during the year after his suspension.

The realisation had had him channelling the 'I'll do whatever it takes' motto he'd been known for during his rugby days into building a sporting goods company. Into making it a success.

Now it was. And yet people *still* thought of him as the bad boy who'd beaten up his opponent seven years ago, and it grated him. So when he'd heard that his old rugby club was being sold, he'd known it was an opportunity. He could go back to the root of it all—to where his problems had started.

The irony was that he needed a better reputation to get the club he believed would change his poor reputation. And Lily was the key to that.

'Let's do it.'

The words were said firmly, surprising him after the brief moment of vulnerability he'd just seen, but he simply asked, 'Are you sure?'

'Yes.'

She gave a quick nod, and then moved her mouth so that it was next to his ear, just as he had done to her earlier. It made it seem as if she was responding to his question—something her action made seem suggestive—and he would have appreciated the strategy if a thrill hadn't gone through his body, distracting him.

'We'll have to tell Caitlyn about this. If she sees us and thinks we're together she's going to freak out.'

She pulled back and laid a hand on his chest—an intimate gesture that had his heart beating too hard for his liking.

'That would probably be best,' he answered stiffly.

It took him a moment to figure out whether his tone

came because of the effect she had on him or the prospect of speaking to his brother.

A fist clenched at a piece of his heart as it always did when he thought of Nathan, but he tried to focus on his task. He took Lily's hand and led her through the crowd of people he no longer cared enough about to know to where his brother and Caitlyn were standing.

Holding Lily's hand sent awareness up and down his arm, but he ignored it. Attraction wasn't something new to him. *There's more with her,* a voice taunted, and again he tried to think of something else. But his options seemed limited to things he *didn't* want to think about, and he sighed, realising he would have to face at least one of them.

His brother won, Jacques thought as they reached the circle of people Nathan and Caitlyn were surrounded by. The easy air that Nathan carried around him—the way it translated into ease around people—had always been something Jacques had admired. Sometimes envied. Until he'd realised that people were overrated. One day they saw you as a hero, doing things they admired—the next those very things were criticised and *that* was how they defined you.

But Jacques knew it was also the easy way Nathan approached their less than stellar parents. How he was still in touch with them when Jacques hadn't seen them in years. How he could still want to be a part of their family after all they'd had to deal with growing up...

He stopped that train of thought when he saw they'd attracted Nathan's attention, and with a slight nod of his head Jacques indicated they go to a quieter corner of the room.

'I'm glad you came,' were the first words from his brother's mouth.

'You knew I would.'

Nathan sent Jacques a look that had a lance of guilt piercing his chest. It made him think about how he hadn't seen either of his parents there that evening—*Surprise, surprise,* he thought, despite the relief coursing through him—and he realised it was disappointment, not accusation, that had Nathan doubting Jacques. And that it wasn't exactly *Jacques,* but their whole family.

While Jacques sympathised with his brother, that feeling was capped by the memory of the thousands of times Jacques had warned Nathan to stop *hoping* with their parents. Jacques had learnt a long time ago that it would get him nowhere. His anger about it had ended his career, after all. Had taught him to stop trying. And, since he hadn't seen them in seven years, he figured he'd succeeded in that.

'Congratulations,' Jacques said, remembering that this was the first time he'd seen his brother and his fiancée since they'd got engaged.

He brushed a kiss on Caitlyn's cheek, enjoying the smile that spread over her pretty face, and then went in for the obligatory handshake and pat on the back with his brother.

'While that was both amusing *and* touching,' Lily interrupted with a small smile, 'I know you both have to do the rounds, so we just wanted to tell you we're going to pretend to be dating so that I can make Kyle feel a fraction of what I felt when I walked in on him and her—' she nodded a head in the woman's direction '—naked.'

By the time she was done Jacques could tell that she was out of breath. Which didn't surprise him, since with each word the pace with which she'd spoken had increased. What *did* surprise him was what she had said— that Kyle had cheated on her. While he'd been amused at being roped in to being a pretend boyfriend earlier, he understood why she'd done it now. And he no longer felt amusement over the situation.

There was a stunned silence, and then Caitlyn said, 'Honey, are you okay?'

'I'm fine.' Lily brushed one of her delightful curls from her face. 'We just wanted to warn you in case you wondered. Or got asked about it. And, while we're speaking about that, we've been dating six months. You and Nate introduced us.'

Jacques's lips twitched at the way their story had evolved, but the amusement faded when he wondered how Kyle could have cheated on someone like Lily.

Someone like Lily? a voice questioned, and he realised it sounded crazy. He barely knew her—she might have cheated on Kyle first. But given what he knew about Kyle and the few moments he'd spent with Lily he highly doubted that *she'd* been in the wrong.

His opinion of Kyle dropped another notch, and the temptation to relive the night he had knocked the man out boiled in Jacques's blood. He frowned, wondering where the intensity of his feelings—a mixture of anger and protectiveness—came from. And then he felt his brother's gaze on him, and looked up into a flash of warning.

Since he'd experienced a surge of protection for Lily himself, he understood it. But it singed him to know Nathan was thinking about Jacques's past with women. And it burned to know his brother's warning was on point, considering what he planned to use Lily for.

'You don't have to worry, Cait,' he said, distracting himself.

He knew Caitlyn was the one to win over if he wanted his plan to work. Caitlyn gave him a quick nod, then turned her attention to Lily.

'You know I never liked him—especially after everything...' She trailed off, glancing at Jacques. Then she quickly said, 'I give my blessing for this fake relationship in the name of payback.'

Caitlyn had sparked his curiosity, but it was forgotten when Lily smiled and his chest constricted.

Simple attraction.

He willed himself to believe that when his skin prickled as she took his hand again. And when she looked back with those beautiful eyes of hers to check whether he was okay with it and his heart raced.

He gave her a quick nod, and she started towards the doors that led to the side of the balcony that held the pool. Before he could take more than a few steps with her, someone touched his arm and he looked back.

'Please...be careful with her,' Caitlyn said, looking at him with eyes that reflected her plea.

'I... I will,' he answered, before he could think to say anything else, and the gratitude that shone from her face had his stomach dropping.

He glanced at his brother, saw the frown that suggested Nathan didn't believe him, and his stomach dropped even further. He turned back to Lily, following her until she stopped next to the pool, and tried not to think about the interaction he'd just had. It made him wonder what it was about Lily that inspired the protectiveness he'd seen in the two people he'd just spoken to—the protectiveness that he'd felt himself.

He cleared his throat. 'Are we going for a swim? I didn't bring my swimming trunks...although I have nothing against stripping down to my birthday suit.'

'What?' she gasped, and a smile spread across his face.

'I'm kidding, Lily. Unless...?' he teased, and enjoyed the way red tinted her olive skin.

The colour made him think of the other women he'd dated—he used that term loosely—who spent hours in the sun trying to get that tone. Something told him that Lily would never spend so much time on such a vain endeavour. Not when he was sure the messy auburn curls surrounding her face hadn't been tampered with. When he was sure her beautiful face bore almost no make-up. Her hazel eyes weren't highlighted by mascara or liner. The blush on her high cheekbones wasn't artificial, nor was the pomegranate hue of her full lips.

As attracted as he was to the outside—he took a moment to enjoy the way her body filled out the dress she wore, just as he had when he'd been coming down the stairs—he found himself more intrigued by what the outside *told* him. How many women did he know who would come to an upper-class party *without* plastering their faces with make-up? How many would leave their hair in its natural state when every other woman had hers sleeked up in some complicated style?

Certainly none of the women *he* knew, he thought.

And her reactions to his teasing were so refreshing. Endearing. It made her feel more authentic. And it made her perfect for his plan.

It also made him realise how little innocence the women he'd spent his time with in the past had had. But then innocence wasn't exactly something he'd been looking for in the past. No, he'd been looking to forget the way he'd screwed up his life. And then the public had turned on him—had destroyed him in the media—and he'd begun to wonder what the point of trying was. If they wanted a bad boy, that was what they would get. And they had—for an entire year. The worst time of his life...

'I don't know why I let you fluster me.' Lily's words tore him from his thoughts. 'I know you're teasing.'

'And if I wasn't?'

She sent a look at him that had him smiling.

'Nice try, but it isn't going to work again.'

'It was worth a shot. How else would I be able to see the wonderful colour your cheeks turn when you're flustered?'

She shook her head, and with her bottom lip between her teeth looked away.

Because he saw the very colour he'd been talking about again, he grinned. 'This is fun.'

'For you, maybe,' Lily answered, but she didn't seem upset. 'What did Caitlyn say to you when she called you back?'

'You saw that?'

She nodded, and it took him a few seconds to decide what to say to her.

'She told me to be careful with you.'

Lily nodded again, her face pensive, and then her eyes shifted to something behind him. She moved closer and gave him a whiff of citrus and summer. It was a heady combination, he thought as his body tightened, and he assured himself that that was the only reason for his reaction.

'Our plan seems to be working.' Her curls shook as she lifted her head to look at him. 'Kyle barely seems to be paying attention to his—'

Her eyes widened and she bit her lip again. The prickle in his body became an ache.

'Date?' he offered, to distract himself, but couldn't help the hand that lifted to tuck a curl around her ear.

'Sure—let's go with that,' she murmured, and fluttered those dark lashes up at him.

The ache was replaced by a punch to the gut.

'Why do I need to be careful with you?'

It suddenly seemed imperative for him to know.

'You don't…' she breathed, and electricity snapped between them.

'Are you sure?'

'No.' She shook her head. 'I'm tired of being treated like I'm going to break. My fiancé cheated on me. I was—' She stopped, and there was a flash of vulnerability on her face before it was replaced with a fierce expression. 'You don't have to be careful with me. Treat me as you would any other woman.'

CHAPTER THREE

JACQUES'S EYES FLICKERED down to her lips, and Lily realised how her request sounded. Under any other circumstance she would have been mortified at the implication of her words. Now, though, she *wanted* Jacques to take advantage of the ambiguity. She wanted to be taken advantage of...

'I wouldn't be pretending to be your boyfriend if you were any other woman.'

His voice broke into her thoughts and she blushed at the direction of them, wondering where they'd come from.

'Why are you doing this for *me*, then?'

The heat she'd thought she'd seen earlier in his eyes cooled into an enigmatic expression.

'Besides the fact that you basically forced me to on the stairs?'

She nodded, feeling her blush deepen.

'At first because I couldn't imagine anything better than making Kyle Van der Ross uncomfortable. Now it's because I want to make him jealous.'

He looked at her, and she realised they were having this conversation in an awfully intimate position. She took a slight step back, to give herself some air—and to prevent herself from being distracted by his scent—

but stopped when he placed a hand gently on the small of her back.

It sent her next question stammering from her mouth. 'Wh…wh…why?'

He smiled at her—a soft smile that was in stark contrast to his intimidating masculine presence—and she wondered what she was missing. A man like Jacques wouldn't be interested in *her*. And even if he was the last thing *she* wanted was to get involved with someone who could shatter the self-esteem she had fought so hard for.

The self-esteem she was *still* fighting for.

'He cheated on you, Lily. And only the most despicable of men hurt the women they claim to love in that way.' His face no longer held an easy expression. 'Besides, I *like* helping you. And before you ask me why, it's because I like *you*.'

'You barely know me,' she retorted. It was easier than acknowledging the truth of his words.

'I know that you had the guts to leave someone who cheated on you. I know that you're loyal enough to come to your best friend's engagement party even though you knew your ex would be here. You're innovative—I don't think I know many other people who would come up with the idea of a stranger pretending to be their boyfriend—and you're thoughtful enough to let your friends know about the charade so that they don't get upset. What more is there?'

He grinned, but she couldn't bring herself to respond. Hearing him describe her like that sent a gush of warmth through her body. But it didn't seem right. Not when she was used to harsh words. Not when she was used to people telling her how she should look. How she should be. And from her parents—from Kyle, too, she'd realised too late—how much *better* she could be.

'Fine—you know things about me,' she said, when the silence had extended a tad too long. 'How about you share something about yourself, then?'

'Sure,' he replied easily, and touched her waist to shift her to the left. 'It's easier for Kyle to see you like this.'

Her skin felt seared at his touch, and her thoughts went haywire for a second. And in that second she saw herself pressed against Jacques, kissing him until she no longer knew who she was.

She shook her head, thinking that she didn't know who she was *now*. This woman having inappropriate thoughts about a man she barely knew was definitely not her. She'd never gone that far—even in her most lonesome of days.

When she'd been overweight it had been easier to avoid attention. And even when she'd lost some of her weight she had still been too afraid to put herself in a situation where men might hit on her.

It had been on the one night Caitlyn had convinced her to go out—in their final year at university—that she'd met Kyle. He'd been the first person to treat her like a woman, and not like 'the girl who lost weight'. His attention had been flattering, overwhelming. She'd fallen hard, and had been swept into his world like a commoner into a castle.

His offhand comments about her looks—he hadn't seemed to have a problem with her weight, but her hair, her face, her clothing were still fair game—hadn't mattered when he could make her feel like the most beautiful woman on the planet with one look. His suggestions as to how she should act, what she should say, how she might do better had been irrelevant when he was treating her to fancy dinners, to expensive gifts.

'What do you want to know?'

Jacques was watching her, and her face heated even at the thought of him knowing what she was thinking.

'How'd you get the scar?'

He frowned, as though he wasn't sure what she was talking about. And then his hand lifted and he rubbed his thumb over the scar. Lily was hit with the desire to do the same, and she clenched her hand, determined not to be caught in this attraction between them.

'I was in a fight.'

'Kyle?'

He smiled, though his eyes were hooded.

'He didn't land a punch that night. No, there have been other fights.'

His eyes glinted dangerously, and her knees nearly went weak.

What is wrong with you, Lily?

'Next question. What do you do?'

'I own a sporting goods company.'

'What does that entail?'

'Well, there's a shop where the public can buy sporting equipment, but mostly we do bulk and international orders.' He slanted a look at her. 'You've never heard of Brookes Sporting?'

'Hard to believe, isn't it?'

He smirked. 'Just a little.'

'And that's what you chose to do after your rugby career ended?'

There was a beat of silence before Jacques asked, 'How did you know I played rugby?'

She only then realised she wasn't supposed to know that.

'You expected me to know your company, but not that you played a popular South African sport? Besides, I'm

sure Nathan mentioned it a while ago…' She trailed off
when she saw he wasn't buying it.

'Really? The brother who didn't think I was going
to come to his engagement party told you I used to play
rugby?'

'Would you believe me if I told you I used to watch
you play?'

'No.'

She sighed. She was going to have to tell him the truth.

'I overheard your conversation earlier, Jacques. I'm
really sorry.'

That explained how she'd known he would follow her
lead when they'd spoken to Kyle, Jacques thought. It also
meant she had heard Jade and Riley's suggestion, which
put his plan to convince her to be involved at risk.

'Is eavesdropping a hobby of yours?' he asked slowly.

'I didn't mean to,' Lily replied primly. 'I was upstairs
because I saw—'

'Kyle and the cheater?'

She nodded. 'And when I walked past the room you
were in I heard the whole marriage thing…'

So she *had* heard it, he thought, but soothed the faint
trickle of panic by telling himself that she didn't suspect
he wanted *her* involved. She wouldn't have agreed to his
suggestion to continue the charade of their pretend relationship at the party if she did. And then Jacques would
have lost the opportunity to ensure that all the wealthy
people who formed part of his brother's social circle—
including Lily's ex-fiancé—saw him and his 'new girlfriend'.

The rest of his plan had originally involved them leaving together at the end of the night. It would have just
been for coffee—though the party attendees wouldn't

have known that—and he would have suggested their pretend relationship continue for just a while longer. But this new information meant he needed to speed up that plan…

'Why don't we get out of here?'

Her eyebrows rose and her cheeks took on that shade of red he liked so much.

'Together?'

'Yeah. We can grab a cup of coffee.'

'Why?'

'I like you, Lily.' Though he'd meant the words to convince her to have coffee with him, he found that he genuinely meant them. Something tightened in his stomach at the knowledge. 'I also think there's nothing more you'd like to do than to get out of here.'

Her face had changed when he'd said he liked her, and though he couldn't quite read it he thought there was a trace of uncertainty there. As if she didn't believe what he said. The tightening in his stomach pulsed, and for the first time he considered how manipulative his plan was. Sure, it wouldn't hurt Lily—but it wouldn't benefit her either. It was entirely for *his* benefit.

But you helped her, too, a voice in his head reminded him. That made him feel better, and because he couldn't afford to dwell on why he should reconsider he chose to focus on that.

'You're right.' Lily's expression was unreadable. 'And buying you a coffee is probably the least I can do to say thank you.'

She was setting boundaries, he realised. Letting him know that she was only accepting his offer because she wanted to say thanks. He wasn't sure why that bothered him, but he didn't have time to ponder it.

'Are you sure you want to leave, though?' she asked.

She looked inside to where Nathan and Caitlyn were standing.

'I don't think Nathan expects me to stay longer than I already have,' he said, ignoring the guilt.

'Do you want to say goodbye?' she asked softly, and he looked down to see a compassion he didn't understand—and didn't want—in her eyes.

'I don't want to interrupt them.'

She watched him for a moment longer, and then nodded.

He reached for her hand, thinking about how easily he could feign affection with Lily and yet struggle with women he was much more familiar with. His skin heated when her fingers closed around his, warning him that his plan might have complications he hadn't considered.

But as he made his way through the crowd of people with Lily he knew that those complications would be worth it when the Shadows Rugby Club was his and he could help place them in the international league. If he could do that it would make up for the fact that he'd *cost* them their place in that league seven years ago.

When he felt like being kind to himself he told himself his actions that night of the championship game that should have determined that place had come from anger. From pain. That night had been the last time he'd seen either of his parents, too. Not a coincidence, considering that *they'd* been the reason he'd got into a fight with a player who hadn't deserved Jacques's attention. Who wouldn't have got it if he hadn't uttered those same words his father had before Jacques had arrived at the game...

'You're such a disappointment.'

The memory of that night still plagued him—still scarred him—but if he could pull off his PR company's ridiculous plan maybe he would finally find some peace.

Maybe he would finally be able to put it all behind him and move on.

'Do you have somewhere specific you'd like to go?' Lily asked once they were outside.

He watched her pull her coat tighter around her, saw her look out around the private estate his brother's house was on, and realised she was nervous.

'I'm not going to kidnap you, Lily.'

She looked at him. 'I know. And I'm going in my own car.'

Smart girl, he thought, even though disappointment lapped at him for reasons he didn't understand.

'My office is pretty private.' He saw something in her eyes, and said, 'You'll be safe, Lily. I promise to behave myself.'

My future depends on it.

She tilted her head, as though she was considering his words. 'So let's have coffee somewhere more neutral, then. I know a place…'

CHAPTER FOUR

'THIS IS *NEUTRAL* for you?'

Jacques joined Lily in front of her store, and looked pointedly at the sign that said 'Lily's' above the glass entrance.

'Relax,' she replied, though the way her heart was beating told her she was probably saying it to herself.

'We're just stopping here for the coffee—then we can take a walk down the beach. It's not too busy this time of night.'

'I usually let a woman take me out for dinner before I do romantic walks on the beach, Lily.'

Her hand froze on the door at his words, and it took her a moment to hear the store's alarm beeping. She hurriedly entered the code, trying desperately to come up with something to say. But her mind only formulated excuses—not the sassy comeback she'd hoped for.

You should have known it wouldn't last, a voice mocked her.

And though she wanted to deny the words she couldn't. She'd thought it was a *good* idea to bring him back to her store and then to walk on the beach. She'd feel better in a familiar place, she'd told herself.

But being in that familiar place had snatched her from the fantasy world she'd been in for the past few hours.

The world where she'd flirted as though she were in a thinner body. As though she had all the confidence in the world. As though she wasn't trying with all her might to value herself.

'This is nice,' he said, breaking the silence. 'It's a coffee shop and a bookstore?'

'Yeah. I love reading and I love coffee, and a lot of the people I know do, too. So I thought it would be pretty great to have a place where you could relax and do both. And, of course, there's the view.'

She was rambling, she knew. A combination of nerves at Jacques being there and the defensiveness she always felt when she spoke about her store.

Her parents' warnings echoed in her head—as did their urges for her to do something more *respectable* than being a store-owner—and she shook it off. She had more pressing things to worry about at the moment.

'Do you have any preferences for coffee?'

'Black, no sugar.'

She busied herself with the task, and for a few moments there was silence.

'You have good taste.'

The milk she was pouring spilled onto the counter. 'Wh…what?'

'I assume you decorated the store yourself?'

She nodded mutely, refusing to look at him in case he wore that amused expression again.

'It's the perfect décor for a shop like this.'

She'd gone with a blue and white colour scheme, to complement the view of the sea that stretched endlessly through the glass entrance. White bookshelves held as many books as she could fit in them—old and new—and lined the walls on either side of the shop. The wooden tables and blue-cushioned chairs were homely, comfortable—exactly what she'd been going for when she'd decorated, though she knew she'd spent hopelessly too much on them.

But she only worried about that when she did her accounts and saw how many negative numbers they had.

'Thanks,' she said, making quick work of the clean-up before handing him his coffee in a takeaway cup. She cleared her throat. 'We don't have to...to do the walk. I just thought it made sense...'

'I was teasing, Lily.'

The smile on his lips made her stomach flip. And then there were even more gymnastics when he lifted her chin.

'You know—that thing I do so I can see you blush?'

She took a step back. 'You mean the thing I shouldn't let fluster me?'

'Exactly.'

She couldn't help a smile at his quick answer. 'How about we take this to the beach?'

She left her coat and her shoes in the store, and a few moments later they were walking on the sand together.

'It's beautiful, isn't it?' he said, looking out to the water.

Waves crashed against the sand at his words, and the reflection of the full moon on the water shimmered, as though thanking Jacques for the compliment.

'Yeah, it is. I remember going on holiday to Johannesburg when I was younger. I refused to go again when I realised there was no beach.' She shrugged. 'Something about a beach just—'

'Calms you?'

'Yeah.' She glanced over. 'Did the same thing ever happen to you?'

There was a bark of laughter. 'That would have involved my parents actually *taking* us on holiday, so no.'

The words surprised her, and if his silence was any indication they had surprised him, too. She wanted to press him—for reasons she didn't want to think about—but before she could Jacques jogged a few paces ahead of her. Lily watched as he threw his empty coffee cup into a nearby bin, and in a few quick movements climbed onto a large boulder.

He grinned down at her when she reached him. 'Join me.'

'Up there? In this dress?' She shook her head. 'I'll pass.'

'How about that one?' Jacques nodded at the boulder next to the one he was on. It was smaller, but she still didn't see herself up there.

'I don't think you understand, Jacques—'

She broke off when he jumped down next to her, threw her coffee cup into the same bin—despite the fact that hers had only been half-empty—and took her free hand.

'Come on—it'll be a good place to talk.'

Helpless to do otherwise, she let him lead her to the next boulder, but stopped when they reached it.

'I don't see how this is going to work.'

'Like this.'

She felt his hands on her waist, and realised his intentions too late—he was already lifting her.

'Oh, no, Jacques,' she gasped. 'I'm too heavy—'

But she didn't get a chance to finish her sentence since her feet were already on the smooth, cold granite of the boulder.

A few moments later, Jacques joined her. 'Did you just say that you were too heavy?'

He barely sounded winded, and it took Lily a while to find her words. She was too busy wondering whether she'd overestimated her weight or underestimated his strength. Since she didn't live in a world where the former was ever a reality, she settled on the second.

'I guess not,' she finally answered him.

'You think you're heavy?'

'I...well... Kyle wasn't as strong as you are,' she finished lamely.

He gave her a strange look, but didn't say anything. Instead he offered a hand, gesturing that they should sit. She ignored the spark that zipped through her at the contact, and snatched her hand back as soon as she was sitting.

'Thanks for agreeing to have coffee with me,' he said when he settled down beside her.

'It was the least I could do after you helped me with Kyle. Even if you *did* throw most of mine in the bin.'

'Sorry...'

Jacques smiled apologetically, but something on his face told her there was more.

He confirmed it when he said, 'I actually wanted to talk to you in private because...'

He took a breath, and she felt a frisson of nerves deep inside.

'I was hoping you would do a little *more* than just have coffee with me.'

'What do you want?' she asked stiffly, hearing a voice mocking her in her head.

Did you really think he was being nice to you because he liked you?

'Nothing we haven't already managed to pull off.' He paused. 'I'd like you to pretend to be my girlfriend.'

CHAPTER FIVE

IT SOUNDED SILLY even as he said it—more so when he saw the look on her face—but he ignored the feeling. *This* was the point of continuing the charade for so long. This was the point of asking her out for coffee.

It shouldn't matter that the easiness they'd shared this past half an hour—the ease responsible for that slip about his parents—had dissipated.

'Are you sure you just want me to pretend to be a *girl-friend*?' she asked quietly.

'Yes. We've done a pretty good job at convincing Kyle. A few more people wouldn't hurt.'

'"A few more" isn't quite the number, though, is it?'

Wondering how she knew, he answered, 'Fine, it's a lot more than a few. But you won't actually be *on* television. I just need the people at the studio to know you exist, so when I mention you on air it'll be believable.'

'What are you talking about?'

'*Latte Mornings*. I have an interview on the show tomorrow morning.' He frowned, realising now that they weren't on the same page. 'What are *you* talking about?'

'I heard your conversation, remember?'

She looked straight at him, and if her words hadn't surprised him he might have acknowledged the way his stomach tightened in response.

'You need a wife, right? Someone who will make you more…palatable to the public for some business deal you're working on?'

'Hold on.' He took a deep breath. 'You don't get to make assumptions about things you overheard—out of context, I might add—in a private conversation.'

Her cheeks flushed, and the spirit that had had her looking him in the eye earlier faded as she averted her gaze. 'I'm sorry that I eavesdropped, Jacques, but I… I can't be your *wife*.'

'I'm not asking you to *marry* me, Lily.'

'Then what *do* you want from me?'

'I just want you to pretend to be my girlfriend. You may have overheard that I'm not entirely willing to marry someone to get the public to like me.' *Not if I don't have to.* 'But you gave me the idea tonight that I could pretend to have a nice, respectable girlfriend and that might have the same effect.'

'And that's the real reason you wanted coffee?'

'Yeah. It isn't that much to ask, considering that I did the same for you tonight.'

He shouldn't feel bad about this. He shouldn't have to defend himself.

So why was he?

'And maybe if you'd asked me straight I would have agreed. But instead you just told me to continue the charade for a bit longer—which *now*, of course, I realise is because you wanted to test whether it would actually have an effect, and not because you wanted to annoy Kyle— and then "coffee".' She lifted her hands in air quotes. 'You manipulated me.'

'And what *you* did wasn't manipulation?' he snapped back at her, guilt spurring his words. The picture she had painted reminded him too much of his father.

'I didn't manipulate you,' she answered primly. 'I told you why I did what I did. I was honest with you as soon as I had the chance to be.'

He shrugged, pretended her words didn't affect him. 'And I'm a businessman. I know how to capitalise on opportunities.'

'This isn't an *opportunity*,' she said coldly. '*I'm* not an opportunity.'

'Of course not.' He said the words before he could think about how they might undermine the cool exterior he was aiming for.

'Then stop treating me like one.'

She was right, he thought, and then remembered that she'd said if he'd been straight with her maybe she would have agreed.

'You're right—and I'm sorry for the way I went about this.'

She gave him a look that told him she didn't entirely trust his words. That look combined with the wounded expression just behind the guard she was trying so desperately to keep up, made him feel a stab of guilt.

He *had* manipulated her. And he should know, since he'd witnessed his father manipulating his mother for his entire childhood. Somehow the man had made his wife believe that telling their children they were disappointments, failures, was normal. That raising them without the love and support parents were supposed to give was acceptable. And his mother, so desperately in love with a man who had only wanted her for her money, hadn't believed she'd deserved more.

That her children had deserved better.

When Jacques had finally managed to convince his mother to kick his father out it had only taken his father a few minutes to change her mind. And now Jacques regretted it. The trying. The hope. The fact that he'd done it on the night of the championship.

It had been the reason he'd been so easily provoked into the fight that had got him suspended for three years. That had lost his team their chance to be a part of the international league they had fought so hard to play for.

It was why buying the Shadows now was so important. And why he needed to make amends with Lily.

'Would you give me another chance to ask you to be my girlfriend? My pretend one, of course.' He wasn't sure why he clarified it, but it made him feel better.

'If you tell me why you need a pretend girlfriend, yes.'

He nodded, and forced himself to say the words.

'Seven years ago I was suspended from playing rugby.' It took more strength than he'd thought it would to say the words. 'I got into a fight that cost my team a championship game and the chance of playing in the highest league they could play in.'

She interlaced her fingers and rested her hands in her lap. 'What was the fight about?'

'It doesn't matter,' he answered, because it was true.

'The scar?' she asked, tapping at her lip.

He wondered what intrigued her so much about it, but only nodded. There was a beat of silence before she spoke again.

'It must have been important if it cost you something that clearly meant so much to you.'

Maybe it had been important to him once—the chance of a family without his father. Now Jacques thought he'd been fighting over something that hadn't been worth nearly as much as it had cost him.

'It doesn't matter," he said again. 'It's only the effect the entire thing had on my reputation that does.' He paused. 'I heard recently from a few business associates that my old rugby club is going to be sold soon, and I want to be the one to buy it. Except I've been told that some of the club's biggest sponsors will pull out if it's sold to me. The only way to prevent that, it seems, is to build a more...*positive* reputation.'

She stared at him. 'You're seriously telling me that people care that much about your reputation?'

'Apparently.'

'And the only thing you did to get this negative reputation was have a fight?'

'One that lost my team the championship *and* an opportunity.'

'Yes, of course—but that's *it*?'

He hesitated. 'Well...'

Jacques really wasn't interested in rehashing the details of the year when he'd spiralled into the depression that had damaged his reputation even more.

'Well...?' Lily repeated, a single brow arching in a way that made him forget the tension of the conversation they were having.

'The year after I was suspended I spent a lot of time... Well, I spent some time on a self-destructive path,' he said once he had steadied himself.

'What does *that* mean?'

'I...' He'd hoped his explanation would be enough. 'I told myself that I didn't care what people thought about me, and I did exactly what I wanted to.'

And yet, ironically, it had been caring about what people thought that had *made* him act that way in the first place.

When she didn't speak after a few moments, he found himself asking, 'Why aren't you saying anything?'

'What did that entail?' she said in lieu of a reply.

He tried to formulate an answer, but nothing he could say would make him look good.

'I can't help you if I don't know the truth, Jacques.'

'Parties. A lot of swearing at journalists. Women.' He ran a hand through his hair, wondering how telling her all this intimidated him more than tackling the largest of men on a rugby field. 'What more do you want me to say?'

'So you were a bad boy?' she asked.

He cringed. The term brought memories he would rather ignore.

'I thought people *loved* bad boys.'

'Maybe,' he conceded, and then considered her comment. 'I think people only love bad boys as an idea. Something or someone far away from them. But they definitely do not when a bad boy, say, wants to date their daughter.'

She tilted her head, and one of her curls sprang over her forehead.

'So you're saying that people don't want you to buy a rugby club because they love the club too much?' She looked at him. 'They don't want you to "hurt their child"?'

He opened his mouth to protest, thinking her oversimplified explanation couldn't possibly be the reason he was in his current dilemma. But after a few moments he realised that that was *exactly* what was going on.

'Pretty much, yeah.'

'And if you have a girlfriend…?'

'If people see that I have a respectable girlfriend—a steady one—maybe they'll like me enough to trust me with the Shadows again.'

She frowned, and he waited as she processed his words.

'You really think that would work?'

No, was his first thought, but he said, 'I trust the people who work for me. If they say having a wife—or a girlfriend—people like will make them see me more favourably, then I believe them.'

There was another pause, and then she asked softly, 'How do you know people will like *me*?'

The hesitancy in her voice scratched at the protective instincts he'd locked away seven years ago.

Look where that had got him with his mother.

'Because you're likeable.'

Her curls bounced as she shook her head. 'No, I'm not.'

'Based on whose evaluation?' When she didn't reply, he said, 'Lily, you asked me to be honest. How about you do me the same courtesy?'

She looked down at her hands and he saw another glimpse of that other side of her. The side he'd seen when she'd claimed to be too heavy for him to lift her onto the boulder. It hit him harder than he might have anticipated, and he clenched his fists to keep himself from comforting her.

He barely knew the woman, and even if he did there was no way he wanted to get involved with her troubles. He'd purposely steered away from relationships to avoid being lured into protecting someone as he'd had to protect his mother. And Lily's insecurities reminded him a little too much of the woman he hadn't seen in seven years.

And yet when Lily answered him he found himself forgetting his own warning.

'I had a...a difficult time growing up. Didn't have that many friends. And then a failed relationship...'

The vulnerable look on her face twisted his heart.

'I mean, *that* must say something about my likeability.'

He watched her face change into an expression that

told him she'd said more than she'd meant to, and then the guard slipped back up again. It took him a moment to figure out how to respond.

'You have Caitlyn. And Nathan. They love you.' He paused. 'And *I* like you, Lily.' He said it again, to make her see that someone who didn't know her as well as Caitlyn and Nathan could like her too. Again, he found that he meant it. 'And you can't blame yourself for what happened with Kyle.'

She tilted her head. Didn't meet his eyes. 'Actually, I can. I didn't see him for what he was. I *let* him treat me poorly. I—'

'Stop!' he said harshly.

Seeing the surprise on her face, he forced himself to calm down. But Lily was doing exactly what his mother had done with his father—blaming herself, making excuses. It had always made his blood heat, just as it did now.

'Don't make excuses for him.'

'I'm… I'm not,' she stammered. 'I just meant that—'

She broke off when she looked at him, and he realised he hadn't schooled his face as well as he should have.

'I'm sorry. I just—'

The tone of her voice sucked all the anger from him. 'You don't have to apologise,' he said softly, unable to help himself as he took her hands into his.

She nodded, and the colour that had seeped out of her face started to return. His stomach turned, and he realised Lily wasn't the right person for his plan. She was too vulnerable…too fragile for him to bring her into the public light.

It had nothing to do with the fact that she awoke feelings in him that he had buried the night he'd written his parents off. Feelings that reminded him of when he'd fought for his mother. Feelings of protectiveness, of tenderness—feelings that had no place in what he wanted to achieve…

'*I'm* the one who should be apologising,' Jacques said, his decision made. 'I shouldn't have asked you to do this.'

'What?'

'You're not the right person for this, Lily.'

He saw her face blanch, was about to comfort her, but then thought better of it. He moved his hands from hers, immediately missing the warmth, and stood.

'I don't think that being in the public eye together is right for either of us,' he finished lamely, but he could tell that under her stony expression she was upset.

'Okay,' she said hoarsely, and then cleared her throat. Her voice was much stronger when she spoke again. 'You're probably right. No one would believe we were together anyway.'

She pulled her legs up and he could see she was contemplating how to stand without his help. He offered it anyway, and she accepted reluctantly—and again, so she could get off the boulder.

With each step back things between them grew more tense. Something inside Jacques grew more unsettled—so much so that he sighed in relief when they reached the pathway leading to her store.

'Thank you for your help with Kyle today,' she said primly, and each stilted word had his chest tightening.

'I was happy to help.'

It sounded strange to him to be so formal after what they'd just spoken about, but he didn't know how else to respond. He didn't even know why her words left him with an ache in his chest.

Silence stretched, making it feel as though there was more distance between them than the few centimetres from where she stood on the pathway and where he stood in the sand. The silence was heavy with disappointment, and it shook him more than he cared to admit. Perhaps because he'd lived with it hanging over his head his entire life. The disappointment that he would never live up to expectations he didn't know.

Like when he'd been hailed as the best player the Shadows had ever had and it hadn't impressed his father.

Heaven only knew what the man wanted from him—or from Nathan, for that matter, since even Nathan's law career had made but a blip on Dale Brookes's radar. But even disappointment implied caring. It implied that his father felt enough for his children to *want* them to achieve certain things. Since Jacques was sure that wasn't the case, maybe it was his own disappointment that his father didn't love them that was bothering him...

He shook his head. *Where had that come from?*

'Jacques?'

'Yeah?'

'I think I'm going to kiss you.'

He barely had time to process her words before her lips were on his.

Heat seared through him and his lungs caught fire.

He heard her intake of breath, realised that she felt the same.

Except that while his reaction had been to deepen the kiss hers was to pull away.

They stood like that for a moment, his hand lightly on her waist, both of hers on his chest. He felt them shaking against him and only then realised that his body was shaking too. Her eyes were wide, and the flush on her cheeks was caused by an entirely different reason than his earlier teasing.

'I'm so sorry,' she breathed, aiming her striking eyes at him.

Stealing his breath. Stoking his desire.

'I didn't mean to—'

This time he interrupted her with another kiss.

His arms went around her waist and he pulled her closer, lifting her from the path until she stood with him on the sand. Somewhere in his mind it registered that the romance of taking a walk on the beach that he'd teased her about earlier shrouded them now—that their first kiss was now on a beach in the moonlight. But then he stopped thinking, consumed by the magic of her mouth.

She tasted like strawberries just ripened. Smelled like a warm day in spring. Something inside him softened at the sensations that came with her kiss. She responded hungrily, deepening it. He heard a groan and realised that it had come from him. Because she was making him forget where they were—who he was and what he had to lose—he fought to slow the kiss. He hoped it would lessen the tension, the urgency, that had built between them.

But his attempt was a vain one, only succeeding in making him want more.

In making him *need* more.

He pulled away from her, his breathing as shaky as hers, and forced himself to take a step back. Forced himself not to be charmed by that just-kissed look on her face. He ignored the fact that her expression was like that because *he* had kissed her—deeply and thoroughly—and reined his emotions in.

'We shouldn't have done that.'

She looked up at him, her hand freezing midway to touching her lips, and he watched her fingers curl into a fist.

He felt as though his heart was right in the palm of that hand.

'No, we shouldn't have.'

She bit her lip, and his body yearned to go back to what they had been doing. It took him a moment to realise that she was doing it to keep herself from saying anything.

'We probably won't see each other after this, so it doesn't matter.' He felt like an absolute jerk saying it— even more so when he saw her flinch. Her words about no one believing that they would be together played in his head again, and he wondered at them. Wondered why he thought his words now had proved the truth of that to her somehow.

'Good luck with the TV show tomorrow. I'm sure everything will work out.'

She turned her back on him and hurried down the path before he could respond. And because he wanted to give her—and himself—some time to process events, he waited before following.

But that time wasn't nearly enough for him to process everything that was going on in his mind. To figure out why his actions that night had shamed him. Especially since they weren't actions he would have been ashamed of at any other time.

Or with any other person.

It was Lily, he realised. Something about her made his actions feel...unethical. *Manipulative.* He hadn't thought he was being manipulative. Or perhaps, more accurately, he hadn't cared. At least not until she'd called him on it. And that kiss had only complicated things between them. He worried that it would affect the self-confidence she had so much trouble with.

Which was why this was for the best. He didn't need to

worry about someone else's self-confidence. He needed to focus. He'd worked too hard to make up for his past to be distracted by a woman. Besides, as much as Lily intrigued him, she needed someone who would take care of her. Someone who would be patient with her insecurities, who would appreciate the spirit that covered them.

Someone who didn't have a million hoops to jump through before people saw him as decent.

And that wasn't Jacques.

It was for the best, he thought again, and didn't examine why it didn't feel like it. Or why realising that he wouldn't see Lily again any time soon made him feel more empty than the task ahead of him.

CHAPTER SIX

LILY TOOK A shaky breath as she walked into the *Latte Mornings* studio. She still wasn't sure why she was there. When she'd got home the previous night she'd convinced herself that she would forget all about Jacques. Especially since she still felt raw because his interest in her—his kindness *to* her—had all been a ploy to get her to help him.

She'd told herself she should have known. *Kyle* had been nice to her once upon a time. It was why she'd fallen for him—and the way she'd learned that niceness was never simple.

But still, it stung.

Jacques's dismissal felt like confirmation that she wasn't likeable. And even though he'd claimed otherwise his actions had shown her the truth. They had amplified all her insecurities and she'd been determined to escape them. She'd been determined to show Jacques she was as right for his plan as anyone else.

So she'd kissed him.

It had been impulsive. It had been hot. It had been everything she'd expected from a man with Jacques's undeniable sexiness and charm. But there had been something more, too. She remembered the scar above his mouth again, the fight he'd said he'd had with Kyle, and realised it had been *dangerous*.

It both thrilled and terrified her that she seemed to be attracted to the danger she sensed in Jacques. And, though she wanted to, she couldn't deny that it was part of the reason she was walking into a television studio at six in the morning to pretend to be his girlfriend.

She knew this plan was a form of redemption for him. She'd read articles about what had happened during his last game. Watched the footage. She'd seen the absolute anger on his face. Felt the danger of it settle in her throat when she hadn't been able to tear her eyes away.

Her instincts told her that that fight *had* mattered, despite Jacques's claims otherwise. And the more digging she had done, the more she'd become convinced of it. The internet was full of what had happened after that fight. His red card…the suspension. The year he'd said he'd been 'self-destructive'. The pictures.

She didn't know Jacques very well, but she knew the man in those pictures wasn't the same person she'd spoken to the night before. The man in those pictures was broken. Completely so. But the man *she'd* met hid that brokenness well…

It had all fuelled her urge to help him. And in an effort to avoid the thought that she wanted to help only because she was attracted to him, she'd realised she could do with *his* help. She *needed* it if she wanted to save the store she'd opened six months ago from going under. And she *had* to save it—or the guilt that anchored her heart to the soles of her feet most days would be for nothing.

Pretending to be Jacques's girlfriend would give her a platform where she could market her store from. To get more customers, to get more income and pay more bills. *That* had been the real reason—at least the biggest one—

she'd got up at four-thirty, got ready and driven almost an hour to the television studio.

Because she couldn't fail with her store. She couldn't fail at her dream. And she sure as hell couldn't prove her parents right and fall even further short of their expectations.

But her steps faltered when she saw the two security guards at the entrance of the studio. How was she going to get past them?

If she tried to talk her way through—told them she was Jacques's girlfriend—she would just seem like some crazed fan. In fact *all* her options would make her seem like that. And even if they did believe her, how would she verify it? She couldn't call Jacques, since she didn't have his number. The only thing she had of him was the memory of the heat their lips had sparked when they kissed. And she highly doubted *that* would get her through...

Her courage failing, she turned to leave.

'Lily?'

She turned back at the sound of her name, her heart beating so fast it might have been sprinting to win a race. Jacques stood just behind the security guards, a cup of coffee from the barista next to him in his hand. Her eyes greedily took him in, which in no way helped to slow down her heart-rate. She'd managed to underplay her attraction to him in her memories, convincing herself that she'd exaggerated his good looks. Even the pictures she'd seen on the internet hadn't swayed that conviction.

Now, though, she was forced to admit that she couldn't have exaggerated Jacques. She had never seen someone look *that* good in jeans and a T-shirt, though the black leather jacket escalated the look. Along with the mussed hair, she saw another reason for his bad-boy nickname...

But the confusion on his face distracted her.

'Hey, babe,' she said, and wondered if the 'babe' was too much. But when she saw the way his eyes widened, she decided to commit.

'I'm *so* sorry I'm late. Can I go in?' she said to the security guards, and after getting a brief nod of confirmation from Jacques they let her through. She walked up to him, steeled herself against the attraction, and gave him a quick kiss.

'I didn't think you were coming,' Jacques said, the slight shock in his eyes at her presence and at the kiss almost immediately cloaked.

'I changed my mind. I didn't want you to go through this alone.' She took the coffee from his hand and sipped. It was strong, without any milk, and she had to force herself not to spit it out. 'Do you think we could get another?'

Amusement crept into his eyes, and he nodded. A few moments later he was back, this time with a coffee that had milk in it—he'd taken note the night before, she thought—and two sachets of sugar.

'Let's swap, *honey.*'

The drawl he used made her lips twitch.

'I know how much you like hot coffee.'

She thanked him as they exchanged their coffees, and then forced herself not to react when he put an arm around her shoulders and the smell of his cologne filled her senses.

'You want to tell me what you're *really* doing here?' he said under his breath as they rounded the corner to where they shot the morning show.

'I'm paying back a debt,' she responded in the same tone.

'You didn't have to.'

They were in the main studio now, and she was briefly

distracted by the busyness of the set. She had never been on one before, and it was a little overwhelming.

She forced her attention back to Jacques, moving in front of him to make it look as if they were talking intimately. In reality, she just wanted to be out of his arms.

'I know, but this is important to you, right?' He gave her a wary nod and she continued, 'So let me do this. It's not like it's real. What's the harm?'

He studied her for a moment, and then he said, 'Thanks.'

'No problem.' When their gazes locked and something sparked she took a step back and looked at her watch. 'What time are you going on?'

'Seven-thirty.'

She nodded, stayed still for a moment. And then, when the silence grew a little awkward, she said, 'It wasn't until I got here that I realised I wouldn't be able to get in. So... thanks for getting yourself some coffee.'

She smiled thinly at him, and turned away before she could become ensnared by his magnetism.

'Mr Brookes? We're ready for you in Hair and Make-up.'

Lily watched as the young woman tucked her hair behind her ears when Jacques directed his attention to her.

'You can follow me,' the girl said quickly, and turned. But then she realised that Jacques wasn't following. 'Is there a problem?'

'No...not unless my girlfriend has to stay out here?'

The girl's eyes widened, and her black hair whipped from side to side as she looked at Lily and then back to Jacques again.

Though it was strange hearing Jacques call her that, something fluttered inside Lily at the thought. Something that was lined with pride, with satisfaction. With a thrill.

She tried to ignore it.

'Um…sure, you can both follow me.'

Decidedly less confident, the girl led them to a room that looked exactly like the rooms Lily had seen in movies. Jacques was settled into the chair in front of one of the mirrors, and she sat herself on the couch opposite the chair. The man who was doing Jacques's make-up was tall and lanky, with bright green spikes all over his head. There was barely an introduction—though she did learn the make-up artist's name was Earl—before he began putting foundation on Jacques's face, and she couldn't hide her smile.

'Something amusing you, Newman?'

She met his eyes in the mirror and found her smile broadening. 'Why would you think that, Jacques?'

'Maybe because of that ridiculous smile on your face?' He closed his eyes as he said it to allow Earl to put foundation around them.

'Fine—you caught me. But I was only thinking how wonderful it is that I don't have to do your make-up for you today. Thanks so much, Earl.'

Earl glanced over at her, his expression amused before he schooled it and got back to work.

'You're ruining my reputation, Lily,' Jacques growled, and Lily felt a thrill go up her spine.

She loved the banter, the easiness of the conversation they were sharing. It seemed that having a conversation with Jacques as his pretend girlfriend was a lot easier than having one as his friend. Although, to be fair, she could hardly call whatever she and Jacques shared a *friendship*. Perhaps 'alliance' was a better word.

'Are you going on with him?' Earl asked as he put some wax on his hand and vigorously rubbed it through Jacques's hair.

'No, no,' she said quickly. 'I'm just here for moral support.'

'And you're doing a great job, babe.'

She shot Jacques a look that she hoped told him he was laying it on a bit too thick, but Earl didn't seem to notice.

'You two are quite sweet. Not who I would have pictured you with, Bad-Boy Brookes, but maybe that's a *good* thing.'

Earl pulled at a few more strands of Jacques's hair, then nodded. 'You're as ready as I can make you. I'll go check how long it'll be before you have to go on. I'll be right back.'

He had barely walked out of the room before Lily spoke.

'That nickname has quite a ring to it.'

Jacques got out of the chair and came to sit next to her. He knew just as well as she did that he was too close, but since he seemed to want it that way Lily refused to indulge him by moving away. She just shifted her weight so that she was leaning to the other side.

'It's not one I'm proud of.'

'Nor should you be, if all the articles I read last night were true. Particularly the one that had the headline: *Bad-Boy Brookes's Year of Debauchery.*'

He turned towards her, the look in his eyes dangerous. 'I'm not sure what's more disturbing. The fact that you looked me up, or that you've mentioned that horrible headline.'

She flushed, but refused to look away.

'I had to know what—or who—I was agreeing to support. And I'm glad I did it. I now understand why you need me.' She paused, sensing the tone of the conversation would change if she continued talking about the things she'd learnt the night before. Unwilling to lose the easiness between them, she said, 'Besides, now I'm prepared if some woman tries to gouge my eyes out.'

'It's not *that* bad,' Jacques said, hoping his blasé attitude would mask his embarrassment.

'Yeah, you're right. I mean, the articles didn't make it sound bad *at all*,' she teased. 'Only about ninety per cent of them used the name "Bad-Boy Brookes" when referring to your personal life—the other times they used it to refer to your willingness to do whatever it took to win a match. And it was also *only* used if you were seen partying with more than one woman over a single weekend. So you're right,' she said again. 'It really wasn't that bad.'

She stood, and Jacques's eyes moved over her. The jeans she wore highlighted the curves of her hips, and he stood quickly so that his eyes wouldn't be drawn to them any more. Not that it made him uncomfortable. He had always been the type of man who appreciated the female body, and he wasn't afraid to show it. Except that Lily... Well, she wasn't the kind of girl who inspired the lust he was used to.

His eyes travelled over her body one more time, and he felt the result of it in his chest, his gut, and then his body. No, he thought again, not the type of lust he was used to at all...

'But then, of course, there was that photo shoot.'

Her eyes widened, her cheeks glowing with that wonderful colour he'd grown to like so much the night before, and he grinned.

'Which one? My agent at the time had me do quite a few.'

'The underwear one,' she said in a high-pitched voice , and avoided his eyes.

His smile grew broader. She hadn't intended telling him she knew about that, he thought. So why had she?

'Yeah, that was at the peak of my career. One of my favourites. Body didn't croak then like it does now.'

'Are you fishing for compliments?'

She still wasn't looking at him, and he took a step closer.

'Only if you have them.'

'Somehow I think your ego can handle it if I don't offer them to you.'

'Maybe my ego, but not my heart. I need to hear my girlfriend compliment me. Just once.'

Her lips twitched, and she brought her eyes back to his. 'You *know* you look just as good now as you did then. Even though I haven't seen you in your underwear recently.'

'We could change that.'

The joking air between them immediately turned into a sizzle. He hadn't intended to say the words, but he hadn't been able to stop them when she'd spoken. And damned if he didn't mean them. He could see it as clearly now as he had during their kiss last night. The chemistry, the attraction... He wanted it more than he could say. It was almost as if he...*needed* it.

The thought jolted him, and he took a step back. Forced himself to take control again.

'Is it going to be a problem for you?' he finally said, to change the subject.

'What?'

Her voice was a little breathy—just as it had been after their kiss—and he had to steel himself against the desire.

'My dating history?'

She shook her head quickly, causing the curls she had tied up at the base of her skull to bounce.

'Of course not. It's not like we're *really* dating. I have no emotional investment in this whatsoever.'

Her face had gone blank with the words, and for the first time since he'd seen her that morning he wondered why she was there. *Was* she paying back a debt?

He searched her face for a clue that there was more, but saw nothing.

And that had his instincts screaming.

There was something else—something more—but he wouldn't know what until he asked her.

Before he could, they were interrupted.

'Mr Brookes, they want to go through your questions one last time.'

Earl had come back, and with one last look in Lily's direction, Jacques walked out through the door. He forced himself to focus on what he was there to do, and went through the questions he'd previously been emailed with the producers one last time.

He knew his PR firm had given the studio those questions, which was why he'd agreed to this appearance in the first place. It was also why neither Jade nor Riley was there yet. He was confident enough about his answers—answers they had coached him through—to have them there only for the interview itself.

He knew the questions off by heart by now: how was his business going? Particularly his international expansion? Did he have any news about his personal life?

He hadn't had much of an answer for that when they'd first spoken about it, but now he would casually mention his relationship with the lovely Lily Newman, and send her a loving look on camera, after which the host would go on to talk about his past rugby career.

Did he miss it? Did he regret the way it had ended?

Since he did, he would say so, and the sincerity of

his words—according to his PR firm—would be a great segue into his plans for buying his old club. Hopefully seeing him in a stable new relationship, doing a popular family show would boost his image enough that the club's sponsors wouldn't pull out if he bought it.

But he didn't want to spend any more time thinking about the hoops he had to jump through to get people's approval. When he was finished with the producers he walked out of the room—and paused when he saw Lily.

Her arms were folded over a loose red top, a patterned white and red scarf perfectly accessorising the effortless look. She looked a little out of place, he thought, and watched her brush one of her tight curls from her face. It didn't seem to matter that the curls were tied at the nape of her neck. They found a way to frame her face regardless.

She turned to him, smiled , and his heart slowed, nearly, *nearly* stopping. His lungs constricted and he felt as if he'd been kicked in the stomach.

It took a moment for him to recover. The smile on her face disappeared and she took a step forward, but he raised a hand and waved her away, not sure he could have spoken to her if she had come to face him.

What just happened? an inner voice asked, but he shook his head, unable—unwilling—to answer that question. He couldn't afford to. Not minutes before his interview.

And yet when he was called on to the set he had to actively *force* himself to focus on what he was about to do.

He dismissed the insecurity that threatened, reminding himself that he was good at playing games. He'd made an entire career of it, hadn't he?

He could pretend to have a girlfriend, and he could pretend to be someone the public wanted him to be. The way he played only mattered if he didn't score the try, he reminded himself, and no matter what happened he *would* be scoring this try. He *would* be the one to buy his club.

It had saved him from the anger he'd felt at home—had given him an outlet for the frustration he'd felt with his family. But when he'd realised his family wasn't worth it he'd let that anger control him. He'd let it ruin the thing that had always given him meaning. Purpose. But he would make up for it—for the mistakes he'd made before he'd known any better.

'Welcome back to *Latte Mornings*!' David, the host of the television show's sports segment, spoke the moment the producer gave the signal. 'Today's guest needs no introduction. He is one of our biggest rugby legends, who earned respect during his rugby career because of his phenomenal talent. Mr Jacques Brookes. Thanks for being here, Jacques.'

Game on.

'Thanks for having me.'

David went through the questions Jacques had prepared for, only going off-script to make a joke or to comment about something Jacques had said. He didn't once mention Jacques's suspension, which was a relief, since Jacques had worried about that before the interview. Now, though, Jacques was more concerned about the questions regarding his personal life. He wasn't sure he wanted to know why that was the case…

'So, Jacques, tell us about what's going on in your personal life? Are you still breaking hearts?'

David laughed, and for a moment Jacques wanted to wipe the smile off David's face. *Why* would the man remind people of one of the things Jacques wanted them to forget?

'Well, actually, I've been dating someone I think may

be the one.' He looked over at Lily, smiled, and watched as a pretty flush covered her cheeks.

He was still astounded at the fact that something that simple—that natural—could wind his insides with attraction.

David raised his eyebrows. 'That wasn't the answer I was expecting, but that's great. How long have you two been together?'

His mind blanked for a moment, and his accelerated heart-rate suddenly had very little to do with his attraction to Lily.

'Er…six months?' He glanced at Lily, and she nodded and smiled.

He felt steadier. He'd remembered that six months was how long she'd told Kyle they had been together, so the timing would be consistent in their world of pretence.

He realised that his answer had sounded unsure, so he laughed and looked back at David. 'I was just making sure I got it right.'

'Of course. We wouldn't want you to get into trouble.'

David smiled at the camera, and Jacques resisted the temptation to roll his eyes. He didn't care much for David's sometimes over-the-top media personality, but he knew it got the ratings, so he ignored it.

'Tell us a little more about your girlfriend…?'

David's eyebrows rose again, and Jacques answered, 'Lily.'

'Lily. What a beautiful name.'

David smiled over at Lily, and when Jacques's eyes followed he saw her return it with a shy smile of her own.

'Tell us more about her. What does she do for a living? How did you two meet?'

Jacques wasn't sure how long he sat there, his brain telling him that he should have anticipated this line of questioning *before* he'd mentioned her. Suddenly he realised he knew nothing about her except the little she'd offered—and that wasn't nearly enough to maintain the pretence.

Gears shifted in his head, and he forced steel into his gut as he tried to resist the decision his mind had already made. He *had* to do this, he thought. It was the only way he wouldn't destroy his plan with his faux pas.

'I'd love to tell you more about her, but actually I think this would be a great opportunity to introduce her to the public. Lily, could you come over here, please?'

CHAPTER SEVEN

PLEASE TELL ME I'm dreaming, Lily thought when Jacques called her over. It certainly seemed like one of those horrible dreams—going on a live television show that almost the entire South African population watched, unprepared. Especially with everyone on set looking at her expectantly.

She felt someone touch her back, and then the coat that had been in her hands was replaced with a microphone and her feet were moving, one at a time, until she was under bright lights and next to Jacques.

Up close, she could see something in his eyes that she couldn't place her finger on, but it didn't matter when she was pretty much living her worst nightmare.

'It's *lovely* to have you with us, Lily.'

David broke the silence, and his eyes told her he was as surprised—possibly even as annoyed—as she was at her being on camera.

'Thank you,' she said softly, and it took Jacques moving the hand that held the mike for her to realise she hadn't spoken into it. Feeling the heat in her face, she cleared her throat and repeated the words into the mike.

You have to stay calm, Lily, she told herself. *Be confident. This is your chance to do exactly what you came here for.*

'Am I in trouble?' Jacques asked, breaking the tension her little fumble had caused, and he casually put his arm around her waist, pulling her closer.

She couldn't deny that it calmed her—which she might have appreciated if *he* hadn't been the one to put her in this position in the first place.

'Definitely!' she answered through numb lips, and resisted looking around when she heard a chuckle go through the studio.

'Is this the first time he's done something like this, Lily?' David asked her, and she idly thought that he must have recovered from *his* shock.

'Yes. And the last time, too, if I have anything to say about it.'

Another chuckle went through the studio, and she felt herself relax slightly. She *would* survive this, she thought, and then she would take her time and enjoy killing her pretend boyfriend.

'We've been pretty private for the most part.'

Jacques spoke up, and she looked down at his smiling face. Noted that the smile was more apology than amusement.

'Which is why there hasn't been anything on social media? Or in the gossip columns, for that matter?' David asked, and drew Lily's attention to the fact that in the world that they currently lived in, relationships were all over social media. And, since Jacques was a public figure, there should have been *some* sign of their relationship somewhere.

Jacques's hand around her waist tightened, and she wondered whether he could tell that she was beginning to panic.

'I think when you have something this special you don't really want it to be in the public eye.'

It would have been a sufficient answer, but Lily found herself saying, 'And since I knew that Jacques was a public figure, and I'd heard about his...his past, I wanted to take it slow and keep it between us for as long as possible. I guess that will end after today.'

David smiled at her, and then sobered. 'And his past doesn't bother you?'

'We all have pasts, David. They make you the person you are. But they aren't the entirety of what defines you. Jacques is one of the best people I know. He works harder than anyone. His business ethic is impeccable. He does so much for the people he cares about, and his charity work—' which she'd read about only a few hours ago '—clearly shows that he doesn't need to know those people personally. If I had let whatever had happened in his past affect my answer the day he first asked me out I wouldn't ever have got to know the other sides of him.'

There was a long pause after she spoke, and she looked down at Jacques to see warmth in his eyes. Her cheeks grew hot again.

'Well,' David said eventually, 'it really does seem like you know a different Jacques to the man we're used to. But that might not be a *bad* thing.' David winked, and then continued, 'We have to go to an advertisement break now, but when we come back we'll talk to Jacques a little bit more about that past we've just touched on.'

When they were off the air Lily's legs began to shake. A delayed reaction, she thought, and was incredibly grateful that it hadn't happened while they were still live. Before she knew it Jacques's arms were around her, drawing her into a hug while keeping her steady, and she wondered if he had sensed her instability.

'Thank you,' he said.

His sincerity sent a shiver through her, and she folded

her arms around him so that their display of affection didn't look strange.

But she didn't respond, unsure of whether the mike he still had pinned to his top was on and if anyone would hear her say what she really wanted to. She drew back after a moment, her body prickling with awareness even though she wanted to kill him.

'All this attention has made me a little shaky. I think I'll wait in the make-up room, so you can't call me back on air again.'

Lily made sure that there was a lightness to the tone she used as she spoke, making it sound teasing and not like the warning it really was. But when she looked at Jacques she saw acknowledgement of her real intentions.

She took a deep breath and walked to the make-up room, aware that people were now watching her. She pretended not to notice, and breathed a sigh of relief when she saw that no one was in the room. She closed the door behind her, locked it, and then sank onto the nearest couch.

Her hands were shaking, she realised, and curled her fingers into her palms to stop them from making her seem like she wasn't calm. Even though no one was there, and even though no one would see her panic, she still felt the compulsion to pretend not to be vulnerable.

It was a defence mechanism she had developed to survive the bullying at school. And it was one that had kept her from seeing the person Kyle had really been. From seeing what their *relationship* had really been. Because if she could pretend everything was okay, even to herself, then surely it would be. It *had* to be.

But that had never been the case. For her younger self being overweight had meant bullying from her peers. And being an introvert who didn't know what she wanted for the longest time had meant her parents had never understood her. How could they when they were extroverted, successful professionals who'd always known exactly what *they* wanted?

Her solution had been to pull back, to be someone no one would notice. That was why Kyle's attention had been so flattering. But then he'd tried to make her believe that who she was wasn't enough. And because it had been so easy to believe him, it had taken seeing him with another woman to realise that she *was* enough.

No, she thought, that wasn't true. It had taken seeing him with another woman to make her realise that she *should* be enough, and that *she* needed to believe it.

She'd been doing a pretty good job of it, she thought, until she'd gone on live TV unprepared and all the insecurities had come rushing back. Now everyone would be watching her, judging her. She looked down at the clothes she was wearing and started to shake again. They made her look even frumpier than she usually did, and the confidence she'd had when she'd chosen them washed away.

All the reasons she'd had for pretending to be Jacques's girlfriend didn't seem to matter any more. Especially when she realised she hadn't even had the chance to promote her store when she'd been on air. All she had done was boost Jacques's ego even more.

But wasn't that the reason he'd brought her on the show in the first place?

She took a few more deep breaths to calm the anger pumping through her veins and walked to the door, avoiding the mirrors in the room so that she didn't have to be reminded—*again*—of how terrible she looked. When she opened the door Jacques was standing there, hand in the air, ready to knock. She plastered a smile on her face, not wanting the sacrifices she'd already made to be undone, and brushed a kiss on his cheek.

'How did the rest of the interview go?'

She forced cheer into her voice and slipped her hand into Jacques's, gently pulling him towards the exit. She assumed since he was there that his interview was done, and she didn't want to stay any longer and pretend she loved a man she wasn't even sure she *liked* at that moment.

'Great.'

Jacques walked with her, though she could sense the resistance in him. They didn't speak for the rest of the short walk to the exit, but Jacques stopped before they could walk past security.

'I have to stay and meet with Jade and Riley. The PR firm reps.'

She nodded, remembering their conversation last night—though it seemed a longer time ago—and brushed another kiss on his cheek as goodbye.

Hopefully for ever.

'Will I see you for dinner later?' he asked, threatening her hopes of never seeing him again. But then she realised that she *wasn't* really his girlfriend, and that this was his attempt at seeing the non-girlfriend Lily again.

And *that* she could refuse.

'I'm working late tonight, honey—remember? You can call me later.'

She waved at him and walked out of the studio, knowing full well he didn't have her number.

CHAPTER EIGHT

'YOU ARE SO lucky I had a deadline this afternoon or I would have called earlier.'

Lily briefly closed her eyes at Caitlyn's irate voice on the phone and locked the front door of the store. It was just before seven, and normally Lily would have taken the store's accounts outside and enjoyed the sound of the sea lapping against the pier and the laziness of Friday evening as she worked.

But today she'd exposed enough of herself to the public.

'I'm not sure I would use the word "lucky",' Lily replied, gathering her things. She just wanted to get home, soak in the bath and forget the mistakes she'd made that day.

'Oh, trust me, you're definitely lucky,' Caitlyn disagreed. 'But that luck has run out and now I want to know exactly what's going on with you and my future brother-in-law.'

'There isn't anything going on with me and Jacques.'

'Really?' Caitlyn demanded. 'Because I'm watching a clip of you defending his past right now. It currently has four hundred thousand views.'

'Cait,' she said wearily. 'Please. I can't deal with snippiness today.'

Lily wasn't surprised her friend had called, demanding answers. She'd already had to deal with her mother's hurt because Lily hadn't told her she was dating again. And by 'deal with' Lily meant 'lie to', since she couldn't possibly tell her mother it was all a charade. She'd managed to talk around it, but that conversation alone had taken up a substantial part of her energy.

But then she'd had to conjure up more for her work day. Because as soon as she'd walked in Terri and Cara, her staff, had demanded why *they* hadn't known. And then people had begun to recognise her, and the store had grown busier than it had ever been before.

'I'm sorry, Lil. I'm just worried about you. You barely know Jacques. Hell, *I* barely know him.'

'I know. I *know*,' Lily repeated more definitely. 'I'm sorry for snapping. It's just been a…a long, long day.'

'Don't apologise.'

Lily could almost see the hand her friend was waving her apology away with.

'At least not to me. Besides, I keep telling you that you don't have to say sorry for bringing the fire. I love it when you do.'

She paused, and Lily sensed her hesitation over the phone.

'Will you tell me what's going on now?'

Lily sighed, and quickly explained everything that had happened in the past twenty-four hours. The only thing she left out was the kiss—she didn't need Caitlyn to remind her of how much she had messed up, and that was the part she was most embarrassed by.

Caitlyn didn't say anything when Lily was done, and her heart pulsed. Her silence was out of character, which meant that Caitlyn wanted to say something she knew Lily wasn't going to like.

'Cait, just tell me what you're thinking.'

'I don't want to...' Caitlyn sighed. 'Fine. Look, I just want you to be careful, okay? I don't really know that much about Jacques, and even when I pressed Nathan about him last night he wouldn't tell me any more than he already had. I just... Well, I don't think he's the person you should move on with. Especially not after Kyle.'

Lily felt annoyance, but pushed it aside. She didn't know why she'd felt it in the first place.

'I'm not moving on with Jacques. This...it's pretend.'

'Are you sure?'

She waited a beat, and then answered, 'Yes.'

'And if you go on with this pretence you'll be fine with all the attention?'

Lily knew Caitlyn wouldn't be her best friend if she didn't know everything about her—well, mostly everything, she corrected, thinking how she'd never told Caitlyn about the way things had really ended with Kyle. But it irked her that her friend knew just where to hit.

'Actually, I take that back. You *have* to be fine with all the attention. You're in this now. You have to keep this illusion going until Jacques's deal is signed, and perhaps even after that.'

Though she desperately wished that Caitlyn was wrong, the feeling in the pit of her stomach told her that her friend was right. She'd known it the minute she'd got that call from her mother.

'I'll figure it out,' Lily breathed, and heard Caitlyn sigh again.

'Just be careful.'

'I will be. Thanks.'

There wasn't much to say after that, and when she'd said goodbye Lily locked up and made her way to the parking lot. She kept her jersey tight around her, despite the early summer heat, and kept her head down. She didn't want to be recognised. Not only because she'd had enough of it that day, but because she didn't know what to expect if one of Jacques's more devoted fans found her.

'Lily.'

Her first instinct was to grab for the pepper spray in her handbag. But though it took her a moment, she recognised the voice.

Jacques was leaning against the car that was parked next to hers. He'd changed his T-shirt from white to blue, abandoned the leather jacket. She felt a flash of disappointment, but shook it off.

'Hi…'

His deep voice rumbled, and her train of thought was derailed. And for that reason, she said, 'No.'

'No, what?'

'No, I'm not interested in whatever you're here to say.'

'Give me a chance.'

'No.'

She shook her head and walked past him to the driver's side of her car. A hand closed over her arm.

'Can we go somewhere private to discuss this, before we draw an audience?'

She knew he was right—that people would recognise him and then perhaps her sooner or later—but she couldn't bring herself to agree.

'We don't have anything to discuss. I did what you asked. Debt paid. Now we can move on.'

'Lily, please. I just need a few minutes. *Please.*'

Her heart softened, though her mind urged her to stay strong. For a minute she struggled between the two. But one look at his face had her sighing.

'My flat is twenty minutes away.'

'Mine is ten.'

She frowned. How had he always been that close to her and yet had only now managed to disrupt her life?

'Fine, I'll follow you.'

Lily was grateful for the short drive, since it didn't give her enough time to indulge her feelings about going to Jacques's flat. So she ignored the slight churn of panic in her belly. Ignored the rapid beat of anxiety in her chest. She'd experienced them often enough with Kyle to recognise the signs of anticipating an argument.

Instead she focused on her breathing. And as she parked her car in front of the sophisticated building in Jacques's secure estate she gave herself a pep talk. But she didn't speak in the elevator they took up to his flat. She didn't comment when he let her in and the first thing she saw was Table Mountain. When the first thing she heard was the crashing of waves.

Jacques put on lights, though it was only just beginning to grow dark then, and she got a better view of the glass that made up one side of his flat. Part of it was a sliding door, she realised when he opened it, and took a step closer. It looked out onto the beach, and the steps leading down from the balcony of the flat went directly to the sand. Having specifically rented her shop at the beachfront for its calmness, she appreciated Jacques's choice. Even though he probably didn't really live there, she thought, looking at the inside.

Grey laminate floors stretched across the open-plan room. Soft white furniture was arranged in the living room to face the spectacular view, with a light brown carpet and white dining room set just behind it. The kitchen was next to that, designed in white and grey to match the colour scheme of the entire flat. Lights beamed softly in the roof above the living room and kitchen, and an intricate fixture hung over the dining room table, illuminating it intimately.

It looked like the homes she'd seen in magazines—visually beautiful, glossy, and so very perfect. Except it didn't *feel* like a home. It didn't have the cosiness a home with a view like his should have.

'You're upset because of the interview today.'

It wasn't a question, and she braced herself for the inevitable.

'You already seem to know the answer to that.' She saw the confirmation on his face. 'Why am I here, Jacques? For you to point out the obvious?'

'No, I wanted to…to apologise.'

The way he said it made her think that wasn't the real reason she was there. She thought about Caitlyn's words, thought about her own reservations, and *knew* he didn't only want to apologise.

'I shouldn't have ambushed you this morning. I just… I didn't know what to do when they started asking questions about you.'

'*And* you thought having me on camera with you could only help your aim to buy the club.'

'Yes.'

He was watching her closely and she shifted.

'But that doesn't mean I don't feel bad about it.'

'*Do* you?'

'I do.'

'At least you're being honest.' And sincere, she thought, looking at his face.

'I'm sorry if I upset you.'

The words seemed more genuine now.

'I also wanted to thank you.'

He took a step forward, and instinct had her moving back. Then, because she didn't want it to seem as if she was afraid of being close to him—he *didn't* affect her that much, she assured herself—she stepped out onto the balcony.

The fresh air immediately eased some of the tension in her chest.

'Why do you want to thank me?' she asked when she heard him step out beside her.

'Our interview has gone viral.'

Ah, there it was. The real reason she was there.

'Yes, I've heard,' she said dryly. 'So you're saying thank you because we're all over social media?'

She could feel him watching her, and her heart hammered.

'Yes,' he answered, leaning against the railing as he'd done the night before at Nathan's. 'But more because the comments people have made are positive. My PR firm is very happy.' He paused. 'People really like you, Lily. And because of that they're starting to really like *me* again, too.'

She almost laughed. 'I'm glad it's working out for you.'

'You don't believe that people like you?'

'It doesn't matter what I believe.' But he was right. 'You got what you wanted.'

Jacques pushed himself up, his face revealing no emotion. 'Why don't you just say what you really want to say, Lily? Say what you mean.'

She looked at him. 'You used me.'

'*You* were the one who showed up at the studio today.' His voice was low. 'I didn't ask you to. In fact I'm pretty sure I remember telling you that you weren't the right person for it.'

His words sent a jolt through her.

'I know that. And I realise now that it was a mistake.' She forced herself to calm the anxiety pumping through her at the confrontation, told herself she was doing the right thing.

'But I showed up there because I chose to—which means I actually had a say. You took that away from me when you called me on to *live television* without checking with me first.'

A flash of regret crossed his face, but Lily refused to be swayed by it. She might as well say everything she needed to now.

'I would have never agreed to that if you'd asked me, and in my book that means you used me.'

The regret was gone from his face now, replaced by a stormy expression that she might have been wary of if she hadn't expected it.

But instead of the fire she knew he was capable of, he simply said, 'You knew what this would entail when you agreed to do it.'

She waited for more, but there was nothing. She shook her head.

'Why can't you just say that you shouldn't have done it? And then you can apologise sincerely—not because what you did *upset* me, but because you did it at all.'

He still didn't reply.

'I know the real reason you wanted to talk is because you need me,' she said. 'And because I'm already in two minds about helping you, it would probably be best if you stop with the silent treatment.'

CHAPTER NINE

THERE WAS A part of him that appreciated her temper. It was so different from the insecurity he could sense just beneath the surface, and the honesty was refreshing. But a bigger part of him was disturbed that Lily's words were describing his father.

Again.

From the moment he'd met her he'd been treating Lily as his father had treated his mother. Manipulating her, using her. But, unlike his mother, Lily had called him out on it both times. She wasn't as similar to the woman who'd raised him as he'd thought, Jacques realised. But did that matter when *he* was acting like his father? Someone he'd fought all his life *not* to become?

'I'm sorry I used you.'

'Thank you,' she answered softly, and he had to take a moment to compose himself. To protect himself against the emotions—the memories—he'd always managed to keep far, far away from his daily life.

Until he'd met Lily.

'So, will you help me now?' he asked when he was sure he had control of himself again.

'If we're being honest, I really don't want to.'

She looked at him, and his heart ached at the vulnerability he saw on her face.

'So I apologised for nothing?'

'No, you apologised because you want to be a decent human being.' She shot him a look that had him smiling and shook her head. 'You were kidding. Okay, well... A sense of humour.'

She shook her head again, and looked out to the beach.

'When you get over your surprise, how about you tell me what's going on?'

'I told you—I made a mistake this morning. And now I realise how big.'

'Because people are recognising you?'

'Yes, but more than that, too.'

She angled her shoulders so that he couldn't see her face. Again, his heart pulsed for her.

'My parents called this morning. They wanted to know why I hadn't told them we were dating.'

She turned back to him now, and his heart's reaction became harder to ignore.

'What did you say to them?' he asked, to distract himself.

'I lied.' She shrugged. 'What *could* I tell them? That I was pretending to be your girlfriend for a business deal? They would be so disappointed in me. And I've disappointed them enough.'

The words to ask how were at the tip of his tongue, but he stopped himself. He didn't want to become more invested in this woman. Not if he could help it.

'We're in this now, aren't we?' She looked up at him. 'We have to keep this going until the deal's done. Until people lose interest.'

Since it was exactly what he'd wanted, he thought he should confirm it to her with excitement. But instead, he found himself saying softly, 'Yeah, we do.'

She crossed her arms, sucking in her bottom lip in

such a defeated way that he couldn't help it when his words came tumbling out.

'Why did you do it? I'm not talking about the reason you already gave me.' He brushed off the explanation he knew she had ready. 'Sure, maybe you *did* come through this morning because you wanted to thank me or pay off a debt. But that wasn't the only reason.'

She tightened her arms around herself, and he knew he'd been right.

'You're *invested* in this somehow.'

Her face paled, but barely so. If he hadn't been so enthralled by the colour of her skin, by the features of her face that were so effortlessly breathtaking, he wouldn't have noticed.

Stop.

'No, I'm not.'

'Yes, you are.'

'If there *was* another reason, Jacques, why would I share it with you?'

She had straightened her spine, and he felt satisfaction pour through him. *This* Lily he could handle.

'So there *is* another reason?'

'Oh, for goodness' sake.' She threw her hands up, and then put them on her hips. 'If I tell you, you'll just use it as leverage to force me to keep the game going.'

Guilt burned in his stomach, but *that* he could easily ignore.

'You were the one who said that we have to go through with this. And telling me might remind you why you decided to do it in the first place. It might even give you the motivation you seem to need.'

Her eyes fluttered up to his, and he felt a punch in his gut at the emotion there. At the fire that sparked between them for the briefest moment.

Her hands fell from her sides—defeat, he thought—and her expression softened. And something gleamed in her eyes that made the voice in his head which was so concerned about his feelings when it came to Lily shout all the louder.

'What do you see out there?' she asked, gesturing to the beach.

He frowned. 'People?'

'Exactly. It's a Friday evening. People are going home from work after a hard week. They come to the beach to relax, enjoy a cocktail. Maybe read a book and unwind. And yet here *I* am with you.'

It took him a moment, but he got there.

'Your shop…?'

'Should be open—yes. I should be using the opportunity. Capitalising on it.' She paused. 'I used to. For a few months. But then keeping the store open at night took more money than I had.'

He waited for the rest, though he'd begun to put two and two together.

'I *was* at the studio this morning because I owed you. But I was also there because of that.'

She looked at him with a quiet strength he wondered if she knew she had.

'I've put more into this place than you could possibly imagine. I've sacrificed so much.'

She took a deep breath.

'My store is failing, Jacques,' she said in a voice that broke, and the expression on her face told him she thought *she* was failing, too. 'I'm barely staying afloat being open during the day. If I don't get more customers I won't be able to afford to pay the rent, or the electricity bill, or the rates. Not to mention pay my two staff members and the millions of other things small business owners need to pay.'

She shook her head, looked him in the eye, and he saw the fatigue. But then she straightened her shoulders again.

'So I thought if you mentioned my name, my occupation, it would drive more people into the store during the day, which might let me pay for keeping the store opening during the evening. I thought pretending to be your girlfriend would help my business.'

'So you were using *me*, too?'

'No!' she said sharply. 'I didn't trick you into doing anything you didn't want to. *You* were the one who wanted me there, and I saw how that might benefit the place I love so much. But I would never have done what you did to me.'

He knew he shouldn't have said those words the moment they'd left his lips, but he hadn't been able to help it. And now he wondered why he couldn't just let it go. Why he couldn't admit he'd been wrong.

'You didn't tell me any of that before I did the interview. *You* didn't even mention it when you were on TV.'

'I know.' She sighed. 'I didn't think it through properly. If you hadn't gone to get coffee I would have probably realised that and gone home before I embarrassed myself. And then I was on TV and I couldn't think straight. It was like a nightmare come true.'

'But you managed to defend me so well that people are saying I'm lucky to have you.'

'That's why I was there.'

Suddenly he remembered how struck he'd been when he'd seen her just before the interview. And how much what she'd said during the interview had meant to him. There was something about Lily—about the two of them together—that took Jacques completely out of his comfort zone.

And into a zone that forced him to *feel*.

'I don't always make the best decisions.'

Her words dragged him out of his thoughts. 'I'm glad you made this one.'

'I don't know if I can say the same,' she admitted softly.

'Well, you made the decision.' He stepped closer to her. 'And you were more prepared than I was when you did. Reading up on me, however creepy, shows me your decision wasn't entirely rash.'

Her lips curved, and the tension in his shoulders slackened.

'The things you said…they really helped. No one has ever said something like that about me.' Her eyes fluttered up at him and he quickly added, 'Not in public, I mean.'

'Yeah, I figured that when people kept asking me, "Is Jacques really the way you said he was on TV?" Mostly girls with hearts in their eyes, but it's something.'

'So you had more people in your store today?'

She sighed, gave him a look that told him she knew what he was doing.

'Yes.'

'It can keep being like this, Lily.'

'Yes, I *know* if I pretend to be your girlfriend some more my store will be a lot busier,' she said flatly. 'I know I don't really have a choice, Jacques. You don't have to keep trying to convince me.'

'Thanks for the confirmation. But I thought… Well, I was thinking about more than that.'

He wasn't sure why he'd faltered when his idea was actually a good one.

'I can help you use the momentum of this publicity to get regular customers. I can help with your business plan, with the accounts—with pretty much everything your shop needs to stay successful when this is all over. I can even give you a loan—'

He broke off when she stepped back abruptly.

'I don't want your money, Jacques. You can't *pay* me to do what you want me to.'

CHAPTER TEN

'I'M NOT PAYING YOU,' Jacques answered with a frown. 'I'm just offering you a loan to help get you on your feet again.'

'And would you have offered me that loan if you didn't need my help?'

Her breathing was much too rapid, and she forced herself to inhale and exhale slowly.

'No, I suppose not. But—'

'Then don't do it now,' she snapped, and turned away from him so that he couldn't see the tears in her eyes.

She suddenly felt incredibly tired. The interview, the store, the public, and now this conversation... She'd told him things she hadn't intended to because—well, because he'd *listened*. Maybe he even cared.

But that was just an illusion, she thought, and *she* was the magician, weaving a world where she believed in things that didn't exist. Like someone who was genuinely interested in her worries, her cares.

And his offer of money... It reminded her entirely too much of the way her relationship with Kyle had ended. If she accepted money from Jacques, as she had from the Van der Rosses, all the regret she'd felt since then would have been a lie. She would have been lying to *herself.* It would make her just as bad as she already thought she was for taking that money in the first place…

'I'm sorry, Lily, I didn't mean to offend you.'

'No, *I'm* sorry. I shouldn't have…' She took a breath. 'It's just been…so lonely. Who'd have thought starting a store would be lonely?'

She'd meant it as a joke, and was horrified when her eyes burned. Because it *had* been lonely. And carrying the burden of the store's fate alone…

She couldn't turn to her parents—they'd just say *I told you so* and try to make her see where she'd gone wrong. Because in their minds *she* would be the one in the wrong.

As she always was.

When she had complained about being bullied at school they'd asked her what *she* had done. When she'd broken off her engagement they'd asked her what *she* had done.

There was constant disapproval from them. A constant expectation of failure. Especially when the things she wanted were so different from what *they* wanted.

'I don't want your money, Jacques. But I *will* accept your help with my business skills. I want you to train me, show me where I'm going wrong. But that's all.' She paused, watched his face for his agreement. When she saw it there she nodded in response.

'Is the money thing…? Is it because of Kyle?'

Her insides felt as if they'd been dipped into an ice bucket. 'What?'

'He had money. I thought maybe you didn't want to be reminded of it.'

The ice defrosted, but her body still shook.

'You're right. I don't want to be. I just want that part of my life to be over.'

He was quiet for a moment, and then he said, 'It's been bothering me for a while. You and him together.'

His face was clear while he spoke, but something in his eyes made her belly warm.

'I can't see it.'

'Because he's rich and handsome and successful and I'm just okay-looking with a struggling store?'

'Stop that,' he commanded. 'I don't want to hear you talk about yourself like that any more. And I sure as hell don't want to hear you make him sound like he's some kind of prize.'

She felt a flush stain her cheeks. 'I'm sorry.'

'And stop apologising. You have nothing to apologise for.'

He walked towards her, and her heart sped with each step he took.

'I'm going to say this once, because you need to hear it.'

He lifted her chin with a finger, forcing her to look into his eyes.

'You are the most…*captivating* woman I have ever met. Your hair makes me want to slide my fingers through it so I can see the curls bounce back.' He pulled at one, as if to illustrate his words. 'Sometimes when I look into your eyes I feel like you're looking through me. And that doesn't scare me—even though it absolutely should. And those lips…'

He brushed his thumb over them, making her tremble.

'They make me regret stopping last night. Every time I see them I want to taste them again, to check whether they're really as sweet as I remember.' He lifted his eyes to hers. 'Don't tell me you're "okay-looking" when you have that effect on me. When I have eyes, Lily.'

There was a pause while she tried to catch her breath.

'We have an audience.'

His fingers grazed her chin again, tightened slightly when she tried to turn her head to look at what—who— he was talking about.

'This won't look nearly as genuine if you check to see where the cameras are,' he murmured, tucking a curl behind her ear and moving so that there was no more space between them.

Any hope she had of catching her breath again disappeared. Not because of the cameras—though somewhere at the back of her mind she *was* worried about being photographed after a hard day's work. No, that didn't bother her as much when she was still recovering from the seduction of his words. From the proximity of his body.

The fresh, manly smell of his cologne filled her lungs. The easy way he touched her made her see only him, hear only him. She wanted to shake her head clear, to beg the logical part of her mind to take control again.

But all her senses were completely captivated by him.

His hand wrapped around her waist, lightly at first, and before she knew it she was pressed against his body.

'Is this what our arrangement is going to look like?' she managed to ask, and his eyes darkened.

'I really hope so...'

It was as if he had no control over his body, and his lips had touched hers before he had finished speaking.

She *did* taste as sweet as he remembered, and it made every regret he knew he'd have when he could think again worth it. He fought against the heat that demanded passion and slowly explored her mouth, relishing every feeling, every thrill that went through his body.

His hands made their way up over the back of her waist, loving how the curves of her body felt under his touch. Loving the quiver that it sent through Lily's body. His right hand moved further along, brushing the side of her breast and making them both shudder. The sane part of him—the one that reminded him they were being watched—was the only thing that kept his hand from lingering there, and it finally made its way to its intended destination.

He slid his hand through her curls and tilted her head to give him better access to her neck, pulling his lips from hers so that they could memorise the feel of her pulse against them. The moan that he heard in return made him abandon his resolve to take it slowly, and when he took her mouth this time their kiss was more passionate, more dangerous.

He would never have his fill of her, he thought, and his hands gripped her hips to pull her even tighter towards him.

The shock of desire his action brought made him break away, and he took a step back, fighting to control his body. And when that didn't entirely work he just wanted to control his lungs.

'You are...'

Lily looked rumpled and it made him feel better when he saw the way her chest heaved just as his did.

'Dangerous, Jacques. You make me...'

She didn't continue her sentence, but her words helped sober him from the drunkenness of passion.

'Feel?' he finished for her. 'I make you feel, don't I?'

Her shake of the head didn't matter when he knew it was the truth. She did the same thing to him.

'I'm sure we've given those watching more than enough to talk about,' she said, instead of answering him, looking at the small crowd that had gathered behind the fence around his property. 'How did they even know we were here?'

'We're standing on a balcony, Lily,' he replied dryly. 'And we were talking for the better part of an hour. It wouldn't take much for people on the very busy beach to notice us.'

'Okay, fine. Let's go back inside, then.'

They walked back into his flat, and he closed the door so their audience would lose interest.

And then he watched her gather herself, and found he was utterly taken by her.

By the simple green dress she wore that flared out at her waist. By the hair that was tied to the top of her head in a bun, curls spiralling out wherever they could manage it.

She didn't look like any other woman he knew, he thought. And *damn* but she drew him in like no other woman ever had.

'Would you like to have dinner with me?'

'No, no, no,' Lily said quickly. 'There is no part of me that wants to do that after that kiss.'

'It was just pretend, Lily. It wasn't real.'

'I'm not interested in trying to convince you that you're fooling yourself if you want to believe that. But I *will* say that we need to draw a line if I agree to go through with this.'

'I thought you'd already agreed?'

'I can change my mind.'

She watched him for a moment, and Jacques wondered how now, during the most important deal of his life, he'd found the only woman who stood up to him.

'Look, I'm not going to pretend like there isn't an at-traction between us, because clearly...' She waved a hand between them and his lips curved. 'But I don't want to pursue it. And I don't want you to either.'

The seriousness of her tone faded the remnants of his smile, and for the first time he heard the plea in her voice.

'Those are my conditions,' she said after a pause, and when she looked at him his heart stuttered at the confirmation of her plea. And although there was a part of him that wanted to tell her he couldn't accept those conditions, he nodded.

'That's fair.'

'So you agree?' she asked, eyebrows raised. 'Anything that happens between us from now on is strictly business. We can't complicate things by letting pleasure cloud our judgement.'

He was surprised by how much he didn't want to agree with her, but he nodded.

'If that's what you want, yes, I agree.'

'It is what I want,' she confirmed, though her tone made him think she wasn't as convinced as she wanted to be. 'Then I will have dinner with you. Because you're not calling me on to live television again just because you don't know enough about me.'

'That's why I suggested it.'

At least it should have been.

'Could I just have a moment to freshen up?'

'Sure.'

He showed her to the bathroom, and then tried to gather his thoughts. He needed to focus on his task. It hadn't left his mind once in the few months that he'd been trying to secure the sale, and yet with Lily he constantly needed to remind himself of it.

It was just too easy to get caught up in getting to know her. In wondering how she could afford prime retail property with modern and expensive décor on Big Bay Beach in Cape Town when she didn't have the money to sustain her store. She must have got the initial money *somewhere*. And after her reaction to his offer of a loan he thought it had to be connected.

And then there was her plea to keep things professional. After the way she'd dodged his question about Kyle, Jacques knew he was the reason why she'd asked.

Maybe he would have reacted the same way if his fiancée had cheated on him. But he'd never had a relationship last long enough for him to know what being in one felt like. He'd never wanted to be responsible for another woman's feelings. He'd had a lifetime's worth growing up with his mother. It was just a bonus that avoiding relationships meant he never needed to worry about how much of his father he had in him. About whether he was as cold, as oblivious to his partner's feelings.

And since Lily now had him suspecting that there was a little *too* much of his father in him, it was for the best that he just focus on business. On the deal that would help him make peace with his past.

He'd made progress. The TV interview that morning had had an incredibly positive influence on his image. But he didn't know if it was enough. So he would spend more time with Lily, and then hopefully Jade and Riley would tell him his reputation had been restored and the sponsors had changed their minds.

And if they hadn't...

You'd marry her?

His gut turned at the thought, and the strength of his resistance stunned him. There was immediate panic because of it, and he forced himself to breathe. Told himself it was only because marrying her would go against what they'd agreed on. It had nothing to do with the fact that marrying her would definitely be manipulative, knowing what he knew now. Their attraction. Her vulnerability. The protectiveness she inspired in him...

He turned when he felt a hand on his back, his heart thudding at his thoughts.

'Are you ready?'

'Yeah,' he answered, and cleared his throat when he heard the rasp of his voice. 'There are still a few people outside, though, so maybe we should stay here. I'll pour some wine.'

He wasn't suggesting it because he needed to compose himself. And he wasn't heading to where he kept his alcohol because he needed it to help him do that.

If he needed to marry Lily, he would. It was business, after all. But because of their agreement he'd talk to her first. That was fair, wasn't it? And it wouldn't be manipulative then, would it?

It made him feel calmer, that decision—until a voice asked him what had changed. He hadn't liked it when Riley and Jade had suggested marriage, but he'd believed he would have done it if he'd had to. And definitely without reservations over *who* he was marrying.

So the question wasn't *what* had changed, but who had changed *him*.

And really, he thought as he looked at Lily, should he even bother answering that question?

CHAPTER ELEVEN

'YOUR FLAT IS LOVELY, by the way,' Lily said to break the tension.

Tension she'd thought had started to subside before she'd freshened up.

'Thank you. Though I don't know if I should believe you, based on your tone.'

Something in *his* tone told her something had changed. But she was determined to keep things civil between them, and she wasn't sure if she could if she asked him about it.

'It really is lovely,' she insisted, settling on the safe subject. 'It just doesn't feel like you live here.'

'Why not?'

'You don't have a table on your balcony,' she said, and her pulse picked up—just a little—at the attention he aimed at her. 'That would have been the first thing I would have done when I moved in. I would eat my breakfast there, my lunch… Actually, I'd probably use any opportunity I could to appreciate that view.'

'I can appreciate the view fine from here,' he responded in a low tone.

She turned, saw that he was looking at her, and blushed. 'We had an agreement.'

'We still have the agreement. But I don't think it would

do any harm to flirt.' He grinned, but something felt off. As if he was saying the words on autopilot.

'Maybe not for you,' she said, and then closed her eyes. She hadn't meant for that to come out.

She held her breath, waiting for him to respond, and then sighed when he just said, 'You're right, though, I don't live here.'

She turned back at the proximity of his voice, took the glass of wine he handed her.

'Where *do* you live, then?'

'Near the office. I spend more time there than at home anyway.'

'Because you have nothing to go home to?'

There was a pause. 'Maybe.'

He gestured for her to take a seat, and she did, nearly groaning when the couch enveloped her aching body. It reminded her that she should be at home, soaking in a bath and drinking a glass of wine *there* instead of with Jacques.

She realised then that he hadn't really answered her question. It *had* been a little invasive, she considered. But it had fallen so freely from her lips because it was true in her own case. When she was at home her mind had nothing else to do but think about how she had failed in her life. How her parents had been right…how she should have never thought she was good enough to run a successful store. How running a business required business acumen, not the creative mind *she* had.

And when it was done with that her mind would start on how she should have just left Kyle without a backward glance, instead of accepting money so that she felt as if she'd paid with her soul.

'Maybe we should start with something a little…

less…' she suggested when her thoughts made her chest tighten.

'I think that would be for the best,' he answered, and sipped from his wine glass. 'Tell me about your family.'

It was an innocent question, but she felt a wall go up around her heart. She had to tell him *something*, though.

'There's nothing out of the ordinary there,' she said slowly. 'My mom used to be a paediatrician. She's retired now, but she still helps out at the local hospital three days a week. My dad's a couple of years younger than her, so he's still working. He's an engineer.'

'What kind?'

She tilted her head, a smile tickling her lips that he'd thought to ask.

'Civil.'

He nodded. 'Siblings?'

'None. I'm the only child.'

He frowned. 'It doesn't sound like you're happy about that.'

She'd heard that, too. The slight dip in her voice that had tainted her words. But what could she tell him? That her parents, with their engineering and medical degrees and professional stability, had expected her to follow in their footsteps from a young age? That when she'd proved to be different from them they hadn't been able to adjust? That instead they'd just tried to apply to her the mould they were used to and hadn't seen how it had eroded her confidence, her self-worth?

'No,' she answered him. 'My parents have…' She stopped herself, and cleared her throat. 'It's nothing.'

A single raised eyebrow sent her heart jumping.

'It's something.' There was a pause. 'Lily?'

His tone was a mixture of forced patience and genuine curiosity, and she knew if she were talking about anything else it would have made her smile. Now, she chose her words carefully.

'They just…their expectations of me are a bit high.'

'Why?'

She lifted her eyes at the softness his voice had now, felt the warmth in his gaze right down to her toes.

'They're very…rigid. Things are straightforward for them. Simple. Do you want to be a doctor? Study for a medical degree. Engineer? Study engineering.' They were simple examples, but she saw that he understood what she meant. 'I'm not straightforward.'

'And they can't understand that.'

'No, they can't.'

'I understand not living up to your parents' expectations.'

She looked up to see Jacques staring out at the beach. When he looked back at her she once again saw that stormy expression in his eyes.

'But the more important question is whether you've lived up to your expectations of *yourself*?'

She'd never thought about it, she realised in surprise. *Had* she lived up to her own expectations? Did she even *have* expectations of herself? Her mind scrambled for an answer and she bit her lip. She had goals and dreams. Why were they so difficult to remember now?

Because they're so closely tied to other people's expectations of you.

She frowned. Was her store failing because her parents had expected it to so she did too? Did she believe that she could do better, that she could *be* better, because that was what Kyle had expected of her? What did the money she'd accepted from Kyle's family—the first decision she'd ever made for herself—say about her expectations of herself? What did it *make* her?

'Have *you*?' she asked, desperate when she looked at Jacques and realised he saw too much. 'Lived up to your own expectations?'

Though his expression gave nothing away, she saw the hand holding his glass of wine tighten, and she realised the answer was no.

It made her feel better—a little less vulnerable—and because it did she said, 'Fortunately no one will be asking us that question.'

She nodded at the relief she saw in his eyes.

'But they might expect you to know that my parents live about an hour away from here, in Langebaan. And they'll expect me to know about *your* family. I already know Nathan. How about you tell me about your parents? Other than their ridiculous expectations of you, of course.'

She'd said it lightly, but his face hardened, a light going out in it.

'Neither of my parents work. They have money—a lot of it—that my grandfather made in the mining business. They keep busy, of course, but they don't have jobs.'

'Oh,' she said slowly, processing this new information.

It reminded her that Nathan worked for the Van der Rosses not only because he was a good lawyer, but because he had the connections to get into the biggest law firm in the Western Cape. It made his humility, his good nature, so much more appealing.

'Where do they live?'

'Somerset West.'

'And since you live on the opposite side of Cape Town that puts a nice distance between you and your parents,' she said, and saw confirmation in his eyes before something else eclipsed it…guilt? Because she thought it was, she added, 'I'm not judging. It's the same with my parents.'

'Distance helps. You don't have to constantly be reminded of how you've fallen short.'

He understood, she thought.

'Not that it matters in my case, since I haven't seen them in seven years.'

'*Seven* years?' He nodded, but didn't meet her eyes. 'That's when…'

'When I destroyed my career?'

Now he looked at her. 'Yes.'

The admission was difficult for him, she saw, and felt a little relief at that. They were on the same page, then, sharing difficult things with each other. She still worried that she had told him too much. But it felt good finally to admit that she couldn't be what her parents wanted her to be. It felt good finally to talk to someone who understood. Caitlyn didn't, and since she was Lily's only friend there hadn't been any other options.

Now there was Jacques.

She didn't quite know how to feel about that. So she settled on something a little more familiar.

'So, how about we get to that dinner you promised me?'

Jacques's lips curved into a smile. It broke some of the tension he felt about his surprising admission. The tension that had started when he'd realised she was changing him.

And he'd only known her for two days.

'I usually have my housekeeper prepare meals for me when I know I'll be staying here,' he said, and took her wine glass from her as she tried to get out of the hole the couch had created for her body.

He'd bought the piece of furniture specifically because it had that ability, which felt like heaven after a tough rugby practice or match. But watching her struggle now gave him a new appreciation for it. Her cheeks were flushed as she tried to scoot her way to the edge of the seat. Though it helped to get her feet closer to the ground, it made her dress ride up, exposing her thighs.

A ball of fire dropped in his stomach, turning his amusement into something more serious. Something more dangerous. It rooted his feet to the ground even as it woke every nerve in his body. She hadn't noticed this new development, and the more she moved the higher the dress went.

Eventually she sighed and, without looking at him, lifted a hand for his assistance.

It took him a moment to move—to force his body to behave—and then he set their wine glasses on the table and quickly took her hand, pulling her up without paying attention to the force he used. Though it helped her out of the seat, it also made her lose her balance—and before he could totally comprehend what had happened she had fallen against his chest.

His arms went around her, steadying her, but when she looked up at him, the colour of her skin still tinged with pink, rational thought flew out of his mind. Their eyes met, and the heat that always simmered between them turned into a boil. His arms tightened, pulling her closer to his body. Her curves fitted perfectly there, he thought, and the air in his lungs thickened. Her eyes had widened, but she hadn't protested at their proximity. Instead her arms had wound around his neck, and those full lips of hers had parted.

He remembered their taste from that afternoon, when he'd kissed her for what he'd told her was the public's sake. But it had really been because he'd had to know whether the attraction, the pull he felt for her was real. And now that he knew it was—now that he could acknowledge that despite all his playboy-like dating years he'd never wanted another woman as intensely as he wanted Lily—he wondered how their kiss would be.

Whether now that they were in his flat, away from the public, their kiss would turn into something more. Something that would sate the nagging need he felt for her...

'Jacques!' She interrupted his thoughts in a hoarse voice. 'You...*we*...we promised.'

Somewhere at the back of his mind it bothered him that she'd had to remind him—*again*—of that promise, that agreement they'd made only a few moments earlier. It seemed vague, faded—just like the goal that had consumed his mind from the moment he'd learned the Shadows Rugby Club was for sale.

The realisation made him step back, put some distance between them.

But still his body yearned.

'I'm sorry.'

'Me, too,' she answered, and something in her voice— her eyes—made him wonder if she was apologising because they had stopped things before they got...*interesting.*

There was a long pause, and then he heard her release a shaky breath. The sound revved him into action. 'So. Food?'

'Yeah—what do you have?'

He forced his mind to focus and picked up his wine, downing it even as he wished for something stronger.

'I didn't tell my housekeeper I was coming,' he said, only then realising that he didn't have much to offer her.

'I think there's some lasagne left over from when I was here last week.'

'Did you invite me to stay here for dinner without having dinner to offer me?'

Embarrassment stirred beneath the desire he'd felt just a few moments earlier.

'Yes. But to be fair I wasn't exactly expecting this. I thought we'd go out.'

'Do you have any ingredients to make something?'

He walked to the kitchen, checked in cupboards that held only cutlery, crockery and the few items he needed to make coffee.

'I'm afraid not.'

She stared at him for a while, and then a smile crept onto her lips.

'What?' he asked, as his mouth twitched to mirror hers.

She shrugged. 'It's just nice to know you don't think things through sometimes either. You know—like the rest of us normal people.'

He smiled at her, but her words had scratched at a wound he'd thought he had buried a long time ago. He'd always wanted to be *normal*. Normal children had normal families. Normal families had fathers who cared about their sons and didn't brush them aside for something—anything—better.

He pulled the fridge open with enough force that the door swung from his hand, hitting the counter and then his arm. Since there was nothing in it there was no damage, but he had to close his eyes to control his anger. To control *his* damage.

'I was only teasing,' Lily said from behind him, and he turned, his heart softening when he saw the uncertain look on her face.

'I know. I was just thinking that I should have something for you other than this.'

He gestured to the fridge. It held only a half-empty bottle of orange juice. It was a lame excuse, and they both knew it, but Lily didn't call him on it. Instead she watched him, the look of uncertainty fading, leaving only a shadow of vulnerability on her face.

He could see that vulnerability every time he looked at her, he realised. It was the reason he hadn't wanted her to take part in his plan in the first place. And it was the reason she was the *best* person to take part in his plan. She was *real*—with real feelings, real emotions.

She had the same concerns he did—that she had fallen short of the expectations her parents had of her. And while he was sure that was because she hadn't had the courage to tell her parents to adjust those expectations, his concerns were a result of years and years of trying but never succeeding.

Once he'd realised nothing he did would ever mean anything to Dale Brookes—would ever make his father *love* him—he had stopped trying. But he hadn't given up on his mother until the night of the championship game. He hadn't been able to believe that after everything Dale had put her through—after everything she'd seen the man put him and Nathan through—she'd stayed with him after he'd promised her for the umpteenth time that he would change.

Not even the taunts his father had aimed at him after his mother had decided not to leave had given her a clue that he wouldn't *ever* change. And after that night—after the subsequent events that had ruined his career—he had cut ties with his parents. He'd put away those protective instincts he'd felt for his mother. Had vowed never to apply them to another woman.

Except Lily.

'How about that lasagne?'

She interrupted his thoughts and he frowned as he tried to remember what they were talking about.

'Let me check.' He checked the freezer, saw there was nothing in it, and closed it again. 'I'm sure there aren't any people outside any more. We should go out.'

'Because there's no food in your freezer?'

'Are you mocking my hosting abilities?'

'Who? Me?' She fluttered her eyelashes. 'I would *never* do that to my oh-so-gracious host.'

He eased with the banter. 'What do you feel like eating?'

'What's the closest place?'

He frowned. 'It doesn't have to be close. We can drive somewhere nice—'

'No.' She cleared her throat and pulled the jersey she still wore tightly around herself again. 'Let's just get something at the closest place.'

It took a moment for him to put all the pieces together.

'You don't *want* us to be seen in public?' When she looked away, he shook his head. 'Lily, that's not a realistic expectation for this whole plan. We're—'

'Just not tonight, okay?'

It was a plea that went straight to his heart.

'I've given people enough of me today. And I look fa—' She stopped, looked at him with uncertainty and then finished, 'I look frumpy in this dress.'

'No, you don't,' he said immediately. 'And you weren't going to say that.'

'What?'

But she'd walked into the living room, away from him, and he realised she knew exactly what he was talking about.

'Yesterday you said you were too heavy for me to lift you.' He was talking to himself mostly, but when he saw her face he knew his gut had been right. 'Lily, were you going to say *fat*?'

CHAPTER TWELVE

'No,' she answered quickly. 'Of course not.'

'Why on earth would you think that?' he asked her, dismissing the obvious lie.

She wanted to be flattered by the incredulous tone he used, but her embarrassment was too much for her to think of anything else.

'We should probably get going.'

Please don't push, she thought, and while the minutes passed repeated the plea in her mind.

'There's a place we can walk to from here. It's secluded…intimate. Something only the residents around here know about.'

Relief pummelled the reply from her mouth. 'Yes, that sounds perfect.'

He nodded. 'We can go down there.' He gestured to the balcony stairs.

She followed him down the steps, through the gate he'd opened in the fence that no longer had to keep out a crowd. Her feet felt heavier with each stride. It didn't take long for her to realise the weight had nothing to do with the sand they were walking on, but guilt.

Guilt for avoiding his question. For lying to him. She didn't *want* to tell him, but she felt compelled to and she wasn't sure why. Though she wanted to ignore it, his silence made her feel as if he was pulling back. It sent waves of panic through her that soon took control of her tongue.

'I was overweight for a very long time.' Her insides shrivelled at the words, but she knew it was too late to stop. 'I lost some weight when I started university, and then a little more while I studied. It was hard.' She cleared her throat when her voice suddenly went hoarse. 'I've been struggling to keep it off since then.'

He didn't respond, but gripped her hand. The warmth from it spread through her body.

'You still feel like you're overweight?'

'I…' She took a deep breath and was grateful for the slight pressure from his hand. 'I'm not perfect. I'll never be a supermodel.'

'And in your mind that means you're fat?'

She flinched at the word, just as she had the first time he'd used it. But it was her own fault. She'd thought it first—had almost said it—and she couldn't shy away from it now because it offended her But it brought back such memories—hurtful ones that made her want to fade into the background.

Before she could respond, he stopped, and put a hand around her waist, pulling her in to his side.

'We're here.'

She'd been so lost in thought, so lost in the difficulty of their conversation, that she hadn't seen the beach torches that led to a small wooden deck. The deck seated four tables of two and four, then led into a beach cottage that had been renovated into a restaurant. Paraffin lamps lit the deck, lining the two steps that led up to it and the wooden banister that surrounded it.

Jacques's hand still held hers as they walked up the steps and she saw the beach-themed green and blue interior of the restaurant. A stocky young man greeted Jacques with enthusiasm, with recognition, and seated them at the only free table on the deck.

'This is... Wow, it's beautiful.' She looked out to where the moon lit the sea, and only then saw the small dance floor just beyond the deck. 'Do people actually *use* that?'

He shrugged. 'I've never actually been here to see that.'

'But you *have* been here before. With other women, of course, considering the waiter is now discussing you with his friend over there.'

She nodded her head to where the man was animatedly speaking to another waiter, gesturing in their direction.

'He might just be a fan of mine.'

'He might be,' she agreed. 'But since the other waiter just sent me a knowing glance I suspect I'm right.'

He smiled, but didn't meet her eyes. 'You are.'

Though she wasn't surprised, she *was* a little annoyed—too much for someone who supposedly didn't care about Jacques's past.

And then he said, 'But you're the first I've brought here at night.'

'And that's important because...?'

'Because night-time dates set the tone for the rest of the evening. This kind of place...it's intimate.'

Her heart pounded at the implication.

'And the waiter you pointed out just took a picture of us. He'll probably post it to all his social networks.'

That's more realistic than thinking he wants to be intimate with you, Lily.

'So "secluded" and "intimate" don't necessarily mean private?'

'We aren't supposed to be private, Lily,' he reminded

her. 'But I can ask him not to post it. To delete the picture, even. I doubt his boss would want him taking pictures of the restaurant's patrons anyway.'

'You'd do that? For me?'

He didn't meet her eyes. 'For both of us. We still have a month until the club's sale is finalised, and I think we've had enough exposure for today.'

But she knew he'd just given her that reason because he couldn't admit he *would have* done it for her. It had her insides glowing.

'It's fine—let him post it. What harm could it possibly do after all we've already done today?'

He nodded his thanks, and then called the waiter over to order wine.

It gave her time to think about why his words had warmed her so much. They shared an attraction, yes. And if she hadn't lived the kind of life she had perhaps that would mean something. But attraction didn't last. Reality would soon catch up with them—just as it had with her and Kyle. And Jacques would soon realise—just as Kyle had—that Lily simply wasn't enough.

She'd thought about it a lot after she'd broken off their engagement.

Lily knew she would have made Kyle a decent wife. She'd passed her degree—a Bachelor of *Arts*, much to her parents' chagrin—at one of the top universities in the country, so she'd have been able to engage with his peers without embarrassing him. She had lost weight, so she'd looked fine, she supposed, but not good enough that she'd threaten any of the supermodel wives of the business acquaintances Kyle would have to charm. And she had been easily manipulated—which had probably been a huge part of her appeal. Easily bullied.

Lily would have done almost anything Kyle had asked because—well, because he'd asked her.

She could remember the times when she hadn't responded favourably and had had him pressuring her. She'd given in so quickly, terrified he would leave if she didn't. And yet despite all that Lily had clearly still lacked *something*. And that something had been significant enough that Kyle had turned to another woman to get it.

No, she thought again. Jacques's interest in her wouldn't last for very long. Not once he found out she wasn't anything more than a prop in his charade.

But she could enjoy the present. She could enjoy the fact that she was in a restaurant—a beautiful one she would never have discovered otherwise—with a man she liked. And, being in the present, Lily didn't have to think about the context that word 'liked' was being used.

'You're perfect, you know,' he said when the waiter had left, so sincerely that she regretted that he wouldn't want her soon. 'Your body, your weight… You don't have to worry about it.'

'Thank you,' she said softly. And then, because the way he was looking at her gave her gooseflesh, she continued, 'Like I said, I've lost a lot of weight. Now I try to keep what I eat appropriate, so that I don't gain it again.'

'That isn't the only thing you do.' Jacques's voice was low. 'You wear clothes you think hide your body. And even then you pull at them so they don't cling where they aren't supposed to.'

He paused when the waiter arrived to pour their wine. As soon as he was gone, Jacques continued.

'You worry about what people think about the way you look. So much so that you put a jersey on during a warm evening just in case someone sees you. Am I right?'

Her vocal cords wouldn't work. Not that there were any words for her to say after Jacques's little speech. It stunned her—shook her—that he was so perceptive. That he'd seen things she hadn't paid much attention to. She cringed that she hadn't been able to hide them. Felt the mortification balling in her stomach coated by anger.

'The judgement in your voice... Is that because you think I shouldn't care what people think?'

His brow furrowed. 'I wasn't *judging* you, Lily. But I do think you could worry a little less about it.'

'Because that's worked so well for *you*?'

It was a low blow—one she'd made deliberately, out of anger. But when she saw him recoil she immediately felt ashamed.

'I'm sorry. I shouldn't have said that.'

'But you were right.'

He shrugged, and she could almost see the weight that lay heavy on his shoulders. It made her feel even worse.

'No, *you* were right. I... I said that because I *know* you're right. And yet somehow... Well, some scars just don't go away.'

'Kyle?'

Again his perceptiveness was disturbing.

'Yes. But he was in a long line of others.'

'Then *why* did you date him, Lily?'

Because his tone was pleading with her, and because he was asking her for the second time—third, if she counted the night they'd met—she told him.

'He was interested in me. After years of no one wanting me, of feeling like I wasn't enough at home or at school, this successful, attractive man wanted *me*. So I ignored all the signs that told me he was just like the people who had bullied me in my childhood. It took catching him cheating to finally open my eyes.'

She didn't blame him for the silence that followed. But that didn't help her feel less exposed.

'I didn't realise…'

She lifted her glass to her lips, saw that her hands were shaking. 'Why would you?'

'I never liked him.'

He said it in a gruff voice, and it made her smile.

'You have good instincts.'

'And you blame yourself for *not* having them?'

Her fingers curled around the stem of the wine glass. 'No, I don't. My gut knew all along that he wasn't the right person for me. I just didn't listen.'

Because she'd already told him too much, she told herself there was no point in holding back now.

'I blame myself for believing that I couldn't do better.'

'But you know now that you can.'

It was a statement that told her he wouldn't accept any other.

'Yes.'

'Lily, you have to *mean* it.'

'I *do* mean it.'

'No, you don't. You may believe it in part, but something's keeping you from believing it fully.'

She felt a door slam shut in her heart.

'Let's order.'

CHAPTER THIRTEEN

IT TOOK JACQUES a moment to realise he'd been shut out. Another to deal with the rush of emotions that realisation brought. The anger was there, and the frustration. As was the curiosity. But the feeling that was strongest was the desire to make her *believe*. She didn't have to be defined by people's opinions. By one decision.

You're trying to convince yourself.

He shook it off. He didn't need to indulge thoughts that came from nowhere. But he *did* need to say something—this *one* thing—so that he wouldn't have to think about it over and over that night when they'd parted.

He waited for her to order, knowing she would use that as an excuse if he didn't, and placed his own. When the waiter had left, he said, 'You're a strong woman, Lily. Even if you don't believe it right now, some day you will and I'll have told you first.'

He'd wanted to reach out, to lay a hand over hers, but the look on her face had his hand sticking to his thigh. Her eyes were glossed with emotions that he felt in his own chest, her face a picture he didn't think he would ever be able to forget.

There was surprise, yes. But there was also hope. Pleasure, too. All because he had seen something in her that he now realised had been whittled away after years of being bullied.

What he wouldn't have given to see that look on his mother's face just once...

'Thank you.'

He nodded, unable to find words when his mind, his heart, were in turmoil.

'So, the flat...' She cleared her throat. 'Why did you buy it if you don't spend enough time there to have more than half a bottle of orange juice in your fridge?'

Grateful for the change in topic, he answered, 'I bought it after my first big rugby pay-cheque. The club is based down the road from here. It made sense to live close by. I could walk to and from the daily practices, and I was able to leave my car behind when we had away matches.'

'But you don't spend much time there now. So why do you still have the flat?'

'Because...because it reminds me of the happiest times of my life.'

There was another beat of silence, and then Lily said, 'That's why you want the club, too? Because it represents something good in your life?'

'Are we going to spend the whole evening talking about things that make us uncomfortable?'

He reached for his wine, drank it in one gulp. When he set it down he saw that she was watching him. She gave him a small, comforting smile.

'Seems like we can't get away from it.'

'We could if we just stopped now. If we talked about something innocuous like the weather.'

'It *is* a lovely evening,' she agreed, lifting her wine in a mock toast.

He smiled, then sobered. 'What do you want to know?'

His own words would have surprised him if he hadn't felt the shift that was happening between them. And, though he'd resisted it from the moment he'd first felt it, it still seemed to have power over him.

It still seemed to compel him.

'I want to know what really happened the night of that game,' she said, as he had known she would.

'I got into a fight, got a red card—my team lost and I got suspended.' It sounded crass, but it was the only way he could tell her.

'I know. I read all that in the papers. What I want to know is *why*?' she said softly. 'It's clear how much that time in your life meant to you. How much it *still* means to you. What could have happened to make you give it up?'

He took a deep breath, opened his mouth, and then shook his head.

He tried again. 'I told you my grandfather was in the mining business?'

She nodded.

'That was my mother's father. He spent years building his business, and the family name grew with it. By the time he retired he was a millionaire, with his name appearing on every rich or most successful list in South Africa.'

He paused and ran a hand through his hair.

'It meant people knew the family name—who they were. Here and overseas, since my grandfather had started trading abroad. If you aren't careful, having that kind of money and power tends to make people take advantage.' Another pause. 'My mother wasn't careful.'

He stopped, tension tight in every part of his body. He didn't look at her. He didn't want to see the empathy he knew would be there.

'She was an only child—my grandmother died during

childbirth—and my grandfather sent her overseas to live with his sister while she went to school.'

He took another breath.

'She got pregnant with me there. My grandfather was furious. She'd just finished school. With his connections, my mother would have had the world at her feet.'

He lifted his eyes to hers.

'He made it clear that she couldn't come back here. Not when she was unmarried and pregnant.'

She nodded, making him see she was familiar with the inflexible values of past generations.

'My mother decided to get married to spare my grandfather the embarrassment. It wasn't too bad for her, considering how much she loved my father. He just didn't love *her*.'

Anger still heated his blood at the thought.

'But he loved her money. There's no proof that he planned the whole thing, but I *know* he did.'

He could almost taste the bitterness on his tongue.

'We moved back to SA and my grandfather died a few years later. My mom had just fallen pregnant with Nathan, but my father's lack of interest in us become clear when my grandfather was no longer around. He didn't have to pretend to be a family man any more. My mother had inherited most of the money—the rest was in a trust fund for us—but since they were married her money was his, too.'

He shook his head when he realised he was saying too much.

'You didn't ask to know all this.'

'No,' she agreed. 'But since you've told me there must be a reason.'

He nodded, and tried to build up his nerve to tell her the rest.

'I watched my father treat my mother—and us—poorly for most of my life. I tried to get her to leave him, but she was clinging so hard to the memory of the man he had been when he was wooing her—when he was pretending to be someone he wasn't—that she wouldn't. Until she found out he'd been lying to her about the money he was spending. She could take his uninterest and harsh words, but lying about money was too much for her.'

He shook his head, still not quite believing that *that* had been more important to her than her children's well-being.

'I got her to consider making him leave, and on the night of the championship we packed his bags. We were kicking him out. But when he found out it didn't take long for his charm to soften my mother's defences. A few words, compliments, promises, and she took him back. Not even my begging was enough to make her reconsider.'

He felt Lily's hand over his, and looked down to see it was covering his clenched fist. He forced himself to uncurl it and took a deep breath. He wasn't done yet.

'He turned on me that night. Said things I don't want to remember but can't forget. No matter how much I try.'

He took another breath as the memories flew through his mind.

Failure. Disappointment. Useless.

'I wasn't fighting the opposing team that night, Lily…'

There was a beat of silence before she said what he couldn't bring himself to.

'You were fighting your father.'

Lily's heart broke when he nodded, and she entwined her fingers with his, squeezing. But the moment was interrupted when the waiter brought their food, and she pulled her hand away, grateful for the break in the tension.

A small wave of guilt flowed through her when she looked at the burger in front of her, but since it was accompanied by a salad—and she hadn't eaten since lunch—she figured it was okay.

'Why did you never go back?'

'It was too late. I got suspended for three years—the maximum for what I did. Even if a team had wanted me, being out the game that long meant I wouldn't have had the same skills.'

'I'm sorry.'

He shrugged. 'It doesn't matter now.'

'But it *does*,' she said, wondering why he was pretending it didn't after everything he'd told her. 'Isn't that why you're doing this? Because of how much it means to you?'

She could see he was considering it, so she gave him time and dug into her meal. The burger was juicy, soft, and for the first time in a long time she found that she was enjoying a meal without feeling guilty.

'It does matter,' he said as she bit into a piece of lettuce. 'Because that loss—my red card—set the Shadows back years. In the past seven years they haven't made it to another championship. They lost their chance at playing in an international league because of me. If I buy the club I can change that. I *will* change that.'

'Yes, you will,' she said, seeing the determination in his eyes.

But it made her worry about what her part in his plan would cost her.

'Knowing what you know about my past...' She cleared her throat. Reached for her wine when the action didn't do anything to help the sudden dryness that was there. 'About my…insecurities, would you have still called me on to live TV today?'

A mixture of emotions played over his face. 'I… I don't know.'

There was a long pause.

'Why not?'

'Because there's a part of me that wants to protect you. But there's another part…'

'That wants this so badly you can't afford to protect me.'

It wasn't a question, but disappointment still soaked through her heart when there was another pause.

'I've wanted to prove myself for as long as I can remember. I've been working *seven years* for it.' He took a breath. 'I'll do everything I can to make sure you don't get hurt during this, Lily.'

She nodded, but couldn't reply.

'Lily, please.' Regret filled his voice. 'I'm sorry.'

'Don't apologise,' she answered, once the ache in her chest had subsided. 'You've been honest about your intentions. At least you have been this evening.' She exhaled shakily. 'I know this is important to you. And since you've been working so many years for it, it seems selfish to expect you to sacrifice it when you've only known me two days.'

'That's not…' He sighed. 'I don't know what to tell you, Lily. Except that it feels a hell of a lot longer than two days.'

He was struggling, she realised. It sent a shiver of hope through her. But then her mind offered her a look into the future.

She'd continue the charade with Jacques, convincing herself that he had feelings for her—developing feelings for *him*—deeper and more intense than anything she'd felt for Kyle. And then Jacques would get his club and he'd no longer need her.

And she would have to nurse the pain of the worst heartbreak of her life.

No, she thought, her heart aching even at the prospect of it. It was better to stop that hope from developing into something more dangerous now.

'Don't worry about me,' she said into the silence. 'I can look after myself.'

She could—and she would.

'You…you still want to do this? Even though—?'

'Yes,' she interrupted him. 'I'll still help you, Jacques.'

'Why?'

'Because it's time I faced my fears. And…because you need me to.'

She said nothing about reminding herself that there could be no hope for them.

'Have I told you how amazing you are?'

It was a line, she knew, but when she looked into his eyes she could almost believe it was true.

'Now, *darling*, there's no need for flattery. We're already dating, aren't we?'

CHAPTER FOURTEEN

AND SO THEY WERE.

For a month Lily dated Jacques Brookes. She went to charity events. Corporate events. She was wined and dined in Cape Town's most expensive restaurants. Showered with public displays of affection. Treated like royalty.

It was so similar to what she'd experienced with Kyle that she knew she should have pulled back. And if she'd *felt* anything similar to what she had when she'd been with Kyle maybe she would have.

But she didn't. Because there was one significant difference: Jacques.

The conversation they'd had the night they'd had dinner at the beach had clarified things. Lily knew what Jacques expected of her—knew why—and that made it easier to focus on their professional agreement. To lock away all those strange feelings that had been stirred the first two days they'd known each other.

She also couldn't deny that the attention their relationship got contributed to her focus. The pictures of them kissing on Jacques's balcony had been in the papers the day after they'd been taken. The photo of their 'intimate' dinner had been shared more than a hundred thousand times on social media after the waiter had posted it. Their interview snippet now had over a million views.

Their relationship had been sealed in public.

She didn't have time to think about personal feelings when she was dealing with all the interest in her. Customers now wanted pictures, signatures—though heaven only knew why they wanted them from *her*. She was just the girlfriend, not the actual celebrity.

When it became too much she reminded herself that she was facing her fears. She reminded herself that growth was never without pain. And she repeated that to herself when people began to poke into her past. When people who had never been her friends came forward to testify about how wonderful she'd been to them.

And, worst of all, when they discovered that she'd once been engaged to another of Cape Town's most eligible bachelors. The media had hounded her on that one, and more than one outlet had questioned the sincerity of her interest in Jacques.

Since that wasn't the kind of attention Jacques was hoping for, she'd expected him to step back. To tell her that he couldn't afford to be with someone who gave him negative press.

But he hadn't.

Instead he'd had his PR firm release a statement defending their relationship. He shut down any questions about her past when they were together, and held her tightly against him as he did so. As if he knew that she needed the comfort, the reassurance. And each time he would check that she was okay, Lily found that she was. Because although she would be shaking, Jacques would be holding her hand. Protecting her.

He'd said he would, and he'd kept his word.

And *that* was the real reason she was okay.

Jacques had even asked Jade from his PR firm to coach Lily when she could. So Lily knew what she shouldn't say in public—anything about Kyle except that they'd once been engaged and it hadn't worked out—and she knew what she should post on social media.

Those posts were strictly about Lily's, though, since Jade handled anything regarding Jacques and Lily's personal lives and their relationship. Still, Lily had seen an influx of 'likes' and 'follows' on the store's different accounts, and she knew that she would have to utilise them to keep momentum after her and Jacques's fake relationship ended.

That thought had caused a strange twinge in her heart lately, but she told herself it was because of the friendship she and Jacques had settled into. They'd got to know each other better over the dinners they'd shared, and Lily had got to see different sides of Jacques at different events. And sometimes after the events, Lily would watch his old games, his old interviews, and realise just how much he'd given up when his career had ended.

And then there were his business skills. Her respect for those grew whenever she saw him in action, and skyrocketed with everything he taught her about her own business. He'd taken her accounts, her business plan, and each time she saw him he gave her notes and guidelines. He pointed out where she had been going wrong—sometimes shockingly so.

It embarrassed her, and told her she shouldn't have opened a store before she had known all that, but never once did he make her feel like a failure. Even when her own thoughts mocked her—even when she would have fully understood if he called her that—he didn't. He just patiently told her where she should adjust, and how she should do so.

With those adjustments, and the increased traffic the store was getting, things were going surprisingly well. Despite the attention her relationship with Kyle had got, and despite those who called their relationship fake for the sake of Jacques's interest in the Shadows—those who saw through them—Lily was okay. Going out with Jacques was a little less intimidating every time she did it, and the clothes Jade would send her for events didn't scandalise her quite as much any more. Lily even found herself amused that for every one of those who doubted their relationship, ten others praised her for taming Bad-Boy Brookes.

So she ignored her worries. She ignored how, every time she spoke to her parents, she was reminded of the backlash she needed to anticipate when things with Jacques ended. How, every time she spoke to Caitlyn, she had to repeat that she didn't feel anything for Jacques other than friendship.

Because she didn't.

The niggle left behind after each of those conversations didn't mean anything.

And friends did sometimes pitch up at their friend's flats at five-thirty in the morning, Lily told herself as she did just that.

She hadn't been able to sleep the night before, and she suspected it was because she and Jacques would be attending one last event together that night, before Jacques made his bid for the club.

It had made her anxious—more than it should have— because she didn't want to lose her friend, she assured herself. So she'd got up at four, got ready for the day, and grabbed two coffees on her way to Jacques's flat. If she couldn't sleep, she could at least enjoy the sunrise.

With a friend. Who happened to have the perfect view to do that from…

She used the key he'd given her when he'd told her she could stay at his place on the nights she was working late. Between that and the events they were attending she was sometimes too exhausted to make the twenty-minute trip home. And, since Jacques's was less than half that time away, she'd found herself taking him up on his offer. But only the nights she knew he wouldn't be there. Lily wasn't sure she could handle staying in the same flat with him yet.

Yet?

She shook her head, forcing the thought away as she walked down the passage to Jacques's room. He was hosting the charity event that evening—for a Shadows-affiliated charity—at a venue in Big Bay, and had been staying at his Blouberg flat for the past week to see to the final arrangements.

When she got to his room, she pushed the door open softly.

And her heart just melted, pushing thoughts of friendship far away.

He lay on his back, one hand cushioning his head, the other on his bare chest. Though she appreciated the strength of his body—the defined chest, the chiselled abs, the full biceps—the unarmed expression on his face undid her. There was no guarded expression now, no worry lines, no indication that he was thinking about a million other things while he spoke to her.

Now he was just a man who slept. It made her realise, not for the first time, how much his plan required from him. And, while she understood the importance, she worried that it was going to break him in the process.

When she felt her chest tighten and her heart burn—

when she felt that neat little box she'd put her un-friend-like feelings about Jacques into tearing open—she took a shaky breath and walked towards him. She took no more than two steps before he shifted, turning his head in her direction. And though she stilled completely at the movement he opened his eyes, the sides of them crinkling with his smile when he saw her, as though her appearance was perfectly normal.

'Hi,' he said huskily, and her skin turned to goose-flesh.

'Hi,' she responded, and heard the hoarseness of her own voice—felt the intensity of her attraction for him edged with something more—and cleared her throat.

'I'm sorry I woke you, but I want to show you something.'

Now he frowned, and turned his head to the clock next to him.

'Lil, are you *kidding* me? It's not even six a.m. yet.'

Warmth spread through her body at his use of the nickname.

'No, I'm serious. Come to the living room.'

She turned to leave, eager to escape the tension that was rife in her body. It subsided—but only slightly—when she stood on his balcony, with the sight of the waves crashing on the shore and the salty air filling her lungs.

She handed him a coffee when she felt him next to her, saw that he had pulled on the shirt she assumed he'd worn the night before but hadn't closed it all the way, and cleared her throat again.

Forcing herself to focus on why she was there, she nodded her head in the direction the sun. They didn't speak as they watched the sun slowly rise.

Lily wished she could spend more time appreciating the beauty of where she lived instead of worrying. Instead of feeling the constant fear of failure. She watched as the yellow and orange colours spread over the ocean, bringing light and warmth. And when the sun rose high enough that a ray lit over them she sighed, heard Jacques sigh, too.

She felt him move closer to her and she turned, tilting her head back to look up at him.

If she thought her heart had melted when she'd seen him asleep, she had no words to describe what was happening to it now.

'Is it wrong for me to want to kiss you?' he asked, taking the coffee from her hand and setting it on the table he'd added after her suggestion.

One of many things he'd done for her that made her heart melt a little more each time.

'Are there cameras around?' she replied softly, forcing herself to think of what was *real*.

'No.'

'Then why do you want to kiss me?'

He took her face in his hands gently, and it began to feel very real.

'Because you're beautiful. You're kind. You're just… you're amazing.'

She opened her mouth to deny it, but his lips were on hers before she could.

And then she was lost in the romance of kissing a man entirely too handsome to be interested in her.

On his balcony.

With the sun rising behind her.

And then she was lost in the kiss.

His lips felt as if they belonged on hers as they nudged. As they teased. As they sent warmth flowing through her body. And then his tongue joined hers, and she tasted the mint from his toothpaste, the coffee on his lips. She felt the temperature rise, the warmth now heat.

She put her hands on his waist, under the shirt he'd thrown on, and let them skim the sides of him. Her body responded when she felt his shudder, and she closed the distance between them so that she could memorise how those muscles would feel against her. So that when he realised he didn't really want her she would remember what it had been like to feel him against her.

To feel what it was like to have a man like Jacques want her.

He angled her so that she was pressed against the balcony railing, moaning when her hands slid over his abs and back down again. She couldn't think, couldn't breathe with his hands on her. She moved one of her own hands from where it explored his body, so that she could slide it through his hair as she'd wanted to do from the first night they'd met.

And then, when she felt him press even closer to her, she moved that hand to the base of his neck, wanting to taste more, to give more. A deep sound came from his throat, and pleasure thrilled her body at the thought that *she* was the one making him moan. That *she* was the one he was so greedily taking in.

He pulled back, and with fire in his eyes rasped, 'Stop me. Stop me now before we do something neither of us will be able to forget.'

'I don't want to stop,' she said, before reason could kick in.

Desire flared in his eyes as he dipped his head down towards her again.

His mouth was just a breath away when they heard a crash.

Jacques immediately shoved her behind him, but she

moved to see what the sound was, her heart beating hard for an entirely different reason now. At first she saw only a short man with dark hair, sprawled across a bin on the beach. The cause of their interruption. Then, when he pushed himself up, she saw the camera around the man's neck.

'He's taking pictures of us...' she breathed, and shock planted her feet to the ground before she willed herself to move.

She was in the house in the seconds it took for Jacques to take the steps down to the beach. A moment later she heard another crash that she wasn't entirely sure she wanted to know the cause of. She wrapped her jersey tightly around herself, stuffing her hands under her armpits to stop them shaking.

It was still strange to have someone take pictures of her. She was growing used to it at public events, but this kind—the kind that she couldn't prepare herself for, the kind that had photographers climbing fences to get their shot—still felt as if someone had told the world all her secrets.

And it succeeded in reminding her that real intimacy was out of the question for her and Jacques. She wasn't there to make memories she'd never forget. Memories that would probably haunt her for the rest of her life. She *had* to face reality, and that reality was that she was just a prop for Jacques. It made her wonder if he'd known about the camera. If he had kissed her *because* of it.

The hurt stunned her.

'Are you okay?' Jacques said when he walked into the house a few minutes later.

He slammed the doors shut, locked them, and pressed a button that tinted the clear glass.

'I'm... I'm fine.'

'Lily.' He took a step forward, and then stopped when she took one back. 'I took the memory card from his camera. He doesn't have any pictures of us.'

The words told her that he *hadn't* only been kissing her for the camera. And even if her mind still doubted it, her eyes saw that he held a small square memory card in his hand. She wanted to feel relief at that—should have—except that the fact that she'd doubted Jacques told her that she didn't quite trust him.

Was it because she knew those pictures would benefit him? Was that thought even fair? Jacques's actions over the past weeks had shown her that he was willing to protect her. That he was willing to risk losing publicity to do so. So why didn't she trust him?

Because the last man she'd trusted had hurt her, she thought.

And just as quickly she realised that she was scared the man she now loved would, too.

'I… I have to go. The shop…'

She couldn't say any more, too raw from the realisation.

'Okay…' Jacques replied slowly. 'Lil, can we just talk—?'

'No,' she said quickly.

The responding coolness in his eyes had her stuttering through an explanation.

'I'm… I'm already late. I have to go. I… I'm sorry.'

She didn't wait for him to speak. Instead she fiddled with the locks on the door and, when it opened, checked that there was no one else waiting to take her picture. When she was sure, she ran to her car.

She ran because more than anything else she wanted to stay.

And that terrified her.

CHAPTER FIFTEEN

I'll pick you up at seven.

THAT WAS IT. That was all Jacques's message had said. But it was seven now, and Lily had to stop herself from looking at the text message again to check whether she'd read it correctly. If she hadn't she would feel like an even bigger fool, standing there in her store—in front of its glass wall—in the scandalous dress Jade had sent her.

She and Jacques had decided—before the fiasco of that morning—to meet at her store, since the charity event's venue was around the corner from it. But as she looked down at the tight plunging neckline that pressed her breasts together, exposing more of them than the world had ever seen, she wondered if that had been a good idea. It seemed even worse when she considered the way the white dress hugged the curves of her body, barely brushing her knees and leaving nothing to the imagination.

Lily couldn't deny that the dress would draw attention to her and Jacques that night. And, while she had grown to be okay with Jade's other dress choices for that very reason, this one was the worst.

She smoothed at the non-existent creases, and then sighed. She was thinking about the dress because she didn't want to think about that morning. Just as she'd kept busy all day to avoid it. Lily was happy to brush her feelings under the carpet—maybe if she didn't pay attention to them they would go away.

Love doesn't just go away.

A rap on the door brought her from her thoughts—thankfully—and her throat dried when she saw Jacques. He was in a slim-cut navy blue suit, a white shirt open at the collar, his hair swept back in that untidy way she liked. His broad shoulders wore the stylish look effortlessly, his handsomely rugged features making him look so much more masculine—though she didn't know how that was possible.

Her body reminded her about the chance she'd missed with him, and she had to take a moment to compose herself before she opened the door for him.

'Hi,' she said, her knees going weak at the smell of his cologne.

'I'm sorry I'm late. Things were a bit busy today.'

His words were stilted. Clearly that morning wasn't going to be as easily forgotten as she'd hoped.

'That's fine.'

She turned away from him, letting him close the door behind him as she grabbed her handbag. When she looked at him again he was staring at her. Her face flushed.

'Jade was right.' His voice had softened. 'That dress does look amazing on you.'

'Thanks.'

She lifted a hand to her hair, and then brushed at her dress again.

'It's perfect,' he said. 'Lily, you're—'

He took a step forward and she moved back.

'Jacques, no.' She drew a breath. 'Please.'

'You're running.'

She lifted her eyes to his.

'From what? There's nothing to run from here,' she reminded him. *Herself.* 'We're just two people with an agreement, right?'

His eyes flashed. 'Where is this coming from? Things were fine—good, even—until—'

'Until this morning, when we kissed and almost did something to make things a little too real for the both of us?'

She could see that he hadn't expected her to verbalise it, but panic didn't give her a choice. And when he didn't answer her dread took its place, followed by something else that had her eyes burning.

'Let's just go,' she said, when she'd composed herself. 'It doesn't seem like we have anything to talk about anyway.'

She was pushing him away. And for the life of him he couldn't understand why.

Or why it bothered him so damn much.

Jacques grabbed two flutes of champagne from the nearest waiter as he walked into the venue where his charity event was being held. The room had a stunning three-hundred-and-sixty-degree view of the beach and the city through its glass walls—save for the end of the room that held the foyer. Still, it was a design unique to that hotel, which was precisely why he had chosen it.

He handed Lily a glass, and she smiled her thanks. But it wasn't her real smile. Over the past month he'd grown accustomed to the pretend smile she gave to photographers, to the public. He'd seen the smile she reserved only for people she cared about. The one where the skin around her eyes crinkled just a little. He'd seen it because in their private moments she'd aimed it at him.

The fact that she wasn't aiming it at him any more set him on edge. And that edge was quick to turn into anger. Because anger was easier than the longing he felt after their kiss that morning. Or the disappointment at her reaction to it.

Lily shifted next to him, reminding him of where he was, and he realised that she was uncomfortable. Public events weren't enjoyable for her, and unlike him, she wasn't accustomed to pretence.

The things he knew about her past made him realise there was more to it than that, of course, and though he'd already said it that night he repeated, 'You don't have to worry about how you look, Lily. You're gorgeous.'

She gave him an annoyed look.

'You *have* to say that, since your people sent me this ridiculous dress.'

His eyes moved over the white dress that clung to her body, desire trembling through his own.

'I approve of it.'

'Yes, you would. Your plan is more important than my insecurities, after all'

His focus on his plan had been dwindling because of her, so he said, 'That's not fair. You know it isn't.'

Vulnerability settled in her eyes. 'Maybe not. But it should be.'

'Jacques?'

He turned at the voice that interrupted his reply, and forced himself to greet Jade and Riley civilly.

'We're the first to get here,' he said, though it was through clenched teeth. 'I don't think I need to work the party just yet.'

'You *always* need to work the party,' Jade answered, and there was something in her voice that put his back up.

'What's going on?'

'I…er—' Jade glanced at Lily, and then back at Jacques. 'Actually, do you mind if I borrow Lily for a moment?'

His eyebrows rose, but he answered, 'Sure.'

Jade gave him a quick smile, and then hooked an arm in Lily's. Her height put her head barely at Lily's shoulders, making them a strange couple. He watched until they'd disappeared through the doors that led to the foyer and the bathrooms, and then turned back to Riley.

'What was that about?'

'She was trying to get Lily away from you,' Riley answered, and shifted his weight between his feet. 'We got news today that some of the sponsors still aren't convinced. About twenty per cent of them—the ones who aren't coming this evening—aren't prepared to stay on.'

'So?' he asked, refusing to let the panic settle in his chest. 'That's twenty per cent. We have the majority on our side.'

'They're the twenty per cent who contribute sixty per cent of the club's sponsorship.'

Riley named names, and Jacques swore under his breath. He knew exactly who they were—knew the club would take a huge knock if they pulled out.

'So what do we do?' he asked flatly.

'Well, we did some digging, and we think we can get some of them over to our side. They're family companies, and maybe if they see you as a family man…'

It took Jacques a moment to realise what Riley was saying.

'You want me to propose?'

Riley nodded. 'That was always our original suggestion. Of course we didn't anticipate all the good Lily would do to your reputation. People genuinely *like* her. Maybe if we had a bit more time…'

He trailed off, watched Jacques closely. And who could blame him? Jacques thought. He hadn't been open to that suggestion when they'd first made it. *And now you are?* an inner voice questioned, but he shook his head, refusing to dwell on it. Or on the panic about a possible marriage—even a fake one—that had his head spinning.

'How would I even *do* that? I mean, there's no time to arrange a proper proposal…'

Jacques stopped when Riley handed him a small blue box.

'You got a *ring*?' Jacques narrowed his eyes, his heart speeding up. 'How long have you two been planning this?'

'We only got the news today. But we thought tonight would be the perfect opportunity.'

The box felt heavier than anything he'd ever carried, and the weight of it sat on his chest. He stuffed it into his pocket, but that did no good either. He could still feel it there, throbbing against his thigh.

He had to talk to Lily about it. He couldn't do this to her after everything they'd shared. She didn't deserve—

His thoughts halted when he saw Kyle walk into the room.

'What's *he* doing here?' Jacques growled, and Riley shifted next to him.

'I… I don't know.'

'You and Jade *arranged* this event, Riley. How the hell don't you know?'

Anger had him clenching his fists as his eyes flitted between the space where he'd last seen Lily and Kyle.

'He must have bought someone else's ticket. His name wasn't on the guest list.'

'You'd better hope that's true.' Jacques turned to Riley.

'Because if I find out this was a scheme to get more money for this event…'

'It isn't,' Riley said quickly. 'We wouldn't do that.'

'I know that if this event is a success it's more likely that the club will come to me,' he said in a low voice. 'And that your firm will get a bonus for helping me secure it…'

'I promise, Jacques. This wasn't us.'

Though his colour was pale, Riley's voice was firm. It told Jacques he was telling the truth.

'I need to find Lily. Excuse me.'

'There's one more thing, Jacques.'

He was already on his way to find Lily, but he turned back impatiently.

'What is it, Riley? I don't have the luxury of time, here.'

His eyes were searching the room for Kyle, but with Riley's single sentence everything in Jacques's body froze.

'Nathan called us a few hours ago to let us know he'll be bringing your father as his plus one.'

CHAPTER SIXTEEN

'WHAT ARE THE chances of us meeting like this?'

Lily thought she was imagining his voice at first. She'd escaped from where Jade had been introducing her to guests in the foyer to the bathrooms. But on her way there, she'd realised it wouldn't have given her the privacy she'd hoped for and had headed to the conference room instead.

But now she turned and saw Kyle, and realised two things. One, he must have followed her, and two, his voice hadn't been her imagination.

'I think the chances were always going to be pretty high, since you must have seen me come in here.'

'I see you've worked on that confidence problem since I last saw you.'

Warning coated his tone, but Lily braced herself against the inevitable fear. And, though it wasn't easy, she found she could do it.

'Why are you here?'

'To see you.' He took a step closer and her breath almost caught. 'To remind you of your place.'

'Don't you have someone else to remind now?'

The bravado was a farce, but it was her only defence.

'I don't have to remind Michelle of her place. She knows exactly what I need from her.'

'I still don't understand,' she said a little desperately. 'Why are you here?'

She wanted him to get to the point. Because the sooner he did, the sooner she would be able to escape.

'I've seen pictures of you and Jacques together,' Kyle spat. 'You're disgracing yourself. And making *me* look bad.'

'That's not true.'

'You were *my* fiancée, Lily. And everyone knows that now. So start acting like someone worthy of being associated with my name.'

'No one cares about me and you, Kyle,' she said, unable to help herself. 'All they're interested in is Jacques. If I need to act appropriately for the sake of anyone's name it would be Jacques's and not yours.'

There was a pulse of silence, and then Kyle closed the space between them. Instinct had her moving back, every brave part of her fading into the fear that had her heart in her throat. A part of her mind was telling her she could simply escape the event if Kyle bruised her, another was formulating the apology she would have to give to Jacques if someone saw her leave.

But she didn't have time to think about it any further. The door opened and in a few quick movements Jacques was in front of Kyle.

'You should leave. Before I remind you of what my fist feels like.'

Lily didn't think she'd ever heard anything sound as menacing. And, considering the look on Kyle's face, she didn't think he had either.

'She's after your money. Just like she was after mine.'

The air in her lungs quite simply froze. But Jacques didn't respond to Kyle's words. Instead he said, 'I'm going to say this one more time, and then I'm going to act on it. And, no, I *don't* care if people speculate about it when they see you leave with a bloody face.'

Jacques sent Kyle a hard look.

'They're all aware of my reputation.' There was a short pause, and then Jacques repeated, 'Leave—before I make you leave.'

Kyle didn't stay any longer to tempt fate, and when he was gone Lily's knees went weak. In one quick movement Jacques's arms were around her, steadying her.

'It's okay,' he said softly. 'He's gone. And he won't be back.'

'How do you know?'

'Because I told you I would protect you. And that means making sure Kyle never gets to you again.'

At his words, she rested her head on his chest and for a brief moment closed her eyes. She wished they could stay like that, away from the realities of the world. But she knew they couldn't. Not when Kyle's presence had reminded her of something she'd managed to avoid thinking about in the past month. Not when she knew Jacques would ask her about it.

She took a step back, asked a question to delay the inevitable. 'How did you know where we were?'

'I saw him arrive, and then I got distracted.' A shadow passed over his face. 'When I couldn't find him again— or you—I began to look for you. And then I found you.'

'Thank you.'

'What was he talking to you about?'

She turned her back towards him, needing the time to compose herself. She told herself she needed to do this—not because Jacques had asked, but because *she* needed to tell him.

She needed to do this for herself.

When she turned back, he was watching her with expressionless eyes.

'When I found Kyle cheating on me I was devastated. Not because I loved him—which I realised after a few weeks—but because it gave my insecurities more grounds than they'd had in a long time.'

Her voice faltered with those words, but she cleared her throat.

'And although Kyle begged me to go back to him—though he told me that he'd just made a mistake—I couldn't believe him. You don't make a mistake like that when you love someone.'

Get to the point, she told herself.

'When he realised I wasn't coming back he began to buy me things. And when I sent them back he told me I could have whatever I wanted. That it would be my "choice".'

Bitterness washed over her tongue.

'And when *that* didn't work he threatened me.'

She saw the fist Jacques made in response to her words, stifled the hope that flared inside her. It didn't mean anything.

'I told him if he didn't stop I would go to the police, and I was on the way there when his family's lawyer called me.' She took another breath—for courage. 'He wanted a meeting. He told me that the Van der Rosses wanted to "solve" the situation without involving the police, and that he would ensure Kyle stayed away from me. By then I just... I just wanted it all to go away.'

She still cursed her naiveté.

'So I agreed to the meeting, and when I got there Kyle's parents were there, too. They were never...fond of me. They thought I was beneath their son, that I was too dowdy, too...common.'

And she'd proved them right, she thought with a pang.

'Though they were perfectly nice to me. Told me they were so sorry about how everything had ended with me and Kyle.'

The rest came out as a rush. She couldn't bear the silence, the tension that pulsed from Jacques.

'And then they told me that they'd give me whatever I wanted if I signed a non-disclosure agreement. I just had to agree never to speak about Kyle's philandering ways—especially since his father was pitching to an important client with solid family values—and I could ask them for anything.'

'And so you asked for money?'

The flat tone broke her heart.

'I didn't. Not at first. I asked them why they thought it was necessary. Whether they really thought I would ruin their business because Kyle had broken my heart. And my self-confidence, which was really the case.'

She closed her eyes, and then shrugged.

'Though they only actually said something about "covering all their bases", I realised that it was because they didn't think much of me. The look on his mother's face... I knew what they thought of me, and it made me feel so...*worthless*.'

She bit her lip, tried to stop the tears from coming.

'So I asked for something that would make that feeling go away.'

She paused now, and looked at Jacques's face. His expression made her attempts not to cry useless, and she brushed at the tears.

'My store,' she continued when she'd cleared her throat, 'was something I'd been working on for years. I knew I would never have enough money to start it if I didn't take the money from them. So we agreed on an amount and I signed the document.'

So now he knew, she thought, and folded her arms as she waited for him to respond.

'That's why you didn't want to take the loan I offered you?'

'Yes.'

There was a pause.

'I have to propose to you.'

'What?'

He shoved his hands into his trouser pockets. 'I don't have the Shadows' most important sponsors on my side. Riley told me that they might be swayed if I propose to you.'

'And you...what? Want my permission?'

'Yes.' His tone was clipped. 'I didn't want to put you on the spot again.'

Her heart wanted to soften at his words. At the confirmation that things between them had changed. That *he'd* changed. But how could it when he couldn't even look her in the eye?

'I appreciate you asking me. And...and I know this is important to you. So of course I agree.'

'Thank you.'

He nodded and then turned away.

'Jacques, please. Say something. Anything. Tell me you're disappointed in me. That you can't stand it that I took money from them.'

He turned back. 'Is that how you feel about yourself?'

A sob escaped from her lips. *'Yes.'*

'Would you do it again?'

'I didn't even want to take a loan from *you*, Jacques. You know the answer to that.'

'Why not?'

'Because taking that money has stripped away my confidence, my self-worth.' She was purging herself now, she thought. 'Because I've belittled my success by taking it. Because the lack of success in the months before I met you eroded every belief I'd had that owning my shop would make me feel better. That it would make me feel like I was more than what other people thought me.'

It would have felt *so* good if she'd finally been able to make a success of something. If she'd finally been able to prove her parents wrong. The engagement had been the only thing they'd approved of in her life, and she'd disappointed them once again when she'd told them it had ended.

She hadn't told them Kyle had cheated on her. It wouldn't change the fact that they saw her as a failure. That she saw *herself* that way...

'Oh, here you are.'

Jade popped her head into the room, and her smile faltered as she looked from Lily to Jacques.

'I'm sorry, I've interrupted something...'

'What do you want, Jade?' Jacques asked tersely.

'I was actually checking to see if this room was free, not looking for you. Yet. But there *are* a few people...' She trailed off. 'I can stall them if you like?'

'No, that's fine,' Lily said. 'I'll go.'

She avoided Jacques's gaze as she walked out of the room, too embarrassed by her confession to look at him.

She spent a few minutes in the bathroom, composing herself and freshening up.

When she returned to the event she thought she could fake her way through trivial conversation. Until her eyes settled on Nathan and something inside her sagged with relief.

'It's nice to see a familiar face here.' She kissed him on the cheek.

'I know how you feel,' Nathan answered, but when he gave her a smile it seemed distracted. 'It's almost like old times.'

His eyes shifted over the room and she remembered that Caitlyn wasn't with him. That she wouldn't be for the rest of the night.

'I didn't think you would come without Cait. She told me she had a deadline for tomorrow morning.'

'I wasn't going to. But I changed my mind last minute.'

'Did you bring Kyle?'

'What?' Nathan's attention was now on her. 'Kyle's *here*?'

'He was.'

'Are you okay?'

'Yes,' she answered, and found that it was true. 'Your brother helped.'

And that was the reason she was okay.

'Is Kyle still alive?'

She smiled, though she could tell Nathan was only half-joking.

'He is. But he won't be bothering me again.' She was pretty sure of that.

There was a moment of silence and then Nathan closed his eyes. 'Lily, I didn't bring him, but I think he was here tonight because of me. I mentioned it to him earlier today. I'd just decided to come, and was telling him I couldn't work late on a case. I'm so sorry!'

'It's okay.' Her heart was beating at its normal rate again. 'It worked out in the end.'

And she needed to find the man who'd ensured that. They needed to talk.

'Will you excuse me, Nate? I have to find...'

Her voice stopped working when she saw a man walking towards them. Dark skin, dark hair peppered with white, a strong, muscular build. If it hadn't been for the fact that he was clearly years older Lily might have thought she was looking at Jacques. And then, when he stopped in front of them, she saw Nathan's face.

Her heart began to thrum uncomfortably in her chest.

'Dad,' Nathan said, confirming her suspicions. 'This is Lily. Caitlyn's best friend and—'

'Jacques's girlfriend.'

His deep voice held a hint of an accent—British, she thought—and it reminded her, again, of Jacques. But there was something beneath the tone that sounded off to her.

You're bringing your feelings for Jacques into this, an inner voice told her, but she shook it off. It was too complicated a thought to consider before introducing herself.

She smiled and offered a hand. 'Yes. It's lovely to meet you, Mr Brookes.'

'Please, call me Dale,' he said, and brought Lily's hand to his mouth.

A shimmer of discomfort went down her spine, but again she shook it off.

'Does Jacques know you two are here?' she asked pleasantly, directing her question at Nathan.

She saw something that might have been shame pass through his eyes—he clearly knew she was actually referring to whether Jacques knew his *father* was there— before he shook his head.

'I don't think so, no. I haven't seen him yet.'

Suddenly it made sense to Lily. Nathan had been looking for Jacques. To warn him? No, she thought. He could have called him to do that. This was some kind of...*ambush*, she thought, and anger simmered through her veins.

'I should probably find him, then,' she said, and heard the coldness in her stilted tones.

'Are you looking for me, my love?'

An arm snaked around her waist, pulling her closer until she was moulded to Jacques's body.

'Yes, I was.'

She brushed a piece of hair away from his face and he looked down at her, just as she'd intended. He smiled, but by now she knew when it wasn't genuine. Even if she hadn't been able to tell she would have known it by the hard glint in his eyes.

'Well, I'm here now.' He turned his head to the two men in front of him. 'And I see Nathan's introduced you to my father.'

There was a pause.

'Why are you here, *Dad*?' He said the word in a mocking tone.

'I heard you needed some help with your...*investment*.'

Dale had used the same tone as Jacques, and Lily felt Jacques's arm tighten around her.

'You told him that?' Jacques asked Nathan after a moment.

Lily saw Nathan's slight nod, saw the apologetic look in his eyes. It told her that maybe Nathan hadn't meant to ambush Jacques. Maybe he'd wanted a reconciliation. But that didn't seem to be the direction their conversation was going in.

'Well, I don't need your help. Haven't needed it in a very long time, if I recall.'

'Yes, the success of your rugby career tells me how *well* you're doing in your life.'

The muscles under Lily's hand hardened, coiled, as if she was touching an animal that was about to pounce.

'My rugby career may not have ended in the way I

had hoped for, but it made me into a much better man,' Jacques replied in a measured tone. 'I'm going to buy my club—without your help—and I'm going to turn it into something I never could have while I was just playing for it.'

Determination fortified every word, sending pride bursting through her body.

'Trying to convince me, son, or yourself?'

'That's the trouble with you, Dad. You never really got to know me,' Jacques said easily. 'If you had, you'd know I never say things unless I believe them. It's called *conviction*—though you wouldn't really be familiar with the word.'

His arm dropped from Lily's waist, and he took her hand instead.

'You'd also know that I no longer feel the need to convince you of anything.'

With those words, Jacques pulled at her hand and they walked away.

CHAPTER SEVENTEEN

THERE WAS NO time for him to process his thoughts. There hadn't been since Jade had interrupted his conversation with Lily. And now he had his feelings about Lily's revelation and seeing his father again swirling through his head—all before he needed to speak to the people who held his fate in their hands.

'Stop.'

Lily tugged at his hand, stopping him in a relatively empty corner of the room.

'I have my speech soon. And the proposal...'

She drew in a breath at his words, but shook her head and then angled him so that his back was to the crowd.

'I know. But you have to take a moment to breathe. Pretend you're stealing an intimate moment with the woman who's about to be your fiancée.'

She was right—he needed to breathe. He needed to deal with the rush of emotions that was making him feel nauseous *before* he spoke to the crowd.

Suddenly he became aware of the way his chest was heaving, and because he didn't want to be he focused on Lily. 'I heard the way you said "fiancée". It scares you.'

'Of course,' she answered breathily. 'Doesn't it scare you?'

'No.' *Yes.* 'It's not real.'

'Someone should tell my heart that,' she murmured. Her eyes widened and she quickly followed that with, 'It's beating so fast at the prospect.'

Focusing on her words—on the possibility of what they might mean—was helping to distract him. 'Mine is, too.'

'You don't have to say that to make me feel better.'

'I'm not.' And he realised he wasn't.

'I thought you weren't scared?'

'I'm not. But that doesn't mean I'm not nervous.'

As he said it he realised that there was more to his confession. That it coated something he didn't fully understand yet.

'I'm sorry for the way things turned out tonight,' she said.

'It's okay,' he answered, and looked down at her.

As he did so, he realised that he'd been avoiding it since she'd told him about accepting money from Kyle's family. His heart immediately softened—he worried that it had weakened—and he felt the disappointment that he'd felt at her words disappear.

That was why he'd avoided looking at her. Because though her confession should have made him doubt her—he had experience with people who thought money was the most important thing, after all—he didn't. He *couldn't.*

And he found himself feeling even more for her.

'Is it really okay?' She shook her head. 'Kyle pitches up here, and then your father. It's like the past is trying to make sure we remember it.'

She gave him a small smile.

'For what it's worth, I'm really proud of you. I was worried at first. I saw your face when you joined us. But then you *spoke* and I could tell it was just occurring to you. I was so proud.'

He felt as if her words had switched on a light in his body. It warmed him even as it pulsed in his chest, and he realised that the desire to hear those words from his father had driven him through most of his life. Even when he'd been convincing his mother to leave he'd still wanted to hear it.

And though he'd realised long ago that it wasn't going to happen he hadn't accepted it. Not until he'd heard Lily say it and felt that desire go free inside him.

'It looks like you're up,' Lily said, nodding her head to where Jade was trying to get Jacques's attention.

He gave Jade a quick nod, and then tried to formulate something to say to Lily. But he found he couldn't. His brain was a mess from the things he felt, and from those he thought he should feel but didn't.

So he focused on his responsibilities. They'd become too vague for his liking, and the urgency of the plan he had been so set on had faded into the background over the past month. But tonight would change that, he told himself a little desperately. He would put all the distractions aside and charm whoever he needed to.

Starting with that proposal.

'Thank you, Tom,' Jacques said, when the MC handed him the mike after his introduction. 'Let's all give Tom a hand. He's doing a terrific job, hosting this evening's proceedings.'

Applause rang out and Jacques's eyes moved over the crowd. His gaze settled on Nathan, who was standing alone on one side of the room, shoulders hunched. Though Jacques was still angry with him, he knew his brother had just wanted to help.

But, considering that Jacques no longer saw his father, he also knew that Nathan's attempt at reconciliation hadn't worked. Just as Jacques had always told him.

He went through the formalities, thanking everyone for attending and introducing the charity they were supporting that evening. While a representative for the charity said her thanks, Jacques's heart started beating faster. As he handed the woman a large cheque and posed for the required photos his lungs felt heavy. And when he finally held the mike in his hand to end his speech his entire body shook.

But he ignored all of it, and focused on the face of the woman he was about to fake propose to.

'I know many of you here remember me as the man who ended the Shadows' path to the internationals. The man who threw away his career in a fight that shouldn't have happened. It's shaped your opinion of me. And *that* has shaped my opinion of myself.'

His heart thudded for different reasons now.

'It has also driven me. Because I wanted to prove...'

He trailed off, thinking about how he'd wanted to prove that the public's opinion of him was wrong. How he'd wanted to prove his father wrong.

'I wanted to prove that I was more than the mistakes I'd made. That those mistakes didn't define me. That desire has allowed me to build a successful company. It's given me a perspective that's helped me support charities like the one we're here for this evening. But, most importantly, my journey in not letting the past define me has led me to my girlfriend, Lily.'

The first thing he saw when his eyes rested on her was that colour on her cheeks that had drawn him in the first time. The second was the smile she sent him. Though the uncertainty, the traces of fear, were visible to him, it was the sweetest, most encouraging smile he'd ever seen.

And the words that came from his mouth no longer seemed to be pretence.

'There have been times when I've focused so much on *wanting* to be a better person that I haven't actually *been* a better person. And she has helped me see that. Her calling me out on my bad behaviour has given me no choice but to learn from the past. Which is probably why you have all seen a better-behaving Brookes instead of Bad-Boy Brookes.'

He waited as a chuckle went through the crowd.

'But perhaps more importantly is the fact that she's *shown* me how to learn from my past.'

He thought about how she'd refused his money—taking it would certainly have been easier than the training she'd asked for instead—and about how it made sense now that he knew about Kyle.

'I wish you could see yourself the way I see you.'

He walked down the stairs towards Lily now, taking the microphone with him.

'You would be able to see your strength, your beauty.'

A path opened up as he walked towards her, and when he stopped in front of her he could see the hope shining through her uncertainty. It scared him, and something urged him to stop. But he couldn't. Not yet.

'And you'd know that you've exceeded any expectations I had of you or our relationship.'

He knew how much those words would mean to her, but when her hope shone even brighter it glossed all his feelings with a deep fear he couldn't understand.

'I can't imagine my life without you, Lily,' he said, almost automatically now, refusing to hear the truth of the words.

Instead he pulled out the box Riley had given him earlier and went down on one knee.

'Will you marry me?'

CHAPTER EIGHTEEN

IT WASN'T UNTIL that moment that Lily realised just how much she wanted him to be saying those words for real.

The desire for it shook her, but she didn't let it distract her. She breathed a 'yes' and applause erupted around them. Jacques smiled at her, but there was a storm in his eyes that made her heart hurt without her even knowing why.

He slid the ring onto her finger—a simple stunning solitaire—and pulled her into his arms. Heat pricked at her eyes when she felt the stiffness of his arms, the tightness of the muscles in them, but all the years she'd had of pretending to be okay when she wasn't helped her smile and accept the kiss he brushed on her lips.

The rest of the evening went by in a blur of congratulations and a tension that she knew she wasn't imagining. Not when she could sense Jacques pulling away from her. Not when she recognised it because she'd done the exact same thing herself earlier. And while a part of her wanted to hope that they were doing it for the same reason—that he was in love with her, too—Jacques's behaviour was edged with a coldness that warned her against hoping that.

The thought troubled her so much that she escaped the party as soon as she saw an opportunity to do so. Her opportunity came when Jade and Riley whisked Jacques away to speak to a sponsor they apparently needed on their side who'd arrived unexpectedly. The crowd had thinned by then, and no one seemed to notice as she slipped out of the hotel to the beach just beyond it.

When she was far enough away that no one would see her—when she was sure that she hadn't been followed—she closed her eyes and accepted the truth that she'd been running away from since that morning.

She was in love with Jacques Brookes.

Panic gripped her throat, and when she opened her mouth to breathe a sob escaped. She laid a hand on her throat, forced air into her lungs. Forced herself to think. Why was she afraid of falling for Jacques? Because she'd told herself that she needed to stay away from him? That she needed to love herself?

Perhaps, but she knew those resolutions had come from the Lily who'd been treated so poorly by her ex-fiancé. By the Lily who'd thought she deserved to be treated that way. Who had *expected* it because she didn't think she deserved more. But that Lily had slowly been whittled away. She'd been replaced with a Lily who hoped that she *did* deserve more. She'd been replaced with a Lily who had experienced what it was like to be treated well. Who had experienced a good relationship for the past month.

Yes, it had been a pretend relationship for the most part, but Lily thought that their *friendship* hadn't been pretend. The respect they'd shared, the way Jacques had treated her, the things he'd said to her, about her—those hadn't been pretend.

Or had they?

Didn't Jacques deserve more than her? Didn't he deserve someone who was proud of her body, of herself?

Someone with all the confidence that *she* struggled to muster? Someone who felt as if she were enough? Someone who could actually live up to his expectations?

Someone who could live up to her *own* expectations?

She was reminded of when Jacques had asked her about those expectations. She'd realised she didn't *have* expectations of herself—not her own. She only had those that had been invented by those around her.

But now she knew she wanted to be successful. For herself and not just to prove someone else wrong. She wanted to think more of herself. It would be a process, but at least now she believed that she deserved more than an emotionally abusive fiancé. She wanted someone who saw her as more than who *he* wanted her to be. She wanted someone who saw her for who she was.

She wanted Jacques.

And if she ignored her uncertainties—if she looked at the facts, at the evidence—she thought that he wanted her, too.

But he didn't want to.

'Lily? I've been looking all over for you.'

She turned to the man she loved. Saw the look on his face, saw the confirmation of her suspicions, and her heart broke.

'I'm sorry. I needed some air.'

The words sounded distant—as if she was pulling away again—and the door he'd hidden his feelings behind opened.

He slammed it shut.

'Did things go well with the sponsor?'

'I think so. They asked about my plans for the club.'

'Which is a *good* thing, right? It means they're considering your business aptitude and not your personal life.'

'Yeah, probably. But Jade and Riley think my personal life is the reason they were interested. They think the sponsors caught the proposal.'

'That was the plan, wasn't it?'

'Yes, it was.'

So why was he annoyed by her response? By her sudden aloofness?

'It's all there is, isn't it?' Jacques said through a clenched jaw. 'This plan of ours. This *agreement*.'

She tilted her head, and it stole his breath how much he wanted to tuck those curls behind her ear. How he wanted to pull her in and melt that coolness.

'Are you trying to bait me, Jacques?'

'What could I possibly achieve by doing that?'

'My temper? I could lash out at you and give you a reason to deny those feelings you've realised you had for me.'

'I don't… There are no…'

'No feelings?'

'No.'

She laughed. 'Of course. There were no feelings when we kissed this morning. Or when you said those things tonight. No, that kiss actually *was* for the camera. And tonight—that was just for the audience, right?'

'Now you're trying to bait *me*.'

'Is it working? Because I'd really *love* to talk to the man I've fallen in love with instead of whoever *you* are.'

It took him a minute to process what she'd said. Another to think up a response. 'How…? You can't…'

'I don't blame you for thinking that.' She folded her arms, looked out to the ocean. 'I've been trying to deny it since this morning, when I realised it.'

'Since this morning?' he repeated.

Now he knew why he'd felt her pulling away. She didn't like her feelings any more than he liked his.

Why did that upset him?

'We always knew about the attraction between us,' he said steadily.

'The *attraction*?' she scoffed. 'I *wish* this was just an attraction. That would make things *so* much easier.'

'What do you want from me, Lily?'

'I want you to admit that there's more between us than an "attraction". I want you to admit you feel something for me.'

That door he kept those feelings behind vibrated again, and he was having trouble keeping it shut.

'You don't want that, Lily. You're just confusing all of the...the show with real emotion.'

You're making up excuses for yourself.

'Don't do that.'

Her voice was measured, but he could hear the anger.

'Don't belittle my feelings. I've spent my life trying to convince myself that I have a right to them.'

'I wasn't trying—'

'Do you think I *wanted* to tell you the truth about my store? About Kyle? Do you think that I told you how it made me feel because we're *friends*? Because we're attracted to each other?' She shook her head. 'No one knew about that. And not just because of the papers I signed.'

'Then why did you tell me?'

'Because I thought you would understand. You know what it's like to think about your past with shame. This whole charade has been so that you could make up for it. I wanted your help with my store for the same reason.'

She drew a ragged breath.

'And I told you because I wanted you to know. To love me despite my mistakes.'

The door was flung open at her words, and he knew that he *did* love her. He knew that he'd known from the moment they'd kissed. That he'd had it confirmed while he'd been proposing.

But still he couldn't bring himself to say the words.

Instead he said, 'I meant it when I said you've shown me how to not let the past define me.' He exhaled. 'I don't judge you for accepting the money. I can't because…because I *do* understand it. The shame. The determination not to let a mistake define you.'

'But?'

'But…you've distracted me from it.'

'I've distracted you from what?'

'From my *plan*,' he said desperately. 'From showing the world that I'm more than my mistakes. Than my failures. Than the disappointment.'

'Showing the world or your father?'

He didn't respond. He couldn't. Because she was right.

'Seeing him tonight reminded you that you've been doing all of this for *him*, not the world. That all those things—mistakes, failures, disappointment—are things you're trying to convince *him* that you're not. And maybe even yourself.'

'Stop!' he said sharply, feeling her words piercing his heart.

'I understand it, Jacques.' She moved closer to him. 'I'm trying to convince myself that I'm not those things either. That *I'm* not a failure.'

'You're only a failure because *you* keep telling yourself that, Lily.'

The words were harsher than he'd intended, but he just wanted her to stop. To stop reminding him of the pain he'd managed to avoid for so long. He didn't listen to the voice telling him that it wasn't Lily, that it was seeing his father that had unlocked the pain. All he knew was that he *felt*—and *she* was making him feel.

He couldn't distinguish between the feelings. Not any more.

'You keep thinking about the things you've failed at. But have you looked at what you've *succeeded* at? You had problems with your weight, so you lost it. You had a relationship that you realised wasn't working for you, so you left. The shop you opened was struggling, so you found a way to make it work for you. Yes, you've failed. You've made mistakes. We *all* have. But we need to look at how we've dealt with the failure and mistakes. *That's* what defines us.'

There was silence after his little speech, and he realised his chest was heaving. He used the time to gain control of his breathing again—to gain control of *himself* again.

'Are you going to look back at this night and think it's a mistake, Jacques?' Her voice was soft. Deceptive. 'Because if you can't give me a reason to stay, to listen to the things you're saying, you might find something else to define yourself by.'

CHAPTER NINETEEN

LILY DIDN'T KNOW what she expected after her words.
All she knew was that she didn't have to stay—not any
more—if there was nothing to stay for.

But she knew she hadn't expected a kiss.

He was standing in front of her before she could reg-
ister what was happening, and then he slid a hand behind
her neck and pulled her in until his mouth found hers.
Heat immediately flared at the touch, but the greed their
kisses had held before had been replaced by emotion. She
didn't know what it meant—didn't know if he was telling
her he had feelings for her or if he was saying goodbye.

She pulled back. She didn't need any more memories
of him if it was goodbye.

'I need you to *say* it, Jacques.'

'I… I can't.'

He rested his forehead on hers, but she stepped back,
unable to stand being near him any more.

'Why not?'

She hated the heat that prickled in her eyes. Hated it
even more that her heart softened as she saw the battle
on his face. But she *had* learnt from her mistakes. And
that meant she could no longer hope for things in a relationship that she would never get. She could no longer

stay with someone who couldn't be honest with her. She deserved more.

So when he didn't answer she didn't make any excuses. She just cleared her throat and said, 'We'll have Jade leak a story that we've gone away to celebrate our engagement. Just for the two days before you make your bid for the club. I'll let Terri and Cara know, and they can take care of the store for me. And then you can make your bid, get your club, and people will see us less and less. An appropriate amount of time will go by and we'll announce our break-up.'

'Lily, please—'

'No, Jacques. I know better than anyone what you're willing to do when you really want something. And if that something was me, you'd be able to say so.'

It hurt, the truth of that realisation. But she needed to face it.

'It's the least I deserve after doing all this for you.'

Because she had to believe that, she walked away from him. She only stopped to slip her shoes back on in front of the hotel, and then climbed into the first taxi she saw. She kept her composure until she reached her flat. Until she stripped off that ridiculous dress, kicked off those ridiculous shoes and climbed into the shower.

And then she let the tears come.

They turned into heart-wrenching sobs too quickly, but they helped steady her. And when the water turned cold she *felt* steadier. She let the water wash the tears from her face and then focused on the rest of her body. When she was done, she made herself a cup of tea, gripping the mug for the warmth and comfort it provided.

She was proud of herself. There was an ache in her chest that grew more painful with each beat of her heart, but she was proud. From the moment she'd met Jacques she'd told herself she couldn't be interested in him—in anyone, really—until she knew her self-worth.

It was the only way she knew how to survive what she'd been through with Kyle.

How to ensure that it would never happen again.

She couldn't be treated the way Kyle had treated her again. She couldn't be manipulated as she'd been by his parents. She wanted to think of herself without shame, without disgust. And the only way she knew how to do that was to stand up for herself.

Jacques hadn't treated her the way Kyle had. And after that night at the beach he'd no longer manipulated her. But in her heart she knew that if she'd accepted the little that Jacques had offered her she would have been undermining her worth again. She wouldn't have been standing up for herself, or for the love she now believed she deserved.

So she was proud of herself.

Even when a voice taunted her that she'd failed at *this* too she stayed proud. And she banished those thoughts by remembering the way Jacques's face had glowed with something he didn't even know when he'd proposed.

It had made her almost believe he'd meant all those things he'd said to her. That she *had* been showing him how to learn from the past. That maybe her determination to do that *had* been an example to him. Even if she hadn't always succeeded, she'd tried. And wasn't that something?

And maybe she could believe that he thought she was strong—something she'd never thought of herself before. And that she was beautiful—something she'd never given herself a chance to believe before. But what had meant the most was what he'd said about her exceeding his expectations—something she'd never, ever experienced before.

She hadn't even cared that everybody had been looking at her. The only thing she'd seen was that look on Jacques's face...

She stilled.

She hadn't cared that everybody had been looking at her.

That was in such stark contrast to what she'd felt only a month ago at the television show. Then, she'd *hated* the thought of people looking at her in normal clothing. But tonight she hadn't cared that everybody had been looking at her in a tight dress. She hadn't been thinking about what anyone might have thought about how she looked in it. She hadn't cared about her weight.

It was a victory she'd never thought possible. A victory that she knew had come from the time she'd spent with Jacques. His easy acceptance of her, his compliments, the way he'd forced her to see herself as he did—even if it had been harsher than she would have liked, she thought as she remembered what he'd told her that night—it had all been part of the reason she was in love with him.

It was the reason she'd laid everything on the line and told him how she felt.

Though she'd thought them all gone, another tear fell down her cheek.

Had she given up the man who'd shown her how to love herself?

Were the reasons she had worth the sacrifice?

She didn't know. But when things had ended with Kyle she'd promised herself she would learn from the experience. And she knew she had. But, as Jacques had told her, she needed to stop dwelling on the past. She needed to learn from it and move on.

She could no longer expect to fail. She could no longer accept others' expectations of herself as her own. She needed to stand firm in her confidence, in her newly discovered self-worth. She needed to stop letting her past mistakes define her.

She would pay back the money, she told herself. It didn't matter that it might take years. What mattered was that paying it back would allow her to take back the integrity she'd lost. What mattered was that she would finally be able to appreciate her hard work, her success, if she did.

What will you learn after Jacques? an inner voice asked.

Lily closed her eyes. What she'd learnt *during* her time with Jacques was easy, she thought.

But all she had for after was a pain in her chest, mocking her for thinking she could move on to 'after' at all.

Jacques wondered if he would ever forget how it had felt when Lily had walked away from him on the beach. How it had felt to know he had feelings for her but being unable to say it.

It had been two days and he hadn't forgotten it.

Hell, not even the news that he'd got the club had banished the memory.

He'd given it time. He'd thought that maybe the misery of the past two days had just delayed the excitement, the happiness. But it had been nearly five hours now, and the satisfaction of getting everything he'd always wanted was still missing.

Because it was only what you thought you wanted.

He pushed up from the table he'd put on his balcony after Lily had suggested it to him. It was true. He'd *believed* he'd wanted the club. He'd believed it so much that he'd resisted his feelings for Lily because she'd distracted him from it. Because she'd distracted him from the plan that had driven him for *seven years*: to ensure that he wasn't defined by his failures, by his mistakes.

Or by the man who loved money more than his own children.

Jacques's fingers tightened on the balcony railing he was leaning against.

He'd spent so much of the past seven years trying to prove his father wrong. But the truth was that Jacques had also been trying to prove that who his father was didn't define *him*. That the man who would tell his son he could never mean as much to his mother as *he* did— who would call his son a failure and a disappointment— didn't dictate who Jacques would become.

When he'd realised he had treated Lily in those first two days when they'd met like his father had treated his mother, something had shifted inside Jacques. And he'd seen a change in himself over the past month. He hadn't cared as much about his plan as he had about Lily. His wish for the world to see him as someone better than he'd once been had become less important than him being better for Lily.

And then he'd seen his father, and he'd been able to stand up to him. He'd been able to set aside his feelings for the parent who'd dismissed him—who'd been the reason his mother had dismissed him, too—and he'd bought his club, just as he'd told his father he would.

He'd thought it had been possible because he'd changed so much over the seven years since he'd last seen the man. But the real reason had been the change he'd experienced over the past *month*.

With Lily.

For Lily.

Because although she'd thought she wasn't good

enough for him, *he* was the one who had needed to work to be good enough for *her*.

His actions two days ago had shown him he still wasn't good enough for her.

Now, he didn't know why sticking to his plan had been so important to him. Of *course* he still wanted the opportunity to make up for his mistakes. Rugby—the Shadows—had been there for him when he hadn't had anything, and he would do all he could to show his gratitude for that. But since the night they'd spent at the beach restaurant he'd been resisting his feelings for Lily.

He hadn't been acknowledging it, but he'd changed—and that was because of his feelings for her. Feelings he now knew had grown with every moment he'd spent enjoying her company and her uncertain feistiness.

Her point of view had always given him something to think about. And he had genuinely enjoyed seeing how her mind, eager and quick to learn, grasped the aspects of business that he'd taught her.

He'd never been interested in relationships. When he'd discovered rugby—when he'd discovered he was *good* at it—it had become all he'd been able to think about. It had been easier to focus his attention on work than on relationships. Than on love.

Part of him realised now that it was because of the fear witnessing his parents' relationship had instilled in him. And maybe that was why he'd clung to his plan instead of opening up to Lily. It had *still* been easier to focus on work, on things that didn't force him out of his comfort zone.

But Lily had forced herself out of *her* comfort zone to take part in his plan. She'd put herself in the public eye despite her insecurities for *him*. Before she'd really known him. Just because it had been important to *him*.

And he didn't even have the courage to admit that he loved her.

He didn't deny it any more. He was in love with Lily. It still terrified him, but the past two days had shown him something even more terrifying—a life without her.

The fear of that thought had been eclipsed by excitement now. By hope.

She'd always seen a side of him that no one else had bothered to see. He'd known that the moment she'd said those things about him on the talk show. And he knew that was something special. He'd fought for years for the world to see something *she* had seen within twenty-four hours.

Lily had told him she knew how hard he fought for the things he wanted.

It was time he showed her that he wanted *her*.

CHAPTER TWENTY

LILY FLUCTUATED BETWEEN the devastation that had her spending hours in bed and a busyness that had resulted in a spotless house and a fridge filled with food she knew she would have to share with Caitlyn and her parents—as soon as she'd built up the courage to see any of them and explain what had happened with Jacques.

She hadn't heard from him since that night on the beach, but whenever the phone rang her heart jumped with the hope. And then she would see that it wasn't his name or number—like now, when her display showed Caitlyn's name—and she would sink back into the devastation.

'Hello?'

'Wow, you sound terrible.'

'Thanks, Cait.'

'Not in the best of moods, are you?'

Caitlyn's cheery voice grated on her, and Lily clenched her jaw.

'Aren't you supposed to be engaged or something?'

The annoyance turned into devastation once more.

'Yes,' she hiccuped.

'I know it wasn't real, but I saw a clip of it on television again this morning—it's been on about every hour since it happened—and it looked really sweet. Not as sweet as *my* proposal, of course, but then, mine was real—'

'It *was* really sweet,' Lily interrupted, not in the mood for her friend's energy. 'Listen, Caitlyn, I'm not feeling—'

'Actually, Lil, I'm calling for a reason.' There was a pause. 'I'm worried about Nathan. He hasn't been… Well, he hasn't been himself for the past few days. And I know it has something to do with him wanting to smooth things over between his father and Jacques.'

'Yeah, their dad was at Jacques's charity event.'

Caitlyn sighed. 'I know. He wouldn't tell me anything about it.'

'Probably because it didn't go well.'

'I thought so. I heard Jacques was staying at his beach flat so I came by, hoping we could talk, but he isn't here. Could you…? Could you please come by and open up for me? I don't want to wait outside his flat and risk the chance of being branded as "the other woman" if a photographer sees me.'

'You don't know when he'll be back?' Her heart thumped at the prospect of running into him.

'No…please, Lil.' Caitlyn's voice had gone hoarse. 'I'm really worried about Nathan.'

Lily's resistance melted. She couldn't leave her friend in the lurch. 'I'm on my way.'

She clicked off the phone and dragged herself to the bathroom. She showered, shoved her hair into a bun on the top of her head, and stared at her clothing options.

She was engaged, after all. She couldn't look the way she felt. The thought had her selecting a pretty white and pink floral dress and adding a pair of pink button-shaped earrings.

Twenty minutes later she was walking towards Caitlyn at Jacques's flat.

'You're a life-saver,' Caitlyn said as soon as she saw Lily.

'Sure,' Lily answered, and handed her friend the key. 'You can let yourself out.'

'I won't need the key. Jacques can let me out.' Caitlyn frowned. 'Besides, don't *you* need it?'

'I…'

She'd wanted to give Caitlyn the key and escape as soon as she could, but she couldn't answer Caitlyn's question without telling her the truth. She didn't quite have the energy for that.

'Yeah, of course. I'll just let you in, then.'

She took the key back and pushed open the door.

And froze when she saw Jacques.

His gorgeous face was set in a serious expression, his muscular body clothed in fitted black pants and a light blue shirt. He held a gift-wrapped box in his hands, and she idly wondered if it was for her.

And then she began to put the pieces together. Caitlyn's cheerful tone at the beginning of their telephone conversation, the fact that she didn't look nearly as upset as she'd sounded earlier.

'You missed your calling,' she told her friend.

'I'm sorry, Lil.' Caitlyn had the grace to look chagrined. 'It was a favour. For family.'

With one last apologetic look she left. Leaving Lily alone with Jacques.

She closed the door behind her, not wanting anyone to witness whatever was going to happen between them.

'Thank you for staying.'

'Did I have a choice?'

'I… I didn't know if you would have come if I'd asked.'

'I don't know if I would have either.'

Everything inside her was coiled and twisted. She didn't know what to do to make it go away.

'I was hoping we could talk,' he said, and took a step closer.

'About what?' Then she realised what the day was. 'You made your bid today.'

When he nodded, she set her handbag on the couch.

'How did it go? Or are they still making their decision?'

'I got it.'

'Congratulations.'

'Thank you,' he answered, but something in his tone sounded off. 'I really mean that. None of this would have been possible without you.'

'Then why don't you sound happy? It's everything you've ever wanted, isn't it?'

'I thought so. Until I got it and it didn't make me feel the way I thought it would.'

'I don't understand.'

He set the gift down on the coffee table and took another step towards her. She took a step back, unsure whether she would be able to handle it if he came any closer.

His eyes dimmed at her movement, and he shoved his hands into his pockets.

'When you got your shop…did it make all the trouble you'd gone through worth it?'

'You already know the answer to that.'

'Humour me.'

She took a deep breath. 'It felt like it was worth it at first. When I signed the lease on the property…when I decorated it. It was mine. But then… But then reality set in, and I couldn't escape what I'd done to get it.'

'And then it didn't seem worth it any more?'

'For a while. But since I met you things have been

going better. I've told myself I'll pay back the money, and that's made it a little easier to live with myself.'

'When did you make that decision?'

'Two nights ago.'

His eyes searched her face, as though he was looking for something there, and she shifted her weight. Tucked a curl behind her ear.

'Do things…not seem worth it any more to you?' she asked.

He smiled, but she could see the touch of sadness behind his eyes.

'Not so much, no.'

'Why not?'

'Because I sacrificed something much more important to get it.'

Though her heart-rate spiked, she asked, 'What?'

He didn't answer her for a moment, and Lily thought she'd been foolish to ask.

'I told you…you distracted me from my plan. And I meant it. I'd spent years fixated on making a name for myself other than the bad one the world had given me.' He paused. 'When I heard the club was going to be sold I was sure that it would be my chance.'

'I know all of this.'

'Yeah, you do. But you don't know that the reason I was successful in the end was *you*. Not because you helped my reputation—I think we could have chosen anyone else for that and my reputation would have improved.'

This time she didn't move back when he took a step forward.

'I succeeded because *you*, Lily Newman, showed me how to be someone I've been trying to be for years in one month.'

Speechless, she watched as he walked back to the table and picked up the box. She took it from him wordlessly.

'What...?' She cleared her throat when she heard the hoarseness of her voice. 'What is it?'

'Open it. Please.'

It was a plea, and though there was a part of her that was still in shock she was helpless to resist it. She tore the paper open with shaking hands, opened the box and felt the pieces of her heart that were already broken turn into a million more.

He'd given her a beautiful picture frame—wooden and hand-made. She recognised Caitlyn's artistry in it, and knew her friend had created it with Lily in mind. But it wasn't the frame that had Lily choked up. It was the picture it held.

It was a photograph of the exact moment she'd told herself to focus on for the past two days. The moment she recalled when she wanted to think of something happy. When she was brave enough to face what she had lost.

It was a picture taken at the charity event, of when Jacques had proposed to her. He was on his knee, looking up at her with an emotion on his face that was similar to the one it held now. She traced his face, and then looked at her own. Looked at the light, at the hope that shone in her eyes. She saw her eyes focused only on him, though there were so many people looking at her.

When a sob threatened, she put the lid back on the box. 'Why would you give me this?' she rasped, shaken.

'I told you that night that I wished you could see yourself the way I saw you. This picture *shows* you how I see you.'

'I don't know what you want me to see, Jacques,' she said desperately. 'I can't tell what that look on your face is.'

He lifted her chin, forcing her to look at him.

'It's love, Lily. I love you.'

And he kissed her.

He'd thought saying the words would be hard. But once he'd seen her they had come effortlessly. He'd kissed her because he'd been able to tell she didn't believe him. And he'd thought maybe if he could show her...

The moment his lips touched hers there was no more thinking. No more rationalising. He should have known that by now, and yet he was constantly surprised by the way her kiss could consume him.

By the way her *taste* could consume him.

After days of uncertainty—of wondering if he'd ever be consumed by that taste again—he felt more urgency, more greed than he would have liked. For a moment he considered allowing it. He considered letting passion dictate the kiss. But he wanted to show her more than passion. He wanted to show her that there was more than the attraction he'd claimed had always been between them.

She already knew about that. What she *didn't* know about was his love for her. What she didn't know was the intimacy he craved to have with her.

Slowly he deepened the kiss, and with each movement he showed her. With each stroke of his tongue, with each caress of his hands, he opened his heart to her. He showed her that he was hers, and only hers.

And for the first time he discovered that love was more potent than any attraction.

'Stop!' she said breathlessly as she pushed him away.

Somehow they'd ended up against the wall, and when he moved back he wished *he'd* had it behind him to steady him. 'What's wrong?'

'What's *wrong*?' she repeated. 'Jacques, you've had my best friend trick me into coming here. You tell me you got your club, but that it hasn't made you happy. And then you give me this gift, tell me you love me, and kiss me until I don't know who I am...'

Her chest heaved, but he couldn't tell if it was from their kiss or her words.

'You've got what you wanted and it hasn't made you feel the way you wanted it to. So...so maybe you're just moving on to the next thing. What happens if this—if I—don't make you happy? Do you just move on again? Because that...well, it won't work for me.'

'We weren't even a real couple and you made me happier than I've ever been, Lily.' He took her hands in his. 'I know you're worried that this is a rash decision for me, but it isn't. I haven't been able to stop thinking about you.'

He could see that he wasn't convincing her, and panic gripped his heart. But he took a deep breath and reminded himself that he always did whatever it took to get what he wanted. That meant that he needed to fight for Lily.

And *that* meant laying it all on the line.

'I resisted it from the moment we had dinner on that beach and I saw the person you really were. I resisted it through every dinner after that, through every event when I saw you fight against your insecurities. When I saw you overcome them.'

He took a deep breath.

'I fought it because I'd seen what a terrible relationship looked like. I was terrified that I would be like my father—that whatever relationship I was in would turn out to be like my parents. So I stayed away from them.'

'And had multiple partners instead?'

He winced. 'Yeah.'

'So what changed?'

He could tell he had her attention now, and the panic began to subside. 'I met you.'

'As simple as that?'

'As *complicated* as that. I've told you that you changed me, Lily. I mean it. Fear kept me from telling you this before, but I love you.'

Her eyes shone with tears, and her voice was hoarse when she asked, 'And this is not because you're looking for the high you hoped to get when you heard you'd got the club? I'm sorry it didn't feel the way you wanted it to, but...but that can't be the reason you've realised you love me.'

'Not that alone, no,' he agreed. 'I realised I loved you when you called me out on the beach.'

'You love me,' she repeated.

'I do.'

Her eyes began to shine with that hope he'd seen when he'd proposed to her. So he took the box from her hand, opened it again, and handed the frame to her.

'What do you see in that picture?'

'You're proposing.'

'What do you see on my face?'

Tears gleamed in her eyes when she looked at him. 'Is it...is it love?'

He set a hand under her chin, brought her head up to look at him. 'Tell me what you see on my face now, Lily.'

'You mean it?' A tear ran down her cheek. 'Don't do this if you don't mean it.'

'I *do* mean it,' he said quietly, and lowered his hands to her arms. 'Do you want to know what *I* see in that picture, Lil?' He didn't wait for an answer. 'I see a beautiful, kind, caring woman. One who sacrificed her own insecurities to help someone get what they thought they needed.'

He pulled her closer to him.

'I see a woman who has fought to overcome all the things life has thrown at her. Who has used her failures, her mistakes, as lessons. Who showed *me* how to do that too.'

His arms went around her waist, and he closed the distance between them until she was gently pressed to his body.

'I don't want to make *this* mistake, though, Lily. Because I don't know how I'd come back from it. I don't know how I could learn from it when it would be the worst mistake of my life.'

'I didn't know how I could learn from it either,' she whispered. 'I told myself that I could use it as a lesson to be better in the future, but I didn't know how.'

'So we won't make this mistake?'

'No, we won't.'

She looked at him with those beautiful eyes, more piercing now after her tears.

'I love you, Jacques.'

He rested his forehead on hers. 'I've never heard anything that's made me happier in my life.' He took another moment to appreciate it, and then he said, 'I could never imagine being married to someone after seeing what my parents went through. But that's because I'd never loved anyone. And then I met you—I fell in love with you—and I imagined it all so easily. In fact I can't *stop* thinking about it.'

He held his breath, hoping she understood what he'd meant.

'Me either.'

It wasn't the answer he'd hoped for, but the words sounded like trumpets in his ears.

He had a chance.

'I think about a future with you,' she said. 'I look at this gorgeous ring—even though it's pretend—and it undoes every resolution of mine to move on. It undoes every thought of mine that I *can* move on.'

She paused.

'I always thought I didn't deserve the good things in life. And I'd accepted it.'

'You didn't accept what I offered the other night.'

She smiled. 'That was *your* fault. You showed me that settling for anything less than what I wanted wasn't right. Every time I thought something demeaning about myself I heard your voice telling me to snap out of it. Or reminding me of all the things I've achieved. I wouldn't have been able to survive with just a part of you, Jacques. I wanted *all* of you.'

Her eyes flashed with uncertainty, and then the look was replaced with boldness.

'And I think maybe I *deserve* all of you.'

'You do, my love,' he said in relief. 'I'm the one who doesn't deserve *you*.'

'No, Jacques. We're stronger than that now. Together we're stronger. And we deserve each other.'

'Say it again, Lily. Tell me you love me again.'

'I love you.'

She'd barely said the words before his lips were on hers again. This time there were no reservations. This time there was passion. There was greed. There was urgency. But there was also love and intimacy. He gave just as much as he took, his passion fuelled by their acknowledged feelings. By their love.

And then he pulled back.

'I love you too.'

With those words all the turmoil inside her was calmed. All the insecurities faded. And she believed that she deserved this happiness. She deserved this happiness with the man she loved.

'You're a pretty lucky man, Mr Brookes,' she said, looking at the picture again. Now looking at it didn't hurt. 'Some people would say you have it all.'

'Those people would be right,' he replied, grinning. He pulled her in for a hug, his head resting on hers. 'Though you have to admit *you're* pretty lucky too.'

Her cheek rested on his chest, the picture still in her right hand, and she smiled. 'Oh, I know I am. Haven't you read the papers? *I'm* the one who tamed Bad-Boy Brookes.'

He chuckled. 'Yeah, you did. And I'm looking forward to a lifetime of it.'

Her heart sped up and she pulled back, setting the picture on the table.

'Do you mean...?'

'You can't possibly be surprised.' He smiled. 'How do you like that ring?'

'I'm pretty in love with it.' Her heart bursting, she asked one more time. 'Do you *really* mean it?'

'With all my heart, Lily. I can go down on one knee again if it would convince you?'

Lily looked at the picture again, saw the expression on his face. The real one since the emotion she hadn't been able to identify before now had a name. And then she looked at her own face again, and her eyes filled with tears.

'It was real, wasn't it?' she whispered.

'It was, but I'd like to ask you again anyway.'

She smiled when he went down on one knee, this time holding her hand with the diamond ring on it instead of inside its box.

'I love you, Lily. You will *always* be my real redemption. Will you marry me?'

'I can't imagine wanting anything else more.'

He grabbed her, twirled her around. And when they kissed Lily knew that the only thing that would define them in future would be their love for one another.

* * * * *

If you loved this story, check out
A MARRIAGE WORTH SAVING by Therese Beharrie.
Available now!

If you're looking forward to indulging in
another proposal of convenience story,
featuring an enigmatic sheikh, then you'll love
SARAH AND THE SECRET SHEIKH
by Michelle Douglas.

Praise for Vicki Lewis Thompson

"It's a wonderful sexy romance, with some very appealing and likable characters, and I'm definitely going to delve into more of the Thunder Mountain Brotherhood series." —*Harlequin Junkie*, Top Pick, on *Cowboy Untamed*

"The tongue-in-cheek, sweet yet sensual and comfortable family feel... remains until the last page. *Cowboy After Dark* is a story that will keep you smiling." —*RT Book Reviews*, Top Pick

"Thompson continues to do what she does best, tying together strong family values bound by blood and choice, interspersed with the more sizzling aspects of the relationship." —*RT Book Reviews* on *Thunderstruck*

"All the characters, background stories and character development are positively stellar; the warm family feeling is not saccharine-sweet, but heartfelt and genuine, and Lexi and Cade's rekindled romance is believable from beginning to end, along with the classy, sexy and tender love scenes." —*Fresh Fiction* on *Midnight Thunder*

"Vicki Lewis Thompson has compiled a tale of this terrific family, along with their friends and employees, to keep you glued to the page and ending with that warm and loving feeling." —*Fresh Fiction* on *Cowboys and Angels*

DO YOU TAKE
THIS COWBOY?

BY
VICKI LEWIS THOMPSON

First Published in Great Britain 2017
By Mills & Boon, an imprint of HarperCollins*Publishers*
1 London Bridge Street, London, SE1 9GF

© 2017 Vicki Lewis Thompson

ISBN: 978-0-263-92321-6

23-0817

Our policy is to use papers that are natural, renewable and recyclable products and made from wood grown in sustainable forests. The logging and manufacturing processes conform to the legal environmental regulations of the country of origin.

Printed and bound in Spain
by CPI, Barcelona

A passion for travel has taken *New York Times* best-selling author **Vicki Lewis Thompson** to Europe, Great Britain, the Greek isles, Australia and New Zealand. She's visited most of North America and has her eye on South America's rain forests. Africa, India and China beckon. But her first love is her home state of Arizona, with its deserts, mountains, sunsets and—last but not least—cowboys! The wide-open spaces and heroes on horseback influence everything she writes. Connect with her at www.vickilewisthompson.com, Facebook.com/vickilewisthompson and Twitter.com/vickilthompson.

To all my loyal readers who've loved
the Thunder Mountain Brotherhood, thank you!
Your emails and Facebook posts mean so much to me!

Chapter One

Drew Martinelli walked backward up the steps of the ranch house to the porch while keeping her camcorder focused on the couple strolling toward her hand in hand. Cade and Lexi's wedding was four days away and they'd hired Drew to create a video illustrating their love for each other, their appreciation of Thunder Mountain Ranch and their gratitude to both sets of parents. They planned to give a copy to the two couples at the rehearsal dinner as a surprise.

Because they'd wanted to shoot it at the ranch Cade grew up on, they'd had to get his foster parents, Rosie and Herb, to leave for the afternoon. They'd sent them to town on a somewhat bogus errand to pick up more decorations for the wedding. Drew knew Rosie and Herb pretty well by now. She doubted they believed the decorations were necessary but they'd played along, probably realizing something secret was going on.

Drew had begun the video down at the barn with Lexi and Cade tossing hay at each other. Next she'd followed them out to the pasture where they'd played tag with their horses, Hematite and Serendipity. She'd shot footage in the cabin where Cade had lived with two of his foster brothers as a teenager.

Then she'd walked with Cade and Lexi to their own recently constructed cabin and recorded Cade fixing lasagna. Cade's ability to cook must be a big deal because the two teased each other unmercifully during the process. Drew had struggled to keep from laughing, which would have been picked up on the mic.

A last shot on the ranch house porch would be the finale. Drew turned slowly to keep them in the frame as they climbed the steps. Cade sat in one of the roomy Adirondack chairs lining the porch and Lexi nestled on his lap.

As they'd planned, Drew crouched down and zoomed in on Lexi's face. Bits of hay stuck in her brown curls and her cheeks were flushed. Drew had a hunch Lexi's parents would totally lose it when they saw the joy and happiness in their daughter's eyes. Even Drew was a little choked up.

Lexi's warm smile completed the image. "Thank you, Mom and Dad, for always supporting me in everything I ever wanted to do and for welcoming the man I've chosen to share my life with. I love you both so much."

Drew's throat tightened. She didn't often become emotionally invested in her video subjects, but Lexi and Cade had become friends as well as clients. She slowly panned over to Cade. Wow. The big cowboy was clearly moved. That level of intensity wasn't common in the men she'd photographed.

He cleared his throat. "Mom and Dad, you took me in

when I had nowhere else to go." He cleared his throat a second time. "There's not enough thanks in the world for that. Because of you I became a man worthy of this wonderful woman. I love you more than you'll ever know."

Blinking back tears, Drew widened her camera's focus to include Cade and Lexi as they turned to each other and leaned in for a sweet, lingering kiss. Then she switched off the camera, reached for the tissue in her pocket and blew her nose.

When she looked up, Cade and Lexi were watching her in obvious bemusement.

"You got me." She tucked the tissue back in her pocket and stood. "That's one of the most touching scenes I've ever shot. Your folks are gonna turn into faucets when they see this."

"That's the idea." Lexi slid off Cade's lap.

"Yep." Cade got up and scrubbed a hand over his face. "I don't know about anybody else, but I could use a beer."

"Me, too." Lexi glanced at Drew. "Do you have time?"

"Sure, but what if Rosie and Herb come back and catch me here?"

"We'll say that you and I had more details to iron out regarding the wedding video."

"Okay, that works. Let me put my stuff in my truck."

"Oh, and you can meet Austin," Lexi said. "He's probably still working on the kitchen sink that got clogged while we were cleaning up after lunch. Thank God Austin was here or Herb would have stayed home to fix it and our plan would have been wrecked."

Cade laughed. "And we all know Herb would never have left me to do it."

"We do?" Drew looked at him. "Why not?"

"Sorry, Drew. I keep forgetting you haven't been around forever." Lexi slid her arm around Cade's waist.

"My husband-to-be has many talents but he's so not a handyman."

Cade shrugged as if he'd accepted that minor flaw long ago. "I didn't get that gene. Austin, though, he's good with tools."

"Is he the brother who just flew in from New Zealand?"

"Two days ago. Austin Teague. Nice guy." Lexi waved Drew toward her truck. "Get rid of your stuff. Your beer will be waiting for you in the kitchen."

This Austin person would be in the kitchen, too, apparently. Drew was eager to talk with someone who'd been halfway around the world, especially when he'd lived in a place she'd love to video someday.

She stashed her equipment in her truck and headed back to the house. She'd looked forward to meeting Austin ever since Rosie had mentioned him during a discussion of the wedding setup. They'd needed a head count of the foster brothers who'd be participating in the wedding.

Over the years Rosie and Herb Padgett had taken in quite a few boys, who at different times in their lives had ended up at Thunder Mountain Ranch. Cade had been one of their first foster boys, and it seemed that the whole family was excited about his wedding.

The ceremony would be held in the barn, a trendy wedding venue choice these days. But this ceremony would be unique in that the horses would remain in their stalls. Cade and Lexi were very much into horses and they loved the idea that the ranch's equine population would attend the wedding. This way Cade's cat, Ringo, could even be there if he chose.

Human guests would be seated on benches facing the barn's wide front door, which would be open. Instead of an arbor placed in the open doorway as a backdrop, the foster brothers in attendance would stand in a semicircle behind the minister.

Not all of Cade's foster brothers could make it to the wedding, but at last count at least nine would be standing in that group. Drew couldn't wait to film this ceremony, which promised to be more visually interesting than most.

She walked into the ranch house without knocking. People didn't stand on ceremony at Thunder Mountain, and while the living room was comfy and inviting, the large kitchen with its sturdy oak table was the heart of the house. She found Cade and Lexi sitting there, each with a bottle of beer. Two other open bottles were on the table along with a large bowl of chips.

Drew figured one beer was for her and the other must be for the man who was half-hidden under the kitchen sink. All she could see were scuffed boots, wear-softened jeans, a silver belt buckle with a kiwi bird etched on it, and a small section of skin that told her he was shirtless.

"Hey, Drew," Cade said. "That would be Junior's legs sticking out from under the sink over there. He says he'll be done in thirty seconds, tops."

She frowned. "Junior?"

"The name's Austin, ma'am." He wiggled partway out from under the sink, wiped his hand on his jeans and thrust it toward her. "Pleased to meet you."

"Hi, there." She walked over, leaned down and shook his outstretched hand. She tried not to stare, but *oh... my...God.* She had the urge to race back to her truck and fetch her camera. Abs and pecs like that should be captured on film and preserved for posterity. She was also amazed that he could fit those broad shoulders into such a small space.

On top of that he was blond and blue-eyed. Even his

chest hair was blond, although a little darker than the sun-bleached, close-cropped hair on his head. Because of her Italian heritage, she'd spent her life surrounded by dark-haired, dark-eyed people. She had a weakness for men who looked like Austin.

As they shook hands he smiled. "Really glad to meet you," he murmured.

"Same here." Lord help her, she sounded breathless. He probably got that a lot.

"Be done in a jiffy." He released her hand, scooted back under the sink and bumped his head on the pipe. "Ow."

"Are you okay?" She leaned down to peer into the cabinet.

"Yes, ma'am. Didn't watch where I was going is all."

"He'll be fine," Cade said. "Junior's practically indestructible."

"The name's *Austin*." His voice echoed a bit coming from under the sink.

"Why do you call him Junior?" Drew walked over to the table and Cade got up to pull out her chair.

He winked at her. "Because it's his name."

Lexi leaned over and gave him a light punch on the arm. "He's all grown up now. Retire the *Junior* thing."

"Yes, *please*," came the voice from under the sink.

"So I take it he was Junior when you all lived at the ranch?" Drew took a sip of her beer.

"And still is, as far as I'm concerned." Cade grinned as he went back to his seat. "I don't care how big he gets, he'll always be Junior to me."

"No respect." Austin slid out from under the sink and rose to his glorious height, which had to be at least six-three. "I go and sell my truck so I can buy a plane ticket to attend your wedding and this is my reward—still stuck with the same old crummy nickname." His dramatic sigh made his chest heave in a most arresting way.

"*I* call you Austin," Lexi said.

"Yes, you do, Lexi, and I appreciate the support."

Cade tipped his chair onto its back legs and picked up his beer. "The way I heard it, you didn't sell your truck to buy a plane ticket. You sold it because you wanted to buy a new one over here instead of shipping your old rattletrap across the Pacific."

"Technically, yes, but some of the proceeds went toward the ticket, so my statement stands."

"So you're staying?" Drew hadn't been clear on that but it was the best news she'd heard all day.

"Yes, ma'am. New Zealand was great, but I missed Wyoming."

"And me," Cade said. "I know you really missed me."

Austin laughed, flashing beautiful white teeth. "Can't live without you, bro."

"And FYI, your beer's getting warm the longer you stand there working your jaw."

"Let me wash up." He turned back to the sink.

Much as Drew would have loved to admire the ripple of his back muscles as he scrubbed his hands clean, ogling would be inappropriate. She redirected her attention toward Cade and Lexi. Why was she here, again? Oh, yes. "I think we got some great stuff today. I'll edit it as soon as I get home and email you a link to a preview."

"Good." Lexi reached for the chips. "I'm really excited to see it."

"So am I." Cade returned his chair to its original position so he could also reach the chip bowl. "By the way, I was impressed that you walked up the steps backward while you filmed that last part. I'm not sure I could have done that."

"I know I couldn't," Lexi said.

"My years of playing hockey probably helps. You have to have eyes in the back of your head to play that game."

"You played hockey?" Austin joined them at the table.

"Yes, and I was really, really lucky that I got to. Some parents organized a Montana youth league and my brother and I were both in it. I don't think that league exists anymore. For three years I lived and breathed hockey. Every night before I went to sleep I recited that famous Wayne Gretzky quote."

Austin picked up his beer and reached for a chip. "I don't think I know that one."

"I do, more or less," Cade said. "Instead of following the puck, you need to anticipate where it will be and go there."

"Aha!" Lexi looked as if inspiration had hit. "*That's* why you're such an excellent videographer. You're always a little ahead of the action. I couldn't put my finger on why your videos are so much better than others I've seen and I'll bet that's the secret."

Drew's cheeks warmed. "Thank you. I never thought of it that way but if I manage to pull it off I'm glad."

"Montana, huh?" Austin's gaze had remained on her ever since he'd come to the table. "Where in Montana?"

"Billings. My parents own an Italian restaurant there."

"I love Italian food. Do you like to cook?"

"God, no." She shuddered. "I'm probably the least domestic woman you'll ever meet."

"But you're great with a camera," Lexi said. "Plenty of people make videos but you make memories."

"What a lovely thing to say." Drew savored the compliment. "Any chance you'd be willing to put that in a review on my website?"

"Absolutely! I wish I'd thought of it before."

"No worries. You've been busy planning a wedding."

"Reviews make a difference," Austin said. "The company I worked for always asked for them at the end of a ride."

"Horseback ride?" Drew made a guess based on where he'd grown up.

"Yes, ma'am."

"What made you go so far away from home?" She'd done a little bit of traveling related to her videography but she'd never considered relocating to a different country. His willingness to seek out adventure added to his appeal.

"*Lord of the Rings.* When I saw those movies I stayed for the credits. That's when I made up my mind I had to go to New Zealand." He popped another chip in his mouth.

"How old were you?"

"I must've been around thirteen."

Cade nodded. "Oh, yeah, you were thirteen, all right. I remember it well. You drove us all crazy with your fixation on those movies and New Zealand." He looked at Drew. "Watch out for Junior. Once he gets an idea in his head, he's like one of those bullet trains in Japan."

"That's not such a bad thing." Drew sent Austin a glance of solidarity. "Nothing wrong with being highly motivated to attain a goal."

He tipped his head in silent acknowledgment.

"True," Cade said. "But if you've booked a seat on that train you'd better be sure you want to go where it's headed." He looked over at Austin. "I'm flattered that you came back for the wedding, but surely you have other reasons for relocating to your old stomping grounds. At least I hope you do. I can only be entertaining for so long before I run out of material."

Austin rotated his bottle on the table and smiled at Cade. "The new truck's a clue, bro."

Cade gazed at him and then he blinked. "I'll be damned. I should have figured that out."

Lexi turned to Drew. "I have no idea what they're talking about, do you?"

"No." But she was intrigued. Austin was clearly a man who knew what he wanted and went after it. He hadn't allowed the ties to his foster parents or his foster brothers to stop him from pursuing a dream that had taken him halfway around the world.

She, on the other hand, had felt obligated to stay in Billings far too long. She was the oldest and her large family seemed to depend on her for support and advice. But in the past year or so she'd felt smothered by their neediness. She'd been desperate to get away and discover who she was outside of that boisterous clan.

Over the Christmas holiday she'd talked her way into teaching a six-week course in videography at Sheridan's community college. That had justified moving her base of operations from Billings to Wyoming in January.

Through Molly Radcliffe, who worked at the college and was Cade's cousin, she'd met Rosie and Herb. That connection had brought her business and friendship. Today it had brought her in contact with Austin. He probably had something to teach her about making bold moves toward an exciting future.

It sounded as if he had a grand plan for his decision to come back home. That put him several steps ahead of her. As of now, she was making it up as she went along.

She knew what she didn't want—to be dragged down by so many family obligations that she lost track of her own goals and who she was besides oldest daughter and big sister. Austin had already made that journey away from his people. Maybe hanging out with him would give her the gumption she needed to do the same. And whether his spirit of adventure rubbed off or not, he was pretty to look at.

"So why is the truck a clue to your current plans?" Lexi asked.

Austin hesitated and exchanged a quick glance with Cade.

Cade flashed him a smile. "You're the one who said it."

Austin cleared his throat and faced Lexi. "Well, a man who's starting out fresh needs a decent ride to…to…" He sent Cade a look that was clearly a plea for a little help with this explanation.

"A man's truck is like his alter ego," Cade said. "You can tell a lot by what he chooses to drive. Junior, here, is ready to project a more polished image."

Austin let out a relieved sigh. "Exactly."

Drew figured it was a guy thing. She didn't care what Austin chose to drive. She just wanted to be in the passenger seat.

Chapter Two

Drew left far sooner than Austin would have liked, but she had to get home and edit the video and he was all in favor of that. He wanted her to finish it because he had other plans for how she'd spend her evening, assuming she wasn't seeing anyone. When he'd first slid out from under that sink, he felt as if he'd been struck by lightning.

The view from the floor had been spectacular—long, tanned legs that ended in a snug pair of jeans shorts and above that a bare, toned midriff and a white halter top that had gaped a little when she'd leaned over to shake his hand.

But he hadn't focused on that because he was a gentleman. Instead he'd gazed into eyes that were a beautiful deep brown and gleamed with interest. Excellent. Mutual attraction.

She wore a silver pendant consisting of a freeform heart, a large pearl and several little diamonds. He'd noticed it because it had swung toward him when she'd bent down. It looked expensive, and yet she'd worn it when she was dressed very casually. That interested him, too.

He munched on chips and sipped his beer while Cade and Lexi discussed the video they'd just made and how awesome it was going to be. When he heard Drew's truck pull away, he turned to Lexi. "Does she have a steady guy?"

Cade sighed. "Look out. Bullet train."

"Not necessarily." Austin sat up a little straighter. "She seemed interested in me. It might go nowhere, but what's wrong with checking things out if she's available?"

"I don't think she's with anyone," Lexi said. "When I asked if she wanted to bring a guest to the wedding she said no."

"That's great." He got up and retrieved his phone from where he'd laid it on the kitchen counter. "I'd like her number." He settled back in his chair and clicked on his contacts page. "What's her last name?"

"Martinelli." Lexi took out her phone.

"That explains the big brown eyes and the Italian restaurant." He typed in her name. "Ready when you are."

Cade tugged his hat down over his eyes and groaned. "If you give him that number, I guarantee he'll dial it right now."

"So what?" Lexi scrolled through her contacts. "If she doesn't want to go out with him she can always say no."

Leaning both elbows on the table, Cade studied Austin. "When are you fixing to get that courtin' truck?"

"That *what*?" Lexi looked up from her phone. "Is a courtin' truck what I think it is?"

"Yes, ma'am." Cade took a long pull on his beer.

She turned to Austin. "Are you really buying a new truck so you can impress women?"

"Not *all* women. Just certain ones."

"Let me put it this way, Lexi." Cade put down his beer. "When you attended that riding clinic in Denver last year you took cabs to get around, right?"

"Right."

"How did you know a cab was available?"

"The roof light was on."

"Well, Junior here has his light on."

"I do not." Austin glared at his brother. "That suggests I'll take the first one who comes along, and that's not how I—"

"Isn't Drew the first one who's come along?"

"Yes, but we still don't know if she'll go out with me."

"What if she does?"

"Then I'll have to go truck shopping pretty soon."

"Wait, wait, wait." Lexi waved her hands in the air. "You two are speaking in tongues. Could you both use your native language, which also happens to be mine? What the hell are you talking about?"

Cade reached over and covered her hand with his. "I called it his courtin' truck because Junior is looking for a wife."

Lexi swiveled in her seat to look at Austin. "You are?"

He hadn't planned to lay out his plan this soon but he also couldn't beat around the bush with Lexi. She was like a big sister to him. "Yes, ma'am."

"See?" Cade gestured to him. "I knew he had another reason for coming back to Wyoming besides our wedding."

"Austin." Lexi put her hand on his arm. "Please tell me you didn't get this idea because of our wedding invitation. There's such a thing as wedding fever. When I was twenty-two I tried to get Cade to propose because of peer pressure. You probably don't remember that."

"Oh, I remember, all right. That's when he took off for Colorado." At seventeen, Austin had been devastated when his idol had driven away from Thunder Mountain Ranch. Lexi hadn't been the only one with a broken heart. "It wasn't just the invitation, although that made me realize all I was missing and I didn't want to miss this. But I've been thinking about moving back and settling down for quite a while now."

"You're only twenty-six. You have lots of time."

"I know. The thing is, I'm sick of getting involved with someone when it'll never go anywhere. Every woman I dated in New Zealand told me flat out she wasn't relocating. That made perfect sense. Their families were there and it's a beautiful country."

"All right." Lexi seemed relieved. "Then *ultimately* you want to get married, but you don't have a timetable or anything." She smiled. "It's not like you'll ask Drew out now and propose next week."

"I certainly wouldn't plan on it."

"Good, because—"

"But what if she's perfect? What if we're perfect for each other? Life's short. We don't know what's going to happen." He'd learned that early. Both his parents had died in their thirties. "I don't believe in putting things off if taking action is the right decision."

Cade glanced up at the ceiling.

Austin knew he didn't fully agree, but Drew had liked that he was focused. Didn't mean she'd go out with him but he thought she would. He didn't get many refusals when he asked a lady out.

He glanced at the phone in Lexi's free hand. "So can I have the number?"

She looked at him for a moment longer. "Yes. Just—"

"Just what?"

"Nothing." She squeezed his arm and moved her hand away. "Ready?"

He touched the screen to refresh it. "Yes, ma'am." He entered Drew's number. "Do you think she's had time to get home?"

"Probably not."

"Then I'll wait." He put down his phone and picked up his beer. "It sounded like you were both happy with how the filming went."

"I think it went great," Lexi said. "I'll know for sure once we see the edited version, but I meant what I said about her work. She's phenomenal."

"Good to know. Now that I understand how to run a trail ride company, I've been thinking about starting one. A good video on a website would be a big help."

Cade leaned forward. "Gonna go into business for yourself?"

"I'd like to. I'll have to begin small, work with one of the local stables, maybe get a business loan, but I think that's all doable."

"Absolutely," Lexi said. "I'm sure Rosie and Herb would let you stay here for a while, which would save money on rent."

Austin had been thinking the same thing until meeting Drew. "They probably would and I've considered it, but I'd rather get an apartment in town."

Cade gave him a knowing look. "That doesn't surprise me. I—" He paused as the front door opened.

"Anybody home?"

"Hey, Zeke!" Cade pushed back his chair. "We're in the kitchen having a beer. Come on back and I'll get you one."

"Don't mind if I do."

Austin left his chair to greet his foster brother, one

he'd liked okay but had never felt close to when they'd all lived at Thunder Mountain. Zeke Rafferty had kept to himself and all the guys had figured it was because his dad had committed suicide. But Rosie said that Zeke had come out of his shell ever since discovering he was about to be a father.

It seemed that Rosie was right, because the rugged cowboy who'd always looked slightly ticked off came in all smiles. "Hey, Austin!" His handshake was firm and enthusiastic. "I swear you're a lot taller than I remember."

"Not much taller, but I filled out a little."

"I'd say so. How was New Zealand?" He took the beer Cade handed him. "Thanks, bro."

"I loved New Zealand but I got homesick."

Zeke nodded. "I can understand that. New Zealand's a long way from Wyoming. Listen, I came over hoping you'd be around. As you've probably heard, I've been the caretaker at Matt's ranch for the past few weeks."

"I did hear that." Their foster brother Matt Forrest was starring in his first major film and he'd used the sudden influx of money to buy a ranch adjoining Thunder Mountain. "Matt's premiere was another reason to come back. I want to go to LA with everybody next month."

"Yeah, with all the people going, we might end up renting a couple of vans instead of flying. Anyway, my situation is changing and I'm looking for someone to take over for me at Matt's. I thought you might be interested."

"That could be a good deal for you, Junior," Cade said. "Free room and board."

Austin thought about it for less than two seconds. Good deal or not, it would mean he'd agreed to take care of someone else's place instead of moving toward buying his own. He might have to start with a tiny apartment, but it would be his. Paying his rent on time would establish his creditworthiness when he applied for a home loan.

He gazed at Zeke. "Much as I'd like to help, staying at Matt's doesn't fit in with my plans. Sorry." He noticed that Lexi and Cade exchanged a look. At one time he would have followed any advice either of them had given him. But he'd had four years of being completely on his own. He still respected their opinions, but he no longer felt obligated to make decisions based on what they thought.

"That's okay." Zeke shrugged. "Just thought I'd ask." He moved to the table and took a seat. "Somebody will turn up."

"They will." Cade walked to the refrigerator. "Who's ready for another beer? Junior?"

"In a little while, thanks. If you'll all excuse me, I need to make a phone call." He left the kitchen and walked through the living room and out to the porch. Now that the moment was here, he had to decide where he'd take Drew if she agreed to go out with him.

Then it came to him. Plopping into an Adirondack chair, he touched the screen and put the phone to his ear. Damn it, he got her voice mail. "Hi, this is Austin Teague. I enjoyed meeting you today and was hoping you'd have some free time tonight." He gave his number and disconnected.

He knew she was going home because she had a video to edit, so she might have been engrossed in that and hadn't heard the phone. Or maybe she automatically let every call go to voice mail. Then again, she might have turned off her phone. She might—

His phone chimed and her name popped up on the screen. Heart pounding, he answered. "Hi, Drew."

"Hi, yourself." She sounded happy. Interested. "Didn't expect to hear from you so soon."

"Didn't you?"

"Well, okay, I sort of did. What did you have in mind?"

He didn't dare tell her what was in his mind this very minute. He'd already started imagining what it would be like to kiss her.

"Austin? Are you there?"

"Yes, ma'am. Sorry. I'm on the porch and got distracted by…" He glanced around for an excuse. "A butterfly."

"I can understand how that could happen. They're beautiful, aren't they?"

"Yes, ma'am. Anyway, here's my thought, if you're available for dinner. We'll have a cookout."

"Where?"

"There's a nice little spot on a far corner of the ranch property. Since you're not into cooking, I'll handle that."

"Sounds like fun."

"I can pick you up."

"That's totally unnecessary. I'll meet you there. What time?"

He glanced at the time on his phone and quickly calculated how long he'd need to set things up. "Is seven too late?"

"Seven's perfect. That will give me time to finish the video and send the link to Cade and Lexi. I'll see you then."

"Great!" He disconnected the call. He'd just given himself a heck of a lot of work to do in a short time. This was his deal so he wouldn't raid the Thunder Mountain kitchen for what he needed.

But he had a transportation problem. His foster mom and dad had been generous with the loan of their truck but they weren't back from town. He really did need to buy that courtin' truck Cade had teased him about, but he certainly wouldn't be doing that between now and seven tonight.

As if in answer to his silent plea, Herb and Rosie drove up and parked in front of the porch steps. Austin got up and went around to the passenger side where Rosie was to see if he could help with her packages.

His foster mom was a short, rounded lady who had decided to be a blond for the rest of her life. She was the kindest woman Austin had ever known, but tough enough to keep her foster boys in line. Most of the time there had been at least ten boys living in the log cabins down in the meadow. They'd all known that Rosie was the boss around here.

She'd already opened her door but he was able to take her shopping bags and give her a hand down. She was perfectly capable of doing all that herself, but she'd taught her boys to be gentlemen. They'd practiced their manners on her because usually she'd been the only available woman.

"Are you the sentry?" she asked as she stepped down from the truck's running board.

"The sentry?"

"You know. The lookout. The person watching for us in case we got home before whatever was happening was still happening."

"Oh. No, ma'am." Then he realized he hadn't contradicted her assumption that something secret was going on. "I mean, nothing's happening. Nothing at all. Zeke's inside talking to Cade and Lexi. That's about the size of it."

"I saw Zeke's truck parked down by the barn." Herb, a wiry man who'd finally surrendered to wearing glasses in his later years, chuckled as he walked around the truck to join them. "We dawdled in town as long as we could but finally ran out of things to do other than cruising Main Street. That looks a little strange for a couple of sixtysomethings."

"Like I said." Austin tried to blot out the image of Drew because she was part of the secret. "Not a single thing going on, except the sink's fixed."

"Thank you!" Rosie beamed at him. "By the way, now that some of my boys are back, they sometimes get together for poker. If they ask you to play, you might want to think twice."

"Yes, ma'am, I already know I'm lousy at poker. Some of the guides got me into a game and ended up with all my tip money for the week."

"I'm sorry to hear that. But at least now you know it's not your thing."

"Nothing wrong with being a bad liar, son." Herb clapped him on the shoulder. "So are you saying it's okay for us to go in the house?"

"Absolutely. But now that you're back, would it be possible for me to borrow the truck to run a few errands?"

"Sure thing." Herb handed over the keys.

"And would it be okay if I used a Coleman stove for a little cookout on the back twenty tonight? I'll get the food, but I'll also need to borrow some tongs and a pan or two."

Rosie smiled at him. "This sounds like it could be a date."

"It is." And now he was in the soup because she'd probably ask who he'd asked out and how he could possibly have met someone when he'd been in town exactly two days. He was saved when Zeke, Cade and Lexi came out the front door.

Amid much laughter and teasing, Rosie and Herb

promised they wouldn't try to uncover whatever surprise was in the works. Lexi wanted to see what they'd bought in town so Austin handed her the bags and excused himself to go put on a shirt. That finished, he grabbed his hat and wallet and headed out the door, his shirt still unbuttoned. He was eager to get away before he had to answer any more questions that would bring up the subject of Drew being here.

But Lexi had to call out to him. "Does this mean she said yes?"

"She did."

Rosie lifted her eyebrows. "So who's the lucky lady?"

"I'll let Lexi explain it." Touching his fingers to the brim of his hat, he hurried around the truck, hopped in and made his escape.

Chapter Three

Drew pulled into the ranch's circular gravel drive exactly at seven. The sun had dipped behind the Bighorn Mountains, but there was still plenty of light to see Austin sitting on the porch in one of the Adirondack chairs. The picture he made in his gray Stetson, yoked Western shirt, boots and faded jeans was exactly why so many women fantasized about cowboys.

That outfit, especially on a man built like Austin, made her feel safe. Like the knights of old, he would leap on his horse and ride to her rescue. Even though she didn't need rescuing, she still loved the idea of a cowboy hero who'd protect her from the bad guys and look great doing it.

He left his chair as she shut off the motor. Anticipation thrummed through her veins as he came down the steps with the slightly bowlegged stride common to men who'd spent most of their lives on horseback. Oddly enough, she hadn't dated cowboys while living in Montana.

In high school and college she'd hung out with the art students and at home her life had revolved around the family restaurant. She'd dated some artist types and a couple of chefs but no cowboys. Thunder Mountain, however, was chockablock with them.

She moved her purse to the floor of the passenger side out of habit. Nobody would break into her truck to steal it while she was parked here. She tossed the keys down there, too, and opened her door. She'd started to climb out when he rounded the front of the vehicle.

"Let me help you down."

Amused, she waited. She couldn't remember the last time someone had made that offer. He knew perfectly well she was capable of getting down by herself. But when he held out his hand, she was charmed.

"I like your hair like that."

"Thanks." Most of the summer she'd worn it in a braid or a ponytail but she'd decided to leave it down tonight. She was on a date, after all.

"I'm glad you could make it."

"Me, too." She put her hand in his and the controlled strength in his grip sent a shiver of pleasure up her arm. "Fortunately the editing went well and I had time to finish the video." Then she glanced around, not sure who might be within hearing distance. "Did you have to dream up a story to explain to your folks how we ended up going out tonight?"

"I have Lexi to thank for that. She told them you came out today to check on some details for the wedding video." He let go of her hand once she had both feet on the ground.

"That will give them another hint, though." She breathed in the scent of his aftershave. "They know something's going on."

He sighed. "You're right. Now they might think it involves a video. My mistake. If we'd met in town I could've snuck away without explaining I was meeting someone."

"I didn't think of that, either, so I'm as much at fault as you." Something else occurred to her but when she gazed into his blue eyes she lost her train of thought.

He smiled. "Not letting you shoulder any of the blame, ma'am. I complicated things, case closed."

Ah, that smile. And speaking of shoulders...

She remembered what she'd been about to say. "Actually, Lexi took a risk when she invited me in for a beer. When I pointed out that Rosie and Herb might come back and find me there, she came up with that cover story she used to help you out."

"Yeah?" He brightened. "I didn't know that."

"And if she hadn't invited me in for a beer, you and I wouldn't have met."

"So it's all Lexi's fault?"

She laughed. "Pretty much."

"Now I don't feel so guilty. I just thought a cookout would be more fun than a boring restaurant meal."

"You've got that right. I was thrilled with the suggestion. I've spent so much time in Martinelli's that I don't care if I never eat in another restaurant again."

"Then I'm glad I thought of it."

"So where are we headed? Backyard barbecue? Fire pit?"

He gestured toward the edge of the porch. "We'll take the ATV out to the back twenty."

She looked and sure enough, a green-and-brown ATV was sitting there. She'd been so focused on his handsome self she hadn't noticed it. "The back twenty? I've only heard people refer to the back forty."

"They do." He started walking toward the ATV. "But this ranch isn't that big so we have the back twenty. We joke about it, but I have great memories of the place. It's where we used to camp out when we were kids. Or I should say, when I was a kid and was allowed to tag along with the big guys. I came here when I was nine. Everybody else was a teenager."

"And so they called you Junior."

"Mostly Cade." He stopped next to the ATV and turned to her with another one of his endearing smiles. "I don't mind it as much as he thinks I do. I did back then, but now…now I think he says it because he likes me."

"I'm pretty sure he likes you." She wondered if Austin had any idea how appealing he was. "Cade strikes me as the kind of guy who only teases people he likes."

He nodded. "These days, probably so. But you should have heard the way he said *Junior* years ago when I used to bug him to death. I followed him everywhere. Looking back on it, I wonder why he didn't deck me. I'll bet he wanted to but I was a lot smaller and he'd never have beat up on someone smaller."

"Then he must like you, because you've grown enough for him to beat up on if he wanted to."

"Guess so." He laughed. "Come to think of it, yesterday he said now I was too big to mess with, especially since he's hit thirty and is losing muscle mass."

"So if he's thirty, how old are you?"

"Twenty-six."

"Huh." She decided to go for full disclosure and get it over with. "How do you feel about having a cookout with an older woman?"

"I don't care how old you are."

"For the record, I'm twenty-eight."

He shrugged. "Two years is nothing." He turned toward

the ATV, but then swung back to her. "Unless you're not happy about going out with a younger guy. Some ladies would rather date someone older than they are. I've run into a few of those."

Silly women. "I'm not one of them."

"Good to know." He swung one long leg over the ATV. "Climb on behind me and we'll get this show started. Oh, and hold on tight. I won't be going fast but we'll hit some bumps along the way. Can't help it. The rain's done a number on the road."

She needed no encouragement to wrap both arms around his solid torso and scoot against his firm backside. Riding on the back of an ATV with Austin immediately became her favorite outdoor activity. What a great excuse to get up close and personal with a guy who not only looked good but felt even better.

The ride ended long before she was ready to let go of him. He pulled into a clearing with a boundary marked by rocks spaced a few inches apart. Beyond them the brush, mostly sage, grew three to four feet high.

But now they'd stopped and she felt obliged to climb off, darn it. She had a nice buzz going and she had the crazy urge to ask if that had been as good for him as it had been for her.

When he just sat there while he took a couple of deep breaths, she had a feeling it had been.

"Lordy." His low chuckle was followed by a long sigh. "Maybe I should have taken you to a restaurant in town, after all."

"Oh?"

"I knew I was attracted to you, but I thought I could manage a short ATV ride. Turns out it affected me more than I thought it would." He climbed off the four-wheeler and faced her. "But everything's under control now." He gave her a sheepish smile. "I promise you're safe with me."

She met his gaze. "If it makes you feel any better, the drive turned me on, too."

Heat flared in his eyes.

She felt obliged to add one more fact. "But we just met."

"Only hours ago."

"At this point it wouldn't be about you and me as individuals with histories and personality quirks. It would be like strangers scratching an itch. Not that there's anything wrong with that, but I—"

"I didn't invite you out here to scratch an itch. I'm past that stage in my life."

"Good. So am I. Come to think of it, I never went through that stage." She noticed a folded blanket on top of a metal ice chest but that was probably so they'd have a place to sit. "I've always wanted to get to know someone first."

"Exactly."

"It's good we're agreed on that." Definitely good. Maybe. Except he wasn't some guy she'd met in a bar. She knew his foster family. She knew he'd been to New Zealand. She knew he could fix a clogged sink. "I see you've toted everything out here already, so let's have our meal and swap stories."

"That was my plan." He gestured toward the campsite he'd set up. "Welcome to our dining room. That little fire pit is strictly for ambiance. I'm using the Coleman stove to make dinner. Cooking over a campfire gives you lots of atmosphere but it can also give you undercooked or overcooked food."

"A Coleman stove sounds fine. I have one myself."

"You do? I thought you didn't cook."

"I don't when I have alternatives, but I camp out quite a bit when I'm shooting nature videos. I love my coffee in the morning and scrambled eggs are nice to go with it. What can I do to help?"

"The cooking's my deal, but you can light the campfire if you want. I left some matches next to it."

"Looks like you thought of everything." She walked over and crouched next to the fire pit where he'd arranged kindling and a couple of larger logs. Extra wood was stacked nearby. She recognized a fire laid by someone who knew what he was doing and sure enough, it caught with one match. "Done."

"Then all you have to do is keep an eye on it and add a log if you think it needs one. You can have a seat on the blanket and I'll get you something to drink."

"I won't object to that." She found a good spot for the blanket, folded it so two could fit and sat down. The clearing had been raked recently but she'd guess the rocks defining the perimeter had been there for years.

"You know what?" He opened the ice chest. "I should have asked you about the wine instead of making an assumption because you're Italian."

"You brought Chianti."

"No, I brought a New Zealand Sauvignon Blanc." He held it up. "The assumption was that you were a wine drinker. Like I said, I should have asked."

"I am a wine drinker and I'm glad it's not Chianti. I can have that anytime just by walking in the back door of Martinelli's and asking for a glass."

"All righty, then." He twisted off the screw top. "It was going to be this or water. I didn't bring anything else to drink." He took out two chilled glasses and handed her one. "I had this when I was over there and really liked it." He poured them each some wine.

"I'm sure I will, too." She lifted her glass in his direction. "Here's to adventure."

"To adventure." He tapped his glass to hers. "That's a good thing to toast."

"I haven't had nearly as much adventure as you, I'm afraid." She took a slow sip. "Nice wine."

"Then I lucked out. Here's hoping the meal works for you, too."

"Since I rarely cook, almost any food made by someone else works for me."

"This is a skillet dish a trail guide buddy created." Setting his wine on the ground beside him, he hunkered down, turned on the stove and began pulling ingredients out of the ice chest. "It's flexible regarding ingredients. Some kind of white fish, vegetables you have on hand and rice."

"Sounds gourmet."

"My friend's a talented guy. Once every two weeks we offered an overnight trail ride. He was the chef on those outings."

"I'm betting you were in charge of the fire."

"Yes, ma'am."

Drew savored her wine. "Your life over there seems exotic and wonderful. I'm a little surprised you didn't stay."

"I wanted to spend enough time there that I felt the rhythm of the place in my bones." He tended his stir-fry dinner. "But I always knew I'd come back here."

"I like that idea—absorbing a place until you feel the rhythm in your bones. That's what I try to do when I shoot a video. I think I'm almost there with Thunder Mountain." She took another swallow of wine. "You're a bit of a philosopher, aren't you?"

"I don't know about that, but ever since I saw *The Lord*

of the Rings I've been into books. I might've read that phrase somewhere so don't give me too much credit."

"What books?"

"Anything about adventure, courage, honor, stuff like that. A librarian steered me toward *The Iliad* and *The Odyssey.* If I'd known that was serious literature I never would have read them. I'd taken enough teasing for *Lord of the Rings.*"

"But you liked them?"

"Sure did." He paused to drink some wine. "My dad was kind of an epic hero. That's probably why I related to those stories."

She went very still. She knew this was important information but she didn't know how to get him to elaborate. Finally, she decided to make it simple. "Would you tell me about your dad?"

His answer was slow in coming, but at last he spoke. "He was in Search and Rescue."

She slowly let out her breath and waited for the story to unfold.

"A minor avalanche had trapped a family of five. My dad was on the team that went in to get them out." He kept his attention on his cooking, carefully stirring the mixture in the pan. "They rescued everyone except the family dog. My dad went back for the dog and a second avalanche hit. The dog jumped out of his arms when he saw his family and ran to them. But when he jumped, he threw my dad off balance. He couldn't get up fast enough."

"That's rough."

He switched off the burner and put a lid on the pan. "It was rough, especially because I was only six and idolized him." Standing, he reached into a basket next to the cooler and took out plates, napkins and utensils.

"My mom must have been torn apart by the news, but she said all the right things to me—that my dad had died doing what he loved and he'd helped save the family and their beloved pet."

She wanted to hug him and offer comfort, even though the event had taken place twenty years ago. Didn't matter. He still felt the loss. She could tell by the catch in his voice as he'd finished the story.

But their relationship was still so new that she hesitated. At least she could help with serving up the meal. She got to her feet. "I'll hold the plates while you fill them."

"Good idea." He handed her the dishes with the silverware and napkins on top. As he met her gaze, his voice gentled. "I know it seems like I got a rotten deal, but compared to the other foster boys, I was lucky. My parents adored each other and adored me. I thank God for that every day."

That was when she realized she only had half the story. His dad died when he was six and he'd come to the ranch when he was nine. She asked the question as gently as possible. "And your mom?"

"She was a riding teacher. A normally steady horse freaked out. She fell off, broke her neck and died instantly."

"Oh, Austin."

"I'm not saying it wasn't awful, because it was. But after my dad died she spent the next three years emphasizing that I should do what I love because nobody knows the future. She loved riding almost as much as she loved me."

"So you went to New Zealand."

"Yes, ma'am. I knew they would have wanted me to."

"Well, then." She managed to give him a smile. "I can't wait to see what adventure you choose next."

He smiled back. "Who knows? You might want to be a part of it."

"You know, I just might."

Chapter Four

As dusk arrived along with a cool breeze, Austin decided they should sit closer to the fire while they ate. He switched on the lantern he'd brought but kept it on low to preserve the ambience. As he settled down next to Drew on the blanket, he could feel the hum of sexual tension moving back through his system.

He did his best to ignore it and tucked into the stir-fry. It had turned out fairly well, which was a relief. Multi-tasking had never been one of his favorite ways to operate and he wouldn't have chosen to cook dinner while telling his life story. But he'd known those facts had to come out, and the sooner the better. If he expected to spend more time with Drew, she needed to hear about his folks.

But he wanted to know her story, too. She'd worn the pearl-and-diamond pendant again tonight with a long-sleeved cotton shirt and jeans. Clearly it was important to her, so he decided to start with that. He mentioned that he'd noticed it when they'd first met.

She glanced down at the pendant as if she'd forgotten it was there. "My grandmother gave it to me for my sixteenth birthday."

"You had it on earlier today, too." Her scent, light and sweet, mingled with the aroma of wood smoke from the fire. It was an arousing combination.

"I wear it every day. I didn't use to, though." She picked up her wineglass and drank what was left in it.

"More?" He reached for the bottle.

"Sure."

"Might as well finish off the bottle." He divided the rest between them. "So when did you start wearing it all the time?"

"After she died last October. Wearing it makes me feel close to her again."

"Ah." He should have guessed something like that. "I'm sorry."

She put down her fork and looked over at him. "Me, too, but she was ninety-three and wasn't well. I miss her like crazy, but that's all about me. She was ready."

"Ninety-three. That's a good run." He wondered if she realized she was now holding on to the pendant and moving it slowly back and forth along its chain.

"She had a full life, although not one I would have chosen. My mother was the youngest of nine children."

"Whew."

"I know. My mom has a framed picture of my grandparents surrounded by all those kids. I would have gone insane with a brood like that depending on me, constantly needing things, but in the picture she looks serene. That's something I admired about her. Our family is huge and when we all get together it's a circus. Nonna Elena took it all in stride."

"Rosie's like that. Growing up, there could've been

ten or eleven of us running around, more if we'd invited our friends over, and she hardly ever lost her cool. When she needed us to behave, though, all she had to do was give us The Look."

Drew smiled. "Nonna Elena had that technique down, too. We used to say she could cut glass with The Look."

"How many of that crew lives in Billings?"

"Most of them." She let go of the pendant, picked up her fork and went back to her meal. "Did I remember to tell you this is really good? I've been so busy eating it I might not have."

"Since you weren't gagging and choking, I figured you were okay with it. Save room for dessert, though. I bought brownies at the bakery while I was in town." He noticed she'd changed the subject. Was that on purpose?

"I love brownies, but I want to finish this, which means I'll be too full for dessert. Can we wait awhile?"

"Yes, ma'am. I'm flattered you like the stir-fry so much."

"It's great."

"Want the recipe?" He grinned at her.

"How about I just talk you into making it for me again sometime?"

"Love to."

"I look forward to it." She went back to eating.

He did, too, but he wanted to find out if the change of subject had been deliberate. "Do you miss living close to your family?"

She finished chewing and swallowed. "Sometimes, I guess." Then she shook her head. "At the risk of sounding awful, no, I don't really miss that. If we were in Billings right now, I could expect several texts tonight wanting info about my date. I'm thrilled that they don't even know you exist."

"Gonna keep me a secret?" He finished off his meal and set aside his plate.

"For now, if you don't mind. I love them all and they love me, but we're too enmeshed, at least in my estimation. I came to Sheridan to escape the lack of privacy and the constant expectations."

"A lot of privacy out here." Seductive privacy that was working on him the longer they sat within inches of each other. By turning his head a fraction, he could study her profile—her high, intelligent forehead, thick dark lashes, prominent cheekbones and plump lips, which he'd longed to taste ever since he'd had his first glimpse of them while lying under the sink.

"Yes, I like this a lot. Much better than a crowded restaurant." She scooped up her last bite and ate it.

"And no obligations."

She put down her plate and gazed at him. "I like that a lot, too."

"For example, just because I brought you out here to this extremely secluded place, fed you a good dinner and served you some excellent wine, you're not obliged to kiss me."

Her full mouth widened in a smile. "Really?"

"Scout's honor. And that's legit because I was a Boy Scout."

"That doesn't surprise me at all. Okay, then I'll point out that just because I showered, changed clothes and drove out here to meet you when I could have spent the evening watching a movie in my grubby old sweats, you're not obliged to kiss me, either."

"Now that's where you're wrong." He laid his hat on the blanket before reaching out to cup her cheek. Her skin felt so delicate that he lightened his touch. "I have a huge obligation after you made all those sacrifices." He rubbed his thumb gently over skin soft as a rose petal.

Her breath hitched. "It was nothing."

"That's not the way I heard it." He leaned closer and watched her eyes flutter closed and her lips part in invitation. "Sounds to me like you went to a lot of trouble to be here."

"On second thought, maybe I did."

"Let me make it up to you." His heart thundered as he brushed his mouth over her velvet lips. He could barely feel her hand as she slipped it around his neck, yet knowing she'd reached for him heated his blood.

He moaned and fit his lips to hers, pressing a little, then a little more. Her grip on his neck tightened a tiny bit. Slowly he began to explore with his tongue, savoring the warm, arousing taste of her. Her jaw slackened ever so slightly. Easy, easy…

Drawing back, he changed the angle, settling down more firmly this time and becoming bolder with his tongue. A tiny whimper, a quick gasp, and she surrendered completely, opening to him with a rush of passion that made him dizzy.

He rose to his knees and cradled her face in both hands. She mirrored him, gripping his shoulders as she balanced on her knees and turned fully into his kiss, her intensity matching his.

Breathing hard, he lifted his head. "We should probably—"

"I know." She gulped for air and leaned back, but she didn't let go of him. "This is crazy."

"Feels good, though."

"It does, but…" She closed her eyes and shook her head. "I think—" She sucked in a breath and let it out again. "I think we need to slow down."

"Agreed." He reminded himself he was in this for the long haul. He combed his fingers through her silky hair and resisted the urge to grip her head and kiss her again. "We met a few hours ago."

Letting go of him, she took another deep breath and settled back on her heels. "We'll deal with this sudden attraction like two intelligent adults."

"One intelligent adult. All my brain cells are swimming in testosterone right now so I don't qualify." But one thought did make it through his fevered brain. "I'm buying a truck tomorrow."

She stared at him. *"What?"*

"I'll have my own truck by tomorrow afternoon." He retrieved his hat and put it on.

"What's having your own truck got to do with anything?"

"It's a guy thing. I don't want to borrow the ranch truck every time we go out. Which reminds me. Are you free tomorrow night?" He sat back and winced at the sharp pinch of unforgiving denim on his privates.

"No, I'm not. I'll be camping at the Pryor Mountain Wild Horse Refuge so I can get more video of the mustangs."

"Oh." He hesitated. Asking her to change her plans seemed pushy, even for a guy who liked to seize the moment. "I've heard about that place. Never been out there, though. Sounds interesting." Maybe she'd agree to put it off. Tomorrow night was his window of opportunity because the following night was Cade's bachelor party. Then they were into the weekend wedding activities with the rehearsal Friday and the wedding Saturday.

"It's fascinating out there. I have a friend who works at the center and she keeps me posted on the herd's activities. Right now the horses are hanging out in an ideal location for the kind of footage I'm looking for."

"You probably need to grab that opportunity while you can." His chances of spending an evening with her anytime soon were growing dimmer by the minute.

"Right. I would have gone this afternoon except Lexi and Cade asked me to film the video for their folks and it had to be edited right away. I like to get out there in the late afternoon and set up camp, so I couldn't see that working out today."

"So how about this. What if I went with you?" It was a bold suggestion, but tough times called for tough measures.

She blinked. "Um, I'll be camping overnight."

"So you'd rather not?" He didn't want to push her. "Look, I realize that might not work for you. Like we've said, we just met." He hesitated. "I could bring my own tent."

"Do you have one?"

"No, but I'd have time to go into town and pick one up."

"That seems silly. Mine sleeps two."

Now there was an encouraging remark. He didn't think they'd spend the whole time sleeping but decided not to say so. "I'd be honored to be your Sherpa. I'm good at carrying things, setting up tents and building fires. I'd bring the food and do all the cooking. And I'll drive us there in my new truck." He was already picturing that it would be black.

"That makes no sense. The ranch is on the way to the refuge. If you come, I should just swing by and pick you up."

"That would be fine." He still needed to buy that truck, but maybe not tomorrow.

"I was planning to leave around four. The best times to film the horses are at dusk and dawn."

He thought about all the time that left in between but again decided to keep his mouth shut about it. Instead he offered her a way out of taking him along in case she had any second thoughts. "If I go along, I promise not to mess with your schedule for getting good videos. But if you'd rather go out there alone, I'll back off. I'd never want to interfere with your job."

She reached out and touched his cheek. "Don't back off. Persistence is sexy."

Capturing her hand, he turned his head so he could place a kiss in her palm.

She moaned softly and pulled her hand away. "And so are you. Let's go back before we both forget this is only our first date."

Chapter Five

Drew put the dirty dishes and anything food-related in the metal cooler while Austin smothered the fire. He told her the ice chest was fairly critter-proof and should be okay until he drove out with the ranch truck in a little while to haul everything back and make sure the fire was out.

"But we can take the blanket." He shook it out, folded it and handed it to her. "If you wouldn't mind holding it on the way back."

"Or I could sit on it. That might make more sense." She wasn't sure why he wanted to take the blanket when he was leaving the rest of the gear, but she'd go along with the plan.

"Actually, I want you to stuff it between us."

"You want me to… Oh, I get it." She managed not to laugh. "A barrier."

"The trip out here was painful, especially going over

bumps." He tugged on the brim of his hat. "Now that I've kissed you, the ride back will be even worse."

"I'm really glad I'm a girl."

He laughed. "Yes, ma'am, so am I. Let's go." He swung his leg over the ATV and sat down.

She climbed on after him and sandwiched the folded blanket between them. "I'll still need to hold on to you." She wrapped her arms around both the blanket and him. Not nearly as much fun as she'd had without the extra padding, but she didn't want to make the poor guy suffer.

"That's okay. I'm just trying to avoid having you pressed tight against my backside."

"What if I drove?"

"That would be worse."

She imagined his arms wrapped around her middle just below her breasts and her bottom nestled in the V of his legs. Her pulse kicked up a notch. "Guess so. Next time we do this you should probably just drive the truck out here and forget about the ATV."

"Next time we do this I don't plan to be in a constant state of arousal. Ready?"

"Y-yes." She managed to get the word out, but her brain had stalled on his last statement. She'd never met a person more goal-oriented than Austin.

She was beginning to understand what Cade meant. Being with Austin was a little like booking a ticket on a high-speed train and she could be in for a thrilling ride. She might regret allowing him to go along on this video trip because of all the ramifications, but she seriously doubted that he'd get in her way.

If anything, he might make things easier because he was more experienced at camping than she was. The more she thought about it, the more she looked forward to showing him something inspirational right here in

Wyoming. Those mustangs were descended from horses ridden by Spaniards looking for adventure two hundred years ago. That should appeal to him.

Mostly, though, she was excited about exploring a relationship with a man, both sexually and emotionally, without her family members knowing about it. They'd met and evaluated nearly everyone she'd dated except a few times when she'd only gone out with the guy once. Setting up this overnight camping trip with Austin seemed strange because he hadn't been vetted. But ultimately it felt liberating.

When they pulled up in front of the ranch house, she was very glad they hadn't continued to make out furiously on that blanket because Rosie and Herb sat on the front porch with a cowboy she didn't recognize.

Austin did, though. "Jonah, is that you? I thought you were driving over tomorrow!"

"Got off a day earlier so I just headed out." The cowboy ambled down the steps toward them.

"And why wouldn't you? We've gotta be more fun than the folks in Pinedale." Austin dismounted from the ATV and then helped her climb off.

"That's the truth, bro."

Drew left the blanket on the seat and turned to meet another returning foster son. His name sounded familiar but she'd heard so many recently that they were all blurring together.

Austin gestured toward the newcomer. "Drew Martinelli, I'd like you to meet Jonah Bridger, Zen master."

Jonah shook her hand. "Pleased to meet you, ma'am. Don't pay attention to that Zen stuff Austin's spouting. I'm not a master of anything. But Rosie and Herb tell me that you're the best videographer in Wyoming."

"That's stretching it, but it's nice to hear."

"Ah, she's just modest." Austin gave his foster brother a hug. "Like you are, bro. With all that meditating you used to do, you must be enlightened by now."

"'Fraid not. I've learned just enough to be dangerous."

"And to conduct Cade and Lexi's ceremony." Austin clapped him on the back. "I'm gonna get a kick out of that."

"Oh, right!" Drew remembered now. "You're the minister."

"With no church and no parishioners," Jonah said.

"So how does that work?" All Drew's relatives had been married in a church.

"I work at a dude ranch, and my boss wanted to offer weddings to our guests. He asked me if I'd be willing to get qualified to marry folks. You can apply online. It sounded like fun so I did it."

Austin nodded. "I can see how it would be fun being the person who launches a couple on their great adventure."

"Then you should get into it."

"Nope, not my thing. I have other plans in the hopper. But I look forward to seeing your performance on Saturday."

Drew realized that she'd heard Austin mention his future plans but he'd never been specific about them. She'd have to ask him about it tomorrow night. Right now, though, she needed to make her exit. These guys had some catching up to do, and at some point Austin had to drive back out to the clearing and gather the cookout gear.

She laid her hand on his arm. "Thanks for a great dinner. I'm going to head home." She glanced over at his brother. "Great to meet you, Jonah."

He touched the brim of his hat. "Same here, Drew."

She raised her voice. "Rosie and Herb, I'm going home. Have a good night."

"Come on up and sit for a while," Rosie called back. "Have some coffee."

"Thanks. I'll take a rain check." She turned back to Austin and smiled. "See you tomorrow afternoon."

"I'll walk you to your truck." He looked over at Jonah. "Be right back."

"Take your time."

She didn't bother to tell him that walking her to her truck, which was only a few yards away, was completely unnecessary. She suspected he'd want to open her door for her and give her a hand up. In truth, she was beginning to cherish that about him.

Once they'd reached the driver's side they had a small measure of privacy. She kept her voice low. "Are you sure you wouldn't rather stick around here tomorrow night and spend time with Jonah? You two seem fairly close."

"We lived in the same cabin once I was old enough to move out of the ranch house. He's a great guy and I'm glad he's here, but the answer is no, I wouldn't rather hang out here tomorrow. I want to be with you."

"All right." The intensity in his gaze made her heart race. "Then I'll see you at four."

He opened her door. "Don't bring any food. That'll be my contribution."

"Understood, but I'll ice up the chest so it's ready for the food. Having a chef along will be a treat."

He nudged back his hat and grinned. "Well, maybe food won't be my only contribution, come to think of it."

"Hey, don't go getting me hot and bothered."

"Do I?"

"You know you do."

"Good." He leaned down and gave her a quick kiss.

Then he helped her into the truck, closed the door and stepped back.

She had to get her keys from under the seat and when she looked out the window he was still there, feet braced apart, thumbs through his belt loops, looking amazing. She gave a little wave and he touched the brim of his hat.

Somehow she managed to start the engine and drive away even though her mind was completely occupied by the image of Austin standing in the driveway. She'd be sharing a small tent with that gorgeous cowboy within twenty-four hours and the concept left her breathless. It wasn't until she'd started down the dark ranch road that she realized she'd forgotten to turn on her headlights.

Austin climbed the steps to the porch where Jonah had resumed his seat next to Rosie. He and Herb each had a beer but his foster mom was sipping from a coffee mug that probably contained her favorite evening beverage, maybe her favorite beverage period—coffee laced with a little Baileys.

She lowered the mug to smile at him. "Did you have a good time?"

"We had a great time. Thank you for loaning me all that stuff. I'd better get back out there and pick it up, though. If I could borrow the ranch truck one more time, that should be it for a while."

Jonah put down his beer and stood. "We can take my truck. I wouldn't mind paying a visit to the back twenty."

"Hasn't changed much," Herb said. "Same scrub brush, same rocks around the perimeter."

"But it must be overgrown with weeds by now."

"It was a few months ago." Herb cradled his beer in both hands. "But this summer I started taking the academy kids out there for sleepovers. They've cleaned out the weeds."

"So that's why I didn't have much to do." Austin had raked a little but the place had looked as if it had been used regularly. Apparently the teens enrolled in the recently launched equine program would carry on some of the traditions the foster brothers had helped create.

"It's great to think of the kids enjoying the same things we did." Jonah walked over to join Austin before turning back to Rosie and Herb. "Listen, if you two want to hit the sack, you can leave my beer where it is. I'll come back to it after we finish up."

"We'll still be here," Rosie said. "Unless you boys dawdle."

"Then we'll see you soon." Austin walked with Jonah toward the barn where Jonah's beat-up truck was parked.

"Drew's pretty," Jonah said.

Austin chuckled. "That doesn't even begin to describe her."

"I know that, but I have to be careful. If I get too detailed, you might punch me."

"No, I wouldn't. I know you better than that. You don't poach."

"None of us ever did. I mean, think about it. I'll bet at one time or another all of us had a crush on Lexi. But once Cade made his move, that was it, hands off." He fished his keys out of his pocket. "I suppose you got the word that we're all considered part of the Thunder Mountain Brotherhood now."

"Cade told me. It's kind of nice, you know?"

"It is nice." Jonah climbed behind the wheel and Austin got into the passenger seat. Neither of them buckled up and they ignored the warning beeps as Jonah shoved the key into the ignition and turned it. "I won't lie. I was jealous of Cade, Damon and Finn."

"Yeah, most of us were."

"But imagine what it must have been like." Jonah put the truck in gear and drove past the front porch with a little friendly honk for Rosie and Herb. Then he headed down the narrow path to the campout clearing. "They were only thirteen. Hell, Finn was twelve. They didn't know there would be other foster boys eventually. No wonder they declared themselves blood brothers so they'd have something to hold on to. I can see how they'd be proud and protective of that status."

"I can, too." Austin settled back in the seat. "I decided to say thanks for including us instead of being a jerk about it."

"Same here. You know, I've missed this place."

"So have I, which is why I'm back."

"I'm thinking about it, too. Mom asked me if I'd like the caretaking job over at Matt's ranch. I'm considering it, but there are drawbacks."

"Yep. Nothing's really yours."

"I could handle that. Possessions aren't a big deal to me. But when Matt comes home and brings his fiancée, I'll feel like the butler."

Austin laughed. "How's your English accent?"

"Lousy. What he needs is a caretaker's cabin. Doesn't have to be fancy. I'd help put it up. If he'll agree to that, then I'll give my notice and move back here."

"And leave your dude ranch without a preacher man?"

"I'll make sure that's worked out before I leave." He glanced over at Austin. "Not to change the subject, but I'm changing the subject. I'm curious about Drew."

"What about her?"

"Mom and Dad said you've been home for all of two

days. I'll admit those muscles you acquired in New Zealand are impressive, but damn, that's fast work, even for someone as focused as you."

"I don't know what to tell you. This afternoon I was under the sink getting rid of a clog. Cade and Lexi came into the kitchen to grab a beer and then the videographer walked in. I scooted out from under the sink and saw my future."

"Your *future*? That sounds like something out of a movie. But then, you've been a dreamer ever since I've known you. The problem is, life doesn't work that way."

"Of course it doesn't if you just let the chips fall. I didn't get to New Zealand by hoping that some magical event would take me there. I worked my ass off, saved my money and made it happen."

"True, but—"

"Drew is no different. Maybe she's not the right one for me, but I have a gut feeling she is. I didn't expect to find her two days after I landed in Wyoming, but what if that's my reward for making the decision to move back and look for a wife?"

"Oh, jeez. You've known her since sometime this afternoon and you already think you'll end up marrying her? What's wrong with you?"

"I know it sounds crazy."

"Yes, it absolutely does. I'm thinking the water in New Zealand has altered your brain chemistry."

"There's nothing wrong with my brain chemistry."

Jonah sighed. "You're not a competent judge of that. When we get back to the house, we're going to have some beers while I convince you to slow down and take stock. Oh, and whatever you do, don't have sex with her. It's impossible to think clearly when you're doing the horizontal mambo with someone. Which reminds me, what was the deal with that blanket wedged between you two on the ATV?"

"We were just goofing around." Austin smiled and decided not to mention the plan for tomorrow night.

Chapter Six

Underwear. Drew stared into her dresser drawer, having a stupid debate with herself. She had some silky panties and bras but they weren't as comfortable as cotton for hiking. They didn't breathe.

But her breathable cotton was white and made her look like a jock. Which she was. Except with the guys she'd dated in Billings, she'd tried to present a different image. That was why she had silk and lace undies in black, red and purple. Maybe that was the reason she hadn't clicked with any of those men. She'd been trying to be someone different.

She glanced at the clock on her bedroom wall. The truck was loaded. She'd showered and shaved her legs with a new razor. All she had to do was get dressed and throw a change of clothes in a duffel and she'd be good to go.

Finally, she grabbed two pairs of cotton panties and two cotton sports bras, one set to put on now and the other to toss in the duffel. She didn't know why she'd spent so much time thinking about it. This was who she was. In fact, she should get rid of the others, bag them up and donate them to charity.

If Austin had a negative reaction to her utilitarian underwear he wasn't someone she cared to spend time with. That would be good to know before they had sex.

When she left her apartment and got into her truck, she had her hair in a ponytail that was pulled through a forest green Rocky Mountain College baseball cap. She'd tucked her tan long-sleeved shirt into some old jeans that allowed her to move easily. She wore her necklace under her shirt with the pendant inside her bra.

Heavy socks and a sturdy pair of hiking boots finished off an outfit that wasn't the least bit glamorous. She hadn't talked to him about footwear. Maybe she should have.

She drove over to the ranch to get Austin. When he walked out to meet her carrying a duffel and a couple of bags from the grocery store, he looked amazing as always in a yoked shirt, brown Stetson and jeans that fit him like a glove. But he was wearing cowboy boots. She should have warned him not to.

She managed to get out of the truck before he came around to open the door. His chivalry was fun and all, but it could slow them down and she didn't want to waste any time getting out to the refuge. "Do you have any hiking boots to wear instead?"

"Not really."

"You didn't hike in New Zealand?"

"No, ma'am. The idea was to ride the trail, not hike it."

"Sorry. We should have talked about this. We'll be parking next to the road and then hiking in to set up camp. It's more than a mile. To film the horses, we'll have to hike some more. Do you have anything else? Running shoes?"

"I have an old grungy pair, but I hate to—"

"You should go put those on while I load the food in the ice chest." She could tell he didn't like the idea. "Really, I'm serious. We could end up hiking a couple of miles to find the horses, maybe more. You'll be miserable in those boots."

"All right." He handed her the bags of food and his duffel. "Be right back."

She let down the tailgate, crawled into the truck bed and loaded the ice chest with the food he'd brought. The supplies included another bottle of the wine they'd had the night before. She had to admit having a guy provide a gourmet meal in a campground setting was arousing in its own way.

She'd finished stashing the food and had closed the tailgate when he came back down the steps in a pair of running shoes that might have been white once but were now a sad-looking gray. They weren't snazzy like his boots but they'd serve him better.

"I'm glad you have those," she said as he approached.

"It's a wonder I still do. They're close to ten years old. I bought them so I could run track in high school."

"Why would a cowboy who doesn't hike want to run track?"

"There was this girl on the team, and I—"

"Okay, never mind." Then she had another thought. "Are you pretending to be interested in these horses? Because I think they're super cool but if you're only going along because of the tent-sharing possibility, then we should rethink this."

He met her gaze. "The tent-sharing element is a huge draw. But I also want to see the mustangs. Before I went to bed last night I used Mom's computer and looked up their history. Exciting stuff."

"Isn't it?" She was pleased that he'd taken the time to research. "They've survived against all odds and that says something about their resilience."

"I'm all about resilience."

Considering his background, he'd have to be. "Then let's go find some Pryor Mountain mustangs." She walked around to the driver's side.

"You bet." He followed her.

Although his insistence on gentlemanly behavior made her want to giggle, she accepted his help getting in. "Thank you."

"My pleasure." He touched the brim of his hat with the tips of his fingers before jogging around the front of the truck and climbing in. "Let's go."

She started the engine and pulled away from the ranch house. "I have a hypothetical question."

"Shoot."

"Let's say that we're being chased by a bear while we're out on the trail and we manage to reach the truck."

"First of all, never try to outrun a bear."

"I actually know that. All right, something else is chasing us. A cougar."

"Can't outrun them, either. And they're really shy so chances are you won't see one, let alone be chased."

"Pretend it's a female who thinks we're threatening her kittens. And she's a little slow. We've managed to reach the truck. Are you with me so far?"

He grinned at her. "I can't wait to see how this turns out."

"How would you handle things at that point?"

"Simple. I'd distract the cougar while you got in the truck."

She was glad to hear he wouldn't insist on opening her door first. "But that's not logical. If we split up and I head for the driver's side and you head for the passenger side, we both have a good chance of reaching safety before the cougar attacks."

"Or the cougar could decide to follow you and I'd be safe and you'd be toast. I'm not taking that chance."

He said it with such certainty that she had no doubt he would react that way. "You'd risk your life for someone you barely know?"

"I'd argue the term *barely know*, but yes, I would. My dad had never met that family he rescued."

"And he made an incredibly selfless sacrifice. Most people wouldn't have. But he was also a trained professional dedicated to that job. We're just out on a camping trip together. You're not responsible for my safety." From the corner of her eye she could see he was smiling. "What?"

"I could ask where this is coming from, but I think I know since your hypothetical question popped up right after I helped you into your truck. You've never dated a cowboy before, have you?"

"No."

"Then maybe I should explain how we operate. We open doors for ladies. We hold their chairs and help them on with their coats. That's surface stuff, but we'll also fight off the cougar if it becomes necessary." He glanced at her and shrugged. "It's what we do."

"That's—"

"Old-fashioned, I know. And you're an independent woman who can open her own door and wants to give the guy you're with a chance to outrun the cougar. I get that."

"I was going to say, 'that's nice.'"

"Yeah?"

"Yeah. I am an independent woman, at least that's my goal, and obviously I can open my own door. I'd feel horrible if I got away from the cougar and you didn't. But knowing you are willing to throw yourself into the breach on my account is nice. More than nice. If that's how cowboys operate, I'm a fan."

"Excellent news." He settled back with a sigh. "I see you left your pendant at home."

"No, I didn't."

"Where is it?"

"Under my shirt. That works better for hiking and filming."

He nodded. "Makes sense."

After that they rode in companionable silence until they reached the outskirts of town. Well, maybe *companionable silence* wasn't the right description because that implied a relaxed mood. Perhaps *alert silence* was more accurate, at least on her part. Once they stopped talking she became aware of how much space he occupied, both emotionally and physically.

She'd had other guys in her passenger seat before but Austin affected her in ways no one else did. He had presence. Maybe it was the strong profile and the Stetson, or the broad shoulders and the massive chest. It could be his aftershave, which reminded her that he knew how to kiss. She wanted to keep looking at him, although she didn't or they'd be in a ditch by now.

His thigh was within touching distance and so was his muscled biceps. She longed to reach over and— Nope, not going there. She'd do well to come up with another topic of conversation before she embarrassed herself.

Driving through town on the way to the interstate reminded her that he'd planned to buy a truck. That should be a safe topic. "Did you go vehicle shopping today?"

"No, ma'am. Decided to go tomorrow, instead. Jonah and I helped Lexi string minilights in the rafters of the barn."

"That will be beautiful for the ceremony. I can't wait to see how the lights look when we do the run-through on Friday night."

"And that will only give you part of the effect. The flowers won't go in until Saturday, although Cade realized the wall vases and velvet bows have to be out of reach of the horses or they'll eat them."

Drew laughed and felt her sexual tension ease somewhat. "I'm sure Cade and Lexi would hate that but it would make a funny video."

"Speaking of videos, Lexi said she loves the one you did of her and Cade."

"I know she does and that thrills me. She sent me a glowing email. Honestly, I would have had to work hard to make a bad video of those two. They're so relaxed with each other and so in love. I guess that's what comes from knowing someone for half your life."

"Then there are couples like Rosie and Herb. Rosie moved here from Illinois to take a job in social services. They met in the checkout line at the grocery store. A month later they were married."

"I'll bet that's unusual, though."

"Maybe. But my parents had only known each other for about six months. My mom said my dad was the love of her life."

Drew glanced over and he was staring out the window. "They sound like terrific people, Austin. I wish they hadn't been taken away from you."

"So do I." He turned back to her and his expression was calm. "But Rosie and Herb are terrific people, too. I'm a lucky guy."

"When you put it like that, yes, you are. And you have a wonderful home to come back to. By the way, you said something to Jonah last night about your future plans. Have you already applied for a job somewhere?"

"I haven't yet, but if I can swing it, I want to go into business for myself. I paid close attention to how the New Zealand outfit ran things and I figure I can handle something similar over here."

"Of course you can!" This was a topic she could dig into. "And I'm here to tell you that self-employment is a great way to go."

"Any advice on creating a website?"

"Sure. I can help you with that." She loved the idea of someone starting a business and Austin seemed like the perfect person to do it. He was personable and had four years of valuable experience to guide him. But his real gift was the focus he would bring to the project.

As they exited the interstate onto the two-lane road that would take them into Bighorn Canyon, Austin described his plans for trailering horses into the canyon for two- and three-day trail rides.

"That sounds fabulous. If you want, I could go along on one of the first rides and shoot video you could use for the website."

"Great idea. I'd pay, you of course."

"Or how about this? Only snippets will go on the website, but I could offer to sell the full video to your trail riders. I'm sure they'd buy it as a souvenir. Then you wouldn't have to come out of pocket."

"Brilliant strategy. Thank you. Now I wish it was May instead of August. There's no way I can get this up and running before winter weather hits."

"But you can use the coming months to put everything in place so you're ready by next May."

"And arrange for a business loan. I should probably apply for a bartending job at Scruffy's for the winter months, too. When I was saving for New Zealand I worked as a waiter until I was old enough to bartend. That gig was way better money. The tips were awesome."

"I'll bet." A bartender who looked like Austin would get tipped well by any women who stopped by Scruffy's. "It's smart of you to launch your business here in Sheridan, where you know so many people. Being connected to Rosie and Herb will give you a huge PR boost."

"I never considered doing it anywhere else. This is home. I'm here to stay."

"Wouldn't you like to travel some more?"

"Maybe someday. For now, I have things to do here and I plan to concentrate on that."

"Well, if there's any way I can help, just let me know. I'm no expert, but I've learned a little about promotion. Then there's bookkeeping and taxes to think about and I can offer some suggestions there."

"Excellent. I appreciate it. I want this to work."

"I'm sure it will." She was surprised that he wasn't including more travel in his immediate vision of the future after experiencing a wonderful place like New Zealand. But maybe that was the secret to his success. He set himself a goal and refused to be distracted until he'd achieved it.

Which reminded her that she hadn't clearly identified long-term goals for herself. When her grandmother had given her the necklace, she'd also given her three words of advice—*Follow your heart*. Drew had hoped getting away from her family would help her do that, but so far she was still living one day at a time.

"I just saw a couple of mule deer scamper up that hillside." Austin peered out the side window. "No cougars, though. Sorry."

"Yeah, yeah, yeah. I know that was a lame example. I've never seen one out here, but I know they're around. Others have reported sightings."

"Just don't run."

"Oh, I won't. Because then you'll end up being mauled and it'll be my fault." She watched for the rock outcroppings that she used as a marker. "We'll be stopping in another mile or so. I get so excited when one of the herds is spotted within a couple of miles of my favorite camping spot. The folks who are monitoring them emailed me today. The horses are still there."

"How often do you make this trip?"

"This is my third time in this particular area but I've camped in other places, so I guess it's seven visits, total. I don't always get good footage. Depends on the horses and the weather. But it's supposed to stay clear through tomorrow."

"I have a feeling this will be a good outing."

She gave him a quick smile. "Hope so." She slowed down and eased the truck to the right shoulder of the road. "We'll take the tent in first and set that up to claim our campsite. I usually haul my duffel along and leave that in the tent, too. Nobody will bother it."

"That works for me." He unbuckled his seat belt and opened the door.

"Austin." She laid a hand on his arm.

"What?"

"I love your cowboy manners, but don't come around and open my door for me. We're close to the road and there's no reason for both of us to be over there."

He let out a breath. "When you're right, you're right. But be careful."

"I will. I'll meet you out there. Go ahead and pull the tent out if you want." She let a truck go by before quickly getting out and walking back to him.

Instead of lowering the tailgate and getting the tent as she'd suggested, he stood by the back bumper and watched her approach as if his vigilance would prevent her from getting run over. He was so manly, so strong and sure of himself that she almost believed he could protect her by keeping her in view.

As her gaze locked with his, she felt a magnetic, sensual tug. She wanted this man and he most definitely wanted her. For one brief moment she considered abandoning her plan to film the mustangs. Her breath caught. That she'd even think such a thing was a wake-up call.

She'd enthusiastically leaped to support his dreams yet she hadn't solidified her own. She needed to be careful.

Chapter Seven

Austin nominated himself to lug the tent, two blankets and a couple of self-inflating camping mattresses to the campsite. Drew wore her backpack full of camera equipment and carried both duffels as she led the way. As he followed her along a faint path, he kept thinking they'd be there any minute but she'd told him the truth about hiking in a ways.

Bringing the food in later would mean another long walk out to the road and back, but at least they wouldn't be able to hear traffic during the night. So far he'd loved every minute of this trip—minus the dorky shoes—and he knew why. For the first time he was beginning a relationship that had the potential to become so much more.

Prior to leaving for New Zealand, he'd never felt right making long-term promises to women because he'd known he would leave. Dating in New Zealand had been the same story—no commitment. That wasn't his style. He craved meaning in his life and especially in his love life.

Drew had worn the pendant from her grandmother again today and he took that loyalty as a good sign. He could never get serious about a woman who didn't care deeply. Drew obviously did.

"Here we are!" She dropped both duffels and took off her backpack as they stood in a little grassy clearing ringed with tall pines. A scattering of wildflowers, including some yellow daisies and purple lupines, gave the area a nice splash of color. Charred pieces of firewood in a small, stone-lined pit indicated that others had been here. She pointed to it. "I built that and I dragged the log out of the forest so there's a place to sit."

"Nice job." He lowered the tent and the mattresses to the ground and put the blankets on top.

"We should probably collect some firewood before we head off to find the horses. Sometimes I've skipped doing that and FYI, it's not easy to find kindling in a dark forest."

"That used to be one of our mantras in New Zealand. *Firewood before food.*"

"We don't need it for dinner, though. Like I mentioned last night, I have a camp stove. But I like a fire to signal other campers that we're here."

"Then we need to get busy." He eyed the long nylon bag containing the tent. It was an older dome model and he remembered struggling with the bendable supports when he'd had one years ago. "I'll bet you've had some fun times setting the tent up by yourself."

She laughed. "I have, but I'm used to it by now." She walked over and loosened the nylon cord holding the top of the bag. "If you want to go look for firewood, I'll set it up."

He wasn't about to go off and leave her to do it alone. He'd promised to be an asset and despite what she'd said about being used to the process, it would go faster with two people. "I'll help."

"Okay, but I have to warn you. This tent has a unique personality. She responds better to coaxing than yelling."

"*She*? Your tent has a gender?"

"Of course. Doesn't yours?"

"I sold mine before I left New Zealand but I never considered it male or female."

"Which means you didn't name it, either."

He stuck his thumbs in his belt loops. "Can't say as I did, but I like the idea. Now I wish I had. Are you telling me this tent has a name?"

"She does. Meet Hestia, the Greek goddess of the hearth."

"I like it. Hestia, I look forward to spending time with you."

"Now, see? That's exactly the right attitude." Drew pulled a blue tent out of the bag. "This will go just fine."

A minute into the job, he was cursing under his breath as he wrestled with the plastic supports. He had to be careful because if he broke one, they'd have a mess. "Hestia's not cooperating."

"I hear you cussing over there. You need to speak nicely to her." Drew began murmuring sweet nothings to the tent, and damned if they didn't get the thing set up a lot quicker.

They worked together to unroll the mattresses and spread out the blankets. Neither of them spoke and he wondered if she was thinking what he was. They were making the bed they were planning to share.

At last they were done. He stood and brushed off his knees. She did the same. They had created a temporary home that would shelter them during the night and provide a place for…he glanced over at Drew and she was looking right back at him. The air between them seemed to vibrate.

Taking a deep breath, she broke eye contact. "You can put our duffels inside and zip it up tight. I need to go back to the truck. I meant to bring my little first aid kit and I left it in the console."

"I can get it."

"That's okay. I will. How about collecting the firewood while I'm gone? I'll bring the hatchet from the truck. Might as well have everything here except the food." The message in her dark eyes was clear. *Let's take a break.*

He doubted she needed that first aid kit but if she went after it she could spend the time cooling down. He'd use the separation to do the same. "I'll see what I can find. Meet you back here."

Turning away from her, he walked toward the tree line. He'd promised her that he wouldn't interfere with her primary mission, to get video of the Pryor Mountain horses. If he screwed that up, then he'd ruin any chance they had of transforming this attraction into something special.

Years ago, he'd learned the value of foregoing short-term gain for long-term reward. He wanted to kiss her in the worst way, had wanted to ever since she'd pulled into the driveway at Thunder Mountain. He'd successfully controlled the urge. He didn't want her to think that all he cared about was getting physical.

That wasn't true. She was easy to talk to and the drive out here had been fun, although he'd spent some time thinking about what they'd likely be doing tonight. Now that they had a tent and a bed, the concept was more vivid than ever. But the mustangs had to be first on the list.

After loading up his arms with small branches, he found a big one and dragged that behind him as he returned to camp. She wasn't back yet but he hadn't expected her to be. Gathering wood hadn't taken long.

Putting the duffels in the tent wouldn't, either, but he did that next and zipped it closed. Too bad he didn't have that hatchet yet. He could work off some tension chopping wood.

When he saw her coming down the trail toward him, his pulse kicked into high gear. Everything about her appealed to him. He liked the graceful way she moved and the mellow tone of her voice. He liked her laughter and her easy way with others. He liked the way she looked in her Rocky Mountain College baseball cap.

She gave him a smile as she approached and he returned it. He thought about walking to meet her but changed his mind and stayed where he was. For the next few hours, he would take his cues from her.

"I see you got the firewood. That big piece should last us a week."

"I'll chop it up for the next campers. That's an interesting combination, a hatchet in one hand and a first aid kit in the other."

"I'm hoping we only have to make use of the hatchet." She put it near the pile of kindling he'd gathered. "I'll take this with us, though." Walking over to her backpack, she unzipped a pocket and tucked the first aid kit inside. "For one thing, it has bug bite cream." She picked up the backpack by its straps.

"Why not let me carry that?"

She paused to glance at him. "I guess you did say you'd be my Sherpa. Okay, thanks." She took a small camcorder out of the front section. "I want to leave this out for quick shots, in case we come upon something unexpectedly."

"Like a cougar."

"Like that." She grinned. "All joking aside, getting footage of a cougar would be awesome. But they're so elusive that chances are slim."

"I've never seen one, either, and I've lived here most of my life." He slipped the straps over his shoulders and adjusted them. "Ready?"

She nodded. "The trail's over this way." She gestured toward a break in the trees. "It's faint and disappears when we go over rocks, so don't lag behind. I'll be concentrating on what's ahead of us and if you stop to look at something I could be out of sight before you realize it."

"I plan to stick like glue." He matched her brisk pace as they crossed the clearing.

"And let's keep talking to a minimum. The more noise we make, the less wildlife we'll see."

"Understood." He fell in behind her on the narrow trail and focused on keeping her in sight. It wasn't a chore. He enjoyed watching her confident strides as they walked along the path.

Speaking of walking, or *hiking*, a word that made it sound more like a manly sport, he concluded it wasn't his thing. There were reasons cowboys didn't hike and he was discovering them all today.

The mountain air smelled piney and fresh like he was used to, but there was something missing. He finally figured out it was the scent of oiled leather and horse sweat. He heard birds twittering like normal, but there was no clop, clop of hooves and the occasional snorting and blowing.

Another thing about this hiking business—it was slow as molasses. It took them forever to wind through the forest, cross a meadow, pick up the trail on the other side and work their way through the trees again. A horse could have made it in less than half the time.

Besides, the view from the ground was terrible compared to the vista he was used to. Elevated by a horse about sixteen hands high, he'd have a much better idea where they were headed and probably catch a breeze easier, too.

He adjusted the straps on the backpack again. It wasn't that heavy, but it was cumbersome. If he had a horse, the equipment could be strapped behind the saddle or tucked into saddlebags.

He suspected trail rides weren't allowed in the refuge, though. Bringing domesticated horses in contact with wild ones might not be a great idea. That didn't keep him from longing for a sturdy mount and his totally broken-in saddle. He'd shipped it over to New Zealand and shipped it back. It was just that important.

But he'd gotten himself into this situation because of the fine-looking woman walking ahead of him, her glossy dark ponytail bobbing with each step. He didn't regret asking to go along on this trip considering he had a good chance of seeing wild horses and spending quality time with Drew.

But he could say with complete assurance that he was not, and probably never would be, a hiker. She was, though. Maybe if he had boots like hers, with all that tread—nah, wouldn't help. He'd still be walking instead of riding.

His mom used to say she felt a little closer to heaven on the back of a horse. So did he. A little closer to her, too, now that he thought about it. He couldn't remember his first ride because she'd held him in front of her before he was a year old. He had pictures to prove it.

A soft flapping noise and the way his shoe was slipping made him glance down. Great. One of his shoelaces had come untied. He was out of practice wearing running shoes and he'd forgotten to tie an extra knot.

That was one of the things he loved about cowboy boots—no laces. They always looked good, too. Even old scuffed ones did because they had character. Old running shoes just looked nasty.

He dropped to one knee and called out to Drew. "Hang on a sec. I need to tie my—"

"Shh." She stopped walking but didn't turn around. "I hear them. And they're close."

He stopped tying his shoe to listen. If he'd been paying attention he would have heard them, too. His breath caught when he spotted dark shapes walking through the trees, pine needles crunching and branches cracking under their hooves. He estimated the mustangs were only about thirty feet ahead of them and closing.

"We need to move away," Drew said in a low voice as she edged off the trail and to the right. But she had her camcorder pointed at the dark shapes threading their way through the forest on their left. "We're supposed to maintain a one-hundred-foot distance."

"Did anybody tell them that?" But he backed off, too, all the while keeping an eye on his dangling shoelace. If he tripped and went down, all hell would break loose. Even trained horses might bolt at a sudden loud crash.

The dappled shade made it tough to identify color but he thought they were mostly bays. Maybe a buckskin or two. There was a gray bringing up the rear. He counted ten but might have missed some. His heart hammered. He'd been around horses all his life but he'd never seen a wild one.

These animals had never felt the weight of a saddle,

let alone the weight of a person. Instead of human rules, they obeyed the rules of the herd in exchange for protection and companionship. They ate what they could forage. They mated and gave birth with no interference from humans.

Seeing them in their natural state affected him on a gut level that likely would make a difference in the way he thought about horses for the rest of his life. Now that he'd had his first glimpse, he'd be back and he'd have on good hiking boots. If he'd been riding instead of walking, the experience might never have happened. Even if it had, it wouldn't have been nearly this elemental. Maybe hiking wasn't so bad, after all.

Drew didn't switch off her camcorder until the gray horse bringing up the rear was out of sight. "They might be headed toward the meadow we just left." Her voice trembled with excitement. "At first I thought I recognized some of them, but now I think this is a band I haven't filmed yet, which is awesome. We might catch them grazing if we backtrack."

"Let's do it. Just have to tie my shoelace." He quickly made a double knot and did the same with the other one. "Okay. Go."

Instead of immediately taking off down the trail, she paused to gaze up at him, her dark eyes gleaming with anticipation. "Cool, huh?"

"*Very* cool. I wouldn't have missed it for the world. Thank you."

"I was hoping you'd love them."

"I do. They're amazing."

"I know." With a quick smile, she turned and started off, her ponytail swinging.

As he followed her, the warm emotion gripping him had a little to do with sexual attraction but a lot more to do with friendship. He and Drew were bonding over their shared appreciation for these mustangs. He let out a slow breath. At last he had the freedom to connect with a woman without thinking he was liable to mess up her life.

Chapter Eight

Because the lighting had been funky when Drew had tried to get footage of the horses moving through the trees, she didn't think she had much of value. But if the herd stopped to graze in the meadow she and Austin had just hiked across, she might get lucky.

Adrenaline pumped through her system, partly because these weren't the horses she'd been expecting. Filming old friends was great, but having a chance to get shots of a different band would be more exciting. Assuming she got some worth looking at, she'd show them to the experts at the Pryor Mountain center in Lovell. Those folks had named and could identify nearly every mustang in the area.

She was also sharing Austin's high following his first encounter. She hadn't realized this trip was a litmus test. She couldn't be friends, let alone lovers, with someone who didn't respect and admire these wild mustangs, which symbolized freedom to her. His dazzled expression had told her all she needed to know.

When they were within ten yards of the meadow, she paused, turned around and motioned him closer. "i need to unload my tripod and my larger camera before we leave the cover of the trees," she murmured. "If they're out there, the less we move and make noise, the better. The breeze is blowing in our direction, which helps."

He eased the pack from his shoulders. "Take what you need."

Maybe if he hadn't said it so softly she wouldn't have had a sudden, vivid image of those words uttered in a different context and a different place, like in their shared tent. Heat scorched her body and she knew her cheeks must be red. "Thanks."

She kept her head down as she slowly unzipped the backpack. The rasp of the zipper took on erotic meaning in the X-rated movie playing in her head. Wrapping her hand around the tripod did, too.

Good grief, why did she have to be blindsided by lust *now*? She'd made it through the drive here and the tent setup, although she'd had to walk off some tension after that activity. Yes, the thrill of seeing the horses moving through the trees so close to them had stirred her blood.

But she'd fought and won the battle with her libido, which had urged her to kiss him afterward. Why had her mind betrayed her during this critical moment when she needed to focus?

He leaned down so his mouth was close to her ear. "Are you okay?"

His warm breath sent her pulse skyrocketing and she gulped for air. "Sure. Why?"

"You're panting."

More warm breath tickled her earlobe, which she'd never realized was an erogenous zone. "Just excited."

"I get that, but you're shaking, too. Did you eat today?"

"Yes." She pulled her tripod out of the backpack and nearly dropped it on his foot. She fumbled it like a football and eventually he gently took it from her.

He lowered the backpack to the ground and laid the tripod on top. "Let's go where we can talk." Taking her by the hand, he led her back down the path.

Every step of the way she wondered what in the world she could say to him that wouldn't make things worse.

When they were a few yards away from where they'd been standing, he grasped her shoulders and gave her a searching glance. "Something's wrong. I don't know if it's low blood sugar or what, but you're *not* okay. Whatever it is, I want to help."

She managed to hold back a bubble of hysterical laughter.

"You're turning red as a lobster. Don't be embarrassed. Just tell me." His grip tightened. "Do you need medication of some kind? Is that why you went back for the first aid kit? Are you allergic to something out here?"

She took a shaky breath. "It's you."

"Me?" He let go of her and stepped back, frowning. "Is it my aftershave? That can't be right because it's the same one I had on last night."

"It's stupid, but suddenly all I can think about is… kissing…you." She was thinking of way more than that but she'd decided against a full reveal.

Slowly his frown disappeared and he began to smile. "I don't call that stupid."

"Yes, it is. The horses are probably out there in the meadow, posing for their close-up, and I'm fantasizing about having sex with you." She clapped a hand over her mouth.

His smile widened. "More than kissing, then."

"I don't want to talk about it. That won't help and I *really* want to get some good video of those mustangs."

Hooking his thumbs in his belt loops, he took a long, slow breath before gazing at her, all teasing gone from his expression. "I want you to get that footage, too. If my being here ruins it for you, that's not good."

"It's not your fault." The concern in his eyes helped settle her down. He didn't want to be a distraction, and that counted for a lot. "Let's try it again, only I'll be in charge of the backpack and the equipment from now on. That should work better."

"Maybe I should cut through the trees and pick up the trail on the other side of the meadow. I'm sure I can find it and then I'll be out of your way."

"But you want to see the horses, too."

"I'll gladly give that up if I can solve your problem by leaving."

"I don't want you to leave. Maybe admitting my issues was half the battle because I'm calmer now. But FYI, if you need to communicate quietly, don't murmur in my ear. Apparently, that gets me hot."

His mouth twitched as if he wanted to smile but was working hard not to. "What should I do, then?"

"Touch me on the shoulder and mouth the words. I'm pretty good at reading lips."

He ducked his head and cleared his throat. "Got it."

"I don't blame you for wanting to laugh. It's pretty funny."

"Yes, ma'am." He looked up. "But in a good way. Ready to go?"

"Yes. I'll lead."

"Yes, ma'am."

She walked briskly toward her backpack and took out what she needed before closing it up and sliding the straps over her shoulders. Once she'd adjusted them, the familiar weight of the pack helped her feel more in charge. She glanced at Austin. "Let's see if they waited for us."

He smiled and mouthed *okay.*

At the edge of the trees, she eased out into the open and sucked in a quick breath. The mustangs were peacefully grazing about forty yards away a little to her right. The light was perfect, bringing out the gem-like green of the pines to form a nice background, especially for the gray horse. The breeze blowing toward her carried her scent away while delicately ruffling a mane here, a tail there. She was in video heaven.

Mounting her camcorder with as little noise as possible, she crouched down and panned slowly across the herd. The gray stopped eating, lifted its head and surveyed the meadow. She identified him as the stallion and that was confirmed as he began to circle the herd. He'd seen her.

Slowly she picked up her tripod and backed toward the trees. She'd become the uninvited guest at the dinner hour. They deserved to eat in peace.

She'd barely stepped into the shade when Austin tapped her on the shoulder. She turned and he pointed to her right, at the edge of the meadow. She'd been so focused on the horses and so certain that she was the harmless intruder that she'd missed the threatening one.

Creeping toward the herd, using low bushes as temporary cover and the breeze to hide its scent, was a cougar. Drew quickly removed the tripod and trained her camera on the cat. Excitement over her first sighting vied with dread for the horses, especially the small buckskin that seemed to be the cougar's target. As an observer of nature and a friend to all creatures, she couldn't intervene. The cougar had to eat and the mustang was prey.

Restlessly circling the herd, the stallion obviously sensed danger but couldn't identify the source. Then the breeze shifted. The stallion's nostrils flared and he trumpeted a warning. The cat leaped and missed the buckskin. Before the cougar could gather itself to try again, the herd took off at a dead run, their thundering hooves making the ground shake as they crashed through the trees on the far side of the meadow.

Drew recorded their flight. After they were gone, she panned the area for any sign of the cat and found nothing. Not surprising.

Austin stood next to her, gazing out at the empty meadow. "I've never seen anything like that."

"Quite a drama." She glanced over at him. "Which one did you root for?"

"The animal most determined to succeed."

How like him to answer that way. She really was starting to know who he was. "I'm not sure which one qualifies. The cougar had it won and then the breeze shifted."

"Yes, ma'am, but that stallion was on his game. He might not have smelled that cat but he knew something wasn't right."

"Because I was out there."

"I don't think you were an issue. I was watching him and he wasn't paying much attention to you. Some animals seem to know when they're in a protected area. He might not have let you walk right up to him, but I don't think humans worry him."

"I thought my being there was why he started circling the herd."

Austin shook his head. "Maybe, but that's not how I

saw it. The cougar showed up right after you went out there. As it started stalking the herd, the little birds that had been flitting around in the bushes got quiet and then they flew away."

"I didn't notice that."

"I'll bet the stallion did. He gets my vote as the most focused. The cat lost its advantage by being too cautious in the approach and waiting too long to spring."

She couldn't help smiling at that. "Is there a slight chance you identified with the stallion?"

"Yes, ma'am." He flashed her a charming, Austin-style grin. "Every cowboy identifies with stallions." He paused. "So what next? Want to track them? Shouldn't be too hard with the way they tore out of here."

She glanced up at the sky. "We're losing light."

"That's a fact."

"And when I was packing the food I noticed you brought another bottle of the New Zealand wine."

"That's another fact. Are you saying you'd like to go back to the campsite and settle in?"

"I'm saying exactly that. But, Austin…"

"What, pretty lady?"

"About the way I reacted a little while ago? I don't want you to get the idea that I'm some desperate—"

"Whoa, whoa. I don't see desperate. I see sensual and giving."

"Thank you. I like that description." She unzipped her backpack. "Let's get going. We need to haul in our food before it gets dark."

His gaze was warm. "Looks like it'll be a pleasure camping with you, ma'am."

"Ditto, Austin." She liked the way they could talk things out. Her small meltdown in the forest could have become a big deal if he hadn't gently put her back on course.

After she'd loaded her equipment into the backpack, he offered to carry it and promised not to murmur in her ear. Smiling, she turned over the pack. She didn't need to be in charge of the expedition anymore.

She had some video gems, though. She wouldn't use battery life to review what she'd taken but no question she'd struck gold. Although her meltdown had caused a minor delay, she'd been on hand to film a cougar's failed attempt to kill a mustang.

If she'd appeared in the meadow ten minutes earlier, everything could have been different. She'd worried about Austin being a distraction. He was, but she couldn't fault him for it any more than she could fault him for being gorgeous. He also might be her good luck charm, someone who helped make things happen.

The hike back took less time than the hike out because she wasn't looking for filming opportunities. Once they arrived, Austin stowed her pack in the tent and they started down the path to the road. The exercise during the day had left her so hungry her stomach was growling.

After all her solo camping, she had to admit having a strong guy around to carry things was nice. He lifted the ice chest out of the truck as if it weighed nothing. Then he set the camp stove and the lantern on top and said he could take it all.

Without help, she usually ended up making two trips to carry the camping gear and another two for the food and cookware. Having Austin along meant they'd brought more stuff, but it also meant fewer trips. She reached into the truck bed for a canvas drawstring bag of nonperishables and another one with her cookware and dishes.

Neither weighed much so she also grabbed the plastic

trash bag she'd stashed a couple of pillows in. She always brought one when she was camping. Camping mattresses worked okay but she hadn't met an inflatable pillow yet that suited her.

"What's the plan for after dinner?" He asked it so innocently that it didn't seem like a leading question.

But she was holding some of their bedding so she wasn't sure. She glanced over her shoulder. "You'll have to be more specific."

His blue eyes darkened. "I do believe you've tuned into the sexy channel again."

"Maybe." She left the bags on the tailgate and turned to face him. "Have you?"

"I have now." He put everything down before walking over to her. "But as it happens, I was asking how we'll keep critters from getting into our food supplies tonight while we're...asleep."

When she saw the heat in his eyes, she grew short of breath. "I have a thermal bag and a rope tucked in with the nonperishables. We'll store any food that will spoil in that and suspend all the bags from a tree branch."

"Good plan. That was my only question." He glanced at the pillows in her hand and smiled. "But thanks for bringing those. Never did like the blow-up kind." He picked up the stacked items and started down the trail.

Oh, that smile. Got her every time. And his nonchalant comment about the pillows... She struggled to breathe normally as she followed him back to camp. The mustangs and cougar had been amazing, but she had a feeling the excitement of that experience would pale next to the adventure awaiting her tonight.

Chapter Nine

By the time Austin and Drew returned to camp, the temperature had dropped enough that they both pulled out sweatshirts from their duffels. Austin chopped wood while Drew used the kindling he'd gathered to start a fire. Once he'd added a few larger branches, they had a decent blaze going. He helped her pull the log bench a little closer to it.

"Nice." She stood back and surveyed the setup. "If you want to begin cooking, I'll get us started with wine and the box of crackers I brought."

"Dinner's already made."

Her eyebrows lifted. "It is?"

"I cooked up a big batch of stew today. Left most of it for Rosie, Herb and Jonah, but the rest is in a pot that can go right on the stove."

"Efficient." Laughter danced in her eyes.

He knew what she was thinking and she was partly

right. He didn't want to waste a lot of time on food prep. While he set up the stove and started reheating the stew, she poured the wine and took a box of crackers out of a canvas bag.

She handed him a plastic goblet when he came over, and he tapped it against hers. "To the mustangs."

"To the mustangs." She took a sip. "Ah." Then she put her cup on the ground, opened the crackers and held out the box. "Hors d'oeuvres."

"Perfect." He sat on the log and took a handful because if he didn't, he was liable to reach for her instead. Once he did that, the whole program would go off the rails.

"This is the life." Setting the box of crackers on the ground between them, she reached inside the neck of her shirt and tugged out her necklace .

Next she pulled off her cap and the elastic band holding her ponytail and laid them beside her. Her hair tumbled to her shoulders and she rubbed her fingers briskly against her scalp until her hair stood out in wild and unbelievably sexy disarray.

He longed to bury his fingers in it and kiss her full mouth… No, they needed food. Food first. Fun later.

She picked up her wine again. "I probably look like Medusa."

"Not even close."

"Anyway, I'll dig up a brush in a little bit and tame this mess."

"Don't do it on my account. I like it that way."

She laughed. "Thanks for saying such a nice thing about my ratty hair. After a few hours of the cap and scrunchie I feel like I've been wearing a football helmet."

"Did you ever?"

"Yes, as a matter of fact. When I aged out of youth hockey I managed to get on the football team as the place kicker. My parents refused to sign the form so I could do kickoffs and field goals. They just knew I'd be sacked and maimed in some way."

He shuddered at the thought of her being tackled by six or seven hefty linemen. "In their shoes, I probably wouldn't have signed it, either."

She sighed. "There were times I wanted to be a boy." She glanced at him. "But right now I'm very glad I'm a girl."

"That makes two of us." He started to reach for the crackers again because kissing her was becoming an obsession.

"Your stew is bubbling."

"Oops." He put down his wine and stood. "Forgot I left it on high."

"You should let me tend it for a while so you can relax."

"No, ma'am." He turned down the heat and stirred the mixture. Fortunately, it hadn't stuck to the bottom. "I signed on to this expedition as the resident cook and Sherpa. Anyway, the stew will be ready before you know it."

"I find it interesting that this time you made dinner in advance." There was a definite teasing note in her voice.

"You probably think I wanted to leave more time for fooling around."

"Yes."

"I do, but also last night I was determined to impress you with my cooking skills. Tonight I don't feel the need to show off and create it in front of you."

"Because you intend to impress me in other ways?"

He looked over his shoulder. Her impish grin tested his restraint and he figured she knew it would. But two could play that game. "Yes, ma'am, I surely do."

"Oh, good grief. Don't try to tell me that cowboys are naturally more virile than other guys."

"I wasn't planning to tell you." He wanted to deliver the next line straight but he almost blew it by laughing. "I was planning to show you."

She groaned in obvious exasperation. "Okay, okay. Stop. You win."

"Allow me to point out that you started it."

"I did, and now I realize how quickly that kind of sexy talk gets out of hand. See, this is why I've never brought a date on a video trip."

"Never?" He looked at her in surprise.

"Never."

"I'm honored."

"You may end up being the first and the last. What happens when our camp is overrun by critters because we're too involved to notice?"

"That won't happen on my watch." He turned off the stove. "I want this trip to go well. I'm hoping we can camp again sometime soon, maybe after the wedding. I want to come back and get another look at those horses."

She gazed at him. "I'd like that, too. Obviously, you appreciate their value."

"They're incredible." So was she, with her wild hair and a sparkle in her dark eyes. If she had makeup on, he couldn't tell. He imagined she might look this way after waking up… He swallowed. "Stew's ready."

She pushed up from the log. "I'll get bowls and spoons if you'll pour me a little more wine. Maybe it will mellow me out."

He decided not to mention that the wine hadn't calmed either of them down the night before. If anything, it had lowered their inhibitions. But despite that, he'd make sure they didn't ignore the basic rules of safe camping because they'd become swamped by their emotions. Before they turned in for the night, the fire would be out and the food would be strung from a tree branch.

Once they were both seated again, with bowls of stew, more wine and the box of crackers between them, he glanced over at her. "I can't speak for you, but I've had a great time so far." He thought it was important to say so before they crawled into that tent. He wanted to establish that the trip was about more than sexual attraction.

"I've had a great time, too." She smiled at him. "How are your feet doing?"

"They're okay, but I need to buy some decent hiking boots for next time."

She paused with her spoon halfway to her mouth. "You'd do that?"

"Absolutely. I'll get some the minute I have a chance to shop for them. Might be after the wedding, though."

"Understood, but if you need help choosing, just holler." She took a bite of stew.

"Are you offering to go with me?"

"Yes, I'd go with you. And by the way, this is delicious."

"Thank you." He ate a spoonful of stew and it tasted even better than when he'd sampled it in Rosie's kitchen. "I admit that for the first part of the afternoon I thought hiking wasn't for me, but I've changed my mind."

"How come?"

"It's the best way to see the mustangs, for one thing. But on the way back I started thinking about trails that are too narrow for a horse but they lead to fantastic views. You've been on some of them."

"How do you know?" She took another bite of her dinner.

"I checked out your website on Rosie's computer

today. First I looked at the mustang videos, but then I found the ones you've taken around here and in Montana. Spectacular."

"Thanks. Last week I sold one to a company that does nature videos."

"Hey, that's great!"

"It is, actually. I'd submitted some before but they weren't interested. This one grabbed them and I've analyzed why that might be, so I can make similar but different ones they might take."

"Excellent plan."

"It's exciting to think about." Her expression grew animated. "Being on their site means I'll reach more people who for one reason or another can't experience nature personally. I'll be able to bring it right into their homes, offices, even schools."

Her enthusiasm for sharing what she filmed touched him. "And what about the folks who will see it and be inspired to go on hikes themselves? You'll be like a nature ambassador."

"I know! I love that. And potentially it could be a good revenue source. I get a percentage of every sale they make from their site. The more I have up there, the bigger those checks will be."

"We should toast that." He picked up his wine glass. "To more video sales."

She touched her glass to his. "And the amazing scenery that makes them possible."

He drank deeply from his wine glass and put it down. "Now I really want those hiking boots so I can be your Sherpa on a regular basis." The future looked bright.

"The only thing is, we're nearing the end of the season for getting good shots."

"I don't see why. You had some great winter stuff on

your site. I loved the one of frozen lakes and waterfalls, blankets of snow over a meadow, the Bighorns covered with snow. Gorgeous."

"It's pretty, but the operative word here is *frozen*. The winter landscape tends to be static. Wildlife is scarce. The episode I sold to them has lots of movement."

"Makes sense, I guess. It's video, after all."

"I had that lightbulb moment when the company chose to buy this particular one. I made it in June when I drove over to Cody to take footage of the rapids, some of it from a raft. I risked dunking my equipment but I lucked out, partly because I had an experienced rafting guide who watched out for me."

"Do you remember the name of the guide?"

"I vaguely remember it was an Irish name, although he wasn't from Ireland. Do you know someone who guides river rafting trips over there?"

"I do, but it would be too much of a coincidence if you got Liam."

"What's his full name?"

"Liam Magee. He's one of my foster brothers."

"That's him! Wow. What are the chances?"

"Well, I do have a lot of brothers." But he saw this as another positive sign that his relationship with Drew was meant to be.

"Liam is terrific. So personable and very good at what he does. Will he be at the wedding?"

"Yes, ma'am. Liam and his brother Grady will be there, along with their wives, Hope and Sapphire. Liam will get a kick out of seeing you again."

"I can't wait to see him again, either, so I can tell him about selling that project. It's very cool that he's your foster brother."

"Sure is." He couldn't wait for this weekend when

she'd meet several more of his brothers. By spending time with his family she'd realize how well she fit in.

But he was a little disappointed that she planned to stop making nature videos until the weather warmed up. He'd been looking forward to helping her. "How soon next spring do you figure you can start filming?"

"Depends on when we get our first thaw. Talking with you has given me an idea, though. If I took a few weeks in the winter and traveled south, I could still get some action shots."

"I guess that's true."

"I'm only part time at the college, so I might be able to leave between the end of my fall class at the college and the start of my spring one."

"True." Her trip would last over the holidays. He'd been looking forward to his first Christmas at home and she quite possibly wouldn't be around. Bummer.

She rested a hand on his thigh. "Don't look so sad. It's not like I'm leaving tomorrow."

He thought she might remove her hand, but instead she rubbed it lazily back and forth. He sucked in a breath. "Drew..."

"I've finished my dinner. Have you finished yours?"

He had no idea, but when he glanced into his bowl it was empty. So was his wineglass. "Seems like I have."

"How long do you think it'll take to critter-proof the camp?"

His pulse kicked into overdrive. "Five minutes."

Chapter Ten

Drew thought Austin was kidding about those five minutes. But she was astounded at how quickly the two of them had the dishes rinsed and put in one bag, the perishables in another with a cold pack and the nonperishables in a third bag. Apparently, they were both highly motivated.

He picked up the bags and the rope. "I'll hang these up if you'll smother the fire."

"Got it."

He started to grab the lantern and paused. "Will you be okay if I take this?"

"Sure. I'll stay right by the fire." She crouched beside it. Because they hadn't added any more wood, the blaze had been reduced to a few coals. She covered them with dirt and stirred the embers with a stick to make sure they were all out.

Starlight bathed the campsite in a silver glow and a

breeze whispered through the pines like a lover's sigh. The flurry of activity after dinner had kept her from thinking, but now she had a moment alone and she trembled with nervous excitement. The first time with a man could be wonderful, awful or somewhere in between.

Austin had joked about his amazing virility and she was inclined to believe he spoke the truth. But she'd never shared her tent with anyone, let alone a cowboy who loomed large and potent in her mind. After poking each blackened ember with the stick and getting no sparks, she tossed the stick away and stood to scan the tree line.

A light bobbed in the darkness as Austin walked back toward the camp. Her heartbeat nearly deafened her. She took a deep breath and tried to convince herself that tonight was no big deal. She'd been with guys before. But not this one. Not this muscled god of a cowboy who could arouse her with a glance.

When he was still several yards away, he stuck the lantern under his chin in a *Blair Witch Project* move. Helpless laughter swept through her, taking with it her case of nerves. As he stood in front of her grinning, she gasped for air. "I can't believe you did that."

"Had to. I could tell from your body language you were wound tight as a new rope." Nudging back his hat, he set down the lantern and pulled her into his arms. "I want you to be relaxed and happy."

"I'm happy."

"That's a start." He lowered his head and claimed her mouth.

And then it was all right, more than all right. If he made love the way he kissed—slow and steady, with exactly the right amount of pressure and a seductive use of his tongue—tonight would be spectacular. She was in the arms of a man who knew what he was doing, and what he was doing softened her as easily as wax touched by flame.

Clutching his broad shoulders, she melted against him, her body curving to fit his solid chest and the proud jut of his erection. His kiss deepened and his tongue made it clear what he intended to happen once they were stretched out in that tent. Her body grew liquid and pliant in response.

She was so absorbed in his kiss that she didn't realize he'd reached under her clothes and unfastened her bra until it gave way. His big hands warmed her skin as he circled her waist and stroked upward to cup her breast. She leaned back, craving the sensation of his fingers flexing and his thumb brushing lazily over her nipple.

Lifting his mouth a fraction away from hers, he took a breath. "You feel like satin," he murmured, nibbling her lower lip as he fondled her. "I'll bet you feel like this all over."

Her breathing grew shallow and she tightened her grip on his shoulders. "Let's go into the—"

"We will." He outlined her mouth with the tip of his tongue. "But first…there's something…" Releasing her breast, he reached for the button on her jeans.

She gasped as he flicked it open "But shouldn't we—"

"Shh." He pulled down her zipper and slipped his hand inside her panties.

"Austin."

He groaned as his fingers eased smoothly into her wet channel. "So ready."

Her resistance ebbed away. "This…this is crazy."

"I know. Let me."

Of course she did. His knowing caress soon turned her bones to jelly but he held her close with one strong arm while he worked his magic. Her climax came quickly and his kisses muffled her cries.

While she quivered in the aftermath, he picked her up and carried her to the tent. Kneeling, he cradled her against his chest as he unzipped the front flap. Then he sat her gently on the blanket.

Dazed and still struggling to catch her breath, she gazed up at him in wonder. No man had ever taken direct charge of her pleasure and she was a little stunned by how easily he'd done it.

"Just a preview," he murmured. "Be right back." He returned in seconds with the lantern and set it beside him. Sitting back on his heels, he untied the laces on her hiking boots and took them off along with her heavy socks. When he'd tucked both her boots and socks inside the tent, he pulled her sweatshirt over her head and laid it on top of the boots. "What about your necklace?"

"I tuck it in a boot." She lifted it over her head. As she handed it to him, she decided it was time to be less of a bystander and more of a participant. "How about you?"

He grinned. "I'm not wearing a necklace." He tugged at the hem of her shirt.

She caught his hands. "You know I'm talking about your clothes. Let me finish so you can undress."

"But I'm having fun taking off your—"

"I'm sure you are, but I also want you naked, cowboy."

"Yes, ma'am." Pushing himself to his feet, he nudged off his running shoes and began unsnapping his shirt while he stood outside the tent.

"You can come in." She scooted over. "I can make room."

"If I get in there, I'll want to go back to working on your clothes instead of mine. I want you naked at least as much as I want myself in that condition and probably more. In point of fact, I don't have to be totally naked, but it's fairly necessary for you to be."

Just like that, she wanted him again. "I get your meaning." As she was about to take her top off, he leaned down and laid his hat brim up against his side of the tent.

She noticed that his shirt was hanging open, exposing that gorgeous chest. Grabbing a handful of the fabric, she tugged him closer. "But you could kiss me again to tide me over."

His voice roughened. "I could, couldn't I?" Dropping to his knees, he tunneled his fingers through her hair and tipped her head back. "Your mouth is one of my favorite places on your sweet body." He settled his lips over hers.

She kissed him back with more hunger than she'd thought herself capable of. Running her palms over his bare skin, she explored the territory she'd first seen when he'd been sprawled under the sink at Thunder Mountain. She'd wanted to do this then. Now she could rub her hands all over that broad expanse of impressive muscles and springy chest hair.

She could also make him groan when she pinched his taut nipples, and gasp when she brushed her knuckles over the tight denim of his fly.

Breathing hard, he ended the kiss. "You're a devil."

"And you like it."

"Yes, ma'am, I love it. But you're still wearing way too many clothes. Are you taking off that shirt and bra or do I have to?"

"I will." She made quick work of the job. "Better?"

"Almost." Reaching behind him, he moved the lantern into the tent. As the light fell on her, he sucked in a breath. "Wow."

She flushed under the heat of his stare. "Now you're

the one wearing too many clothes. You need to take care of that."

"In a minute." Leaning forward, he cupped the back of her head. Kissing her almost reverently, he guided her down to the blanket. Then his kisses moved to the curve of her neck, then the hollow of her throat. At last he raked his teeth gently over her breast until he captured her nipple in his mouth.

She felt the tug deep in her core. Arching into his caress, she whimpered with pleasure. Cradling a breast in each hand, he kissed, licked and nibbled until she was panting and writhing against the blanket.

"Oh, Drew." Continuing his seductive massage, he returned to her mouth and thrust his tongue inside as he nudged her thighs apart with his hips. Locked tight against her most sensitive spot, he began to rock.

Once again, she came apart in no time at all. He made it seem so easy, this matter of letting go. When she opened her eyes, his face was in shadow but she could tell he was smiling.

She smiled back. "I only asked for a kiss."

"I'm a guy who likes to overdeliver." He eased away from her. "But it really is time to get serious about this program. We've fooled around long enough." On his knees again, he took hold of the waistband of her jeans and pulled them off.

Her damp panties came with them and she lay stretched out before him in the glow of the lantern. As his gaze traveled over her, the look in his eyes made her feel like a goddess. She would remember it for a very long time.

At last he cleared his throat. "I had pictured this moment, but my imagination didn't begin to... I didn't dream... You're incredible, Drew."

"Thank you." Warmed by the sincerity in his gaze, she reached over and fingered the material of his shirt. "Are you going to allow me the privilege of looking at you?"

He gave her a crooked smile. "I wouldn't call that a privilege."

"I would. So please finish taking off your clothes."

"Yes, ma'am." He left the tent.

As she lay there impatiently waiting, she heard the faint hoot of an owl. All her solo camping trips had been about lying in the dark listening for those night sounds. This experience with Austin was completely different. She wasn't complaining.

Then he stepped into the tent, his bundle of clothes in one hand and not a single scrap of fabric on his sculpted body. She drank in the sight of him. Her imagination hadn't done him justice, either.

As for the most private part of his anatomy, she'd certainly underestimated in that department. She didn't often find herself speechless, but the sight of Austin's pride and joy swept her brain clean of everything except primitive need.

He turned and leaned down to zip the flap closed. Oh, baby. Her body tightened as she imagined cupping those firm buns while he made love to her. Whew.

Next he stooped and put his clothes on the floor of the tent before unzipping his duffel. She could guess what he was after, and that was confirmed by the rustle of foil and a ripping sound as a packet was opened.

She almost offered to put it on for him but she wasn't that bold yet. Another time. Eventually this ritual could become playful, but not tonight. His labored breathing telegraphed his eagerness. She was excited, too. Just because he'd given her pleasure didn't mean she wanted to forgo this ultimate connection.

She'd expected him to just go for it considering how long the lead-up had been. Instead he lay down on his side facing her and she rolled to her side, too.

He smoothed a hand over her shoulder. "I made a silly boast a while ago. Cowboys can get a little full of themselves sometimes, although if you tell anybody I said that, I'll deny it."

"My lips are sealed." Amazing how he could stroke her shoulder and she could feel a pleasant zing between her thighs.

Lifting his hand from her shoulder, he rubbed his knuckle over her mouth. "Sealing these lips would be a crime against nature. I look at them and think of you eating a ripe strawberry or sipping champagne. Last night I had a very erotic dream about your lips."

Desire hummed through her veins but if he wanted to draw out the suspense, it was fine with her. "Want to share?"

He smiled. "Maybe later, after we know each other a little better."

"Now you're teasing me."

"Let's just say that in my dream you were teasing me."

Desire gripped her in tight fingers. "I don't want to tease you right now. Is that what you're doing?"

"No, ma'am. I wanted to take a little time to explain that once we get started I might… I might not last as long as I'd like. That's part of why I decided to have some fun prior to the main event. I don't ever want to leave a lady feeling frustrated."

"No danger of that." She paused. "Make love to me, Austin."

"My pleasure." He moved between her thighs. "Do you want the light?"

"I like it. I want to see your face while you're loving

me." She stroked his broad chest and discovered it was damp. Holding himself in check hadn't been as easy as he'd made it seem.

"I want to be able to see yours. Twice now I've missed that experience." Slowly he moved his hips forward. "Talk to me, Drew. I don't want to hurt you."

"You're not." Her pulse raced as she absorbed the sensation of being completely and utterly filled. "It's good. Very…good."

"Then I'm going to hold still for a few seconds, get my second wind. I want this to be special."

"It already is." She ran both hands down his back and felt his muscles twitch in reaction. "Don't forget, this is my first time doing it in a tent."

"I did forget." Weight braced on his forearms, he leaned down and placed kisses on her forehead, cheeks and mouth. "Welcome to tent sex." He initiated an easy rhythm.

"Mmm." The friction felt delicious. "I didn't think it would be so different, but it is."

"I think so." He kept moving. "Beds have their place, but there's something elemental about a sexual connection when you're surrounded by trees and animals. You can slide into their rhythm and become part of it."

Looking up, she held his gaze as he loved her with sure, steady strokes. In the distance a wolf howled. Then another answered. Her heart raced as her climax hovered near. "Take…take me there. I want… Oh, yes…*yes.*" With a wild cry, she surrendered to a wave of passion.

Gasping her name, he followed her into the whirlwind of sensation and they clung to each other as they trembled from the force of it. As their breathing slowed, a breeze ruffled the tent and stirred the branches of the pines.

She reached up and cupped his face. "Tent sex rocks."

He smiled. "Knew you'd like it."

"I don't just like it. I love it."

Leaning down, he brushed his mouth over hers. "Even better."

Chapter Eleven

Austin slept better than he had since leaving New Zealand. Camping in the wilderness was part of the reason. But mostly he credited the woman curled against him, the one who'd been so pleased with the first round that she'd happily engaged in a second one after he'd recovered his mojo. They'd heated up that tent good and proper.

Apparently in their semidrowsy state afterward, they'd each pulled a section of blanket around their bodies and cuddled together to ward off the cold. Early morning light filtered through their nylon shelter, and when a soft wind passed over them, it produced the effect of being underwater.

As he debated how long he could lie here before he'd want her again, he heard a noise outside the tent. He quickly recognized the sound of blunt teeth tearing at grass, the thud of a hoof on the ground and a snort. He shook Drew's shoulder.

She mumbled something he couldn't distinguish.

Putting his mouth close to her ear, he shook her again. "Drew. Horses."

"Hmm?" She rolled toward him, looking sexy and rumpled.

He wanted to kiss her in the worst way, but she wouldn't thank him if he did. Instead of kissing, she'd want to take a look outside. "Listen."

She lay still and then her eyes widened.

He kept his voice low. "What now?"

"Stay here."

"What about the hundred-foot rule?"

"I can't help it if they came to our front door." Moving carefully, she put on her clothes. Then she retrieved her small camcorder from her backpack and slowly unzipped the tent flap.

He held his breath as she slipped outside, but the lazy sound of horses grazing didn't change. Dressing as quietly as possible, he kept pausing to listen. He wasn't going out there, but he wanted to be ready if she needed him.

After about ten minutes, she poked her head into the tent. "They're starting to move off," she murmured. "I'm going to follow them as far as the trees. Want to come along?"

"You bet." He crept out into the cold, pale dawn. At first he scanned the ground for loose sticks that might crack in two if he stepped on them. The way was clear so he moved cautiously toward where Drew stood with her camera trained on the herd.

The mustangs had left the camping area, but they were close enough that he could pick out details—a scar on a flank, burrs tangled in a mane, a fresh scrape on a nose. They didn't carry an ounce of fat. Anyone who knew horses would be able to tell that they were as wild as the predators who stalked them.

They drifted slowly toward the line of tall pines, grazing as they went. The stallion stood apart, his attention on the humans. He snorted and pawed the ground.

Drew lowered her camera. "Let's go," she said in an undertone.

Austin nodded and they slowly retreated to their camping site. When he looked back, the horses had moved closer to the trees and the stallion was grazing.

Drew turned around, too, and sighed in relief. "That's better. I had the feeling that if I kept filming, the stallion wouldn't eat. He doesn't know that this funny black thing I'm holding is harmless." She set it on the log next to the fire circle.

"It's probably better if they don't get too comfortable around humans."

"So true." Her dark eyes shone. "But, Austin, I got some *amazing* footage. Between these close-ups and the cougar episode, I'd count this as my best outing ever."

"Good." She looked so beautiful in the soft light of dawn that it made his throat hurt. Her unbound hair was still tousled from their lovemaking the night before, which reminded him of the intense pleasure of sinking into her warm body. Naturally that affected his package.

As if she could read his thoughts, her cheeks turned pink. Then she smiled. "You know what?"

"What?" His voice was a rusty croak.

"I feel like celebrating."

"Thank God." Lacing his fingers through hers, he led her quickly back to the tent. After they crawled in, they had a bit of a rodeo getting their clothes off and they were laughing by the time they managed it.

"The one disadvantage of tent camping." He gathered

her close and groaned. "You feel so great. I want to kiss you all over but I can't."

She snuggled against him. "Why not?"

"Scratchy beard."

"Then it's my turn. Lie back."

Only a fool would disobey that order. He rolled over, bringing her with him. And...dear God, he was in heaven. She nibbled and licked until he thought he would lose his mind. As if her moist kisses weren't enough to drive him wild, her silken hair caressed his skin everywhere she traveled on her erotic journey. Finally, he begged her to fetch a condom from his duffel.

She wanted to put it on him and he was grateful. He was shaking so much he might have fumbled the job. She didn't waste any time doing it, either, which was a blessing because he was fighting for control. Then she was there, taking him deep as she gazed into his eyes.

His breath caught. This moment would be burned into his memory forever. Then she began to move, and the world became a dazzling blur of color and sensation. He tried to hold back, but it was no use. She took him over the edge and followed right after, her cries mingling with his.

When he stopped gasping and was able to focus on his surroundings again, he discovered her braced above him on her outstretched arms. She looked extremely pleased with herself.

Her soft chuckle was low and sexy. "Heck of a celebration."

He smiled. "Yes, ma'am. You sure know how to party." He dragged in a breath. "And now I'm gonna fix you breakfast."

"That would be nice." She combed a lock of hair back from his forehead. "I'll help."

"Ah, but it's my job, remember?" He captured her hand and nibbled on her fingers. "My excuse for tagging along."

"You can do most of it. But let's work on it together."

Oh, how he loved the way she was looking at him. And the way he felt when he was looking at her. He drew her head down and brushed his mouth over hers, careful not to scratch her with his beard. "That sounds great."

It was great, too. She loved the consistency of his scrambled eggs but he'd only brought salt and she preferred pepper. They compromised on the amount of ground coffee in the pot and made it too weak for him and too strong for her. They got their signals crossed as to who was watching the bacon and burned it. They ate it anyway.

The meal was far from perfect but the mood was. They straddled the log facing each other so they could touch knees and gaze into each other's eyes. It was a goofy thing to do but no one was there to see them acting like teenagers who'd just discovered how much they liked each other.

After the food was gone they continued to sit on the log talking about ways they could make the camping experience even better next time. He had no doubt there would be a next time. Visualizing the future, he saw a whole string of next times, whether they ended up camping or hanging out at her place.

Or they could stay at his place once he rented an apartment. Or…their place? Although he knew not to anticipate something so major this early in the relationship, he couldn't help it.

She'd worn her necklace outside her shirt this morning since they wouldn't be hiking. Reaching over, he took the pendant between his fingers. "Your grandmother had great taste."

"I know. She didn't just buy this in a store. She had someone design it."

He smoothed his thumb over the large pearl. "Then she must have had an idea of how she wanted it to look."

"Definitely. And it all has meaning. The pearl is so I'll remember to be kind to everyone because under their protective shell could be a pearl."

"I like that. What about the diamonds?"

"She used to say I was her sparkly girl and she never wanted me to lose my sparkle."

Tugging gently on the necklace, he brought her closer and looked into her eyes. "You haven't. I can see that sparkle right this minute."

She laughed. "I'll bet you can."

"What about the silver heart?"

"That's the most important part of the necklace. She always told me that no matter what, I should follow my heart."

"I would have liked your grandma." He leaned in, eliminating the gap between them.

"She would have liked you, too." She sighed. "We should probably pack up."

"But we'll come back."

"I'd like that."

"Then we will." He kissed her gently, mindful of his stubble.

As they broke camp and lugged everything to her truck, he thought about the next few days filled with wedding activities. The events would present some challenges for finding private time, but he was ready to tackle the obstacles and look for hidden opportunities to be with her.

On the drive back he started with the immediate one, Cade's bachelor party that night. "Obviously, it cuts out dinner and most of the evening," he said. "And no telling how late that will go, but I could come by your place whenever it winds down. Would that work for you?"

She laughed. "Are you asking if you can show up at my door at two in the morning?"

"Yes, ma'am, I suppose it could be that late. When you put it that way, it's an imposition. Never mind."

"You can show up at my door anytime, cowboy." She continued to watch the road, but she reached over and squeezed his thigh. "Anytime at all."

Heat traveled straight to his groin. "Any more of that talk and I'll be looking for a little side road."

"I've been fantasizing about that ever since we left our camp."

He sighed. "But we really can't."

"No, we really can't. We'll already get back later than I expected."

He checked the time on his phone. "And by now the ranch house will be filling up with people from out of town. I should be there."

"Absolutely. And I have an editing job to finish."

"You do? I thought you'd wrapped up Lexi and Cade's video."

"I did. This is a family reunion I shot last weekend. Rosie recommended me for it. I have most of it done but I promised to show them a preliminary version this afternoon."

"Which means you'd be free tonight and I'm not." He couldn't miss that bachelor party, but he wouldn't have to stay until dawn, or even close to dawn.

She flashed him a smile. "Like I said, anytime."

"Count on me, then. I'll be there."

"I'll leave the light on."

That reminded him of the ribbing Cade had given him about being a cab with its roof light on. This situation with Drew didn't fit that analogy at all, though. So what if she was the first woman he'd dated since he'd come back to town? He'd just been extremely lucky to find his soul mate immediately. Sometimes life happened that way.

He looked over at Drew. "Speaking of editing, how soon will you work on the video you took yesterday of the mustangs?"

"Since I won't be seeing you until late, I'll start on it after I finish the reunion one."

"Will you try to market it?"

"I might, although if I do, I'll give the profits to the folks who are doing so much to protect those horses."

"That's a great idea."

"Until now, I wasn't sure I had anything that would sell, but—" She paused as her phone chimed inside the console where she'd tucked it.

"Want me to get that for you?"

"That's okay. It's my sister texting me. I forgot that today she was supposed to hear whether she got an internship in Florence for the fall semester. If I find a good place to pull over, I'll stop for a minute and text her back."

"Florence, Italy?"

"Yep. She really wants the internship. It would be a great experience and it'd also look good on her résumé."

"Is she your only sister?"

"No, just the one closest in age to me. There are six of us, three and three. Like I said, big family. And that's only counting my siblings. The list of cousins goes on forever. No matter where you go in Billings, you're likely to run into a Martinelli. We show up in—" Her phone chimed again with a different tone. "Huh. Now she's calling. She must be really excited."

"There's a spot to pull over."

"I see it." She put on her blinker and moved to the side of the road. "I promise I won't be long." She switched off the engine and took her phone out of the console. "We both have things to do."

"Sure, but an internship in Florence is important stuff."

"It is, isn't it?" She dialed, put the phone to her ear and waited. "Hey, sis! Did you... Oh, no!" She listened for a moment. "I can't believe it." Turning to Austin, she gave him a thumbs-down sign. "They're idiots. Too bad for them." She paused. "I know. It sucks."

Even though Drew had the phone to her ear, Austin could hear her sister crying.

"Here's what we'll do." She met his gaze as she talked. "I'll come up and bring you down to Sheridan. You can be my assistant videographer for the wedding."

He took a deep breath and nodded to show he understood how her plan would impact them. If she needed to help her sister, he'd deal.

"Elise, it's absolutely okay," Drew said. "I could use the help and you know the routine. Meet me at Mom and Dad's and bring a suitcase. Tell Mom that I'll stop and pick up a pizza from the restaurant. Call it in for me, okay? Love you, too. Bye." She disconnected and looked at him. "I'm sorry."

"Don't worry about it. These things happen."

She smiled. "When it comes to my family, they happen *a lot* and if it were anything other than this, I wouldn't get involved. But Elise had her heart set on going to Italy and I can't just ignore her right now."

"Of course you can't."

"Thanks for understanding."

"Family's important." In fact, he was glad to see how much she loved hers. One more thing that proved how compatible they were.

Chapter Twelve

Drew had the rest of her day carefully structured. She'd finish the reunion video in two hours, tops. Then she'd shower and change, drive to Billings in time for dinner, and be back at her apartment with Elise before midnight. It was doable if she dropped Austin off and left immediately.

But when she swung her truck into the circular driveway in front of the ranch house, she realized any plans of a quick exit were down the drain. Rosie and Herb sat on the front porch with Jonah but joining them was her former rafting guide Liam Magee and a pretty blonde woman who must be his wife. Another couple was there as well, probably Liam's brother and sister-in-law.

Austin confirmed it. "Hey, it's Liam and Grady! Perfect. You can say hi to Liam now instead of in the middle of the wedding chaos."

"Quick, tell me the names of their wives again."

"Hope's the blonde with Liam and I think she just published a novel. The redhead is Sapphire, Grady's wife. He sculpts with recycled metal and she's a potter."

"Oh, my God. That's Grady Magee." Drew parked the truck and switched off the engine. "I didn't put it all together when you told me his name earlier, but I've heard of him. His work is in a gallery in Billings. Darn it, they all look like people I'd like to get to know better. I wish I didn't have to rush off."

"You'll probably have more time tomorrow after the rehearsal."

"Not really. I'll be shooting during the dinner, too. My method is to get more than enough and then pick out the gems."

"I see your point, but don't worry. There will be other chances in the future." Austin flashed her a smile as he opened his door. "I have a feeling you'll be hanging out with this family quite a bit."

His statement hit her like a splash of cold water. She'd meant to climb down herself to save time, but she was so startled by what he'd said that she was still sitting in the driver's seat when he opened her door. She wanted to ask what he'd meant by his remark, but now wasn't the time or place.

She let him help her down and automatically thanked him, but her mind was still busy with his comment. He could be referring to her growing friendship with the family through her work, but she didn't think so. His jaunty smile and his confident tone indicated that he saw her as becoming *part* of the family. And he'd be the connection.

Not that she didn't like him. She was crazy about him, in fact. But that didn't mean she was ready for the kind of commitment she thought he was hinting at. Maybe she was imagining things.

He must have sensed a change in her, though, because his smile faded. "Are you okay?"

"Just thinking about all I need to accomplish." Including a heart-to-heart with him, especially considering the imminent arrival of her sister. Good Lord, if Elise got the wrong impression of her relationship with Austin, that story would travel back to Billings. Her mother would start paging through wedding magazines and mailing Drew clippings of dresses and bouquets.

"Then let me grab my duffel out of the back while you head up to the porch. I won't bother with the stew pot and anything else I brought to cook with."

"Right. Just leave it. I'll get everything back to you tomorrow."

"Listen, you have my cell number if you need me for anything before then."

"Thanks. I appreciate it." She wished she didn't have this uneasy feeling that he'd misunderstood her intentions toward him. Now with Elise coming, she would have no opportunity to clear that up.

That said, the sooner she could talk with him, the better. She didn't want him giving his family the wrong impression about their relationship, either. But she couldn't do anything about the situation now and she really was excited to see Liam and meet his wife.

They left their chairs and came down the porch steps to greet her. "Isn't this a great coincidence?" Liam gave her a big grin and a hug. With his dark hair and green eyes, he could have been right at home in an Irish pub, except that he didn't have the accent.

"I'm so happy to see you again!" She hugged him back and then turned to meet Hope. When Drew mentioned hearing something about a novel, Hope lit up. Once again, Drew was sorry she couldn't stay longer and find out more about it.

She climbed the porch steps with them and was introduced to Grady and Sapphire, who were also extremely friendly and complimented her on the video she'd done for Thunder Mountain Academy, the residential equine education center for teens. That turned out to be a perfect lead-in to her news about selling the video she'd made while a passenger in Liam's river raft.

Rosie and Herb were also eager to hear all about it. When Austin came up the steps carrying his duffel, Rosie insisted that everyone should have a seat while she and Herb went to fetch snacks. There was no stopping Rosie when she launched into hostess mode, so in less than five minutes Drew was drinking lemonade and eating peanut butter cookies while participating in an animated discussion of the best way to market creative work.

The gabfest was wonderful and could have gone on for hours. Drew enjoyed every minute but knew she'd have to make her excuses soon or her whole plan would collapse. Finding the right spot to slip in a comment about leaving wasn't easy, though.

Then Austin did it for her. "I'll bet Drew hates to take off in the middle of this, but we need to let her go. She has a work deadline."

She sent him a look of gratitude. "He's right, I do. I have to finish editing the Hayworth family reunion video by four this afternoon. And thank you, Rosie, for getting me that gig. It was wonderful."

"The Hayworths are good people," Rosie said.

"They're terrific and they'd be okay if I took another day or two. But I need to get it done now because something else has come up I need to tell you about. I've asked my sister Elise to be my assistant while I'm shooting the wedding. She's done it before and she's a huge help."

Rosie beamed with pleasure. "What a wonderful idea! I can't wait to meet her. When will she arrive?"

"Actually, I'm driving up to get her tonight. So I really do need to leave." She picked up her glass. "I'll just take this into the—"

"I've got it." Austin smiled as he took her glass.

"Thank you. And thanks for being my Sherpa."

"My pleasure."

Turning, she bid everyone goodbye.

"I'll walk you to—"

"That's okay. Gotta run." She dashed down the porch steps. If she let him walk her to the truck he was liable to give her a quick kiss goodbye. Yes, they'd be on the opposite side of the vehicle, somewhat out of sight of the folks on the porch. But it was broad daylight and everyone would be able to see enough to know what was going on. She wasn't ready for PDA.

What was she ready for? She debated that question on the drive to her apartment. When it had been just the two of them at the campground, she'd let herself enjoy the freedom of having a sexy interlude that her family didn't have to know about. She'd been less guarded with him than the men she'd dated in Billings because he wouldn't be running into one of her relatives on the street.

Instead she'd be running into *his* relatives. She hadn't factored that into the equation. Now that she thought about it, all the Thunder Mountain guys she'd met either had wives or serious girlfriends. She hadn't been introduced to any who weren't in a committed relationship except Austin and his friend Jonah.

If finding a soul mate was a common trend in this group, she didn't want to be a part of it. But had she said anything that would lead Austin to believe she was looking for a permanent arrangement? Whether she had or not, they'd work things out the next time they had a chance to talk in private. In the meantime, she had a schedule to keep.

By sticking to that schedule, she pulled into the driveway of her parents' two-story frame house a little after six. She'd picked up the pizza her sister had ordered from the family restaurant, an extra-large called Everything but the Kitchen Sink.

On the drive from the restaurant it had filled her truck's cab with delicious aromas and she was starving. Other than lemonade and cookies at Thunder Mountain, she hadn't eaten since breakfast.

Elise came out to meet her with arms open wide. She'd had her dark hair cut in an asymmetrical style that was very artsy. "You are the best big sister a girl could ever have." She gave Drew a tight hug. "Mom and Dad mean well, but they're trying to help me find alternatives. They've been on the phone with all the aunts and uncles discussing it."

"Let me guess." Drew returned her hug. "You're not in the mood to consider alternatives."

"Bingo. I want to wallow in my misery. They can discuss and debate this if they want, but I'm taking turns ignoring them or offering ridiculous options." She grinned. "That frustrates the heck out of everybody, so it's probably a good thing you're getting me out of town."

"I had a feeling you'd be ready for a change of scenery."

"And pizza. I'm ready for pizza. It smells amazing. I'll carry it in, okay?"

"Be my guest." Drew was encouraged that Elise had

an appetite. She was slim to begin with, so she couldn't afford to skip too many meals.

Elise took the pizza from the passenger seat and closed the door. "You know what the worst part is? I almost got it. I'm the runner-up. Some master's student from Seton Hill got it, but I'm in second place. Big whoop."

Drew followed her sister up the walkway where they used to play hopscotch. "But that means if he or she can't go—"

"Oh, she'll go. If she applied for it, she has her ducks in a row. Who wouldn't?"

"I hear what you're saying, but stuff happens. Until the boat sails, or the plane takes off, you still have a shot."

"I suppose." Elise climbed the steps to the wide front porch. The wicker rockers that would be taken in with the first snowfall had patriotic cushions for the approach of Labor Day. "But it almost hurts worse if I nurture that hope. And wanting that means I'd like the woman who got it to have something major happen to keep her from going, which would be terrible for her. It's bad karma to wish for that."

"You're right. But you see, I don't care about her. I care about you."

"I know." Elise gave her a warm smile. "That's why I called you first. Where were you when you called back? I heard a lot of road noise."

"I was…" She opened the front door and heard a familiar sound, her mom on the phone and her dad commenting animatedly in the background. "Oh, boy."

"It's been like this all day, except for brief lulls when they both want to discuss what Aunt Fran suggested or Uncle Sid thinks I should do. Then there are Mom and Dad's recommendations."

"I'm surprised you're not twirly-eyed."

"Ah, I shrug it off. But it'll be nice not to listen to it for a few days."

Drew had only been home once since moving to Sheridan and that had been over Easter. Now she was reminded why. She reached for Elise's arm to pull her back so they could take the food and sneak over to Elise's apartment, instead. She'd have another pizza delivered to her parents. But she didn't move fast enough.

Elise breezed into the kitchen carrying the pizza. "Drew's here."

"Thank God!" Her mom quickly disconnected the call with "Drew's here" and hurried over to hug her. "You're just the person we need. Your sister has so many options now that the internship is down the drain, and she needs to narrow the list and pick something before the semester starts. Talk some sense into her."

Drew gazed at her dark-eyed mother, who kept her hair the same ebony shade it had been when she was twenty-five. Plump and vivacious, she had an Italian ancestry to rival her husband's. They were perfectly matched. They both loved food and a juicy emotional crisis. Now that the pizza was here, they could have both.

Drew adored them but never cared to live within a hundred miles of her folks ever again. "What do you say we have dinner first?"

"Excellent plan." Elise plopped the to-go box in the middle of the kitchen table.

Drew headed for the cupboard. "I'll get plates."

"I'll get wine." Her father bounded down the basement steps to the little wine cellar he was inordinately proud of.

"So we'll talk and eat." Her mother got out napkins and silverware. "But taking Elise down to Sheridan isn't a very good idea right now. If she stays in Billings she can start following up on some of these leads. Sid thinks he can pull some strings and get her an internship at an art gallery in the LA area. It wouldn't pay anything, but he knows a family over there who would give her a room for next to nothing."

"Or I could live on the beach." Elise started dishing pizza onto plates. "And pick oranges off people's trees. That sounds like fun."

Their father returned with a bottle of wine. "I don't think you're taking this seriously enough, honey." He plucked a corkscrew from a drawer and opened the bottle with the ease of a master.

"Drew thinks I shouldn't give up on Florence." Elise glanced over at her. "Right?"

"At least not for a few days. I mean, you're the runner-up. Until you know for sure the other person is all set, you—"

"Of course that person is all set," her mother said. "Who wouldn't be? Elise needs to move on, locate a similar position somewhere else, and the sooner the better. Serena is checking on possibilities in New York and Al has a connection with a very prestigious gallery in Cincinnati."

"But Elise needs to intern at a museum, not a gallery."

Elise pointed a wedge of pizza in her direction. "Exactly. And a European museum has far more cachet. So maybe I should book a flight to Italy and hang around Florence looking pitiful. They'll feel sorry for me and decide they need two interns."

Her mom looked aghast. "You wouldn't actually do such a thing, would you?"

Elise shrugged and turned to Drew. "I might. What do you think I should do?"

"I think you should finish eating so we can leave for Sheridan."

Her mom put down her wineglass. "Hold on a minute. I—"

"She just found out today." Drew laid her hand on her mother's arm. "She needs time to get her head around this so she can make a responsible decision."

Her mom glanced at Elise. "Do you?"

Right on cue, Elise's face grew solemn. "Yes. Yes, I certainly do."

"All right, then. We'll brainstorm while you're gone. I'll text you if anything comes up that you need to know about."

Drew shook her head. "That won't work, Mom. She'll be busy helping me with this wedding. It's a big deal and I don't want her to be distracted."

Her mother didn't look happy but she nodded. "We'll just get right on it the minute you get back, then."

"Sure." Elise gave her mom a quick smile.

Drew sighed in relief. Her mercy mission to rescue her sister from a weekend of hell had succeeded. That felt good.

Chapter Thirteen

Austin had looked forward to Cade's bachelor party as much, if not more, than the wedding. At Cade's request, the foster brothers had gathered around the fire pit in the meadow a short walk from the house. For many years, the meadow and the log cabins forming a semicircle behind the fire pit had been their sanctuary.

When Austin had come to live at Thunder Mountain, only three cabins had been here. He'd stayed up at the ranch house the first year because he'd been so young, but then he'd graduated to the cabins. Recently a fourth cabin had been added to expand the sleeping space for the academy students. Normally the teens would be living in the meadow, but the wedding had been scheduled during the break between the summer and fall semesters.

The menu for the night was simple—steak, baked potatoes, beans and beer. Cowboy chow. Austin had been part of the two-man team cooking the steaks. The other chef was Jake Ramsey, a firefighter who'd learned to fix hearty meals for a bunch of guys while on duty at the station.

Finn O'Roarke, who'd flown in from Seattle with his wife, Chelsea, made sure an iced tub of beer remained stocked with his signature brew, O'Roarke's Pale Ale. Several brothers had chopped enough wood to keep the fire going all night once the food was cooked. Now that Drew had other plans, Austin was willing to turn the party into an all-nighter.

The wives and fiancées were up at the house having their own event, leaving the meadow to the men. It was like old times, with their foster father, Herb, rounding out the group to an even dozen. And just like old times, the talk was mostly about women.

Everyone who wasn't in the know wanted to hear Zeke Rafferty's story. Of all of them, he'd been the least likely to marry and settle down. Yet tonight his fiancée, Tess, four months pregnant with their son, was up at the house with the other ladies. The wedding would take place next month and Zeke looked like he couldn't wait.

"I never thought I'd say this out loud, but babies rock." Zeke took a swallow of his beer. "I can't walk past a display of stuffed animals anymore without buying one."

"I hear you, bro." Damon Harrison's daughter had just turned eight months. "We finally bought a hammock for Sophie's room so we had a place to put 'em all. We're way past the teddy bear stage. Or the mammal stage, for that matter. She just got a plush tarantula from her uncle Zeke."

Finn shuddered. "Way to traumatize the baby, Zeke."

"Are you kidding?" He laughed. "She loves it. Nothing scares Sophie."

"I won't let her bring it to the wedding, though,"

Damon said. "Wouldn't want Finn to run screaming out of the barn."

"No, no, have her bring it," Austin said. "I guarantee Drew would love a video of that little cherub scaring Uncle Finn with a stuffed tarantula."

"Yeah, I wanna see that," Jake said. "Definitely YouTube worthy. I can't wait to have a kid. What kind of pregnancy kit is the best?"

Recommendations started flying around, and Austin wondered if he should be taking notes. He'd need to know this eventually. No worries. He'd ask when the time came.

He had plenty of other questions, though. Cade might need this info, too, come to think of it. So he forged on for Cade's sake. "What's the recommended time to wait before having your first baby?"

"Whatever it is," Zeke said, "we blew that call. We got pregnant by accident and didn't figure out until later that we were meant for each other."

"That's called divine intervention," Jonah said.

Zeke laughed. "Don't pull that preacher talk on me. I knew you when you were a hell-raiser."

"Exactly why I asked him to officiate at my wedding," Cade said. "It seemed fitting. But I'm interested in Junior's question. Why do you want to know, little buddy?"

Austin had consumed enough beer that he didn't bother objecting to being called either *Junior* or *little buddy*. "I was asking for you. I thought you might want to know."

"I don't need to know." Cade gazed at Austin. "I freely admit that Lexi is in charge of that program. We'll start trying to get pregnant when she says so. She has to do the heavy lifting."

Finn raised his bottle in Cade's direction. "Wise decision, bro. Let me get you another brewski and we'll toast that comment. It's brilliant." He headed off to the tub of iced beer. "Who else needs a libation?"

"I do," Grady said. A chorus of requests followed Finn's progress over to the tub.

"I wouldn't mind another beer," Cade said, "But I want to dig a little deeper into Junior's question. He's way too focused on this topic considering he doesn't have a fiancée, let alone a wife."

"I don't have one now, but I have a hunch I will soon."

Cade groaned. "I was afraid that would be your answer."

"Never fear, old buddy." Austin gave him a light punch on the shoulder. "She's perfect. Yesterday she took me out to Bighorn Canyon to see the wild mustangs and we got along great."

"But wasn't that, like, your second date?" Jonah thanked Finn for the beer and opened it.

"Yeah," Austin said. "But when you go camping with someone you see the real person."

"There's some truth to that." Cade gazed at Austin. "But here's a bigger truth. Three days ago you didn't know she existed."

"So? Sometimes lightning strikes."

Brant Ellison, the only cowboy in the group who was bigger and more muscular than Austin, cleared his throat. "I know a guy who was actually struck by lightning. He was addlepated for days." Brant smiled at Austin. "You might want to rethink your metaphor."

"Or extend it." Ty Slater and Brant had been best friends while they lived at the ranch and still kept in close touch even though Ty was now a lawyer working in Cheyenne. "Let's say you were hit by lightning and she's the one for you. But it works two ways. She'd have to feel that lightning strike, too."

"She likes me. I know she does."

Damon sighed. "I hope you're not basing that on a few rounds of mattress bingo."

"I'm not! We have way more going for us. She wants to help me get my trail ride business going. She's offered to give me tips on the website design and do a video for it. She said I make her video expeditions easier because I carry most of the stuff. She likes my cooking."

Cade lifted his beer in Austin's direction. "You're ahead of me there, bro. But you're making me mighty nervous with this 'I have a hunch' talk."

"I'm crazy about her and I'm pretty sure she's crazy about me. I see no reason why we won't be engaged within a month or so."

Jonah choked on his beer and Cade groaned.

Austin glanced around at his brothers and they were all staring at him like he was one doughnut shy of a dozen. "What? When it's right, it's right. Life's short, so why waste time? Look at Rosie and Herb. Met, fell in love, got married, bam. That sure worked out okay."

Liam had been silent through the interchange but he finally spoke. "That's a good point, but Ty's right. You have to make sure Drew's on the same page, and I—" He paused. "Well, never mind. I shouldn't poke my nose in."

Austin felt a prick of unease. Liam had spent several days with Drew on that rafting trip and the guy had good instincts about people.

"Please poke your nose in," Cade said. "The rest of us have tried and we're getting nowhere."

"It's just that I got to know Drew fairly well on that rafting trip, and this afternoon on the porch I could tell you were over the moon, but I wasn't getting that level of intensity from her."

"That's because she wouldn't show it in front of everybody." But she had acted somewhat distant after his comment in the truck about spending a lot of time with his family in the future. "When it's just the two of us, she's very...um, affectionate."

Damon came over and put an arm around his shoulders. "I get that. I'm sure you had a rockin' good time in Bighorn Canyon. But you can't jump from that to a proposal without some indication she's thinking along the same lines as you."

"What sort of indication?"

Damon turned to the rest of them. "Indications. What you got?"

"She invites you over to help her trim her Christmas tree," Ty said. "That's what Whitney did. I loused it up, but that was her way of hinting she wanted to take things to the next level."

Damon nodded. "Any invitation into her space is a good sign. Phil invited me to stay at her house, although I didn't handle that opportunity well, either."

"See there?" Austin felt better. "She let me go along on her camping trip to see the mustangs."

Cade gazed at him. "Did you ask to go?"

"Well, yeah, but she was fine with it. Then today she said I was welcome at her place anytime."

"But whose idea was it to go over there?" Cade skewered him with a glance.

"Mine, but—"

"It really does need to be her idea," Jake said. "And even then, you can get your signals crossed, misinterpret what everything means. Has she taken the initiative on anything?"

Austin thought back over the past two days. He'd asked her out to begin with and then invited himself along on the camping trip. He'd suggested going over to her apartment after the bachelor party. "Maybe not. Oh, wait. She volunteered to go along when I bought hiking boots. That was totally her idea."

He considered it a positive sign, but when he took inventory of how it was being received by his brothers, several of them looked ready to bust out laughing. "Well, it's something, right?"

"It's something, all right," Damon said. "But I wouldn't go lining up a preacher based on a potential shopping trip for hiking boots."

"So you're all saying I should back off a little."

"Or a lot," Cade said. "Hell, Junior, your plane landed four days ago! I'll bet you're still jet-lagged."

"I have to back off for the rest of the weekend anyway. Drew's sister will be in town through Sunday."

Jonah clapped him on the back. "Divine intervention."

Austin considered it more of a monkey wrench in his plans than divine intervention, but he respected Drew's need to comfort her sister. Maybe it was a good thing he and Drew were forced to take a break this weekend. They'd be all the more eager to get together next week. But he might let her make the first move.

Drew ate two slices of pizza and then extricated herself and Elise from the house. She and Elise spent most of the drive talking about the wedding and Thunder Mountain Ranch.

"So let me get this straight." Elise scooted down and propped her feet on the dash, something she loved doing whenever she was in the passenger seat and her parents weren't around to chastise her for it. "First this couple took in foster boys and now they're running a coed equine academy for teens. They must be saints to want teenagers around all the time."

"I can't imagine it, either, but they seem to thrive on the constant activity."

"And I thought our family was crazy."

"Our family *is* crazy. Remember that these academy students aren't related. I think that makes a huge difference in the drama quotient."

"Yes, but you said the foster brothers consider themselves semirelated and quite a few of them are part of the mix, right?"

"They are." Drew pulled into her parking space at the apartment complex. "Which brings me to another subject. But let's wait until we get inside to talk about it."

"Is it top secret?" Elise sounded thrilled with the idea.

"Actually, yes." She unbuckled her seat belt and opened her door, which switched on the dome light. She turned to look at Elise. "Before I say anything, you have to pinkie-swear that you won't tell Mom and Dad."

"Ooh, sounds juicy. Are you pregnant?"

"God, no! Bite your tongue."

"It wouldn't be the end of the world. You're twenty-eight and you'd make a great mom."

Drew stared at her. "What makes you say that?"

"You're always taking care of people, like bringing me down here to cheer me up, as if you thought they were driving me nuts with their crazy-ass suggestions."

"Weren't they driving you nuts?"

Elise laughed. "Sort of, but it's like a game to me. They get all serious about my future so I tell them I'm going to be a beach bum. I like going for the shocking statement."

"You pull their chain on purpose?"

"Sometimes." Elise grinned at her. "When the devil in me can't resist. Family drama can be a spectator sport."

"No, it's not! It's distracting as hell!"

Elise blinked. "Not to me." She was quiet for a moment. "But I can see it bothers you. From now on I won't deliberately light any brush fires when you're around."

"Thank you." She gazed at her sister. "Are you saying you didn't really need rescuing?"

"Maybe not the way you thought."

"But you were crying."

"I know, and I was upset, but I'm over it." She reached out and squeezed Drew's shoulder. "That doesn't mean I'm not excited about spending the weekend with my big sis. Let's go in so I can find out what this major secret is about."

Drew locked the truck and led the way up the outside stairs to her second-floor apartment, all the while thinking she might have overreacted by inviting Elise down here. Elise hadn't asked to come, had she? And now there was the issue of Austin to deal with.

Her sister was too observant to miss the chemistry, so the relationship had to be explained before they drove out to Thunder Mountain Ranch the next day. Some sisterly advice from Elise might be helpful before Drew saw Austin again. Maybe Elise could help her figure out where Austin was coming from.

"I have to warn you," she said as she unlocked the door. "The apartment's even more Spartan than the one I had in Billings. My decorating consists of hanging up my Ansel Adams posters and my signed Wayne Gretzky photo."

"Works for me." Elise rolled her small overnight case into the living room, which contained a worn sofa on one side of the room and Drew's video equipment on the other, including a large flat screen, her computer, and various cameras, tripods and lights.

"I'll take the sofa and give you the bed." Drew felt the

need to offer even though she knew Elise would probably refuse.

"Are you kidding? I love sleeping on this sofa. I was afraid you might have replaced it." She plopped down on it and patted the cushions. "This sofa and I have a history."

"You do, at that." Elise had spent the night on it several times, most notably when she'd been dumped by a guy she'd been madly in love with.

"Are you gonna sit down and tell me the secret stuff or what?"

"I am." She dropped her purse onto the desk beside her computer. "After I get us some wine."

"Excellent." Elise kicked off her shoes and curled up on the sofa. "I didn't drink much at Mom and Dad's."

"Obviously as the designated driver, neither did I."

Moments later as they sipped red wine from juice glasses and snacked on trail mix, Drew gave her sister a brief rundown on Austin.

"He sounds great."

"He is great unless he's hoping to lock down something permanent in the near future. If you could observe the situation tomorrow and see if you pick up on that, too, I'd appreciate it."

Elise grabbed another handful of trail mix. "Your instincts tell you he's getting serious, right?"

"Right, but—"

"Then you need to talk to him ASAP and relay your concerns." She popped the trail mix into her mouth.

"But what if I'm wrong?" Drew's stomach tightened. "Won't that seem arrogant to assume he's getting serious if he's not?"

Elise stopped chewing. "What if you're right? Wouldn't

you rather set the record straight before he goes any further down that road?"

"Yes, yes, I would."

"I wish Brian had been more honest with me instead of being afraid he'd hurt my feelings."

"Okay." Drew took a deep breath. "But there's all this wedding stuff going on so I'm not sure when I'll have a good opportunity until next week."

"I wouldn't wait that long if I were you. Is there a good coffee shop in town?"

"Rangeland Roasters."

"Then you could invite him to meet you there tomorrow morning."

"And leave you here by yourself? That's not right after I—"

"Listen, sis." Elise leveled a stern glance at her. "You came charging to my rescue when you thought I was in need. Maybe I wasn't as desperate as you thought, but I'm thrilled to get out of Billings for the weekend. If I weren't here, you could meet this guy, no problem."

"Except without your encouragement, I wonder if I would have set up a coffee date."

"Regardless, it's the right move, and I can certainly manage to amuse myself for a couple of hours while you have a heart-to-heart with your cowboy."

"It's after midnight. How can I invite him this late when we're talking about tomorrow morning?"

"Didn't you say he was at the bachelor party tonight?"

"Yes, but—"

"Text him. He'll be up."

"All right." Drew sent the text and his response came shooting back. He'd be at Rangeland Roasters at ten.

Elise gazed at her. "He's at a bachelor party with his foster brothers, where the booze is flowing and the laughter is loud, and yet he answered your text almost immediately. Any doubts that this conversation is necessary?"

Drew sighed. "Not a single one."

Chapter Fourteen

Austin borrowed Jonah's truck and arrived at Rangeland Roasters ten minutes early. After receiving Drew's text last night he'd almost shown it to Cade as proof that she was into him. In spite of having her sister staying with her, she wanted to see him. Even better, she'd asked him this time instead of everything being his idea.

But he'd decided not to tell Cade about the coffee date. He hadn't said anything about it to Jonah, either. He'd just mentioned an errand he needed to run in town. Jonah had been too groggy to ask questions, anyway. He'd just handed over his keys.

Most everyone had bunked down at the cabins although they hadn't packed it in until around four. Austin had stayed until the end, but he'd cut way back on his beer consumption so he wouldn't be hungover this morning. A shower, a shave and clean clothes had perked him up, although he'd felt a little weary on the drive in.

But now that he was seated at a table by the window and watching the door, an adrenaline rush counteracted his lack of sleep. When he caught sight of Drew, his pulse hammered. He imagined her thinking about the next couple of days without any time together. Maybe she'd decided to fix that problem because she plain liked being with him.

She caught sight of him through the window and waved. He lifted his hand in response. He loved the way she moved, the way her dark ponytail swung with each stride of her long legs. He loved that she was tall and not fussy in the way she dressed. Jeans and a scoop-necked T-shirt looked great on her. She wore the pendant necklace, like always.

Her grandmother had told her to follow her heart. Maybe that was the reason she was here. As she came through the door, he stood and waited for her. He hadn't been aware of smiling until she returned his smile.

"Thanks for meeting me." She stayed just out of reach as she pulled her wallet out of her purse. "My treat."

"Put your money away. It's on me." He was a little disappointed that she was keeping her distance, but Rangeland Roasters had become a gathering place for residents of the town and she might not want to advertise that they were involved.

"But I invited you."

"Let me pay." He stepped closer and lowered his voice. "And then let's get out of here."

"But—"

"Drew, I insist. What do you want?"

"Just regular coffee."

"Nothing to eat? A muffin? A Danish?"

"No, thanks, but go ahead if you're hungry. I'll hold the table."

"I thought I'd get it to go."

She looked uncertain and finally nodded. "Okay."

As he ordered the coffee, he thought about the side street where he'd parked. It was only a block off Main, but not much traffic went that way. He'd chosen the spot on purpose because he hadn't envisioned sitting in the coffee shop if they could go somewhere more private. He'd put the sunscreen over the windshield.

He used a cardboard carrier for the coffee and decided to get one blueberry muffin in case she changed her mind about eating something. When he came back she was standing next to the table as if still guarding it.

"I'm not sure where we could go," she said. "Maybe we should stay here."

"I'm parked a block away. We can sit in the truck."

"The ranch truck?"

He had a hunch why she'd asked. If they ended up making out a little bit and someone noticed a couple kissing in the truck, she wouldn't want it to be the one with the Thunder Mountain Academy logo on the side of it. He hoped they would kiss. This might be the only chance they'd have for a couple of days. "I brought Jonah's."

"Oh. All right, then."

He followed her to the door and managed to reach around and open it for her without spilling their drinks. She smelled more delicious than either the muffin or the coffee. "To the right." He fell into step beside her.

"How was the bachelor party?"

"Terrific. Like old times. How's your sister doing?"

"She'll be fine. I'm glad I suggested bringing her down here, though. Typical of them, my parents are trying to fix this and they're being a little pushy about it."

"Then I'm glad you fetched her. I was surprised to hear from you, though. Happy, but surprised."

"I decided we needed a chance to talk."

He chuckled. "Oh, yeah?" Then he gestured to the right again. "Down here. The dark blue truck at the end of the street."

"I see it."

"Where's yours?"

"On Main. I was lucky and found a spot close to Rangeland Roasters."

Obviously she hadn't been planning to invite him to sit in her truck. "Did you get that reunion video edited in time?"

"I did. Everything's under control."

"I wish I could say the same."

She glanced up at him. "What's wrong?"

"I desperately want to kiss you." He took the keys out of his pocket and stepped around her to unlock the passenger door. "But I know we need to wait until we're inside the truck. I can understand why you wouldn't want to advertise that we're together."

"Austin, I—"

"Just a kiss. I promise not to get carried away." He opened the door and once she was in, he handed her the cardboard tray with their coffee and the muffin. "You can set that on the dash."

"The console would be better."

He smiled. "Not if I'm going to kiss you." He closed the door and walked around to the driver's side, his heart pounding in anticipation. A mere twenty-four hours had passed since he'd held her yet it felt like weeks.

Before he climbed in, he tucked his hat behind the seat so it wouldn't get in the way. Then he noticed that their coffee tray sat on the console. That was a clear signal and his good mood evaporated. "You don't want me to kiss you."

"I do, but first we need to talk about something."

Last night's conversation with his brothers started playing in his head. He'd been so sure they were wrong and that Drew felt the way he did. He took a calming breath, settled behind the wheel and turned to face her. "Shoot."

Her expression softened. "I really like you."

"I really like you, too." He swallowed. "I have a feeling there's a *but* coming after that, though."

"Not really. It's more of a question. Just now you mentioned that we were *together.* Yesterday you said I'd probably be seeing a lot of your family in the future. Am I imagining things, or are you getting serious about me?"

That knocked the breath right out of him. He stared at her as he scrambled for what to say. His brothers were right. He was moving too fast and had jumped to conclusions based on her eagerness to make love to him.

"I think I have my answer," she said gently.

He scrubbed a hand over his face. "I feel like a damned fool. But yesterday you were so…so…"

"Willing?"

"Yes, ma'am. That's a good word for it."

"Then I'll take some of the blame for misleading you. I think I mentioned that in Billings, whenever I dated someone, it became common knowledge in my family pretty fast."

"You did." He didn't think what she was about to say would make him feel any better but he would hear her out. If nothing else, he could get his act together while she talked.

"You're the first man I've been with where I didn't have any comments from the peanut gallery. It was liberating."

Okay, that info made things way worse. "So you

would have been that *willing* with any joker who happened along?"

"No!" She gazed into his eyes, her expression earnest. "I said it wrong. I've been here nearly eight months and haven't gone out with anyone."

"Probably because you were too busy."

"I was busy, but I was asked out a couple of times and I wasn't motivated to date either of them. The minute I saw you under that sink I was a goner. If you hadn't asked me out I eventually would have asked you."

"So you're physically attracted to me?" He'd briefly dated a woman in New Zealand who'd only wanted sex from him. No conversation, no shared meals, no scenic drives.

"Of course I'm physically attracted but I also like you. You have a zest for life. You've had misfortune but you've risen above it. You set goals and achieve them. I admire all that."

"But you still have an issue."

"I like you very much, but I'm not in the market for something permanent."

"Ever?" His hopes and dreams circled the drain.

"I don't know about ever, but certainly not now. I left Billings to get away from family responsibilities that made me feel trapped. I need to figure out who I am and what I want. Selling that rafting video was huge and it could be a good direction for me. I won't know that for a while, though, and in the meantime…"

"You don't want some cowboy putting a halter on you." Cade and the rest of his brothers had nailed it. He wasn't giving up, but he'd better be careful or he'd scare her off.

She smiled. "That's about the size of it."

He had to ask the next question but he was worried

about how she'd answer. "Is this about dating other guys?"

"No."

His shoulders sagged in relief. "I'm glad, but sort of confused."

"Can't we just have fun?" She fiddled with her pendant, sliding it back and forth along the chain. "Why not leave it at that?"

Because he'd outgrown that phase in his life. He'd even told her so on their first date. He'd left New Zealand because that kind of loose arrangement didn't work for him anymore. He'd always preferred situations that had a trajectory, an end game.

Now that he'd found the right woman, he didn't want to waste time just hanging out. He wanted to make plans, create a blueprint for the future. But if he said any of that she was likely to get out of the truck and walk away.

Frustrating though it might be for him to back off and give her time, he had no choice. It was either do that or abandon the whole deal, which was another option. Logically he knew she wasn't the only woman in the world he could love.

But when he looked into her dark eyes with their silent plea for understanding, he couldn't think logically. Instead he pictured giving up the privilege of kissing those plump lips and the intense pleasure of holding her lithe body while they made love. Nope, he couldn't imagine ending everything because she didn't share his vision. Instead he'd have faith that someday she would.

She moistened her lips. "You're being very quiet over there."

"Just making sure I get it." He was focused on her mouth and the sheen on her lower lip where her tongue had swept over it. "We'll be exclusive but don't have any real claim on each other. I guess that means if it stops working for us we won't have to break up because we were never a unit in the first place."

"Exactly. Can you live with that kind of setup?"

"Yes, ma'am, I surely can." He glanced at the cups of coffee, which would be lukewarm by now, and the muffin, which certainly didn't interest him and might not interest her, either. "Want to drink the coffee or move it?"

"I vote for moving it. Meeting for coffee was just an excuse."

"Then allow me." Picking up the cardboard tray, he opened his door and climbed out so he could set it on the hood. Then he got back in the truck. "I'll deal with it later." He reached for her, coaxing her toward him even though they had the barrier of the console between them. "Right now I have more pressing concerns, like giving you a proper kiss."

She leaned over and wound her arms around his neck. Her necklace dangled between them. "An improper kiss will do."

"Don't know if I can manage that in such tight quarters." Cupping her cheek in one hand, he angled his body and settled his mouth over hers. The moment he touched those velvet lips he groaned in frustration.

She pulled back. "What?"

"I feel like I'm kissing you through the bars of a prison cell. I could rip this console out with my bare hands."

"It's not your truck."

"Good point." He released her. "I'm coming around to your side."

"Austin, there's not enough room."

He opened the door and glanced over his shoulder. "We'll make room." Once he opened the passenger door he got her to hold on to the dash and lift away from the seat. He slid underneath her and closed the door. "Now sit on my lap."

"This is a tight fit, Austin. We're not small people."

"No, but we're motivated people. Scoot around and kneel on the seat so you're facing me. Ah, that's better."

She sat on his knees and gazed into his eyes. "You've done this before."

"And you haven't?" He cradled her face in both hands.

"I didn't say that. Making out in truck cabs is part of a Montana teenager's education."

"Then kiss me, lady. Kiss me like you mean it."

"With pleasure, cowboy." She fit her mouth to his.

He swore rockets exploded when that happened. Maybe a car driving by had backfired, but he thought it was the effect of her tongue in his mouth and his tongue in hers. Their kiss was hotter than a campfire. When he reached under her shirt and unhooked her bra she didn't stop him.

But they were still in a public place in broad daylight, so he contented himself with stroking and fondling rather than pulling off her shirt so he could kiss her there, too. His package ached something fierce but he suffered in silence. Or mostly silence. He let out a moan or two.

When she pulled back she was gasping. "We need to stop. Otherwise…"

"Otherwise I'll have to drive you to a motel and that's not how I want our relationship to go."

"Me, either." She pressed his hand to her breast. "But I love it when you touch me."

"I love it more." He gave her a gentle squeeze. "When are you taking your sister home?"

"Sunday afternoon." She arched into his caress. "Ah, that's nice."

"So you'll be back here Sunday night?" He rolled her nipple between his thumb and forefinger.

"Uh-huh."

"Then let me know when you're home again. I'll come over."

"Great plan." She sighed. "I don't want to leave this truck."

"But you have to." With reluctance he fastened the front catch on her bra. "Did you wear this for me?"

"Yes."

"Thank you." He'd take all the encouragement he could get. If she'd worn this bra on purpose for their coffee date, then she'd hoped they'd end up like this, exchanging hot kisses in some secluded spot. She might be putting the brakes on when it came to making a commitment, but he didn't think she'd hold to that much longer.

Chapter Fifteen

Drew reported to Elise that lines had been drawn in the sand. But that hot interlude in the truck made her wonder how defined those lines were. After the way she'd kissed him, he had to know that whenever he was around, she was like a hand grenade with the pin pulled.

Now that she and Elise were on their way to the rehearsal and Elise would meet Austin, Drew felt the need to unburden herself. "I don't want to get serious about him, but when he touches me, I turn to jelly. That could be a problem."

"Are you telling me that if he proposed during a passionate moment you might say yes?"

"I hope not."

"But you're not sure."

"No."

"So don't be alone with him."

"I want to be alone with him. He's sizzling hot."

Elise threw up her hands. "Then marry the guy! He sounds perfect for you, so why fight it?"

"Because marriage is forever. It means in-laws and mortgages and likely it means babies. I'm not ready for that kind of total commitment."

"You may not be, but I'm ready to commit *you* somewhere if you keep this up. You need to decide what you want and stick to it no matter what."

"That's not so easy when Austin's around."

"Come on, Drew. He's just a guy."

"Say that again after you've seen him. He's gorgeous. And on top of that, he's sweet and generous and—"

"You sound like a woman in love."

"I'm not!"

"Are you sure, sis?"

"Yes." But she wasn't sure, and that made everything more confusing.

At the ranch, Drew made sure her sister met the members of Austin's family who were helping prepare for the big day. Then she introduced Elise to Austin when they went to the barn to set up the umbrella lights for the ceremony. He was one of the foster brothers in charge of bringing horses in from the pasture and putting them in their stalls for the rehearsal.

After he'd gone out the back door to fetch another pair, Elise glanced at Drew. "I get it. He's the stuff fantasies are made of."

"That's why I'm so glad you're here, so you can see what I'm up against."

Elise laughed. "In your shoes I'd be up against that cowboy as often as possible."

"Yeah, yeah." Drew set an umbrella light in place. "See if you can find a convenient socket for this baby."

"Got it." She shoved the plug into the outlet. Then

she glanced around to see if they were still alone. "It's the guy's attitude that I really like. He's modest, yet at the same time driven to succeed. Lately I've run into men who endlessly brag about themselves for no reason. They're like the old saying All Hat and No Cattle."

"I know. Austin's initiative turns me on. That's what makes this so complicated." Drew switched on the umbrella lights and one of the horses nickered.

"They really want the horses in here for the ceremony?"

"They do. Lexi's hired one of her riding students to come in tomorrow morning and braid ribbons into their manes so they'll look festive."

"I can't wait to see how this goes."

"Me, either. Hey, go stand where Cade and Lexi will be so I can get a reading." She adjusted the umbrella's tilt. "Looking good. We can start bringing everyone in. I need to mic Cade but otherwise we're in decent shape."

Elise walked back over to her. "Before we do that, let me ask you something. You told Austin where you're coming from, but are you clear about his thinking?"

"The look on his face when I asked if he was getting serious said it all."

"But there are different levels of serious. I know some couples that have been hanging out for years and they never moved in together, let alone married and had kids. They just like each other. Maybe that's all he's looking for."

"That would be great." She smiled at Elise. "Thanks for being here, sis. You're good moral support."

"Back atcha."

Drew took one last look around the barn to assess her lighting setup. "Okay, let's get this show on the road."

Walking to the open barn door, Elise made a megaphone of her hands. "Everyone can come in now! You first, Cade. Drew needs to mic you up."

Cade walked into the barn with a big smile on his face. "I feel like a celebrity."

"You are." Drew clipped the mic to his shirt. "You and Lexi are the stars of the show, but you're the easiest one to hide a mic on because you'll be wearing a jacket."

"And a vest." He fingered the mic's wire. "I might want to run this under the vest instead of under the jacket."

"Right, and I'm thinking I need to put one of your brothers in charge of getting this put on you tomorrow afternoon."

"Ask Damon to come in."

"He understands this stuff?"

"He's a contractor so I'm sure he can manage it. But he's also my oldest friend and I know he'd do it right."

"Then let's get him in here."

Cade went to the door and summoned Damon, who came in and informed them that the sound guys had arrived and wanted to set up.

"You can tell them that's fine." She was interested in seeing how the sound system would work in the barn.

Once Damon came back, he paid close attention to the correct way to attach the mic and the small battery pack. She felt confident she could hand the job over to him for the ceremony.

Damon glanced around at Drew's lighting installation and his brown eyes lit with approval. "You did a great job with the lighting."

"Thanks." Pleased with the compliment, Drew flashed him a smile. "We can let everyone else in now."

"I'll give them the all-clear." Damon left.

Moments later Lexi came in. After admiring the way her husband-to-be was wired for sound, she watched the speakers and amps being hooked up for the musical portion of the ceremony. "Cade, I think it's too elaborate. We don't need the equivalent of a symphony in here."

"It's our big day," Cade said. "We need a big sound."

"Music sets the tone." Jonah joined the discussion. "I'm glad you're testing it tonight. I've seen ceremonies rise and fall on the choice of music."

"I wanted a single guitar," Lexi said. "I was outvoted."

"Interesting idea." Jonah glanced toward the open door where Austin stood talking to Rosie and Herb. "I know we're at the zero hour, but if you change your mind, we have someone who plays guitar."

Lexi perked up. "I'd forgotten that! It's been a few years, but as I recall, he was pretty good."

"Austin plays guitar?" Drew couldn't have been more surprised.

"He doesn't tend to talk about it," Jonah said, "but he's got a nice touch. He picked it up while we were both living at the ranch and apparently played for sing-alongs when he guided trail rides over in New Zealand."

Drew looked over at Austin. She could imagine him with a guitar balanced on his thigh, now that she thought about it. It completed the picture, in a way. "Did he bring his guitar when he came back?"

"He did," Jonah said. "He considers guitar playing as his sideline. He plans to work it into his own trail rides."

"That's very cool."

"Speaking of sidelines," Elise said as she gazed at Jonah. "I'm fascinated by your decision to become a mail-order preacher. I've never known anyone who did that."

Drew blinked. She knew Elise, and her sister didn't make idle chatter without a reason. Something about Jonah had snagged her attention.

"Hey, I like parties." Jonah smiled. "Now that I'm licensed to marry folks, I get to attend a whole bunch of parties."

Elise laughed. "Can't argue with that logic."

Now that Drew thought about it, she realized Elise had been more animated whenever the good-looking minister was around. Interesting. A crush on one of the members of the Thunder Mountain Brotherhood would be an excellent distraction from all the drama about the internship rejection that was going on in Billings.

Damon rejoined the group. "Ready to test the sound system."

"Good. Once I'm in position with my camera mic on, let 'er rip." Drew moved to the area of the barn she'd picked out for obtaining the best shots. She held up her hand. "Go!"

The first chords of the music chosen for the intro filled the space, surging into the rafters as if the structure had been transformed into a cathedral. The horses grew restless, stomping and nickering in protest.

"Tone it down!" Damon shouted.

The volume was reduced, but the horses still didn't like it. Their protest was more muted, but they were clearly not happy as they paced restlessly in their stalls. Drew suspected the ceremony would either include dramatic music or horses, but not both. Given time Cade, Lexi and Herb might have acclimated the animals to this, but they didn't have that kind of time.

After conferring with Cade, Lexi held up both hands. "Stop the music!" That got a laugh. She turned toward the two sound guys. "You have a magnificent system and without horses in here it would be spectacular. But Cade and I decided early on that the horses would be part of the ceremony, so that means the music won't work. We'd still like you to play for the reception. We'll pay you as if you did both. That's only fair."

"Thanks, ma'am," one of the men said. "Then we'll see you tomorrow afternoon." They began packing up their gear.

Next Lexi focused on Austin, who'd taken a seat on the end of one of the benches. "Jonah says you still play guitar."

He rose and stepped into the aisle. His six-three, muscular frame nearly filled it. "I do, but I'm not—"

"Austin, I'm asking you, I'm begging you, to play guitar for our wedding. For the intro you can play whatever you know, but if you can manage it, I'd love the traditional wedding march when I come in."

He tugged on his hat. "Turns out I know that tune."

"You do?"

"Had a couple who wanted to get married during a trail ride in New Zealand. They wanted that music so I learned it."

Lexi beamed at him. "You're a lifesaver."

"I wouldn't say that, ma'am."

"Well, I would. Could you fetch your guitar so we can continue with the rehearsal?"

"I can, but it needs a new set of strings. The sound won't be what I'd want it to be."

"It'll do for now," Lexi said. "Would you have time to get new strings before the ceremony?"

"I'll make time."

"Bless you, Austin Teague."

Drew looked on as Austin blushed, and her heart warmed in a way that could end up being very dangerous.

Elise nudged her in the ribs. "Gotcha, didn't he?"

"I didn't count on the guitar."

"Yeah, we never see those things coming until they hit us between the eyes."

"This doesn't change anything."

Elise chuckled. "Keep telling yourself that, sis."

After Austin returned with his guitar, the rehearsal went well, mostly because Jonah kept everyone on task. His sense of humor combined with his talent for managing a group of people made him perfect for the job. At one point Elise tapped Drew on the shoulder, pointed to Jonah and mouthed, *He's great.*

Drew nodded because she was also impressed. But she had trouble focusing on anyone other than the gorgeous cowboy playing his guitar. Maybe it needed new strings, but Austin compensated beautifully. After the rehearsal Lexi gave him a big hug and Drew would have loved to do the same. But she was working.

Although the wedding reception would take place in the rec hall near the cabins, Lexi and Cade had decided the rehearsal dinner should be around the fire pit, the favorite gathering spot for cookouts. Drew switched to a smaller camcorder so she could video the group walking down to the meadow. Several of the guests helped her out by peering into the lens and making faces during the short hike.

Elise carried Drew's camera bag and swapped jokes with everyone. As Drew had envisioned, her sister fit right in with the boisterous crowd, which was not unlike the Martinelli clan. Maybe that was why Austin's comment about seeing a lot of the family in the future had made her nervous. In her experience, family equaled turmoil and obligation.

Eventually she realized Jonah was keeping pace with them, too, and had started a conversation with Elise about Michelangelo. Whether he knew it or not, he'd found the surest way to her sister's heart. Drew was encouraged that he seemed as interested in Elise as she was in him.

Before Drew had started filming today she'd promised herself not to get more footage of Austin than of the bride and groom. Turned out it wouldn't be a problem because he never came within camera range. At the moment, he was up at the house helping a couple of his brothers bring the food and drinks down to the meadow. Not that she'd kept track of his whereabouts.

Yeah, right. She'd known right where that cowboy was at all times. She'd picked up on the conversation about who would haul down the dinner fixings and she'd heard Austin volunteer. He was keeping himself busy and that was a good thing because it left her free to do her work.

The setting and the upbeat mood of the guests made her job easy, too. In the waning light, she got some great shots of friends gathered by the fire against the rosy hues of sunset. Once the beer and champagne arrived, she recorded toasts and laughter, teasing and hugs.

Then, after the steaks were on the grill and everyone was gathered, Lexi and Cade produced two matching digital tablets loaded with the video Drew had created. Cade handed one to Rosie and Herb while Lexi handed the other to her folks, Janine and Aaron. The four of them chose to gather around one screen instead of turning on both.

As they started watching, Drew was afraid she'd lose it, but somehow she kept filming through her tears. By the time the video was over, the natural light was almost gone so she shut off her camera. Good thing, because she was suddenly besieged by Rosie, Herb, Janine and Aaron as they embraced her and poured out words of gratitude. Elise showed up to take her camera so it wouldn't hit the dirt.

The group hug ended with much wiping of eyes and blowing of noses. Several of the other guests were in the same shape and a slew of emotional toasts followed. When the entire group raised a glass to Drew, she was both choked up and humbled. One little video had brought so much joy.

Elise gave back the camera and wrapped an arm around her shoulders. "You did good, sis."

"Thank you." Drew sniffed and dug in her pocket for a tissue.

"Ever thought of making that your specialty?"

"Not really." She wiped her eyes. "I think the nature videos will be my specialty."

"Okay. Just thought I'd mention it." She looked past Drew's shoulder. "Hey, Austin. Didn't she do great?"

"She sure did."

Drew turned to find him walking toward her, wearing a broad smile. She'd last seen him tending the food on the grill, but then Cade and Lexi had brought out the video and she'd lost track of him. His sudden appearance delighted her and made her wish they could have a little alone time.

He gestured toward the camera. "I noticed you turned it off. Does that mean you're taking a break?"

"Actually I'm finished for the night. Cade and Lexi didn't want me to use artificial light during the cookout so they said when it got dark I should quit. I was about to take this one to my truck and get the other one out of the barn before the food's served." She hoped he'd get the hint.

"Then let me help you."

"Okay." She avoided looking directly at Elise as she retrieved the camera bag her sister was holding. One of them could easily start laughing. Having a sister who knew the score was both a curse and a blessing. "If anyone asks," she said to Elise, "tell them we'll be back soon."

"I will. Take your time." Her sister's voice trembled as if she might lose her cool any second.

Drew glanced at Austin. "Let's go."

He lengthened his stride to keep up with her. "In a hurry?"

"Yes. Wouldn't want the food to get cold." She tucked her camera in the bag and zipped it closed.

"God, no." And then he laughed softly.

His low, sexy chuckle was all it took to send her up in flames. She couldn't wait to get her hands on that cowboy.

Chapter Sixteen

Austin vibrated with the need to kiss Drew and hold her close, but he also didn't want to forget to say what he'd been thinking during the rehearsal and afterward. "Before we get to the barn and I forget everything but kissing you—"

"Oh, is that what we'll be doing?"

"Yes, ma'am, and I wish it could be more. But first let me say that you have an amazing gift. I thought so when I saw your dedication to filming the horses, and then tonight I was bowled over by your talent. I loved watching you work."

"Thank you."

"I heard Elise talk about making something your specialty. Did she mean weddings in general or the Lexi and Cade one?"

"I think she was talking about the one I made for them."

"Then I completely agree with her. Not everyone

would have the imagination or the talent for something like that. I only caught part of it, but judging from everyone's reaction, you nailed it."

"It was mostly their doing. They came across so authentically that all I had to do was capture the emotion they gave me."

"That's my point. Not everyone could. I know people have to be relaxed but they're bound to be because you're so warm and encouraging with them. I saw tonight how you make everyone feel at ease."

"That's easy, though."

"Again, not easy for everyone. You could expand that concept and offer thank-you videos from grandkids to their grandparents, or from a group of students to a teacher, or from employees to a wonderful boss."

"Except I want to concentrate on making the nature videos."

"Well, yeah, I know you do." For some reason, she was resisting the suggestion so he dropped it. "Just a thought. Did you want to get the camera out of the barn now or later?"

"Let's get it now."

"Works for me." He slid back the wooden bar holding the double doors closed and opened one side, his heart pounding. "After you."

She walked into the darkened interior and lowered her camera case to the floor. Then she turned back to him and stepped closer. "Is this what you had in mind, cowboy?"

"Yes, ma'am." His breath quickened. Dropping his hat on top of her camera bag, he pulled her close. "Exactly what I had in mind."

She wound her arms around his neck and snuggled against him. "You left me alone to do my work tonight. Thank you for that."

"Wasn't easy." He cradled the back of her head, splaying his fingers where she'd put her silky hair into a ponytail. "I love watching you work, but I kept thinking about doing this." Leaning down, he brushed his mouth over hers. "And especially this." He delved deep, moaning as he reconnected with the rich sensuality of kissing Drew.

And oh, how she kissed him back. The seductive way she welcomed the thrust of his tongue made him wish she hadn't been so against a long-term relationship. He could kiss her this way for the rest of their lives.

Lifting his mouth from hers, he gasped for breath. "I want you so much. If I thought we could…"

"We can't." She was breathing as fast as he was. "I want you, too, but…just…*kiss me*." She pulled his head down, her mouth hot on his and her body so close he could feel the imprint of her pendant against his chest.

He hadn't dealt with frustration this intense since he'd been a virginal teenager who hadn't dared to take the next step.

Too soon, she backed away, panting. "We have to stop."

"I know." He ran a trembling hand through his hair. "I thought we could just kiss. Take the edge off."

She gulped. "Wrong."

"Get your other camera." He picked up his hat and her camera bag. "I'll wait by your truck."

"Never mind. I'll handle it. You can go back."

"No, ma'am." He dragged in another breath. "I walked you here and I'm walking you back."

"Because of cowboy manners?"

He couldn't tell if she was amused or irritated. "That and respect for Mom's rules. Guaranteed she noticed we left together. If I show up without you, I'll hear about it. I'll wait by the truck."

"I'll be there in a minute."

He stepped out into the cool night air and took a deep breath. He'd promised himself that he wouldn't go beyond a kiss and he'd damn near broken that promise. She deserved more than a quickie in the barn before they went back to the party. Drew was classier than that. Hell, *he* was classier than that.

Most of all, he didn't want to mess this thing up. Their conversation earlier today had alerted him that she wasn't ready to wear matching sweatshirts to the Thunder Mountain Christmas Eve gathering. She also wouldn't be inviting him to move in with her anytime soon.

Leaning against her truck, he evaluated where he was in this relationship. Not where he'd like to be, but not in a hopeless scenario, either. Unlike the lady in New Zealand, Drew liked his personality as well as his body. He could build on that.

"The truck's open." She showed up lugging the camera she'd mounted on a tripod. "If you'd get the door, I'd be—"

"Let me have that thing while you get the door." He lifted the camera away from her. "Where does it go?"

"Eventually it'll go in the back. I have a whole setup there for transporting my equipment but I didn't want to make this complicated. Elise can help me stow everything properly."

"Or we can do it the right way now." Shouldering her camera bag and carrying the heavy video camera, he walked to the back of the truck. "Tell me what goes where."

"Thanks, Austin." She put down the tailgate and showed him where to put the biggest camera.

"Happy to do it." He arranged everything in the bin and stood back so she could close the tailgate. "Now let's get going because I'm developing a strong urge to kiss you again." He took her hand and started off. Then he gave her hand a squeeze. "Is this okay?"

"If your family operates anything like mine, everybody knows about our camping trip by now, so it's not like we're fooling anybody."

"No, we're not. But I thought you didn't want to give people the wrong impression about...about where we stand."

She pulled him to a stop. "I'll admit I used to care what other people thought about my love life, but that's a waste of time."

"I agree."

"But you and I have to be clear with each other. Are we?"

"Yes, ma'am. Totally clear." And he was determined to be patient and wait for her to realize they were perfect together. Then again, a woman who kissed the way Drew did might have a change of heart sooner rather than later.

"Then you're welcome to hold my hand for as long as you like."

"Okay, I will." He didn't add that if he had his way, he'd be holding her hand for the next fifty or sixty years.

"Are you planning to bring your guitar back out tonight?"

"God, no. I managed to stumble through the rehearsal, but I'm not pushing my luck. By wedding kickoff time, I'll have a new set of strings on that baby."

"I should mic it to make sure we can hear it during the video."

"I'm cool with that. But give me until noon to find the strings and tune it."

"I'll be here for most of the day."

"Most of the day? But the ceremony isn't until five."

"I know, but there are lots of important things to film before then. I want to video the arranging of the flowers in the barn and the little girl braiding the horses' manes. Then I need to document the separation of the guys and gals, which is always tricky in a situation like this."

"The women will get the house and the men will get the cabins in the meadow. Except for Herb. I'm guessing he might be a floater between the two camps."

"I'll be a floater, too. After I film the ladies getting dressed I might head down to the meadow and see how many of the guys will let me show them getting duded up in their outfits."

"I don't know. That's sacred ground, brotherhood only."

"I understand. I don't want to be obnoxious about it, but years from now you might all want some candid shots of adjusting each other's string ties and pulling on your fancy dress boots."

"We might. Listen, I should tell you that when I play the wedding march, the brotherhood has talked about humming it along with the guitar."

"Austin, I love that. Gives me cold chills."

"No promises. Not everyone is in favor."

"Talk them into it. I think it would be awesome."

"We haven't told Cade or Lexi."

"Yeah, well, don't. Then you have the option of doing it or not depending how everyone feels at the time. But you have my vote. This wedding is so nontraditional that whatever you decide to do will be fine. I'll just go with it."

Austin squeezed her hand. "That's what I'm talking about. You have a great way of rolling with the punches.

I'm learning from you that good footage of people has to be spontaneous and you've got that part down. I know your heart's set on the nature videos, but—" He caught himself. "Never mind." He was doing it again, pushing for a scenario that she hadn't been enthusiastic about. His motives weren't pure, either, since he favored a plan that wouldn't require so much travel.

"What were you going to say?"

"I was sticking my nose in again where it doesn't belong. This is your career."

"That's true but you're allowed to give an opinion."

"Not when I have ulterior motives."

They were within sight of the group gathered around the fire pit but she pulled him to a stop again. "I wondered about that."

He decided not to waffle on the issue. "You need to follow your heart, like your grandmother said, and if that means traveling south during the winter months, I'll accept that and be happy for you. We have no ties to each other." He looked into her eyes. "And I'll miss you like crazy whenever you're gone."

Her gaze warmed as she studied him. "If I'm totally honest, I'd miss you, too. But that's not a reason to ditch the idea."

"Definitely not." Although he sure liked hearing that she'd miss him and he *really* liked the way she was looking at him. Maybe she'd miss him enough to invite him along once in a while, assuming he could afford the time and expense. But he wouldn't ask her. Like his brothers had said, she needed to do the asking.

He gave her hand a squeeze. "I just hope you won't reject the thank-you video concept entirely. I saw your face when those folks were watching what you'd created.

You captured something precious and I could tell what it meant to you."

Her expression softened. "It did mean a lot."

"Then that's all I'll say on the subject. Let's go grab some food."

Chapter Seventeen

Drew and Austin each got a plate of food and Damon handed them glasses of champagne. "Word is that we have some announcements coming up and you'll need these for toasting," he said.

"Then we'd better find a bench and sit." Austin glanced around.

"Over here, guys." Elise beckoned from where she sat with Jonah. "We saved you a spot."

Drew noted the space between her sister and Jonah on the bench, or rather the lack of it. There would be plenty of room for two more. "Thanks, sis." She walked over and settled down next to Elise, who'd finished most of her meal.

Austin took a seat next to her and leaned around her to smile at Elise and Jonah. "Appreciate it, folks."

Jonah smiled. "No worries. We knew you'd be along eventually."

Drew balanced her plate on her lap. "Were we missed?"

"A few people asked. I told them you were putting away your equipment and double-checking all the electrical connections." She looked over at Drew and blinked innocently. "Did you take care of that?"

"Yes. Yes, I did. Everything's fine." She returned her sister's bland expression. "Listen, I've been thinking about tomorrow. I'll need to be here all day, but you probably don't want to hang out here that long."

"I won't mind a bit. It'll be fun to see everything take shape. I've never spent much time on a ranch. Rosie thinks I should mosey on down here every couple of weeks, but I told her you'd probably get sick of me if I visited that often."

"I would not. I'd love having you."

"I've offered to teach her to ride," Jonah said.

"And I'd really like that." Elise's expression grew animated as she turned to Drew. "You should learn, too. Remember how we used to talk about it and never did?"

"You don't know how to ride?" Austin's eyebrows lifted.

"Too busy doing other sports, I guess."

"So when you offered to shoot my first trail ride, were you just going to climb on a horse without ever having done it?"

She laughed. "Guess I hadn't thought that through. I'm fairly coordinated so I figured I'd catch on pretty quick, but maybe I could use a few lessons so I don't fall off in the middle of filming."

"And you might want to consider logging time in the saddle before you tackle an overnight trip." Austin looked amused. "You have to work up to spending several hours on a horse or you'll be miserable."

"The four of us could go out," Jonah said. "And we

need to do it before the first snow. Let's pick a weekend and—"

"Attention everybody!" Cade tapped a fork against his champagne flute. "Ty and Whitney have an announce—"

"Oh, my God!" Rosie charged over to throw her arms around both of them, knocking Ty's hat off in the process. He didn't seem to notice as he gathered his wife and his foster mom in a tight embrace.

"Boy or girl?" someone called out.

"You'll all have to wait another six months to find out!" Whitney beamed as everyone crowded around with congratulations.

When Austin and Jonah rose to their feet, Drew put down her plate and stood, too. She didn't know Ty and Whitney well, but she'd be happy to add her good wishes to the mix.

"Hold on, hold on!" Cade tapped his glass again. "Hope and Liam also have an—" He wasn't allowed to finish that sentence, either, before pandemonium erupted a second time.

"And we're having a girl!" Liam's deep baritone carried over the noise of the crowd.

His jubilant expression tickled Drew. Such a caring, positive man would make a great dad.

Cade tapped on his glass a third time.

"Another one?" Rosie's face was flushed with excitement as she surveyed the crowd.

"I don't think so, Mom," Cade said, "but I wanted to check before we made the toast. Anybody else have news to share?"

"Not yet, bro." Finn, the brewer from Seattle, wrapped an arm around his wife, Chelsea. "But we're working on it!"

That got a laugh and Cade's nod of approval. "That's

great to hear. Can't have too many grandbabies, right, Mom?"

"Never!" Rosie's eyes sparkled in the light from the fire. "Bring on those Thunder Mountain babies!"

Drew fingered her pendant. Her grandmother had been surrounded by what Drew considered a daunting number of children and grandchildren. But that was a fraction of what Rosie could be looking at in a few years. She seemed ecstatic about it. The image made Drew shiver.

"Cold?" Austin slipped an arm around her shoulders.

"Not really. I just thought about how many little kids Rosie could have running around here before too long."

Austin chuckled. "And she can't wait."

"I noticed that."

"The woman's incredible. I sometimes think not having kids of her own was how it was supposed to be. She turned into a kind of superhero mom. All she's missing is the cape." He gave Drew a squeeze. "Come on. Let's go over and congratulate the happy parents."

She did that, and she was genuinely happy for them because they seemed so delighted with the concept themselves. As she listened politely to a discussion of prenatal vitamins and morning sickness, car seats and portable cribs, she was so grateful that she wasn't standing in either one of those wives' shoes. Having a Thunder Mountain baby was a great big flipping deal, a goal she couldn't imagine having.

She couldn't say the same for Austin, though. He was clearly in the swing of this new stage in the life of Thunder Mountain Ranch. He asked more questions than anybody, or so it seemed to her. If she didn't know better, she'd think he'd already lined up his baby mama.

Maybe he had. He'd said all the right words about having fun without any strings or promises, but judging from his intense interest in the baby news, he was eager to start a family. She was not. By continuing their affair, she was selfishly wasting his valuable time.

The party lasted a little longer after that, but everyone agreed that they all needed to get some rest before the big day.

Before they left, Cade asked for everyone's attention one last time. "I got a special phone call today. My cousin Jack Chance and his mom, my aunt Sarah, are driving over from Jackson Hole tomorrow."

Drew blinked. The reputation of the Chance brothers, co-owners of the Last Chance Ranch, had spread as far as Billings. She vaguely remembered serving one of the brothers at Martinelli's during her waitressing days. It might have been Jack.

"Oh, Cade." Lexi looked at him with shining eyes. "That's fantastic. When were you going to tell me?"

"Couldn't decide the right moment. Didn't want to interfere with the baby news, so this seemed like the perfect time." He glanced around at the group. "Some of you know the story and some don't, but two years ago I didn't think I had any blood relatives. Finding out I was related to the owners of the Last Chance Ranch came as a big shock."

"But you've adjusted, right, bro?" Finn smiled. "Sure seems like it."

"I have, and I feel like a lucky son of a gun to have them as relatives. We invited the whole family, although God knows where we would have put them all considering our limited seating. They couldn't bring everyone because of schedule conflicts, so Jack and Aunt Sarah are representing the family."

"I can't wait to meet them." Rosie gave Cade a hug. "This is wonderful news, son."

"It'll be good to see them again," Finn said. "Chels and I got to spend a few days at the Last Chance two years ago. We'd be glad to introduce them around."

Chelsea laughed. "From what I remember of Jack Chance, he'll need no introduction. The guy's a force of nature."

Yep, Drew decided. She'd served Jack Chance. Martinelli's piped in music from a sound system but they had no dance floor. Jack had insisted on dancing her around the tables anyway when one of his favorite songs had come on. Then he'd left her a huge tip.

"So is that it for startling announcements?" Damon lifted a sleeping Sophie from Phil's arms. "Because I need to get my ladies tucked in for the night."

"And I need my beauty sleep." Lexi gave Cade a quick kiss. "See you at the altar, cowboy."

Cade stared at her. "You're really going home with your parents? I thought you were kidding."

"Not kidding."

"But I'll be all by myself."

"You'll have your cat." She gave him another kiss, this time on the cheek. "Bye, sweetie."

"Damn." Cade looked crestfallen. "Ringo's great, but he doesn't say much."

Austin glanced at Drew. "I'll walk you to your truck, but I need to talk with Cade first. Wait for me?"

"Sure."

"Jonah and I will go on ahead," Elise said. "The truck's unlocked, right?"

"Yep."

"We'll probably take our time. It's a gorgeous night."

"That it is." Jonah slipped his hand through hers as they left the meadow.

Drew took comfort in her sister's enjoyment of this

flirtation with Jonah. It might turn into something or fizzle out, but for now Elise seemed to have forgotten about Italy.

Austin had his arm around Cade's shoulders as they talked. She didn't want to eavesdrop so she moved a little farther away. Snippets still drifted in her direction, though—things like "important day," "fancy dress" and "Lexi's special moment." She concluded that Austin had given plenty of thought to the subject of brides and weddings, too.

His conversation with Cade had obviously cheered up the bridegroom because now he and Austin were laughing like fools. Finn and Ty walked over to get in on whatever it was while Chelsea and Whitney stood together watching and shaking their heads.

"See you jokers later," Austin said as he left the group and started toward Drew.

"Don't do anything I wouldn't do, Junior," Cade called after him.

Finn laughed. "That leaves a hell of a lot of territory!" He added something else that Drew couldn't hear and the guys launched into another fit of laughter.

Austin came toward her grinning. "Mission accomplished. Couldn't stand to see that sad look on his face."

"I know. I realize there's a tradition that the bride isn't supposed to see the groom the morning of the wedding, but when they've been living together isn't that sort of pointless?"

"I think this is about Lexi's bond with her parents. She wants one more chance to go home and be their little girl again."

"Oh." She was touched by his insight. "Then it makes perfect sense. She loves them a lot. That was clear from the way she thanked them in the video. But it does leave Cade alone with his cat."

"He won't be." Austin took her hand and wove his fingers through hers as they started toward the barn. "Since Jonah and I are the unattached ones, we'll spend the night up at his cabin. I suggested it and he liked the idea. I'm sure Jonah will go along with it, too. We'll drink some beer, play some cards."

"That's very nice of you." Holding hands with Austin was a pleasure she was growing increasingly fond of. As they walked she savored the warmth, strength and affection he communicated with that simple gesture. If she ultimately decided to give up that pleasure, that would be a sad day.

"Hey, we're brothers. It's what we do for each other."

"But you'll also get some sleep, right?"

"Worried about me?"

"I am, but I'm even more concerned about Cade from a practical standpoint. If he's dead on his feet and he's the only one with the mic, then the ceremony could suck, which would be disappointing for everyone."

"Tell you what. I'll make it my job to see that he gets some shut-eye tonight. How's that?"

"Helpful. Thank you."

"I noticed your sister and Jonah went ahead of us. That could mean they want to be alone for a while."

"I'm guessing they do."

"Then we should meander along and give them some extra time." He slowed his pace. "Come to think of it, they might be to the kissing stage by now."

"They might."

"Speaking of kissing…"

And here she was, yearning to feel his strong arms

around her and yet wondering if she would only create heartache in the long run.

He didn't seem to notice her hesitation. "The minute I took your hand my brain checked out. It's a wonder I managed that much of a segue."

"I thought it was cute." His use of the word *segue* reminded her of another quality she admired about him. He was literate, and not in a stuffy, self-important way. He'd read books because he'd loved the stories.

He squeezed her hand. "Here's my idea. There's a place in the shadows beside the barn. If we slide into that spot before we get to your truck, Jonah and Elise won't even know we're there."

"I see." She tried to summon the willpower to refuse. She failed.

"I really need to kiss you again before you leave tonight."

Heat suffused her body and she resisted the urge to fan herself. "We should probably discuss something else."

"Like what?"

"Tell me about Jonah."

"Ah, okay. Let me recalibrate some brain cells. Jonah. Somewhat footloose. Man of a million ideas who can't settle on any one of them for long. Drove me crazy until I accepted that he might drift from one thing to another for the rest of his life."

"You don't think being a licensed minister will turn into anything?"

"No, ma'am. He enjoys marrying folks but said he can't settle on one denomination. Most churches expect you to declare a preference."

"True."

"He's good with people and horses. Dude ranch work suits him. Is that enough about Jonah?"

"Is he nice to women?"

"Always. But picky. He must think your sister is special since he's taken an interest."

"She is special. Someday she'll be living in a large city because that's where she'll find the right job. Jonah doesn't seem like a big-city kind of guy."

"He's not."

"But if he's the footloose type…"

"Exactly. They can have some temporary fun." He pulled her to a stop and smiled down at her. "I don't think you have to worry, Drew. He's a good guy. And I'd love to change the subject."

Her pulse kicked into high gear. "Okay."

"Come with me, pretty lady." He led her to their right, avoiding the pool of light cast by the dusk-to-dawn lamp mounted over the barn doors. Then he hung his hat on the end of the hitching post.

They ended up in deep shadow on the side of the barn farthest away from where her truck was parked. She kept her voice down. "Was that hat some kind of signal?"

"Used to be. Don't know if anybody remembers." He pulled her close.

"I can barely see you."

"You don't need to see me." He cradled her jaw in one hand and pressed his thumb to the corner of her mouth. "Just let me in."

She instinctively parted her lips and he was there, the firm pressure of his lips coaxing her to open even more. With a soft groan, he thrust his tongue inside. Then he proceeded to hold her head very still as he ravished her mouth. He took possession of every inch, teasing, nipping and using his tongue in ways that made her writhe against him in frustration.

Shoving her hands in his back pockets, she pressed

her hips tight against his groin and yearned for the barriers between them to magically disappear. He pushed her against the side of the barn and nestled his aroused package between her parted thighs.

Slowly he raised his head. His voice was strained. "Let the record show that I really want you right now." He gulped for air. "But I'm going to control myself."

She took a shaky breath. "Am I supposed to be thankful?"

"I sure hope not." He nudged the aching spot between her thighs. "I hope you're thinking about when we can solve our mutual problem."

"Sunday night." They had issues, but they needed time and privacy to sort them out.

"That's an eternity from now."

"I know."

"But we'll make it." He shuddered. "Not sure how, but…" He sighed. "We will." Touching his mouth very lightly to hers, he gently sucked on her lower lip.

She was definitely wound too tight, because that simple caress nearly sent her over the edge.

Slowly he backed away. "No more." He sucked in air. "No more good-night kisses."

"Just…just as well."

"I'm holding out for a good-morning one."

"Not tomorrow, though. I'll be—"

"I'm not talking about tomorrow."

"Oh."

"When you come back from Billings on Sunday, I want the whole night."

She swallowed. "Okay."

"Good. That's settled." He took a deep breath. "Excuse me while I do a little pacing. I need to walk off some of this tension."

"I understand."

He chuckled. "I doubt that, but thanks for the support." He winced. "Once you're in the truck and on your way, I'll be much better."

"I don't want to startle Jonah and my sister. How did you want to work this?"

"We'll approach the truck while having an animated conversation."

"Not necessary, bro." Jonah came around the corner of the barn carrying Austin's hat. "I left Elise sitting in the truck. Then I saw this and figured I'd hang out by the hitching post until I heard what sounded like normal conversation."

"So you did remember."

"Sort of. I recognized your hat and you were wearing it when Elise and I left the meadow, so if it was now on the hitching post that logically had to be a make-out signal."

Drew pushed away from the side of the barn. "If Elise is ready to go, then I'd better get over there."

"No rush," Jonah said. "She thought you two might linger along the way."

"That's what comes from double-dating with my sister. She knows way too much."

Austin came toward her. "I'll walk you over there."

"Tell you what." She reached up and touched his cheek where his whiskers were starting to grow. "You and Jonah can stand by the barn and watch to make sure I get in the truck and drive away without incident. But you really don't need to escort me over there."

"She's right," Jonah said.

"But—"

"I know that isn't how Rosie taught us, but there are times you need to throw out the rule book."

Austin laughed. "Do you even have a rule book anymore? You've been throwing it out ever since I knew you."

"I have one. It just doesn't look like everyone else's."

Drew filed that comment away. She might need to pay closer attention to this budding relationship and make sure her sister didn't get hurt by some cowboy with a different set of principles. "So is the consensus that I can walk to the truck on my own?"

"Yes, ma'am." Austin glanced at Jonah. "I'm overruled."

"Then I'll leave you both. Have fun keeping Cade company while he waits for his wedding day. Good night." She gave Austin a quick kiss on the cheek and walked away.

When she climbed into the cab, Elise glanced over at her. "I have a crush on that cowboy."

"Tell me something I don't already know." She fished the keys out from under the seat and started the truck. "FYI, according to Austin, Jonah's not the type to live in a big city."

"I figured that out. Who knows? Maybe I'm not, either."

"What are you talking about? All you've ever wanted was a job curating an extensive art collection for a major museum. You're not going to find that job in a small town."

"I know, but losing this internship has made me reevaluate."

"That's fine, but please don't let a good-looking cowboy, who, by the way, has no idea what he wants from life, derail your entire career plan."

"He knows what he wants."

"Like what? I mean aside from the obvious short-term goal that we don't need to lay out in detail."

"He wants a life based on meaning instead of material possessions. I find that sexy."

"Material possessions like fine art?"

"We didn't get into that, but he gave me something to think about—fine art as stuff. It's a concept I hadn't considered before."

Drew groaned. "I'm not liking the sound of this."

"I didn't think you would. But it's not like we're in love or anything so you can stand down, sis."

"Yeah, okay. I'll admit it's a hot-button issue for me so I'm probably overreacting, or projecting, or whatever the terms are."

"I'd believe that. So how are things going with Austin? You didn't look terribly excited during all the talk about babies."

"I'm totally happy for those couples if that's what they want. But that's not where I am in my life. I'm becoming convinced that's where Austin's at, though."

"Honestly, that wouldn't surprise me. You said he's been with Rosie and Herb since he was nine and Rosie loves weddings and kids. I picked up on that immediately."

"So you think I might be right that he's ready to start a family of his own?" She glanced over at Elise. "Even though he says we can just hang out and have fun?"

"Considering his behavior tonight, maybe he is ready to settle down, despite what he's said to you. You have more info to go on now. I'd suggest another heart-to-heart with the man."

Drew sighed. "I'll do that. But the wedding doesn't make that kind of conversation easy. Then again, if it hadn't been for the wedding, he might not have come back from New Zealand when he did."

"Do you regret meeting him?"

She thought about it. "No. I'll never regret meeting Austin. He's one of the good guys." She took a deep breath. "But that doesn't mean we're meant for each other."

Chapter Eighteen

By Saturday morning Austin could see that Cade was a nervous wreck. Playing cards and drinking beer was no longer an appropriate distraction. Since Austin needed a trip to town for guitar strings, he proposed Jonah and Cade go with him. They could fuel up with breakfast at the diner, pick up the strings and shop for some decorative doodads to make the cabin more festive when Lexi returned that night.

Two hours later they arrived back at the cabin with the new strings plus a boatload of scented candles, flower arrangements, various types of chocolates, wine and a teddy bear couple dressed in wedding outfits. The bears had been Austin's idea.

"I'm doing this when I get married," he said as he surveyed the stash on the kitchen table and the kitchen counters. "What a great idea to welcome her with all these goodies."

Cade rubbed the back of his neck. "Hope so."

"If nothing else, she'll be touched by knowing you wanted to do something special." Jonah nudged back his hat. "And you won't have to find a place for anything except the bears. It's not like we've added a bunch of things you'll have to dust."

"That's a good point," Cade said. "I used to think Mom didn't have knickknacks because we'd break them. Recently she told me it was the dust factor."

Austin picked up the two bears. "You don't have to dust these, either. Just whack them together, like this." He gave a quick demonstration.

"Hey!" Cade snatched them away from him. "Don't do that."

"Why not? It's a great dusting technique."

"That may be true, but Cade Bear and Lexi Bear would prefer to have the dust carefully brushed from their furry little bodies." Cade walked over and gently placed them side by side on the sofa. "They don't appreciate being smashed together like a pair of cymbals."

Jonah was cracking up. "*Cade Bear and Lexi Bear*? Are you really gonna call them that?"

"Sure, why not?"

"Because it's not manly. It sounds like you're three."

"No, it doesn't." Since Austin had insisted on the bears he felt the need to defend Cade. "What else would you call them? They're supposed to represent the happy couple. You can't name them George and Sheila."

"Why do you have to name them at all?"

"Because that's what you do with stuffed animals. I had a bear I called Teddy. Not very original but I came up with it when I was around two, according to what my mom told me."

Cade nodded. "I had a bear. Named him Rufus after the character on *Sesame Street*. When I thought I was too old for teddy bears, I gave him to a younger kid."

"Yeah, I did that, too. When my mom died, I wished I had him back, but it was too late. That little kid was attached to Teddy and I didn't have the heart."

Jonah gazed at them. "Well, I didn't have a bear, so I guess that explains it."

"Doesn't have to be a bear," Austin said. "Like you heard last night, Sophie has a plush tarantula. I knew a kid who had a plush snake."

"Well, I didn't have any of those critters. Didn't know there was a naming protocol involved."

Austin couldn't believe that he'd lived in the same cabin with Jonah for years and hadn't known the guy had never had a stuffed toy as a kid. No telling what else Jonah had done without, but it might explain his philosophy about material possessions. He exchanged a quick glance with Cade.

"You know what?" Cade gestured toward the items piled in the kitchen. "We're standing here shooting the breeze like we have all day and we don't. I want to spit shine this cabin before we start putting flowers and candles everywhere and the morning is slip-sliding away."

"That's the damned truth." Jonah seemed relieved for a change of topic. "When are these long-lost relatives of yours going to show up, by the way?"

"They said not to expect them until right before the ceremony. They're checking into a hotel in town because they know we're full up here. If you're asking whether I should be down at the house soon in case they arrive, the answer is no. We need to start the cleaning project ASAP, though."

"I'll help you with that." Jonah jerked a thumb at Austin. "John Denver has to restring his guitar and practice his tunes."

"Yeah, I do."

"Then take that project out to the porch, please," Cade said, "so we don't have to vacuum around you."

"Do you want to vet the songs? Yesterday I was just winging it but you can have different ones as long as I know them."

"What you played yesterday was fine. I trust your judgment. Just don't play stuff like 'Does My Ring Burn Your Finger' or 'Whose Bed Have Your Boots Been Under?' and we'll be good."

"Damn. You just nixed my two favorites."

Cade grinned at him. "Grab your guitar and get outta here, cowboy. And thanks. It'll be great having you play."

"Especially when I launch into 'All My Ex's Live in Texas.' I know you want that one."

"There's the door, Junior."

Austin chuckled as he picked up the box of strings from the kitchen table and grabbed his guitar from the corner of the living room. He also took his phone out to the porch and laid it on the railing so he'd hear it. The men and women staying at the ranch were supposed to remain mostly separated today, but he remembered that Drew wanted to mic his guitar.

They couldn't be testing the mic at the last minute, either. If she didn't contact him by midafternoon, he'd text her. This was important, but it was also a great excuse to see her and maybe steal another kiss or two. He was getting seriously addicted to those kisses.

An hour later he had the guitar tuned and had started through his memorized pieces. None of them were sad songs or even mad songs. He'd never cared for those and Cade knew it.

Sitting on Cade's porch on a sunny day with his guitar balanced on his thigh was almost perfect. A light breeze was blowing and the birds were chirping away. Having Drew in the chair next to him would complete the picture but they were a long way from an idyllic scene like that. Neither one of them had a porch, for one thing.

He'd planned to rent an apartment but now he was thinking a house would be better, a small house with a porch. Porches and guitars were a natural fit. He might be able to find something like that at a rental price he could afford.

Staying overnight in Cade's house had given him a clearer picture of what he eventually wanted, although the place was a little small if Cade and Lexi had kids. He wondered if they'd thought of that. He sure would when he bought or built a house.

The door opened and Cade and Jonah came out with a big bag of chips and three beers. Cade handed Austin one of the beers and leaned against the porch railing while Jonah took the other chair. "This is lunch," Cade said. "We figured after a big breakfast we could survive on a snack until dinner."

"Works for me." Austin put down his guitar and twisted the cap off his beer. "You finished in there?"

"Yep." Jonah ripped open the bag of chips. "We came out here so we won't drop chips on the floor, although it's so clean you could eat off it."

"Am I allowed to walk on it?"

"Only if you take off your boots," Jonah said. "And don't touch anything."

"What'd you do with my duffel?"

"It's sitting by the front door along with mine. My recommendation is we finish our beer, grab our stuff and head down to the meadow so we don't mess up anything in the house. We have to go down there eventually to get dressed, and we can shower and shave in the bathhouse."

Austin smiled. "Like old times."

"Exactly." Jonah sipped his beer. "No telling how often a bunch of us will be together so we might as well make the most of it."

Austin grabbed a handful of chips. "We'll be doing this again before you know it. I'll be inviting the whole crew to my wedding."

Cade choked on his beer.

"Okay, okay. I don't have a date set or anything, but—"

"Or a *bride*." Cade looked at him and shook his head. "Please learn from my mistakes. You rush this thing and you'll live to regret it."

"It all turned out okay for you in the end, though. You're marrying Lexi and you have this great cabin."

"This extremely clean and tastefully appointed cabin," Jonah said.

"You're right, Junior. I have this cabin and a wonderful woman to share it with. But it's taken two very long years to get to this day because I tried to rush the process in the beginning. I'm trying to save you from screwing up like I did." He reached for some chips and dropped crumbs on the porch. "Whoops."

"No worries," Jonah said. "I parked the broom next to the door so we can sweep down the porch before we leave." Then he turned to Austin. "Cade's right. There's no doubt she likes you, but I wouldn't try to sell her on the wedding gig just yet."

Austin sighed and glanced around. "It's just that I know what I want now. I want her and a house, something like this. I'm already twenty-six, and—"

"You're *only* twenty-six," Cade said.

"My dad was thirty-two when he died." He didn't

bring that up often but it might be the only way his brothers would understand.

Cade's quick glance of solidarity showed that he did. "My mom was thirty-five. I get what you're saying. But I guarantee Drew isn't coming from that same place."

"Most people aren't," Jonah said. "And while it's good to know that time is precious, you can't railroad folks."

"Like a bullet train," Cade said with a grin.

Austin rolled his eyes.

"Well, he said *railroad*. You can't expect me to pass that up."

"Obviously." Austin took a long swallow of his beer and rested the bottle on his knee as he gazed at his brothers. "Well, it turns out you're both right. She asked me out for coffee yesterday to find out whether I was thinking long-term commitment already. I didn't mention that conversation last night because I didn't want to hear either of you say 'I told you so.'"

Cade grimaced. "Knowing me, I would have said it."

"Not me." Jonah polished off his beer. "I'd rather say it now when we're all sober. Hey, brother, I told you so!"

Austin threw a chip at him.

"No food fights allowed!" Jonah carefully picked the chip from the porch floor and tossed it into the yard for the birds. "I'll get the broom and both duffel bags if you two losers want to head for my truck."

Austin drank the last of his beer. "What about the bottles?"

"We're taking them and the bag of chips," Jonah said. "When we leave, there will be no trace of us anywhere."

"Except for the candy, the flowers, the candles and the teddy bears." Austin stood. "I'll get my own duffel. I want to take a peek inside."

"Yeah, okay." Jonah opened the door and pulled out the broom. "We did an awesome job if I do say so."

Austin grabbed his duffel and set it on the porch. Then he surveyed the house, or as much of it as he could see from the open doorway. Flower arrangements, bowls of candy and candles in various sizes sat on the coffee table, the mantel and the kitchen table. The two bears on the sofa added the perfect touch and he was glad he'd insisted on them.

"You need to move," Jonah said. "I want to sweep."

"Hang on." Austin went back and picked up his phone from the porch railing. "I want a picture."

"Don't show it to anybody," Cade said. "I want Lexi to be surprised."

"I won't. This is for me, so I can remember what we did." He took several shots. "I wish now I'd bought another set of those bears. You don't find those everywhere."

Jonah clapped him on the shoulder. "I'll make you a promise, bro. When it's your turn, I'll scour the internet for those bears."

"Okay. Thanks." But Austin didn't trust doing it that way. Some things you needed to hold in your hands to make sure they were right. In the next few days he'd go into town and buy another pair of the stuffed toys. It couldn't hurt to have them on hand.

He was still holding his phone when the text came in from Drew. When can U stop by the barn? Need 2 mic your guitar. His world suddenly became several shades brighter. He texted her back to say he'd be there in five minutes.

"What a big smile you're wearing, Junior," Cade said. "Can I guess who that text was from?"

"She needs me to come to the barn so she can mic my guitar."

Jonah laughed. "That's a new one. I've heard *clean the windows* and *mow the lawn*, but not *mic my guitar.*"

"She really does need to."

"I know. Just needling you. Would you like us to drop you off at the barn?"

"I would." He rode in the back of Jonah's truck on the way down and had to keep a firm grip on his hat and his guitar because the ride was breezy and bumpy. It suited his upbeat mood perfectly. He'd get to see Drew again, and with any luck, she'd be alone.

Chapter Nineteen

Drew had picked up sound equipment before driving to the ranch this morning. She'd also brought a wooden stool from her kitchen because Austin would need something to sit on and he might not have thought of that.

Elise was up at the house shooting video with Drew's small camera as the women fixed each other's hair and steamed the wrinkles out of their dresses. Drew liked to include that footage in the final cut, so it was a good thing she had help handling it while she was down in the barn trying to figure out the best spot to put Austin. The music setup was critical and until that was done to her satisfaction she wouldn't breathe easy.

When Austin walked in carrying his guitar, her pulse jumped the way it always did when she saw him. But she was determined to keep their interaction businesslike. She'd thought about him quite a bit today and she'd always come back to the same sad conclusion—his vision of the future was very different from hers.

"Howdy, ma'am." He leaned his guitar in the corner and hung his hat on it before coming toward her wearing that killer smile.

"Did you actually just say 'howdy, ma'am'?"

"I did. I like saying it. Makes me think of the olden days." With no hesitation whatsoever, he drew her into his arms. "I was hoping you'd be all by yourself."

"Elise is taking footage up at the house." Keeping their interaction businesslike wasn't quite so simple when he was used to kissing her whenever they were alone.

"Good." He pulled her close.

"And we have work to do." Somehow she'd ended up with her palms flattened against his broad chest. His heart was beating as fast as hers. "This probably isn't a good idea."

"I think it's a great idea." He cupped the back of her head and leaned closer. "I won't be able to concentrate unless I kiss you first." He captured her mouth.

Kissing him had always made the world disappear, but not this time. All that thinking about their situation had her on edge.

Slowly he lifted his head and gazed down at her. "Drew, what's wrong?"

"I'm just… We need to talk, but there's no time for it now."

His breath hitched. "You're right about that, but we'll have time tomorrow night."

"Yes, we will."

Slowly he released her and stepped back. "Do you still want me to come by?"

She hated seeing the uncertainty in his gaze, but this would be a terrible time to discuss whether they should consider parting ways.

"Yes, please." She put a hand to her chest and struggled to breathe normally. "But I could be late."

"I don't care what time it is. I hope you'll call me regardless."

"Okay."

He massaged the back of his neck and stared at her. "You wore your hair down."

"I didn't want to be quite so casual today. I'll be changing clothes in a little while, too." She took a deep breath. "If you'll get your guitar, we can see if this microphone placement works."

He didn't move. "When you wear your hair down, it curls more. I didn't realize that. I love the way it looks."

"Thank you. But we really need to—"

"Get down to business. I know. It's just that…you're beautiful."

She looked into his eyes and saw everything she'd been afraid he was feeling reflected there. She wasn't wrong about his intentions. The two of them were a train wreck in the making. Pain sliced through her when she thought of how that could hurt him.

He cleared his throat. "Just couldn't go without saying that." He gestured toward the mic. "Ready to test that thing out?"

She nodded.

"I'll get my guitar."

Moments later, she adjusted the sound levels and the position of the mic while Austin played country love songs. He didn't sing the lyrics but it didn't matter because she knew most of them. She also knew he was playing those songs for her.

Concentrating on the sound quality was a challenge when she kept thinking of how he'd looked at her. What a mess. Watching him play tore her into little pieces because he was obviously serenading her. A sweet serenade was the last thing she deserved now that it seemed certain she would break his heart.

"That's probably enough," she said. "I'm satisfied if you are."

He slid off the stool. "The mic's good and I like the acoustics in this old barn. Didn't know if I would. Now if you'll excuse me, I'll head on down to the meadow so I can spruce up for the big event." At the door he turned back. "Listen, whatever it is, we'll work it out. See you later."

When he was gone, she sank down on one of the benches to catch her breath. She was still there trying to sort through her volatile emotions when Elise came back.

Her sister hurried over, sat beside her and wrapped an arm around her shoulders. "What happened?"

"Austin's in love with me."

"He said that?"

"No, but I can see it in his eyes. And he thinks we can work out our differences but I don't think we can. We're on completely different trajectories." She sighed.

"Is there anything I can do?"

Drew shook her head. "Thanks for the offer, though."

"Are you absolutely sure you're not in love with him?"

"I'm not sure at all. The way this hurts right now, I very well might be. But if I do love him, the kindest thing would be to let him go. I have a gut feeling that he wants marriage and babies and I think he wants them soon."

"You haven't asked him, though."

"Not yet. Now isn't a great time to discuss it. But I will, probably after I drive back tomorrow night."

Elise nodded. "That sounds like a reasonable plan." She squeezed Drew's shoulder. "If I know you, and I think I do, you'll feel better once you get back to work."

"True."

"The women are about to put on their finery, which probably means the men will be doing that, too. You wanted one of us in each locker room, as I recall. Which are you taking?"

She didn't even have to think twice. "The women."

"All things considered, excellent choice. I'm not in love with Jonah so I'll have a steadier hand on the camcorder."

"Don't fall in love with him."

Elise smiled. "I can't promise you that, sis. He's pretty cute." She stood. "You have another one of these little dude cameras, right?"

"Yep. In the truck."

"Then I'll take this one since I'm used to it." She peered at Drew. "You okay?"

"Yep."

"Then I'm off to get me some shots of hot cowboys getting dressed for a wedding. Yeehaw!" She left the barn.

Drew smiled. She and Elise had grown up in the same household, but their personalities were completely different. Drew envied her sister's breezy attitude toward life. Elise had hated losing the internship, but she would have been okay, even without Drew rushing to the rescue. But Drew was glad her little sis was here.

She went to the truck to get a small tote and the other camcorder, and then she walked up to the house. Elise was right. Work was a blessing. Her gloom disappeared while filming Lexi getting into her classy wedding dress with the help of Chelsea and Philomena, her two attendants.

After everyone was dressed, Drew slipped into a bathroom and put on what she referred to as her wedding videographer's outfit. The emerald green knit dress with a gently flared skirt paired with low-heeled shoes gave her freedom of movement and the combination was appropriate for all seasons, including Christmas. Her pearl earrings and her grandmother's pendant were her only jewelry.

On the trip from the house to the barn, she met Elise coming back from her filming escapade in the meadow. "Have fun?"

"You know it, sis. Your guy is already down at the barn warming up his guitar, by the way. I'll meet you there after I change clothes."

"See you then." Drew wanted to get inside well in advance of the guests so that she could shoot the benches slowly filling up. During editing she'd increase the film speed for that segment. It wouldn't take up much of the video's runtime and it was a fun prelude to the big event.

Although Elise had prepared her by announcing Austin was already in the barn, her chest tightened with emotion when she caught sight of him. He wore what the brotherhood had chosen for the occasion—black pants and boots, white shirt, string tie, black Western-cut jacket and a black Stetson. His blond coloring with the dark outfit was breathtaking.

He glanced up when she came in and smiled appreciatively. "Nice dress."

"Thank you. Nice outfit."

"Thanks." He held her gaze for one electric moment. Then he went back to strumming his guitar.

She walked over to the corner where she'd positioned her tripod-mounted camera for maximum coverage of the event. She could swivel to the back to catch the action there and to the front for the ceremony itself. Elise would stand behind Cade with a handheld camera to catch shots from that angle.

Her hand trembled slightly as she turned on the camera and listened to the sound of Austin's guitar through her headset. She closed her eyes and took several deep breaths.

She would do this and she would do it well. Lexi and Cade deserved the best she had to give and she wouldn't allow herself to be sidetracked by her worry about the beautiful man over there playing guitar in the corner. But ignoring him wasn't easy when they were the only two people in the barn and she had nothing to do but wait.

Everything was as ready as it could be. She'd already taken video of the ribbons braided in each horse's mane and the flower arrangements hanging between each stall. She'd even filmed the gray tabby strolling through the barn.

The cat wandered over to Austin and rubbed against his leg. Austin stopped playing and leaned down to scratch behind the cat's ears. "Hey, Ringo. Don't know if you'll want to stay for this thing, buddy. Might be too big a crowd for you, but it's a big day for your main man, Cade."

"How's Cade doing?" She hoped Austin and Jonah had helped him relax. Most grooms were a little jumpy, but Cade had seemed more so than most.

"He's fine." Austin met her gaze as he continued to pet the cat. "Thunder Mountain guys are pretty resilient."

That was the exact moment she lost her heart for sure. It wasn't a wise thing to do but she couldn't help it. Austin had been through so much, and his courage in the face of adversity had touched her from the beginning.

She knew that for a man like him, love was a precious gift, one he didn't give lightly. They might not be meant for each other, but dragging out the uncertainty until to-morrow night wasn't fair to him.

She took a deep breath. "Maybe we need to have our talk a little earlier."

"Okay."

"Like after this is over."

"I look forward to it." His attention shifted to the back of the barn as the brotherhood filed in and positioned themselves shoulder-to-shoulder on either side of the back door. They were an impressive group. Austin tipped his hat to them. "Showtime."

And so it was. Drew filmed the guests as they arrived and were escorted to their seats by various members of the brotherhood. She had no trouble picking out Jack Chance and his mother, Sarah. For one thing, Finn introduced them to each of the brothers before seating them.

For another, they stopped to pet the horses on the way to their spots. She couldn't claim to be a horse person aside from her interest in wild ones, but she could recognize the signs. Jack and Sarah obviously loved them.

Curiously, mother and son didn't look related. Jack's chiseled features and dark coloring indicated Native American ancestry. Sarah was fair-skinned with Anglo features and the posture and height of someone who might have walked a runway in her youth. But they were clearly fond of each other and thrilled to be here. Thunder Mountain had taught Drew that biology wasn't the only component in mother-son relationships and maybe not the most important one.

As guests continued to arrive, Austin's gentle rendition of country songs filled the barn with nostalgia. Lexi had been right about using a solo guitar. This was far better than a sophisticated sound system and recorded music.

Damon and Finn ushered Rosie and Herb to a seat

in the front row. Drew glanced at the time and noticed that they were right on schedule. The same two brothers brought Lexi's mother to the front row.

Drew swung her camera to the back again as the rest of the brotherhood filed up the aisle. Several horses nickered as they passed. After all, these men were cowboys who at one time or another had ridden, cared for and loved those animals.

Finally the men reached the front of the barn and formed a semicircle with their backs to the open doors. Late afternoon sunlight streamed in, surrounding them with a golden glow. They looked magnificent and Drew took her time panning across the entire group.

Next Jonah and Cade arrived and took their places in front of their brothers. Jonah was dressed like everyone else, complete with the black Stetson and string tie. He looked more like a riverboat gambler than a man of the cloth.

Cade was the only one with a slight variation to the dress code. The vest he'd mentioned yesterday turned out to be gold brocade, and Drew's eyes misted when she saw it. During the time she'd filmed the women getting dressed, Rosie had given Lexi a gold locket from Cade along with a note explaining the significance of the vest he'd be wearing.

He'd bought it without consulting Lexi and intended it as a silent pledge of a long and lasting love. He planned to wear it again fifty years from today when they celebrated their golden anniversary. After reading his note, Lexi had burst into tears.

Once all the men were in place, Austin launched into a slightly more energetic song for the processional as Chelsea walked down the aisle wearing a delicate gown of turquoise. Philomena, dressed in a deep blue dress that matched her eyes, followed. She pushed a stroller covered in ribbons and flowers.

Sophie perched in the middle of all that finery wearing a crown of flowers and a frothy dress of apple green. She looked like a woodland fairy child, but she sounded exactly like the spirited baby she was as she squealed and bounced in the stroller. Cameras and phones came out and Phil's stepmother crouched in the aisle to get a picture head-on. Drew suppressed a burst of laughter when Rosie left her place of honor and did the same.

As Phil and Sophie took their places, Austin finished up with a flourish. Then he started a very simple version of a well-known melody and began humming it softly. The brothers behind him, including Cade and Jonah, joined in as the audience rose to the sweetest wedding march Drew had ever heard.

As the soft humming drifted through the barn, Lexi appeared on her father's arm. Drew had seen her outfit earlier, but the impact of it here was a hundred times greater. Against a backdrop of weathered wood, she was a glowing vision.

The classic, flowing lines of her white satin dress suited her perfectly. Cade's gold locket nestled at her throat, and instead of a veil, she wore a crown of white flowers over her short brown curls. Her bouquet was also all white except for a single red rose in the center.

The closer she came, the louder Austin hummed and the brothers took their cue from him. They almost drowned out the sound of Lexi's horse, Serendipity, who trumpeted her congratulations as Lexi passed by.

By the time Lexi reached the front of the barn, the brotherhood's chorus of deep baritone voices filled the space to overflowing with a joyous sound of celebration. Lexi obviously loved it. She alternated between tears and laughter, which could be the sign of a perfect march down the aisle.

Austin brought the song to a crescendo and cut it with perfect timing. Silence reigned as everyone in the barn absorbed the beauty of the moment when Cade and Lexi stood gazing at each other. Then little Sophie called out "da-da" and the spell was broken as everyone laughed.

Lexi's dad transferred her hand to Cade's and took his seat, Jonah cleared his throat and the ceremony began. Drew had filmed several weddings, but none had touched her the way this one did. The love between Cade and Lexi shimmered in the air, so real she almost believed it would show up as waves of color on the video.

Her filming strategy was simple—stay focused on the shining faces of the couple vowing to love each other forever and a day. The words made Drew's throat hurt but she didn't have time to question why. She was too busy capturing a precious memory for two people who deserved to have a video to play when that fiftieth rolled around.

After it was over and they hurried down the aisle together to the vibrant tunes pouring from Austin's guitar, after guests and members of the brotherhood had stopped to compliment Austin on his playing, Drew found herself alone with him once again.

Slowly he leaned his guitar against the wooden stool and walked over to her. "You haven't ever asked this directly, but it's probably something you'd like to know."

She took a deep breath. "Okay."

"I want this." He gestured to the decorated barn. "And I want it with you. My brothers would tell me I'm crazy for laying it out, but...I saw how you reacted to this wedding. I don't know a lot of things, but after four years of guiding trail rides I've learned to read people. I saw your face and I think you want it, too."

She opened her mouth to contradict him.

"Don't answer me now. Give yourself some time to think about it." He held her gaze. "Give yourself time to imagine how great we could be together." Then he glanced toward the back of the barn. "Hey, Jonah. Great timing, bro."

Drew stared at the preacher in confusion.

"Happy to be of service." Jonah tipped his hat. "All set?"

"Sure am." Austin looked at Drew. "Before he left I asked him to head back here after giving us a couple of minutes. He'll walk you over to the reception. On the way he's supposed to tell you what a great guy I am." Then he turned and walked out of the barn.

Chapter Twenty

Austin figured he'd blown it, but engineering that moment alone with Drew when the air still vibrated from the excitement of Cade and Lexi's wedding had been too good to pass up. She'd been so into it. Whether she realized it or not, she was a people person like him.

She had enough talent to create nature videos and could probably make money doing it, but filming people was her sweet spot. Building a wonderful life with her would be so easy, at least in his view, but she didn't think she was ready. Typical of him, he'd just pushed her to make a decision.

Good thing the rockin' party going on in the rec hall absorbed everyone's attention and no one noticed he was a wee bit distracted. Like all the other guys, he'd shed his jacket and thrown himself into the action—eating, drinking, toasting and dancing to the music provided by an excellent DJ. But his mind wasn't on the festivities.

Instead he was focused on Drew as she moved around the room with her small camcorder.

Cade was right about him—when he set his mind to something, he was exactly like a bullet train. Jonah had told him that he couldn't railroad people and that was what he'd attempted with Drew, pretty much from the beginning. Now she wouldn't even glance his way and it was his own damned fault.

The rec hall looked great, though. He hadn't seen the place when it was first built but from what he'd heard, it had been a bare-bones structure. Part classroom, part hangout for the academy's teenagers, it had been more functional than attractive.

The students had done a lot toward changing that. The walls were covered with murals, good ones, too. They'd created faux windows on each wall. One looked out on a startlingly realistic view of the Bighorns and another on a pasture with Thunder Mountain horses grazing in it. On either side of the front door, imaginary windows revealed a nonexistent porch lined with chairs.

While he and Jonah had been keeping Cade occupied this morning, the rest of the brothers had pitched in to decorate. Somebody had come up with colorful table-cloths, probably Rosie, but the guys had provided the vases of wildflowers on each table. They'd done a decent job with crepe paper streamers, too. The streamers added a high school prom vibe, but that wasn't a bad thing.

Maybe if he hadn't made his pushy speech in the barn, this night could have been a lot of fun. Drew would have stopped by during her filming and given him a smile. Later they could have slipped outside for a few stolen kisses. He could be wrong that she was deliberately avoiding him, but he didn't think so.

Then he saw her leave her camera with Elise and go out on the dance floor with Jack Chance. Okay, that did it. The guy was a great dancer and he'd taken a turn with nearly every woman in the room, but Drew was supposed to be working, right? And if she took a break to dance with anyone, he wanted to be the one holding her, not some well-heeled dude from Jackson Hole.

Making his way across the dance floor, he tapped Jack on the shoulder. "Cutting in."

"Oh, hey." Jack glanced at him without missing a beat. Then he looked at Drew and raised his eyebrows. "Okay with you?"

Austin clenched his jaw.

"It's okay." She didn't smile, though. Not even a little bit.

"I'll ask you again later. We need to catch up." Jack smoothly transferred her into Austin's arms.

He pulled her close, but not too close, and continued the lively two-step. "Catch up? You know him?" He didn't dare gaze into her eyes or he'd stumble. He was normally a good dancer but he was stretched tight as his guitar strings right now.

"I was his waitress once when he came to Billings to look at horses. He stopped by the restaurant for a bite to eat."

"How long ago?"

"At least five years, maybe more."

Austin's jaw muscles bunched. "Must have been memorable."

"It was. He danced me around through the tables."

"Sounds like quite a guy."

"Austin, he's married with two kids."

"Doesn't mean anything."

"In Jack's case it does. Listen, this is stupid. Let's go outside so we can talk."

He sucked in a breath. "That would be great." Taking her hand, he led her out the front door and into the cool night. "It's chilly out here. Do you need—"

"I'm fine." She faced him. "I've wanted to talk to you, but I wasn't sure what to say. I'm still not sure."

"You don't have to say anything." He shoved his hands in his pockets so he wouldn't reach for her. "Let me apologize for what I said back at the barn. Cade's warned me several times about my tendency to barrel ahead when I've set myself a goal."

"Your goal-oriented personality was one of the things I admired about you."

"You said 'was,' so I guess you don't admire it so much anymore."

"I still do, but what you want from me... I can't give you that. There's nothing wrong with having a plan but you need to find a woman who's ready for marriage. And kids. I assume you want those, too."

"Yes, I'll admit that I do."

"Austin, you've fallen for the wrong girl." Her eyes grew shiny with tears. "And I'm so sorry. I don't doubt your feelings are sincere. I'm...fond of you, too."

"Fond?" His heart cracked right down the middle.

"More than fond."

"Thank God. Drew, we can build on that. I promise not to push you. I'll—"

"But see, I already know what you really want. I've felt your urgency and even if you could dial it back, I'd wonder if you were mentally tapping your foot. On top of that, waiting around for me keeps you from finding someone ready and willing to fulfill your dreams. That's not fair to you."

"Don't worry about being fair to me."

"Can't help it." She smiled and swiped at her damp cheeks. "I really do care about you. I want you to be happy."

"Me, too."

"Then let me go. I'm not the person you need."

"You're making it sound hopeless."

"Because it is. Probably was from the beginning. We want different things."

He hit rock bottom. Since he had nothing more to lose, he decided to be blunt. "I still don't understand. Why are you so against committing to me, or any guy, for that matter?"

"Because I'd lose myself. It was happening in Billings—constant family obligations were distracting me and taking me away from my work. I felt scattered during a time when I needed to be focused on how to build my business. Moving here was a breath of fresh air, a welcome taste of freedom."

"It can still be that!"

"Not if I keep going out with you. I thought we could just have fun, but I realized fairly soon that you want more, plus you have a huge family, bigger even than mine." She took a shaky breath.

"Drew, I promise you they wouldn't—"

"If I became seriously involved with you and by association with your family, guaranteed the expectations would start up again."

"How can you say that? You've known most of them since June. Do they strike you as the kind of people who would do such a thing?" Frustration was a steel band tightening around his chest.

"I can't tell because I'm still mostly an outsider. Things change when you become part of the inner circle."

"I don't see it that way."

She sighed. "I know you don't because you love them. I love my family, too, but they're enough to handle without adding another larger group to the mix."

"You're making some big assumptions about how you'd be treated."

"They're assumptions based on hard-won experience. I'm sorry, Austin. It isn't going to work." She choked up on the last part. "I need to get back to filming." She turned and ran inside.

Disbelief and shock kept him where he was for several seconds. He hadn't even managed to open the door for her. All this time he'd thought if he handled things right he'd succeed. But he'd never had a chance.

When he looked at his family he saw warmth and acceptance, support and love. She saw a situation booby-trapped with obligations. He didn't have a clue how to fight that perception.

It seemed that her family had such a dynamic. He couldn't say because he'd only met Elise. Maybe Drew had felt a duty to bring her down here and cheer her up. But Elise hadn't pulled Drew away from her work. In fact, she'd rolled up her sleeves and helped.

Elise might not be typical of the Martinelli clan, though. Again, he couldn't judge without meeting more of them. But he sure as hell knew that his family didn't smother anyone with responsibilities that kept them from doing their work. Didn't matter. He could say that until he was blue in the face and Drew wouldn't believe him.

He'd made some mistakes in this deal, but even if he'd slow-played it the way Cade had advised, they would have come to this point eventually. Drew didn't think the trap would close until she'd officially become family, so she never would have agreed to be his fiancée, let alone his wife.

He wasn't good at accepting defeat, but this time he had to. At least there was plenty of beer inside that rec hall. That would be his solution for tonight. Tomorrow he'd work out a solution for getting over Drew. He knew in advance it would be one of the toughest goals he'd ever set for himself. Might even be unattainable, but he wouldn't know until he tried.

Elise's crush on Jonah turned out to be more of a blessing than Drew had counted on. Jonah was the big topic of conversation during the drive back to the apartment after the reception and Austin's name never came up. Jonah had also invited them out to breakfast the next morning but Drew begged off, citing the large amount of editing she had ahead of her.

She did have a ton of editing and she tackled it the minute Jonah picked up Elise and they took off. Getting through the rehearsal and the prewedding activities wouldn't be too bad, but she dreaded the footage of the wedding and the reception. Austin would be all through those portions.

Jonah brought Elise back from breakfast before Drew had made it past the rehearsal dinner, which was fine. No one would expect a finished product right away because there was so much. Monday morning she could work on the painful sections.

Elise continued to rave about Jonah on the way back to Billings. With her feet propped on the dash, she listed off all his sterling qualities. "I hope you meant what you said about visiting as often as I want because I'd like to take you up on it."

"Of course I meant it. You were a huge help this weekend and besides, I love seeing you."

"I love seeing you, too. I was sad when you left Billings so this'll be great."

"It will." So far Elise hadn't mentioned Austin. Drew wondered if her sister had sensed there was a rift and didn't want to bring up a touchy subject. That would be a relief.

"The main thing I like about Jonah is that he has his priorities straight." She crossed her ankles and wiggled her feet. "Does it distract you when I have my feet up here?"

"No." She smiled. "I'm used to it."

"Good, because I can relax better this way. Jonah thinks it's funny I do this."

"You put your feet on his dash?"

"Sure, why not? He says it's a working truck, anyway. No fancy muscle car or shiny new truck for that cowboy. He's considering buying a couple of horses, though. Austin asked him if he wanted to be a partner in his trail riding business. Did Austin mention that to you?"

"No, I didn't hear about it. Great idea, though."

"You should do a promotional video featuring both of those guys. Bet they'd get a lot of business from women if you did."

"Possibly, although I'm not sure I'll have time to make them a video." She'd forgotten that she'd offered to go on the first trail ride and film that, too. "I might need to recommend someone else."

"Why on earth would you do that when you… Uh-oh." She let her head fall back against the seat. "Wow, I've been in my own little world but now that I look back on it, I can see things weren't right. I thought you were just tired from all that work, but you and Austin had a falling-out, didn't you?"

Drew tried to calm her breathing. "Not really. We've accepted that we're not right for each other but it's not like we had a fight or anything. It's just over, which is for the best." That speech didn't come out as matter-of-factly as she would have liked.

"So he's looking for marriage and kids, after all?"

"He's looking for a wife who'll fit nicely into his big family. That includes having some grandkids for Rosie to spoil and I guarantee there would be a bunch of other expectations I wouldn't figure out until it was too late."

"What kind of expectations?"

"The same ones we have in our family—last-minute babysitting requests, whipping up an extra dish for the potluck because someone forgot to shop, acting as peacemaker for the family squabbles. You know the drill. I left Billings to get away from all that. Why jump right back into it?"

"*That's* why you left?"

"Yes."

"I thought it was because you got a job at the community college and you'd be closer to the wild horse refuge!"

"That's what I told the folks because I didn't want to hurt their feelings."

"Oh, Drew. I hate that you feel you had to leave because the family was stressing you out. I wish you'd told me."

"I didn't know how. You don't seem to have that problem."

"They bug me sometimes, and I'll probably end up moving somewhere eventually, but not because I have to get away from them." She fell silent.

"Look, I'd appreciate it if you didn't mention this to Mom and Dad."

"I won't. They'd be crushed."

"I know, and I love them both so much. It's just—I needed some space to figure out who I am and what I want. I don't know if I would have made that nature video if I hadn't left, let alone sold it. I really think that's my future, making more of those."

"Could be."

"Elise, I'm sorry if I upset you by saying all that. I don't hate our family or anything."

"Of course you don't. You wouldn't do all those nice things for them if you hated them. Hey, could we have a little music? I think better with music."

"Sure." Drew switched on the radio and punched the button to bring in a Billings station since they were within range now. She wasn't clear on what Elise might be thinking about but she'd be quiet and let her do it.

They were nearly at her parents' house when Elise spoke again. "Fortunately we're a couple of hours away from dinner and I have a plan. Dad will be taking his Sunday afternoon snooze and Mom will be catching up on back episodes of that show she likes, the one with zombies."

"She likes that?"

"She started watching it a few months ago and she's hooked. Go figure. Anyway, let's tell her we feel like climbing into the tree house to see what shape it's in."

"Why would we do that?"

"To see if it's fit for the next generation of kids. She'll buy it. I want to talk about this some more and that's the only place we can guarantee she won't hear us."

"I don't know. If she's watching zombie shows, anything's possible. She might decide to join us in the tree house."

"She might, but I'm thinking she won't. She's never liked heights."

Elise was right. Their mother had no interest in climbing up to the tree house and didn't think it was safe for them, either. But they promised her they'd test each rung of the old rope ladder carefully before going higher.

Drew insisted on going first. "I'm heavier than you. It'll be a better test."

"Okay, but if there are any cool spiders at the top, don't you dare kill them."

"Wouldn't dream of it." They'd both read *Charlotte's Web* and had never killed another spider since. Climbing the rope ladder brought back memories of lazy summers when she and Elise would haul a thermos of lemonade and a package of Oreos up here. They'd read sexy books they weren't supposed to have and talk about the day they'd unlock the mysteries contained in those books.

At the top of the ladder Drew glanced through the opening to the tree house their dad had built at least twenty years ago. "Lots of leaves and one small spiderweb in the corner," she called down. "Let me scoop out some leaves before you come up. Stand back." She climbed in and dumped handfuls of leaves out the door. Finally, she was satisfied. "Come on up."

Sitting cross-legged in her usual spot to the right of the opening, she waited for Elise to appear. She must have swung up that rope ladder like a monkey because in no time her head appeared and then she was in, taking her place to the left of the entrance.

She glanced around. "This is cool. I'm going to come here more often."

"We need to watch the time so Mom doesn't get worried. I forgot my phone."

"Then you really must be distracted. I brought mine." She pulled it out of her pocket and laid it on the dusty floor. "For starters, I want to make sure I understand. You broke it off with Austin because he wants to bring you into the bosom of his family and that freaks you out. Is that the basic idea?"

"More or less."

"What if I were to tell you that you have nothing to fear but fear itself?"

"I'd say you're quoting Franklin D. Roosevelt and it doesn't apply."

"Okay, but I need to say something. Don't get mad at me."

Drew laughed. "You always say that before throwing out something that's going to make me mad."

"And it probably will. Here it is. You're doing this to yourself."

"Doing what?"

"Getting tangled up in our family's problems, babysitting on short notice, making the extra potluck dish. You don't have to do any of that unless you truly want to."

"What are you talking about? It's expected!"

"That's true in your case because you always say yes. In fact, you usually volunteer. But, sis, you're allowed to say no. I do that a lot."

Drew gazed at her. "And you don't hear about it?"

"Sometimes I do. I just smile and say whatever they wanted from me doesn't fit into my schedule."

"I never considered doing that. What a startling concept."

"You're the oldest, so naturally you were conditioned to be the responsible one. I wasn't. It's easier for me."

"And you didn't feel you had to run away from home."

Elise reached over and wiggled Drew's foot. "In retrospect, that wasn't a bad thing. You met Mr. Gorgeous."

"You've been leading up to him all along, haven't you?"

"You know me too well, sis. Look, I was only there for the weekend so I can't say if his family is as needy or downright manipulative as ours can be. I'm guessing they're not, but who knows? The point is, you can hang with them and not give up your focus if you remember that you don't have to do what everyone asks, or suggests, or even intimates that you should."

"That would be completely new territory for me."

Her sister smiled. "Stick with me, kid. I'll teach you the ropes."

"The more you talk, the more I think my response to Austin was—"

"Knee-jerk?"

"Yeah."

"Hey, forgive yourself. And by the way, you're allowed to vote ixnay on the wedding and the babies for now. If he's not okay with that, then you really don't belong with him. But unless I missed something, he didn't give you a timetable."

She thought back over his little speech after the wedding. "He didn't, but I have the feeling he might have one. Besides, when I hear someone say *I want this*, I assume they mean right now."

Elise shrugged. "Explore that question with him, but I've seen the way he looks at you. I think he's open to negotiation and you're in a hell of a spot to strike a bargain that's good for you."

Excitement bubbling inside her, Drew scrambled to her knees. "I have to go back. I have to go back *now*."

"Then do it."

"I'll miss dinner with the folks." Then she laughed as years of obligation lifted from her shoulders. "But it doesn't fit into my schedule!"

"You're getting the idea, girlfriend!"

She crawled over to Elise and gave her an awkward hug. "I love you, sis."

"I love you, too. Now climb down that ladder. I'll be right behind you and back you up when you tell Mom you can't stay for dinner."

Drew was on the road to Sheridan in just under ten minutes. After her breakup speech to Austin, she had no idea what he'd be doing tonight. It wasn't even five o'clock, so maybe he wasn't drowning in his sorrows yet.

She tried never to make calls while she was driving, but this was an emergency. She grabbed her phone from the passenger seat and dialed his number.

He answered on the second ring. "Drew? Are you okay?"

"I'm *very* okay. I'm more okay than I've been in… forever! Listen, I want to amend some things I said last night. Can we meet?"

"Just name the time and place."

His firm, confident response sent heat spiraling through her. "My apartment."

"Give me directions."

She rattled them off. "I'll be there in less than an hour."

"See you then."

She broke speed limits all the way to Sheridan. She noticed a familiar truck in the parking lot. If she wasn't mistaken, it was Jonah's.

She hurried up the outside stairs and found Austin leaning against the wall next to her doorway. She'd kept her keys out because she didn't want to have this conversation in public. "I see you haven't bought a truck."

He smiled, and it was such a beautiful sight. "Couldn't get motivated."

"I thought a new truck was a priority." Her heart pounded as she fit the key in the lock and opened the door.

"Turns out it wasn't." He followed her in and kicked the door shut. Then he sent his hat sailing across the room and pulled her into his arms. "Tell me why you want to amend last night's comments."

"Because my brilliant sister pointed out that I don't have to let people load me down with commitments unless I want them to." She felt a little dizzy from excitement but she pressed on. "She gave me a quick lesson in the power of *no*."

"Is that what you're here to tell me? No?"

"No! I mean, *yes*, but—" She paused to take a breath. "Austin, you really are like a bullet train."

"Damn it, I know. I need to fix that."

"No, don't!" She gripped his shoulders and gave him a little shake, although shaking a man built like Austin wasn't easy. "I love that about you."

"You do?" He gazed down at her in confusion. "I thought that was a big reason you broke up with me. I'm too intense. You think I'll railroad you into doing things you don't want to do."

"But don't you see what I'm saying? If I grow a backbone, if I stand up to you and tell you no, then you *can't*." She smiled. "I'll be bullet-train proof."

"That's a cute way to put it, but you wouldn't have to go through all that if I'd learn to dial it back."

"Don't you dare!"

His eyes widened.

"Don't you dare change that about yourself, Austin Teague. You go after what you want with a single-mindedness that not many people have. It's the reason you'll succeed at whatever you try."

"Are you kidding? I almost lost you!"

Love for him welled up inside her and tears pushed at the back of her eyes. "We almost lost each other."

He gathered her close and his gaze searched hers. "Please tell me we haven't."

"Not if you still want me."

His laughter was choked. "Want you? That doesn't begin to cover it. You're a part of me. I feel you in everything I do. I see you everywhere I look. I can't imagine life without you, but last night, when you said…" He swallowed.

"I was scared."

"Yeah, of me. Of what I'd ask of you."

She shook her head. "Of myself, although I didn't understand it then. Elise helped me figure out that I didn't have to do things on your timetable."

"What timetable?"

"For getting married. And having babies."

His cheeks turned pink. "You're right. I did have one."

"Thought so."

"I don't anymore. I'm learning from Cade's mistakes."

She'd thought she couldn't love him more than she already did, but that statement proved her wrong. Her throat tightened and she could barely get the words out. "Austin, I love you so much."

His breath caught. Then gradually his shocked expression changed, and like dawn breaking, warmth and light filled his gaze. When he spoke, his voice was roughened by emotion. "That's all I need to know." He cupped her face in both hands. "I thought I'd completely blown it and I'd never get to tell you this." He paused. "I love you, Drew Martinelli. I think I've loved you from that first day. You can call me an idiot, but I believe we're destined to be together."

"Then we're both idiots, because I believe it, too." And this time, when he kissed her, the world didn't disappear. Instead it expanded into a lifetime of adventure and love.

* * * * *

MILLS & BOON®

Cherish ™

EXPERIENCE THE ULTIMATE RUSH OF FALLING IN LOVE

MILLS & BOON®

EXCLUSIVE EXTRACT

Artist Holly Motta arrives in New York to find billionaire
Ethan Benton in the apartment where *she's* meant to be
staying! And the next surprise? Ethan needs a fake
fiancée and he wants *her* for the role…

Read on for a sneak preview of
HER NEW YORK BILLIONAIRE
by debut author Andrea Bolter

"In exchange for you posing as my fiancée, as I have
outlined, you will be financially compensated and you will
become legal owner of this apartment and any items such
as clothes and jewels that have been purchased for this
position. Your brother's career will not be impacted negatively
should our work together come to an end. *And…*" He
paused for emphasis.

Holly leaned forward in her chair, her back still board-
straight.

"I have a five-building development under construction
in Chelsea. There will be furnished apartments, office lofts
and common space lobbies – all in need of artwork. I will
commission you for the project."

Holly's lungs emptied. A commission for a big corporate
project. That was exactly what she'd hoped she'd find in New
York. A chance to have her work seen by thousands of people.
The kind of exposure that could lead from one job to the next
and to a sustained and successful career.

This was all too much. Fantastic, frightening, impossible…
Obviously getting involved in any way with Ethan Benton

was a terrible idea. She'd be beholden to him. Serving another person's agenda again. Just what she'd come to New York to get away from.

But this could be a once-in-a-lifetime opportunity. An apartment. A job. It sounded as if he was open to most any demand she could come up with. She really did owe it to herself to contemplate this opportunity.

Her brain was no longer operating normally. The clock on Ethan's desk reminded her that it was after midnight. She'd left Fort Pierce early that morning.

"That really is an incredible offer…" She exhaled. "But I'm too tired to think straight. I'm going to need to sleep on it."

"As you wish."

Holly moved to collect the luggage she'd arrived with. Ethan beat her to it and hoisted the duffle bag over his shoulder. He wrenched the handle of the suitcase. Its wheels tottered as fast as her mind whirled as she followed him to the bedroom.

"Goodnight, then." He placed the bags just inside the doorway and couldn't get out of the room fast enough.

Before closing the door she poked her head out and called, "Ethan Benton, you don't play fair."

Over his shoulder, he turned his face back toward her. "I told you. I always get what I want."

Don't miss
HER NEW YORK BILLIONAIRE
by exciting new author
Andrea Bolter

Available September 2017
www.millsandboon.co.uk